SCOOBY-DOO! TEAM-UP

VOLUME 3

Sholly Fisch Writer **Dario Brizuela** Artist **Franco Riesco** Colorist
Saida Temofonte Letterer **Dario Brizuela with Franco Riesco** Cover Artists
Spectre created by **Jerry Siegel** and **Bernard Baily**
Deadman created by **Arnold Drake**
Aquaman created by **Paul Norris**
Hawkman created by **Gardner Fox**

Kristy Quinn & Brittany Holzherr Editors – Original Series
David Piña Assistant Editor – Original Series
Jeb Woodard Group Editor – Collected Editions
Liz Erickson Editor – Collected Edition
Steve Cook Design Director – Books
Louis Prandi Publication Design

Bob Harras Senior VP – Editor-in-Chief, DC Comics

Diane Nelson President
Dan DiDio Publisher
Jim Lee Publisher
Geoff Johns President & Chief Creative Officer
Amit Desai Executive VP – Business & Marketing Strategy,
Direct to Consumer & Global Franchise Management
Sam Ades Senior VP – Direct to Consumer
Bobbie Chase VP – Talent Development
Mark Chiarello Senior VP – Art, Design & Collected Editions
John Cunningham Senior VP – Sales & Trade Marketing
Anne DePies Senior VP – Business Strategy, Finance & Administration
Don Falletti VP – Manufacturing Operations
Lawrence Ganem VP – Editorial Administration & Talent Relations
Alison Gill Senior VP – Manufacturing & Operations
Hank Kanalz Senior VP – Editorial Strategy & Administration
Jay Kogan VP – Legal Affairs
Thomas Loftus VP – Business Affairs
Jack Mahan VP – Business Affairs
Nick J. Napolitano VP – Manufacturing Administration
Eddie Scannell VP – Consumer Marketing
Courtney Simmons Senior VP – Publicity & Communications
Jim (Ski) Sokolowski VP – Comic Book Specialty Sales & Trade Marketing
Nancy Spears VP – Mass, Book, Digital Sales & Trade Marketing

SCOOBY-DOO TEAM-UP VOLUME 3

Published by DC Comics. Compilation Copyright © 2017
Hanna-Barbera. All Rights Reserved.

Originally published in single magazine form in SCOOBY-DOO TEAM-
UP 13-18 and online as Digital Chapters 25-36. Copyright © 2015,
2016 Hanna-Barbera and DC Comics. All Rights Reserved. SCOOBY-
DOO and all related characters and elements © & ™ Hanna-
Barbera. DC logos, trademarks, characters and all related elements
featured in this publication © & ™ DC Comics. The stories, characters
and incidents featured in this publication are entirely fictional.
DC Comics does not read or accept unsolicited ideas, stories or artwork.

DC Comics, 2900 West Alameda Ave., Burbank, CA 91505
Printed by Vanguard Graphics, LLC, Ithaca, NY, USA.
3/10/17. First Printing.
ISBN: 978-1-4012-6801-5

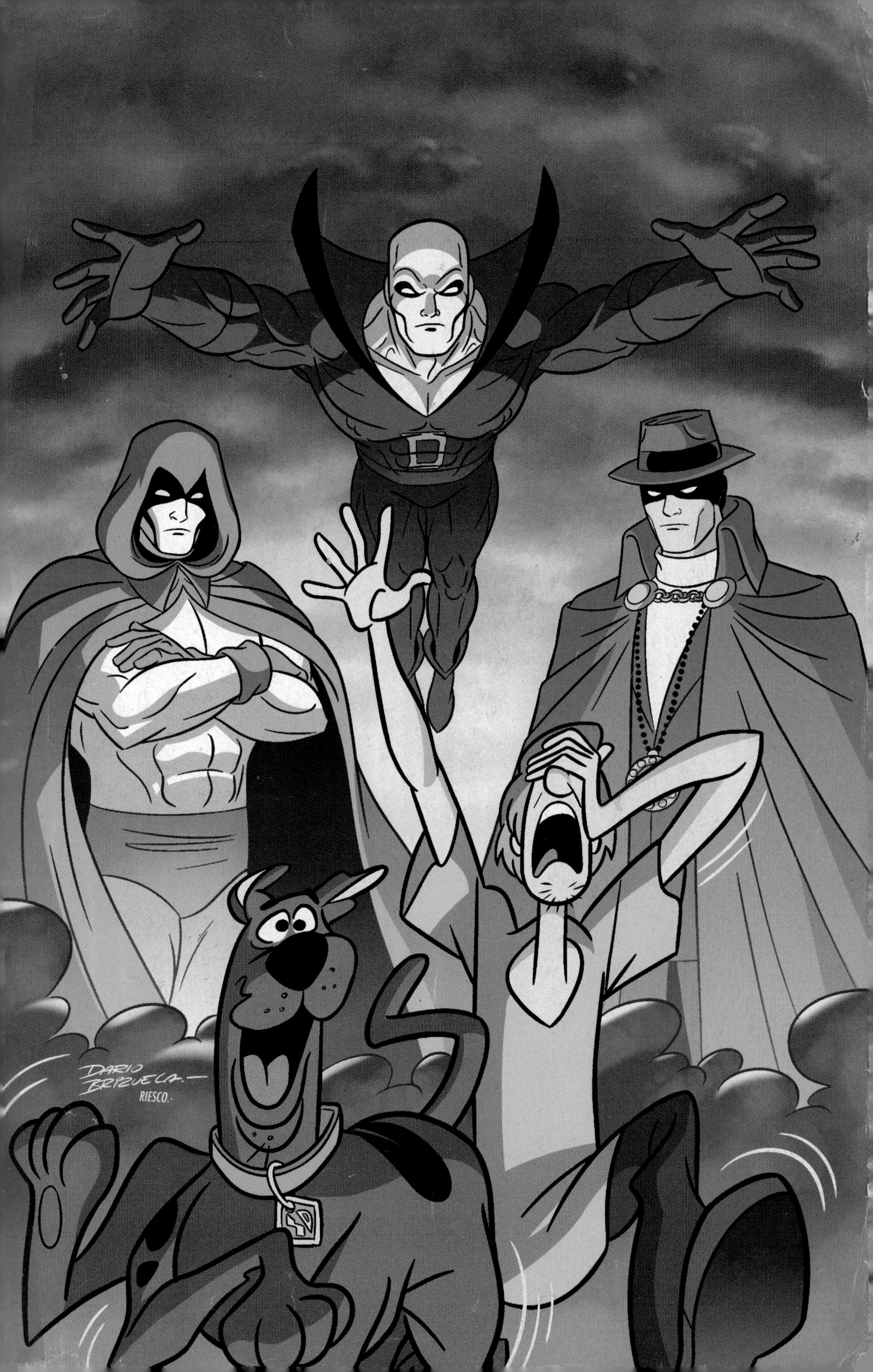
DARIO BRIZUELA
RIESCO.

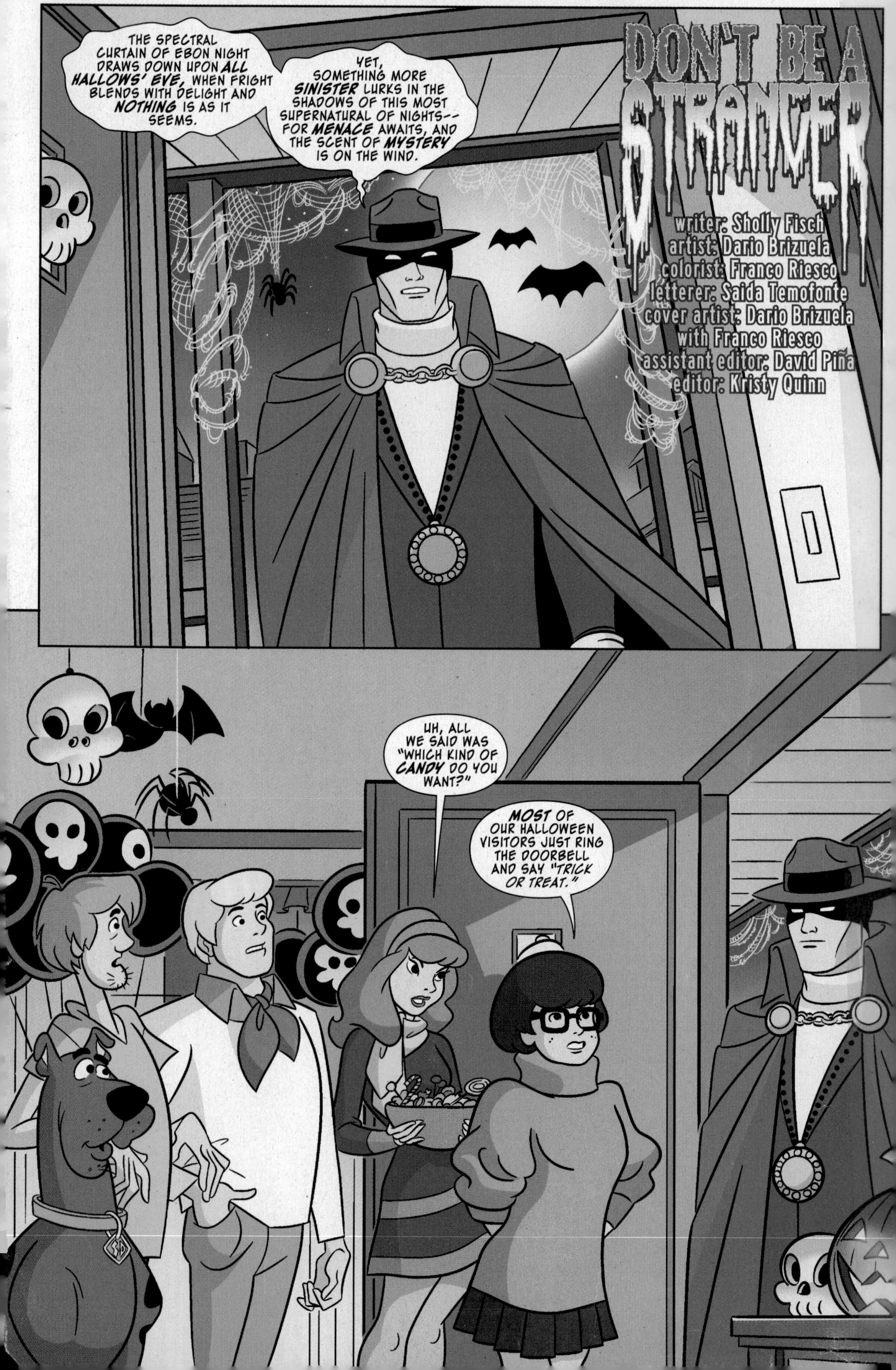
THE SPECTRAL CURTAIN OF EBON NIGHT DRAWS DOWN UPON ALL HALLOWS' EVE, WHEN FRIGHT BLENDS WITH DELIGHT AND NOTHING IS AS IT SEEMS.
YET, SOMETHING MORE SINISTER LURKS IN THE SHADOWS OF THIS MOST SUPERNATURAL OF NIGHTS-- FOR MENACE AWAITS, AND THE SCENT OF MYSTERY IS ON THE WIND.
DON'T BE A STRANGER
writer: Sholly Fisch
artist: Dario Brizuela
colorist: Franco Riesco
letterer: Saida Temofonte
cover artist: Dario Brizuela with Franco Riesco
assistant editor: David Piña
editor: Kristy Quinn
UH, ALL WE SAID WAS "WHICH KIND OF CANDY DO YOU WANT?"
MOST OF OUR HALLOWEEN VISITORS JUST RING THE DOORBELL AND SAY "TRICK OR TREAT."

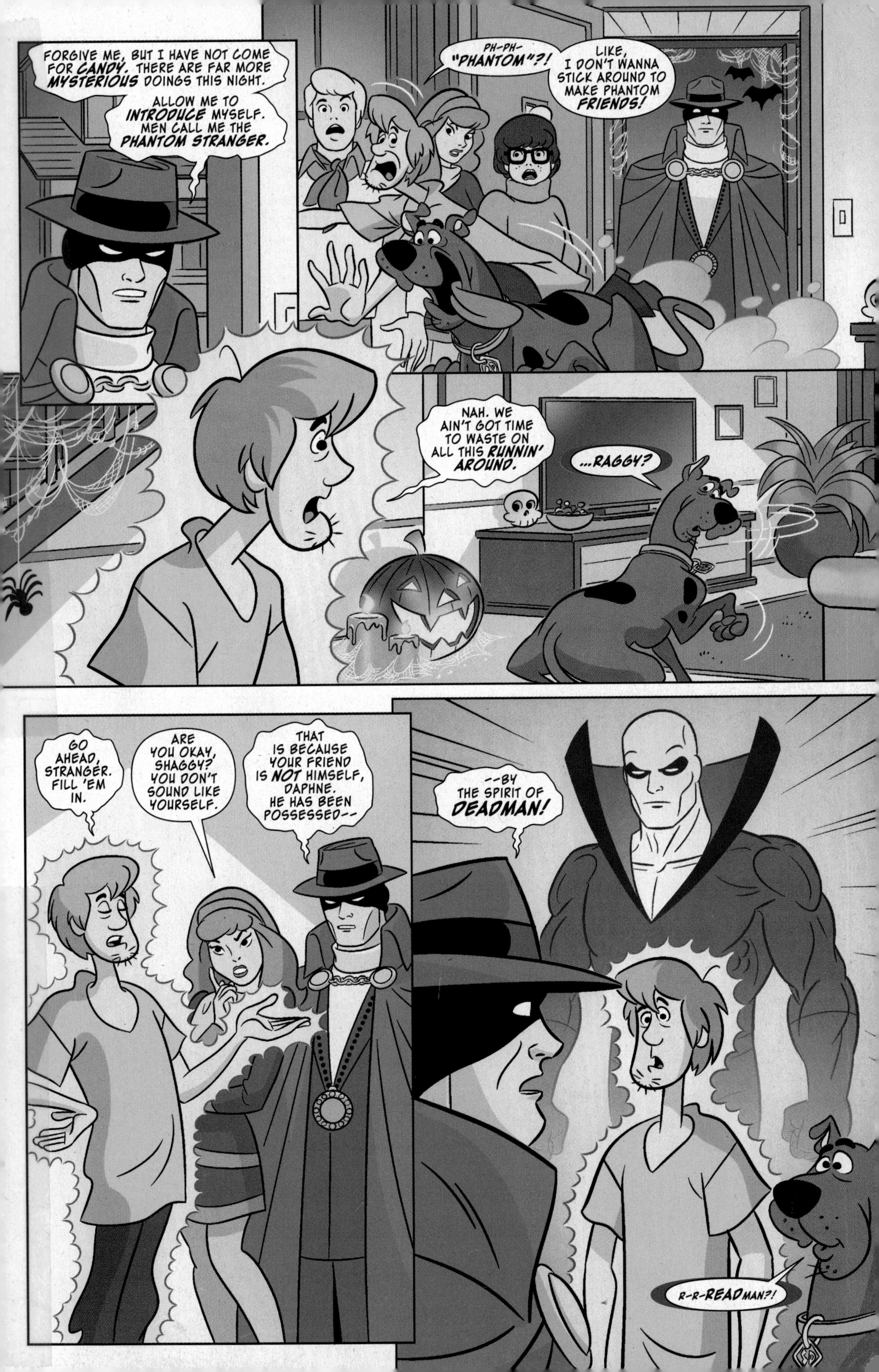
FORGIVE ME, BUT I HAVE NOT COME FOR CANDY. THERE ARE FAR MORE MYSTERIOUS DOINGS THIS NIGHT.
ALLOW ME TO INTRODUCE MYSELF. MEN CALL ME THE PHANTOM STRANGER.
PH-PH- "PHANTOM"?!
LIKE, I DON'T WANNA STICK AROUND TO MAKE PHANTOM FRIENDS!
NAH. WE AIN'T GOT TIME TO WASTE ON ALL THIS RUNNIN' AROUND.
...RAGGY?
GO AHEAD, STRANGER. FILL 'EM IN.
ARE YOU OKAY, SHAGGY? YOU DON'T SOUND LIKE YOURSELF.
THAT IS BECAUSE YOUR FRIEND IS NOT HIMSELF, DAPHNE. HE HAS BEEN POSSESSED--
--BY THE SPIRIT OF DEADMAN!
R-R-READMAN?!

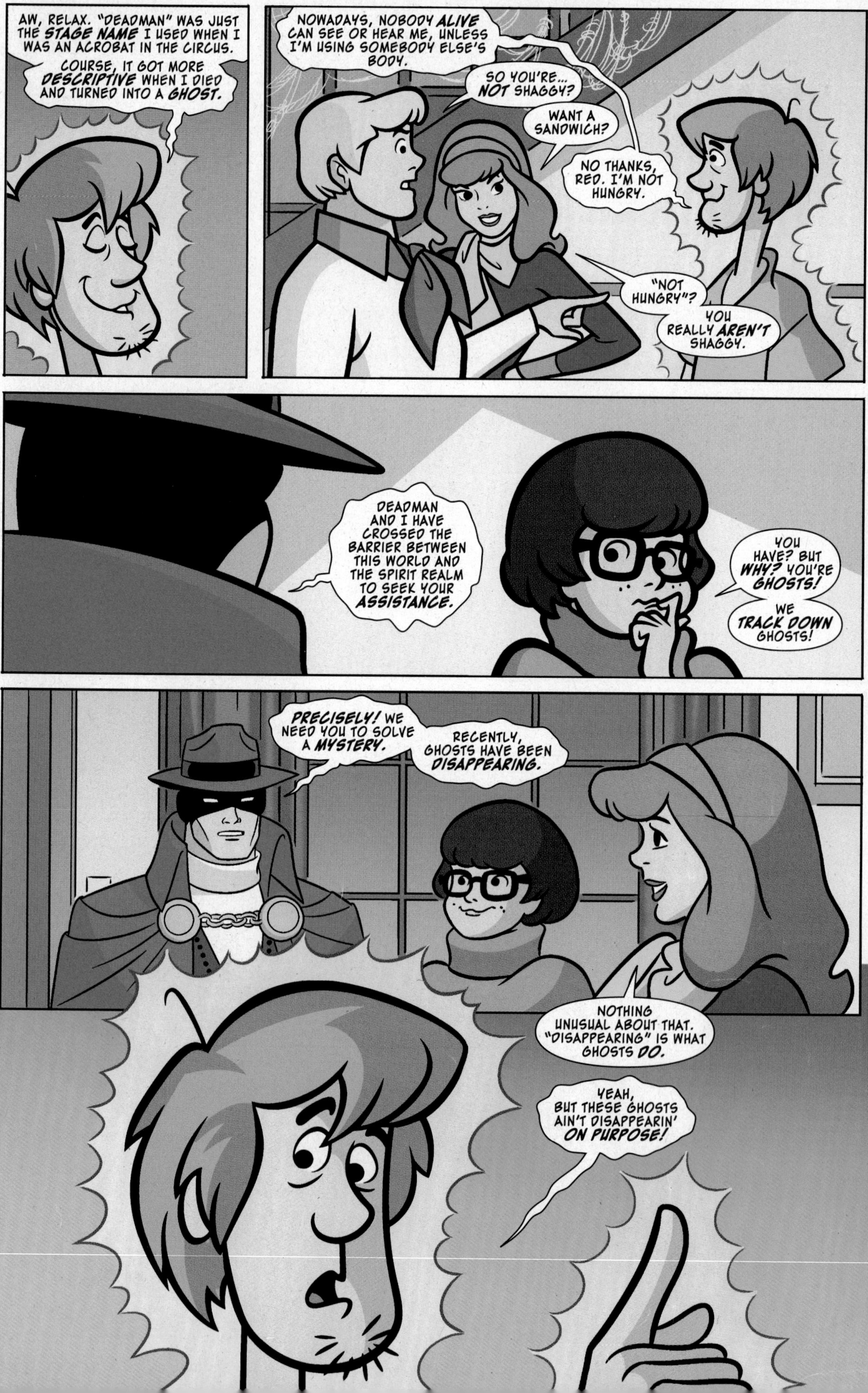
AW, RELAX. "DEADMAN" WAS JUST THE STAGE NAME I USED WHEN I WAS AN ACROBAT IN THE CIRCUS.
COURSE, IT GOT MORE DESCRIPTIVE WHEN I DIED AND TURNED INTO A GHOST.
NOWADAYS, NOBODY ALIVE CAN SEE OR HEAR ME, UNLESS I'M USING SOMEBODY ELSE'S BODY.
SO YOU'RE... NOT SHAGGY?
WANT A SANDWICH?
NO THANKS, RED. I'M NOT HUNGRY.
"NOT HUNGRY"?
YOU REALLY AREN'T SHAGGY.
DEADMAN AND I HAVE CROSSED THE BARRIER BETWEEN THIS WORLD AND THE SPIRIT REALM TO SEEK YOUR ASSISTANCE.
YOU HAVE? BUT WHY? YOU'RE GHOSTS!
WE TRACK DOWN GHOSTS!
PRECISELY! WE NEED YOU TO SOLVE A MYSTERY.
RECENTLY, GHOSTS HAVE BEEN DISAPPEARING.
NOTHING UNUSUAL ABOUT THAT. "DISAPPEARING" IS WHAT GHOSTS DO.
YEAH, BUT THESE GHOSTS AIN'T DISAPPEARIN' ON PURPOSE!

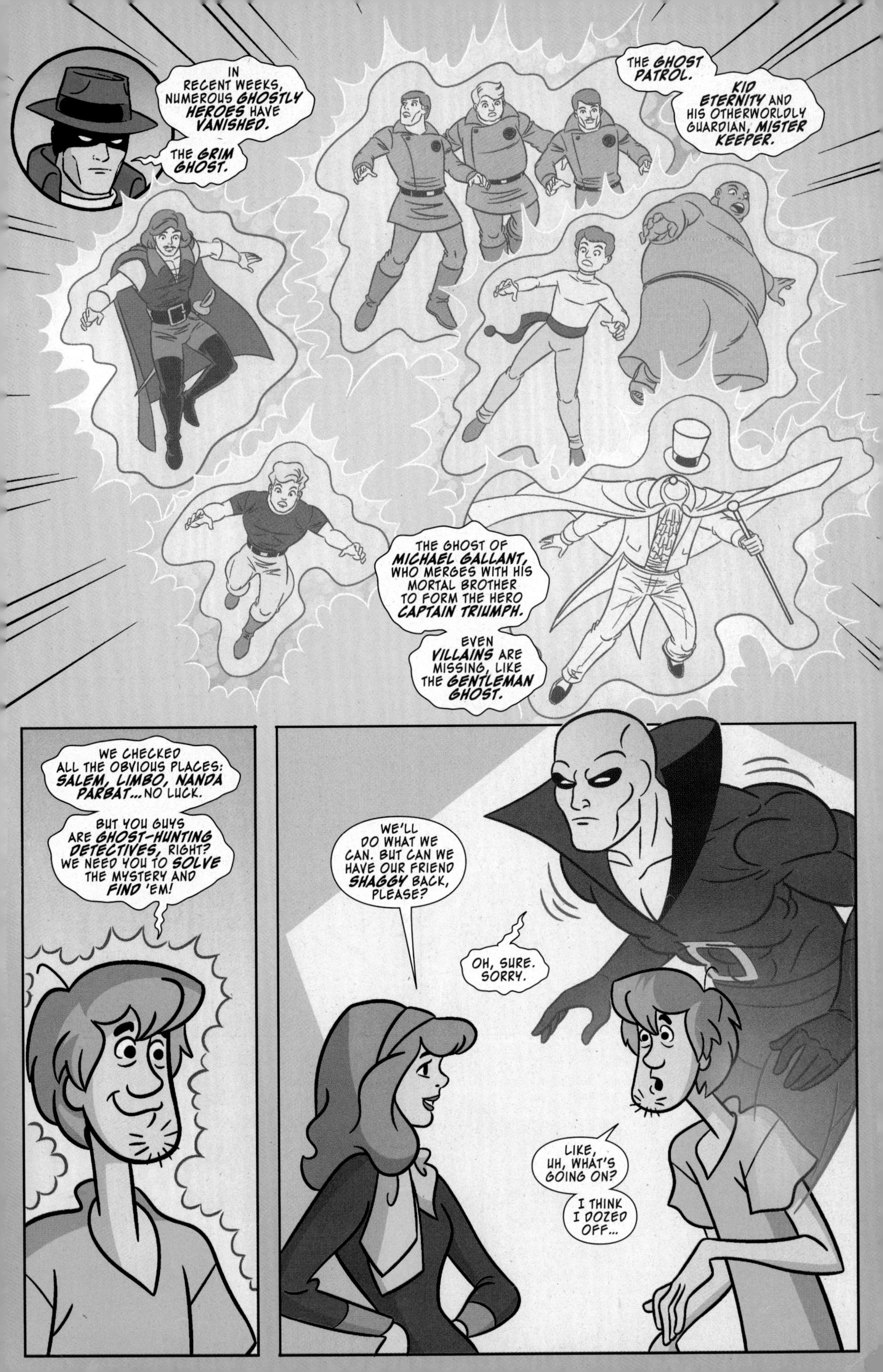
IN RECENT WEEKS, NUMEROUS GHOSTLY HEROES HAVE VANISHED.
THE GRIM GHOST.
THE GHOST PATROL.
KID ETERNITY AND HIS OTHERWORLDLY GUARDIAN, MISTER KEEPER.
THE GHOST OF MICHAEL GALLANT, WHO MERGES WITH HIS MORTAL BROTHER TO FORM THE HERO CAPTAIN TRIUMPH.
EVEN VILLAINS ARE MISSING, LIKE THE GENTLEMAN GHOST.
WE CHECKED ALL THE OBVIOUS PLACES: SALEM, LIMBO, NANDA PARBAT... NO LUCK.
BUT YOU GUYS ARE GHOST-HUNTING DETECTIVES, RIGHT? WE NEED YOU TO SOLVE THE MYSTERY AND FIND 'EM!
WE'LL DO WHAT WE CAN. BUT CAN WE HAVE OUR FRIEND SHAGGY BACK, PLEASE?
OH, SURE. SORRY.
LIKE, UH, WHAT'S GOING ON?
I THINK I DOZED OFF...

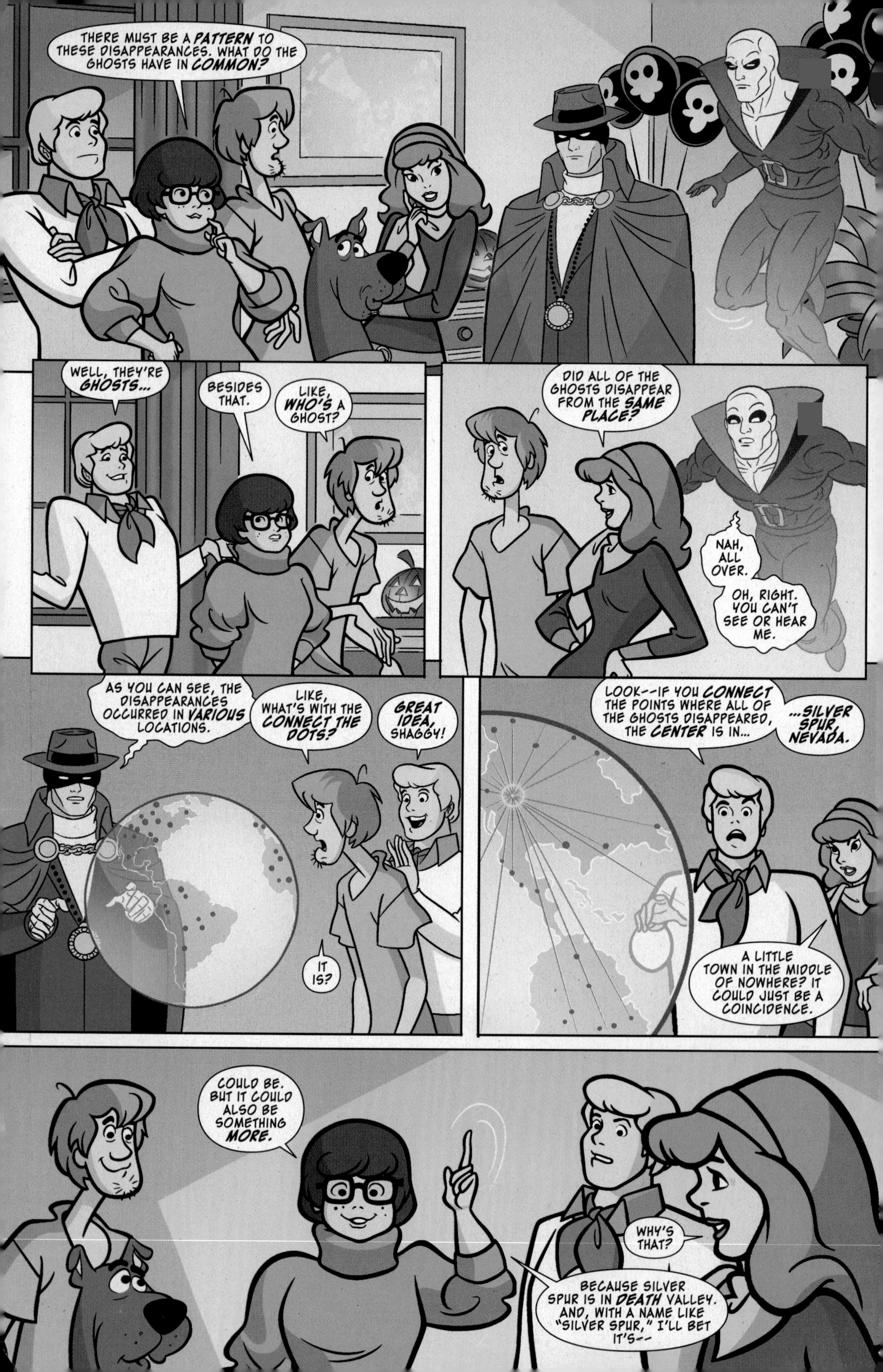
THERE MUST BE A PATTERN TO THESE DISAPPEARANCES. WHAT DO THE GHOSTS HAVE IN COMMON?
WELL, THEY'RE GHOSTS...
BESIDES THAT.
LIKE, WHO'S A GHOST?
DID ALL OF THE GHOSTS DISAPPEAR FROM THE SAME PLACE?
NAH, ALL OVER.
OH, RIGHT. YOU CAN'T SEE OR HEAR ME.
AS YOU CAN SEE, THE DISAPPEARANCES OCCURRED IN VARIOUS LOCATIONS.
LIKE, WHAT'S WITH THE CONNECT THE DOTS?
GREAT IDEA, SHAGGY!
IT IS?
LOOK--IF YOU CONNECT THE POINTS WHERE ALL OF THE GHOSTS DISAPPEARED, THE CENTER IS IN...
...SILVER SPUR, NEVADA.
A LITTLE TOWN IN THE MIDDLE OF NOWHERE? IT COULD JUST BE A COINCIDENCE.
COULD BE. BUT IT COULD ALSO BE SOMETHING MORE.
WHY'S THAT?
BECAUSE SILVER SPUR IS IN DEATH VALLEY. AND, WITH A NAME LIKE "SILVER SPUR," I'LL BET IT'S--

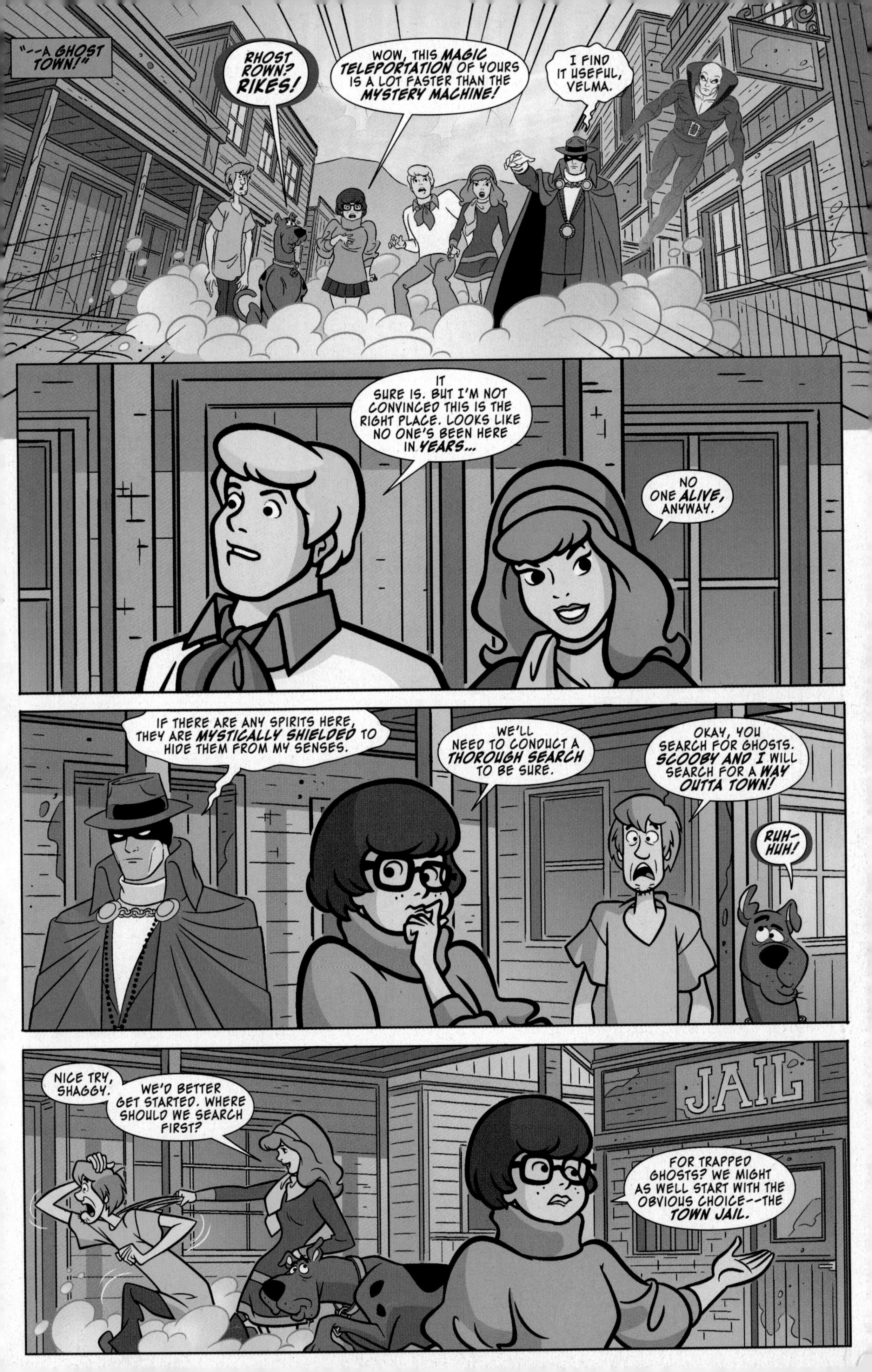

"--A GHOST TOWN!"
RHOST ROWN? RIKES!
WOW, THIS MAGIC TELEPORTATION OF YOURS IS A LOT FASTER THAN THE MYSTERY MACHINE!
I FIND IT USEFUL, VELMA.
IT SURE IS. BUT I'M NOT CONVINCED THIS IS THE RIGHT PLACE. LOOKS LIKE NO ONE'S BEEN HERE IN YEARS...
NO ONE ALIVE, ANYWAY.
IF THERE ARE ANY SPIRITS HERE, THEY ARE MYSTICALLY SHIELDED TO HIDE THEM FROM MY SENSES.
WE'LL NEED TO CONDUCT A THOROUGH SEARCH TO BE SURE.
OKAY, YOU SEARCH FOR GHOSTS. SCOOBY AND I WILL SEARCH FOR A WAY OUTTA TOWN!
RUH-HUH!
NICE TRY, SHAGGY.
WE'D BETTER GET STARTED. WHERE SHOULD WE SEARCH FIRST?
JAIL
FOR TRAPPED GHOSTS? WE MIGHT AS WELL START WITH THE OBVIOUS CHOICE--THE TOWN JAIL.

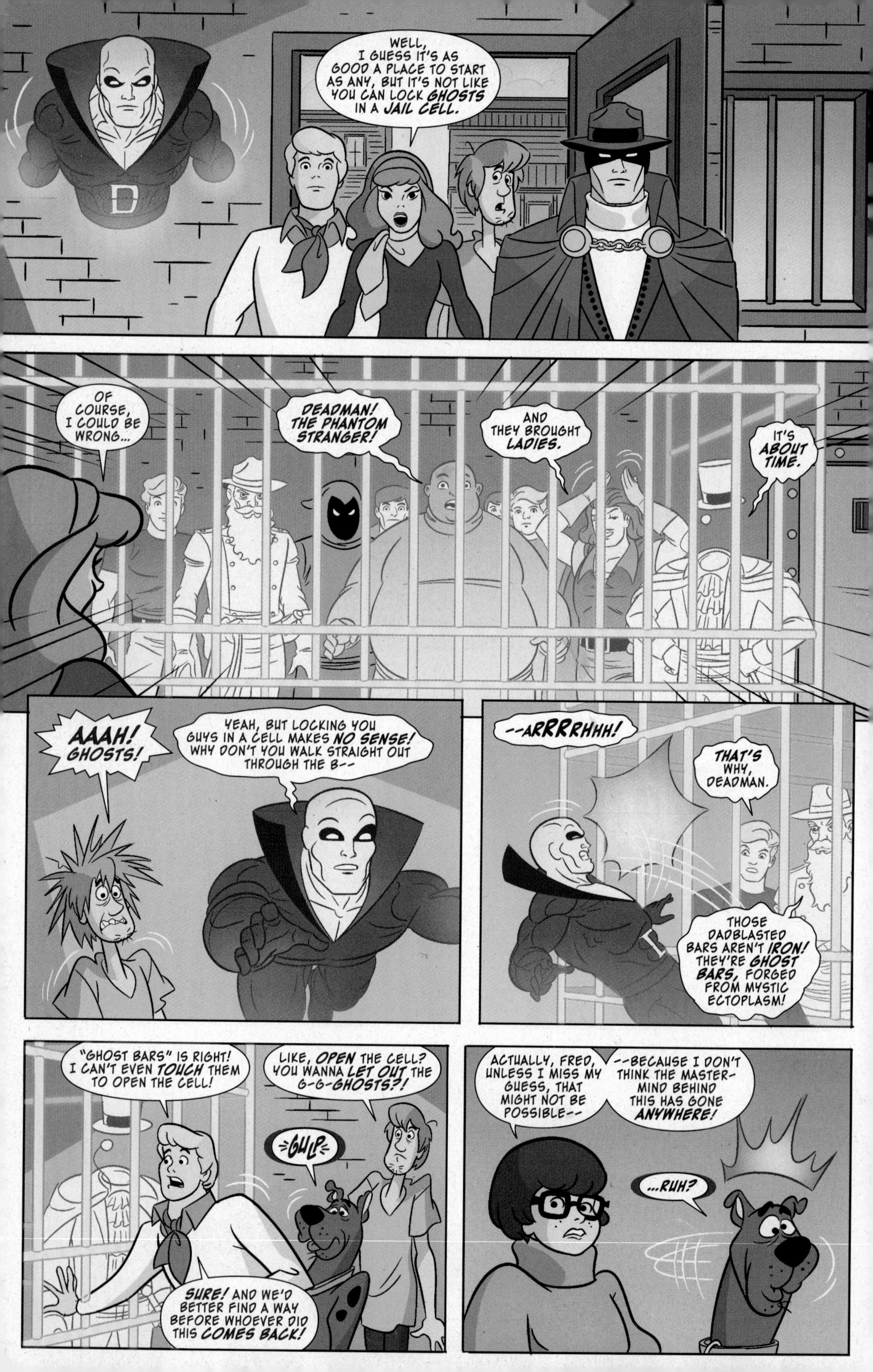
WELL, I GUESS IT'S AS GOOD A PLACE TO START AS ANY, BUT IT'S NOT LIKE YOU CAN LOCK GHOSTS IN A JAIL CELL.
OF COURSE, I COULD BE WRONG...
DEADMAN! THE PHANTOM STRANGER!
AND THEY BROUGHT LADIES.
IT'S ABOUT TIME.
AAAH! GHOSTS!
YEAH, BUT LOCKING YOU GUYS IN A CELL MAKES NO SENSE! WHY DON'T YOU WALK STRAIGHT OUT THROUGH THE B--
--ARRRRHHH!
THAT'S WHY, DEADMAN.
THOSE DADBLASTED BARS AREN'T IRON! THEY'RE GHOST BARS, FORGED FROM MYSTIC ECTOPLASM!
"GHOST BARS" IS RIGHT! I CAN'T EVEN TOUCH THEM TO OPEN THE CELL!
LIKE, OPEN THE CELL? YOU WANNA LET OUT THE G-G-GHOSTS?!
GULP
SURE! AND WE'D BETTER FIND A WAY BEFORE WHOEVER DID THIS COMES BACK!
ACTUALLY, FRED, UNLESS I MISS MY GUESS, THAT MIGHT NOT BE POSSIBLE--
--BECAUSE I DON'T THINK THE MASTERMIND BEHIND THIS HAS GONE ANYWHERE!
...RUH?

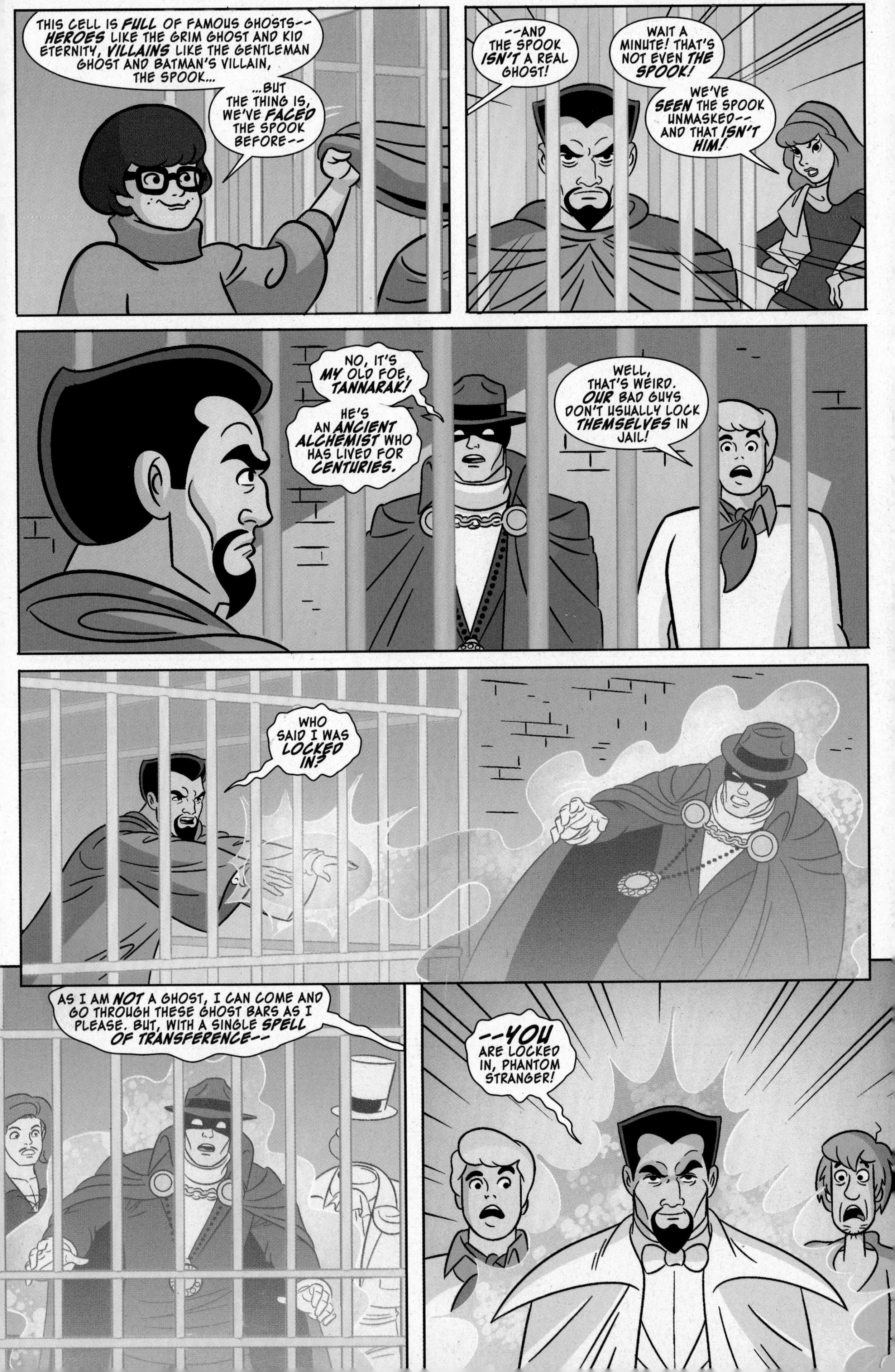

THIS CELL IS FULL OF FAMOUS GHOSTS-- HEROES LIKE THE GRIM GHOST AND KID ETERNITY, VILLAINS LIKE THE GENTLEMAN GHOST AND BATMAN'S VILLAIN, THE SPOOK...
...BUT THE THING IS, WE'VE FACED THE SPOOK BEFORE--
--AND THE SPOOK ISN'T A REAL GHOST!
WAIT A MINUTE! THAT'S NOT EVEN THE SPOOK!
WE'VE SEEN THE SPOOK UNMASKED-- AND THAT ISN'T HIM!
NO, IT'S MY OLD FOE, TANNARAK!
HE'S AN ANCIENT ALCHEMIST WHO HAS LIVED FOR CENTURIES.
WELL, THAT'S WEIRD. OUR BAD GUYS DON'T USUALLY LOCK THEMSELVES IN JAIL!
WHO SAID I WAS LOCKED IN?
AS I AM NOT A GHOST, I CAN COME AND GO THROUGH THESE GHOST BARS AS I PLEASE. BUT, WITH A SINGLE SPELL OF TRANSFERENCE--
--YOU ARE LOCKED IN, PHANTOM STRANGER!

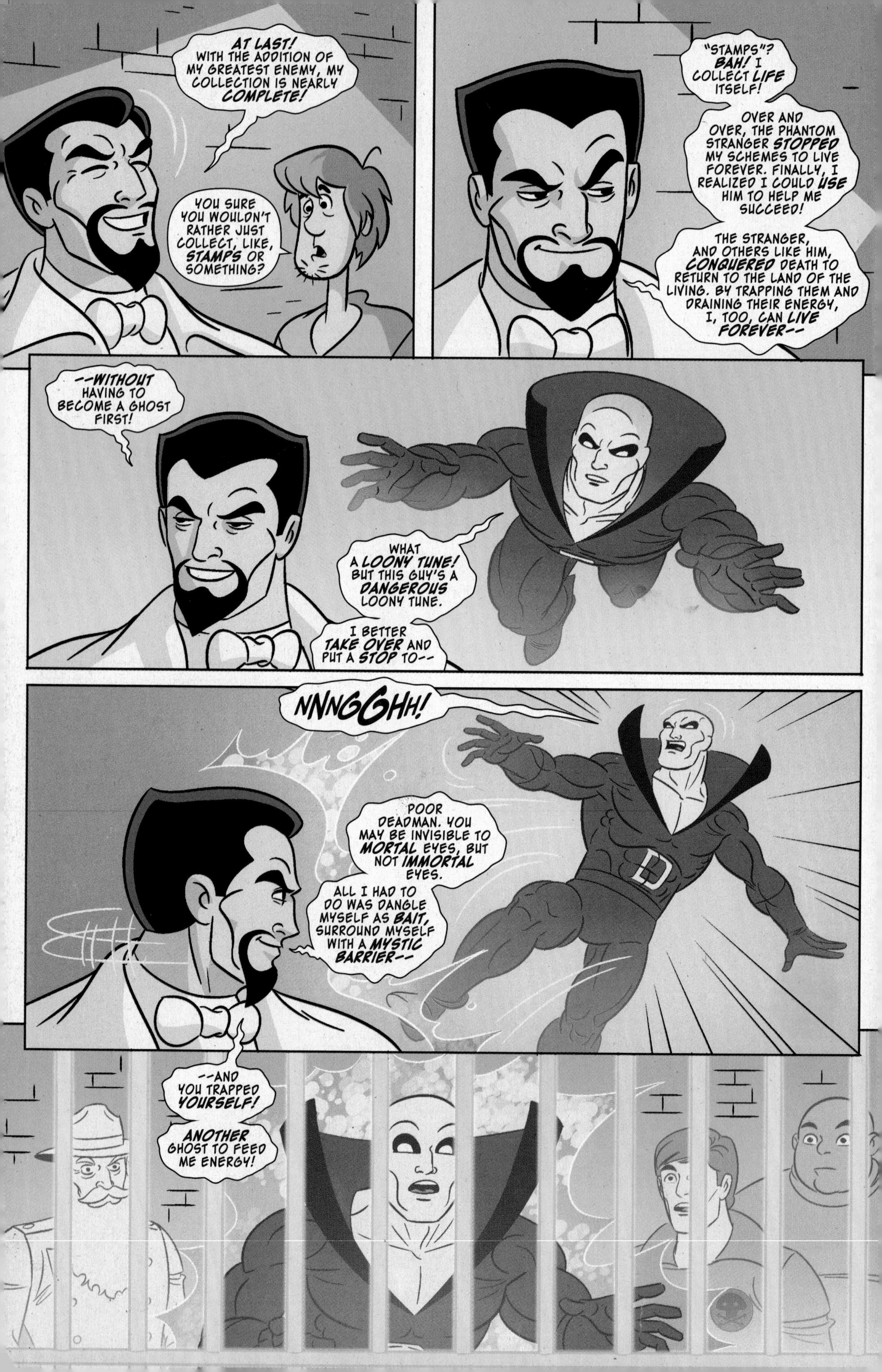
AT LAST! WITH THE ADDITION OF MY GREATEST ENEMY, MY COLLECTION IS NEARLY COMPLETE!
YOU SURE YOU WOULDN'T RATHER JUST COLLECT, LIKE, STAMPS OR SOMETHING?
"STAMPS"? BAH! I COLLECT LIFE ITSELF!
OVER AND OVER, THE PHANTOM STRANGER STOPPED MY SCHEMES TO LIVE FOREVER. FINALLY, I REALIZED I COULD USE HIM TO HELP ME SUCCEED!
THE STRANGER, AND OTHERS LIKE HIM, CONQUERED DEATH TO RETURN TO THE LAND OF THE LIVING. BY TRAPPING THEM AND DRAINING THEIR ENERGY, I, TOO, CAN LIVE FOREVER--
--WITHOUT HAVING TO BECOME A GHOST FIRST!
WHAT A LOONY TUNE! BUT THIS GUY'S A DANGEROUS LOONY TUNE.
I BETTER TAKE OVER AND PUT A STOP TO--
NNNGGHH!
POOR DEADMAN. YOU MAY BE INVISIBLE TO MORTAL EYES, BUT NOT IMMORTAL EYES.
ALL I HAD TO DO WAS DANGLE MYSELF AS BAIT, SURROUND MYSELF WITH A MYSTIC BARRIER--
--AND YOU TRAPPED YOURSELF!
ANOTHER GHOST TO FEED ME ENERGY!

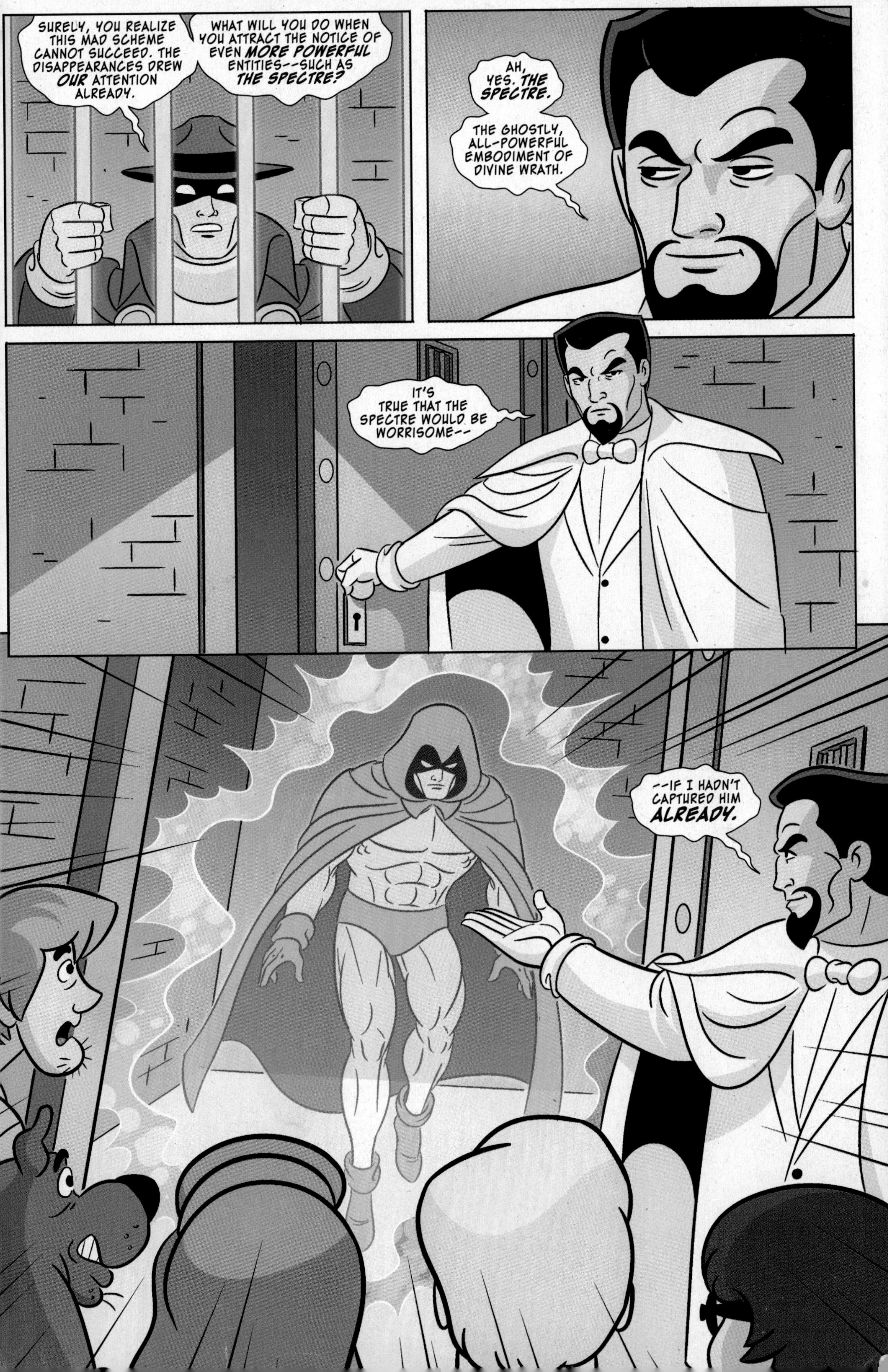
SURELY, YOU REALIZE THIS MAD SCHEME CANNOT SUCCEED. THE DISAPPEARANCES DREW OUR ATTENTION ALREADY.
WHAT WILL YOU DO WHEN YOU ATTRACT THE NOTICE OF EVEN MORE POWERFUL ENTITIES--SUCH AS THE SPECTRE?
AH, YES. THE SPECTRE.
THE GHOSTLY, ALL-POWERFUL EMBODIMENT OF DIVINE WRATH.
IT'S TRUE THAT THE SPECTRE WOULD BE WORRISOME--
--IF I HADN'T CAPTURED HIM ALREADY.

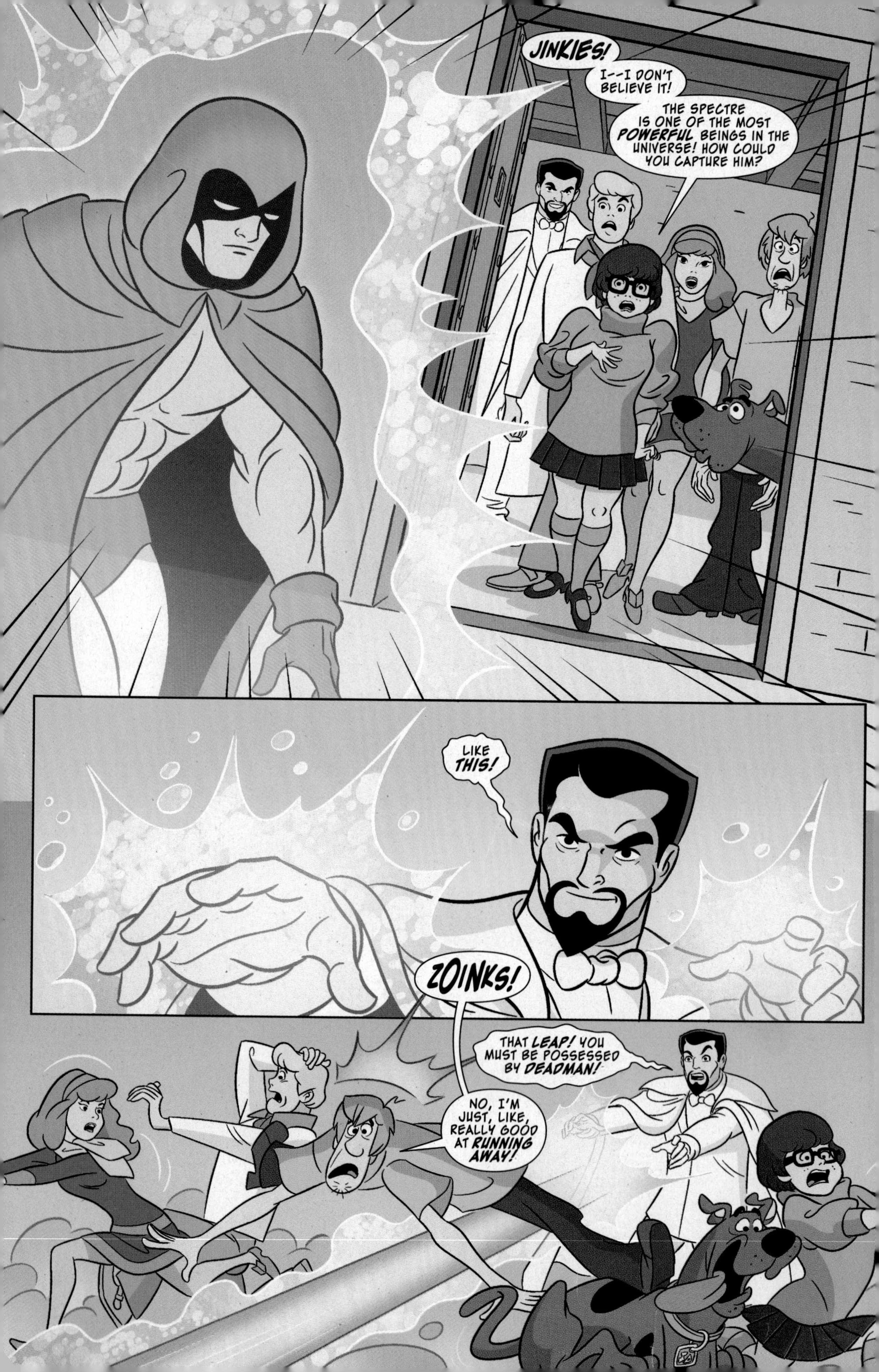
JINKIES!
I--I DON'T BELIEVE IT!
THE SPECTRE IS ONE OF THE MOST POWERFUL BEINGS IN THE UNIVERSE! HOW COULD YOU CAPTURE HIM?
LIKE THIS!
ZOINKS!
THAT LEAP! YOU MUST BE POSSESSED BY DEADMAN!
NO, I'M JUST, LIKE, REALLY GOOD AT RUNNING AWAY!

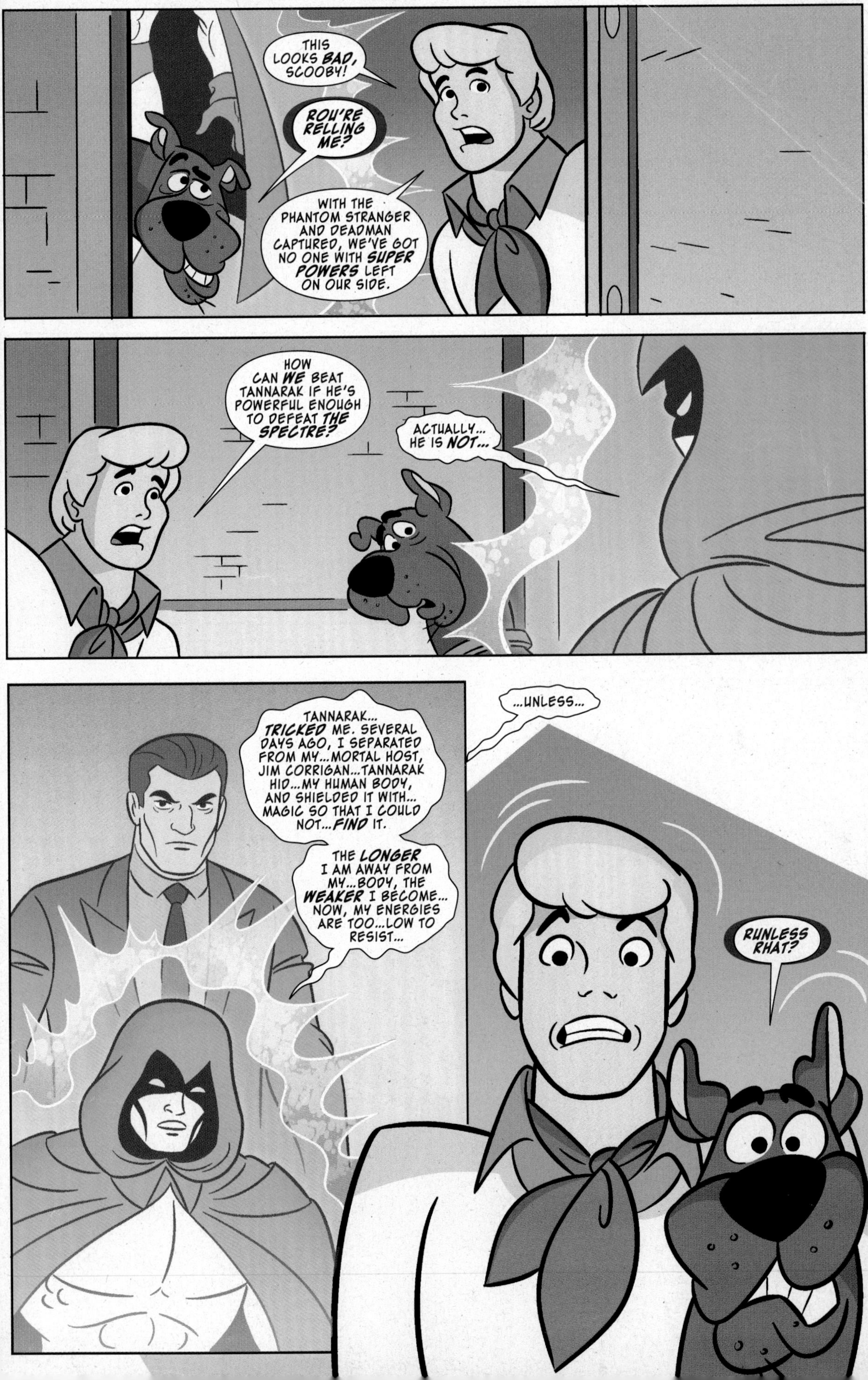
THIS LOOKS BAD, SCOOBY!
ROU'RE RELLING ME?
WITH THE PHANTOM STRANGER AND DEADMAN CAPTURED, WE'VE GOT NO ONE WITH SUPER POWERS LEFT ON OUR SIDE.
HOW CAN WE BEAT TANNARAK IF HE'S POWERFUL ENOUGH TO DEFEAT THE SPECTRE?
ACTUALLY... HE IS NOT...
TANNARAK... TRICKED ME. SEVERAL DAYS AGO, I SEPARATED FROM MY...MORTAL HOST, JIM CORRIGAN...TANNARAK HID...MY HUMAN BODY, AND SHIELDED IT WITH... MAGIC SO THAT I COULD NOT...FIND IT.
THE LONGER I AM AWAY FROM MY...BODY, THE WEAKER I BECOME... NOW, MY ENERGIES ARE TOO...LOW TO RESIST...
...UNLESS...
RUNLESS RHAT?

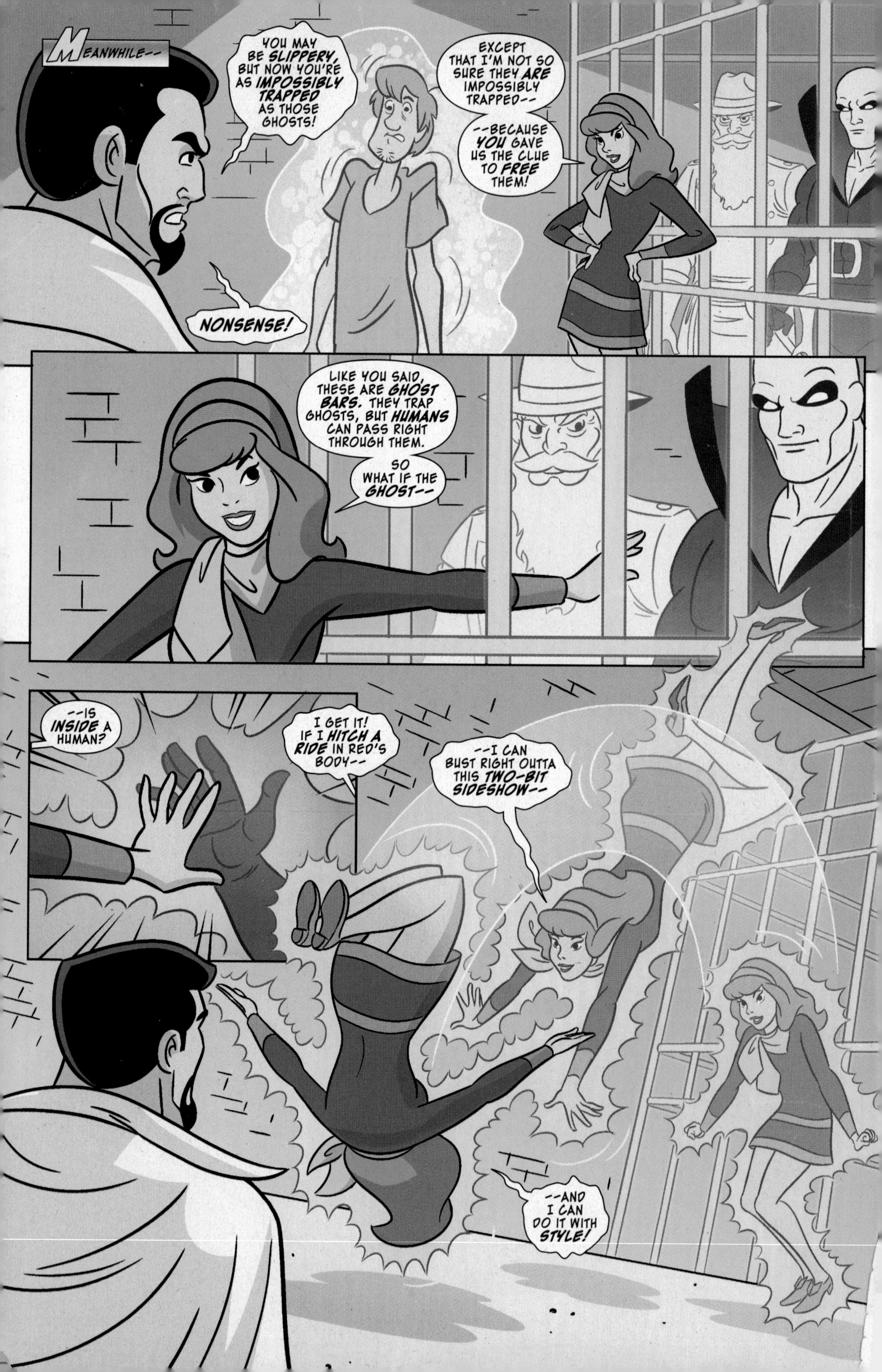
MEANWHILE--
YOU MAY BE SLIPPERY, BUT NOW YOU'RE AS IMPOSSIBLY TRAPPED AS THOSE GHOSTS!
EXCEPT THAT I'M NOT SO SURE THEY ARE IMPOSSIBLY TRAPPED--
--BECAUSE YOU GAVE US THE CLUE TO FREE THEM!
NONSENSE!
LIKE YOU SAID, THESE ARE GHOST BARS. THEY TRAP GHOSTS, BUT HUMANS CAN PASS RIGHT THROUGH THEM.
SO WHAT IF THE GHOST--
--IS INSIDE A HUMAN?
I GET IT! IF I HITCH A RIDE IN RED'S BODY--
--I CAN BUST RIGHT OUTTA THIS TWO-BIT SIDESHOW--
--AND I CAN DO IT WITH STYLE!

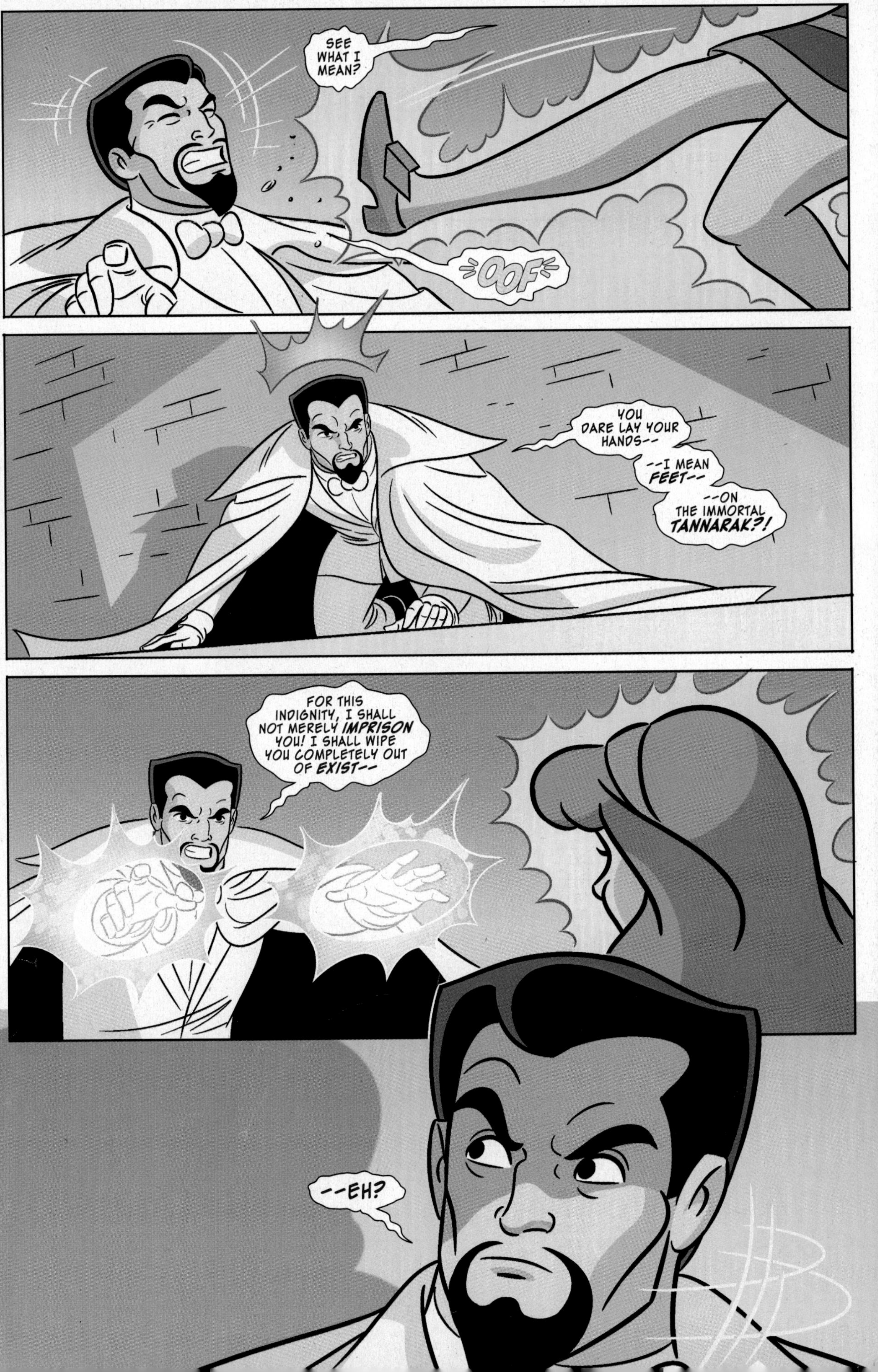
SEE WHAT I MEAN?
OOF
YOU DARE LAY YOUR HANDS--
--I MEAN FEET--
--ON THE IMMORTAL TANNARAK?!
FOR THIS INDIGNITY, I SHALL NOT MERELY IMPRISON YOU! I SHALL WIPE YOU COMPLETELY OUT OF EXIST--
--EH?

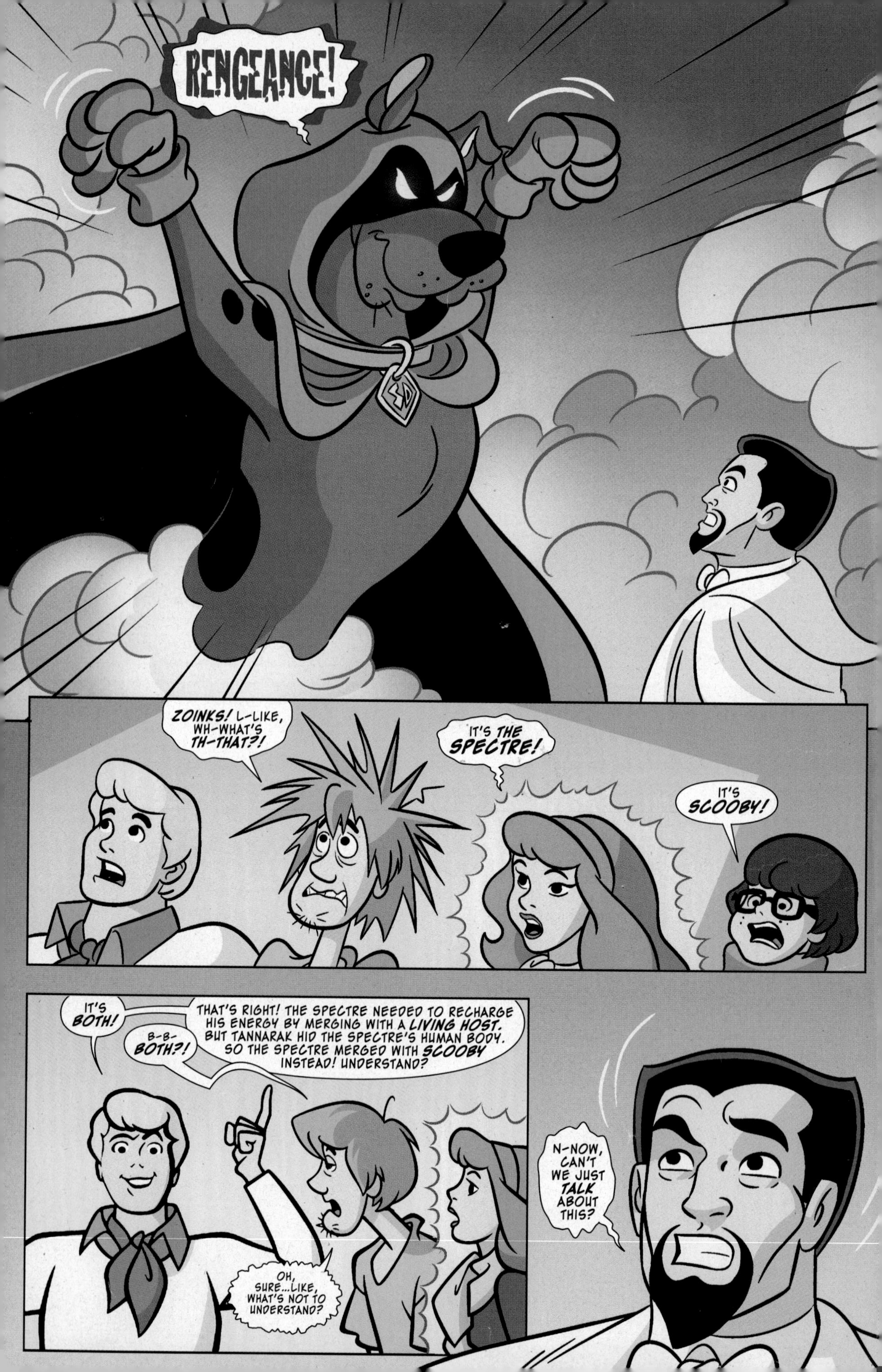
RENGEANCE!
ZOINKS! L-LIKE, WH-WHAT'S TH-THAT?!
IT'S THE SPECTRE!
IT'S SCOOBY!
IT'S BOTH!
B-B-BOTH?!
THAT'S RIGHT! THE SPECTRE NEEDED TO RECHARGE HIS ENERGY BY MERGING WITH A LIVING HOST. BUT TANNARAK HID THE SPECTRE'S HUMAN BODY. SO THE SPECTRE MERGED WITH SCOOBY INSTEAD! UNDERSTAND?
OH, SURE...LIKE, WHAT'S NOT TO UNDERSTAND?
N-NOW, CAN'T WE JUST TALK ABOUT THIS?

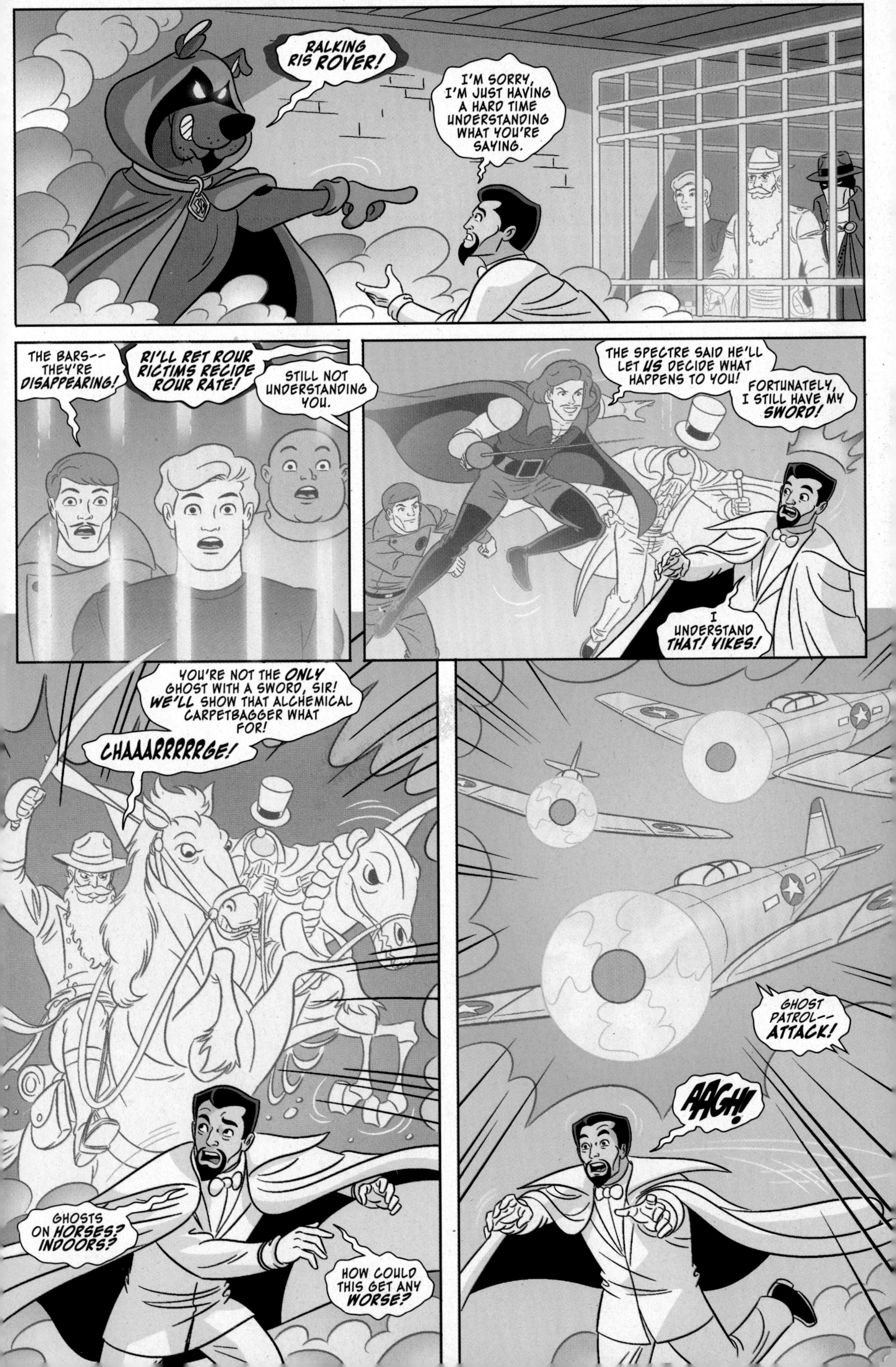
RALKING RIS ROVER!
I'M SORRY, I'M JUST HAVING A HARD TIME UNDERSTANDING WHAT YOU'RE SAYING.
THE BARS-- THEY'RE DISAPPEARING!
RI'LL RET ROUR RICTIMS RECIDE ROUR RATE!
STILL NOT UNDERSTANDING YOU.
THE SPECTRE SAID HE'LL LET US DECIDE WHAT HAPPENS TO YOU!
FORTUNATELY, I STILL HAVE MY SWORD!
I UNDERSTAND THAT! YIKES!
YOU'RE NOT THE ONLY GHOST WITH A SWORD, SIR! WE'LL SHOW THAT ALCHEMICAL CARPETBAGGER WHAT FOR!
CHAAARRRRRGE!
GHOSTS ON HORSES? INDOORS?
HOW COULD THIS GET ANY WORSE?
GHOST PATROL-- ATTACK!
AAGH!

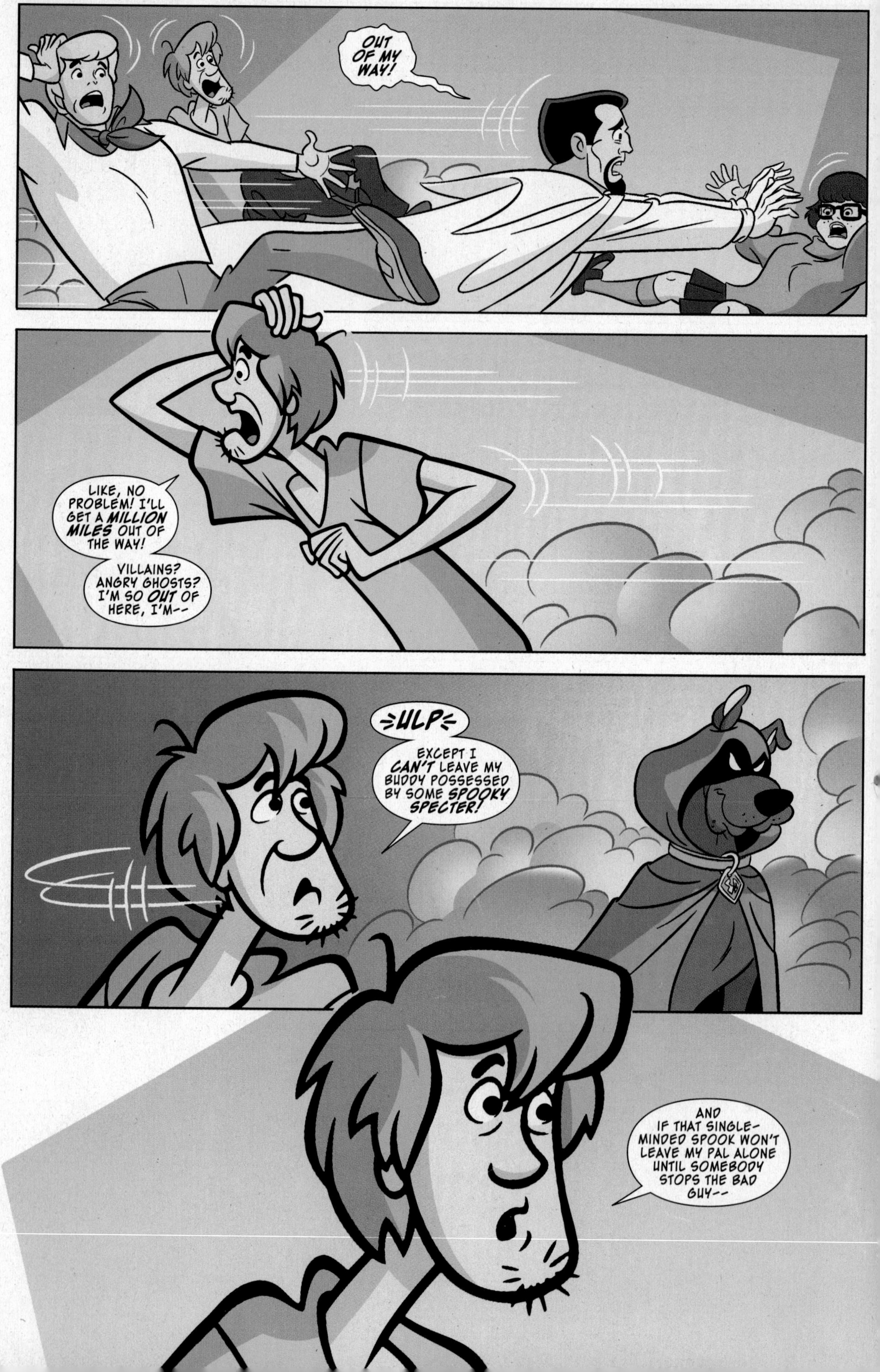
OUT OF MY WAY!
LIKE, NO PROBLEM! I'LL GET A MILLION MILES OUT OF THE WAY!
VILLAINS? ANGRY GHOSTS? I'M SO OUT OF HERE, I'M--
ULP
EXCEPT I CAN'T LEAVE MY BUDDY POSSESSED BY SOME SPOOKY SPECTER!
AND IF THAT SINGLE-MINDED SPOOK WON'T LEAVE MY PAL ALONE UNTIL SOMEBODY STOPS THE BAD GUY--

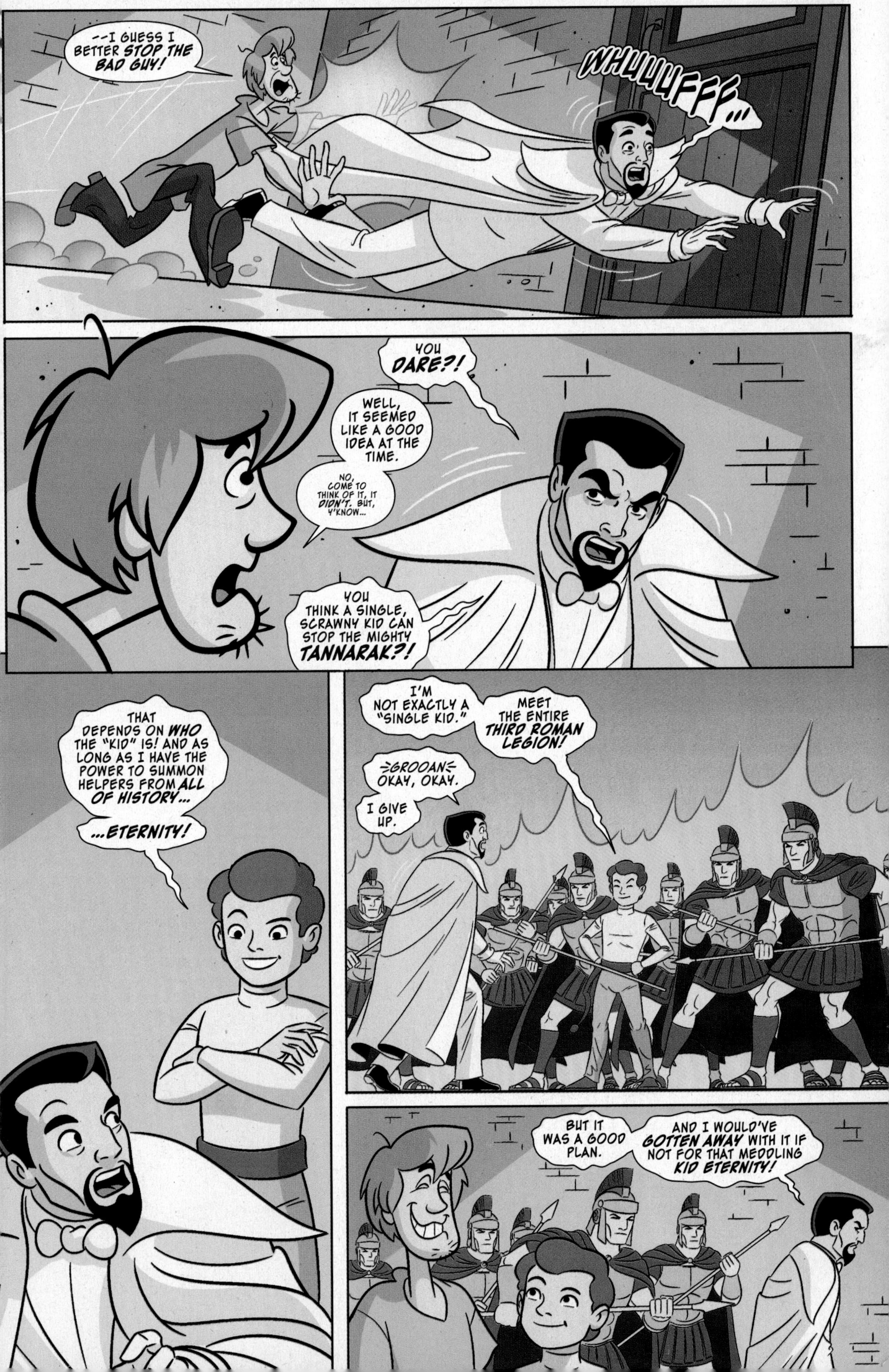
--I GUESS I BETTER STOP THE BAD GUY!
WHULUUFFF...
YOU DARE?!
WELL, IT SEEMED LIKE A GOOD IDEA AT THE TIME.
NO, COME TO THINK OF IT, IT DIDN'T. BUT, Y'KNOW...
YOU THINK A SINGLE, SCRAWNY KID CAN STOP THE MIGHTY TANNARAK?!
THAT DEPENDS ON WHO THE "KID" IS! AND AS LONG AS I HAVE THE POWER TO SUMMON HELPERS FROM ALL OF HISTORY...
...ETERNITY!
I'M NOT EXACTLY A "SINGLE KID."
MEET THE ENTIRE THIRD ROMAN LEGION!
=GROOAN= OKAY, OKAY.
I GIVE UP.
BUT IT WAS A GOOD PLAN.
AND I WOULD'VE GOTTEN AWAY WITH IT IF NOT FOR THAT MEDDLING KID ETERNITY!

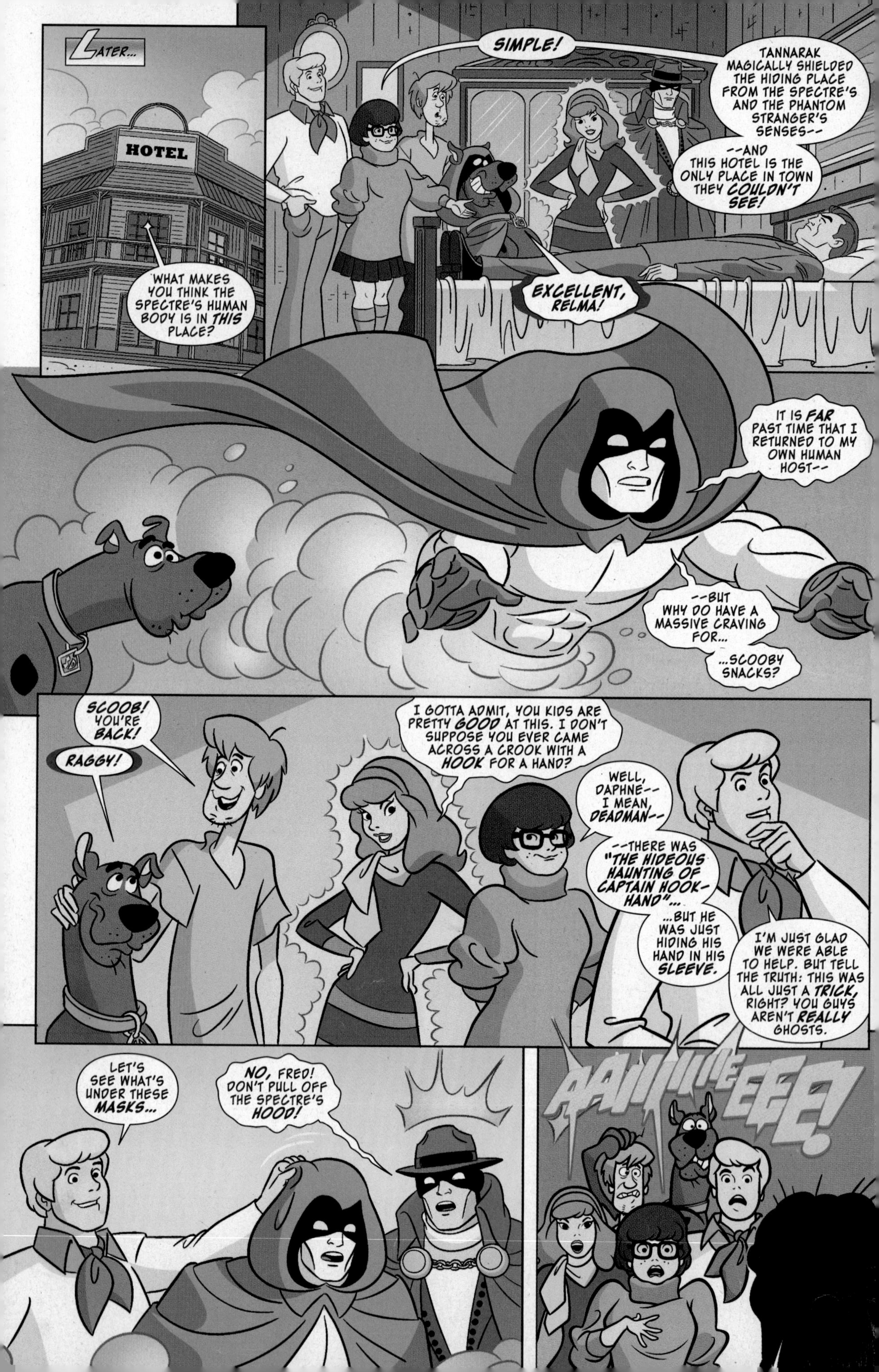
LATER...
WHAT MAKES YOU THINK THE SPECTRE'S HUMAN BODY IS IN THIS PLACE?
SIMPLE!
TANNARAK MAGICALLY SHIELDED THE HIDING PLACE FROM THE SPECTRE'S AND THE PHANTOM STRANGER'S SENSES--
--AND THIS HOTEL IS THE ONLY PLACE IN TOWN THEY COULDN'T SEE!
EXCELLENT, RELMA!
HOTEL
IT IS FAR PAST TIME THAT I RETURNED TO MY OWN HUMAN HOST--
--BUT WHY DO HAVE A MASSIVE CRAVING FOR...
...SCOOBY SNACKS?
SCOOB! YOU'RE BACK!
RAGGY!
I GOTTA ADMIT, YOU KIDS ARE PRETTY GOOD AT THIS. I DON'T SUPPOSE YOU EVER CAME ACROSS A CROOK WITH A HOOK FOR A HAND?
WELL, DAPHNE-- I MEAN, DEADMAN--
--THERE WAS "THE HIDEOUS HAUNTING OF CAPTAIN HOOK-HAND"...
...BUT HE WAS JUST HIDING HIS HAND IN HIS SLEEVE.
I'M JUST GLAD WE WERE ABLE TO HELP. BUT TELL THE TRUTH: THIS WAS ALL JUST A TRICK, RIGHT? YOU GUYS AREN'T REALLY GHOSTS.
LET'S SEE WHAT'S UNDER THESE MASKS...
NO, FRED! DON'T PULL OFF THE SPECTRE'S HOOD!
AAIIIIIEEEE!

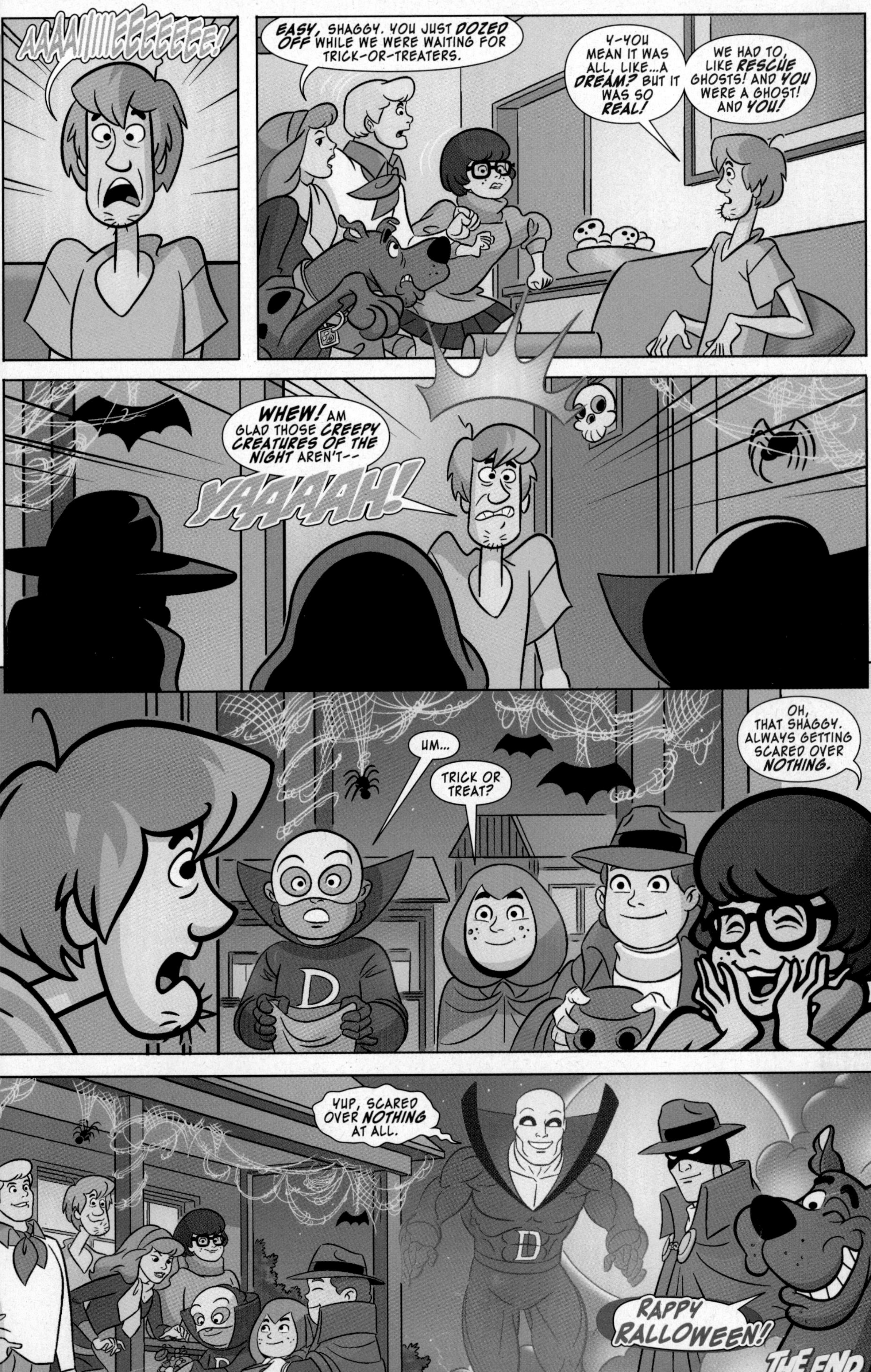
AAAAIIIIIEEEEEEEE!
EASY, SHAGGY. YOU JUST DOZED OFF WHILE WE WERE WAITING FOR TRICK-OR-TREATERS.
Y-YOU MEAN IT WAS ALL, LIKE... A DREAM? BUT IT WAS SO REAL!
WE HAD TO, LIKE RESCUE GHOSTS! AND YOU WERE A GHOST! AND YOU!
WHEW! AM GLAD THOSE CREEPY CREATURES OF THE NIGHT AREN'T--
YAAAAH!
UM...
TRICK OR TREAT?
OH, THAT SHAGGY. ALWAYS GETTING SCARED OVER NOTHING.
YUP, SCARED OVER NOTHING AT ALL.
RAPPY RALLOWEEN!
THE END

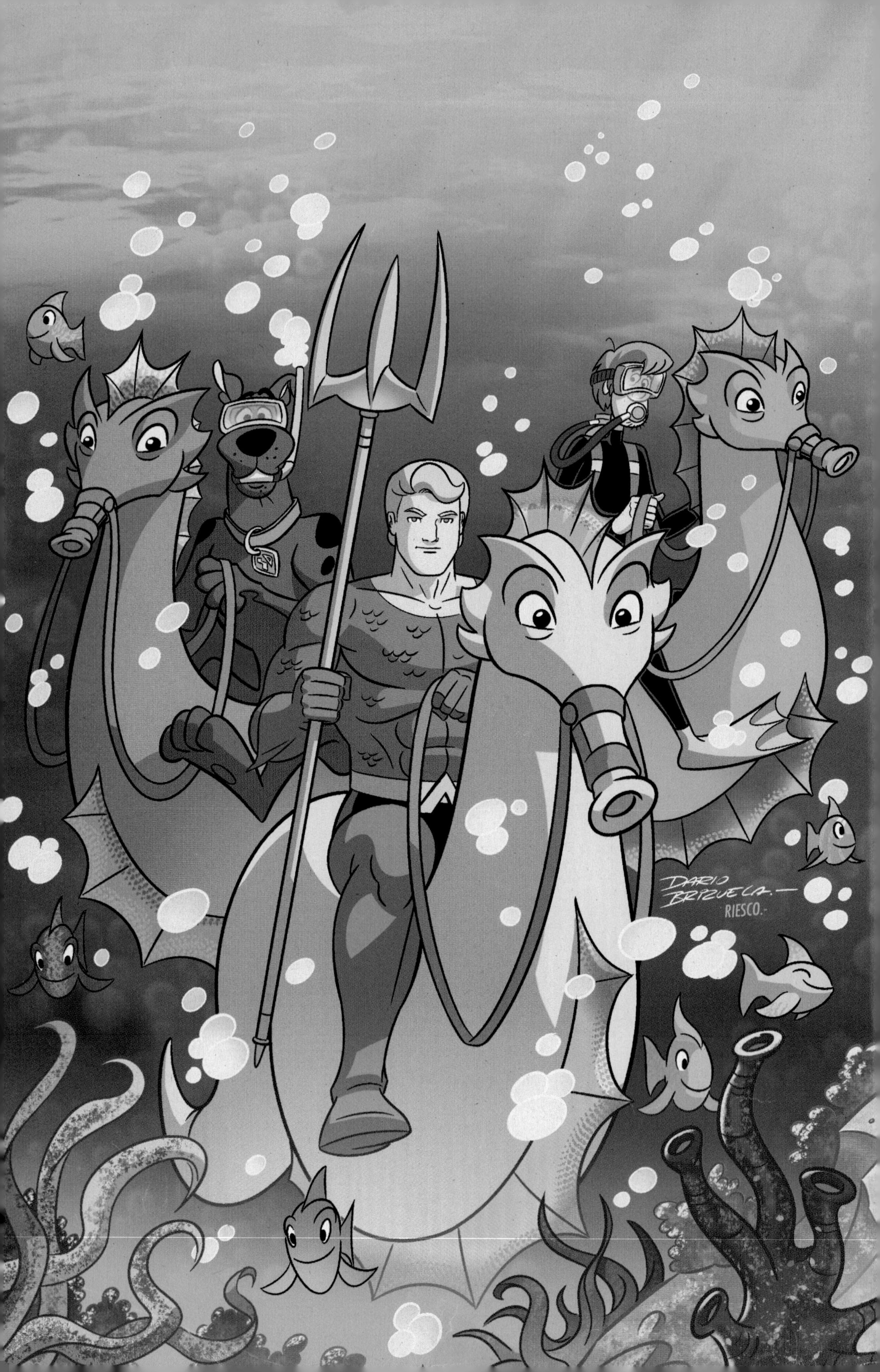
DARIO BRIZUELA.—
RIESCO.-

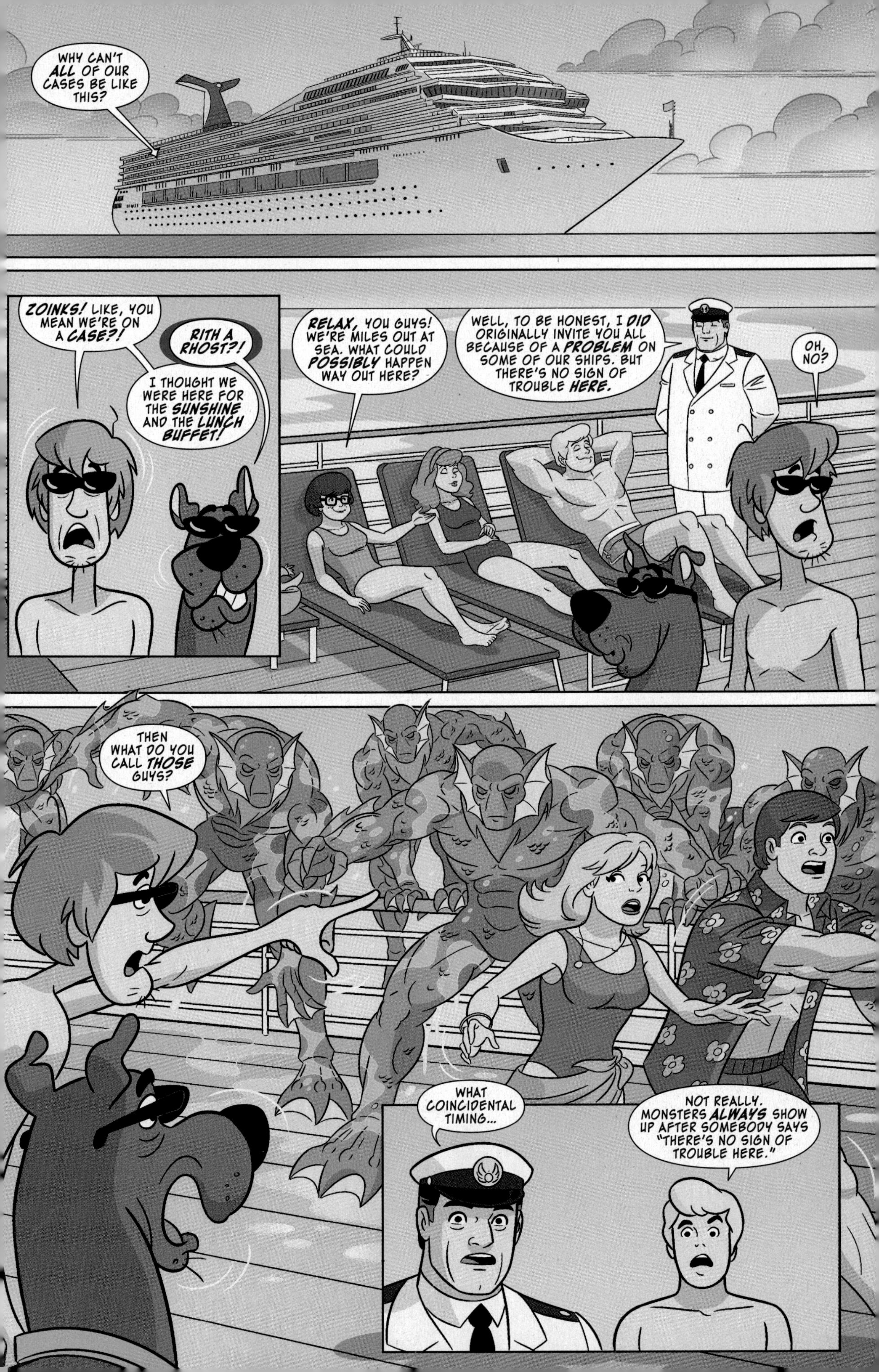
WHY CAN'T ALL OF OUR CASES BE LIKE THIS?
ZOINKS! LIKE, YOU MEAN WE'RE ON A CASE?!
RITH A RHOST?!
I THOUGHT WE WERE HERE FOR THE SUNSHINE AND THE LUNCH BUFFET!
RELAX, YOU GUYS! WE'RE MILES OUT AT SEA. WHAT COULD POSSIBLY HAPPEN WAY OUT HERE?
WELL, TO BE HONEST, I DID ORIGINALLY INVITE YOU ALL BECAUSE OF A PROBLEM ON SOME OF OUR SHIPS. BUT THERE'S NO SIGN OF TROUBLE HERE.
OH, NO?
THEN WHAT DO YOU CALL THOSE GUYS?
WHAT COINCIDENTAL TIMING...
NOT REALLY. MONSTERS ALWAYS SHOW UP AFTER SOMEBODY SAYS "THERE'S NO SIGN OF TROUBLE HERE."

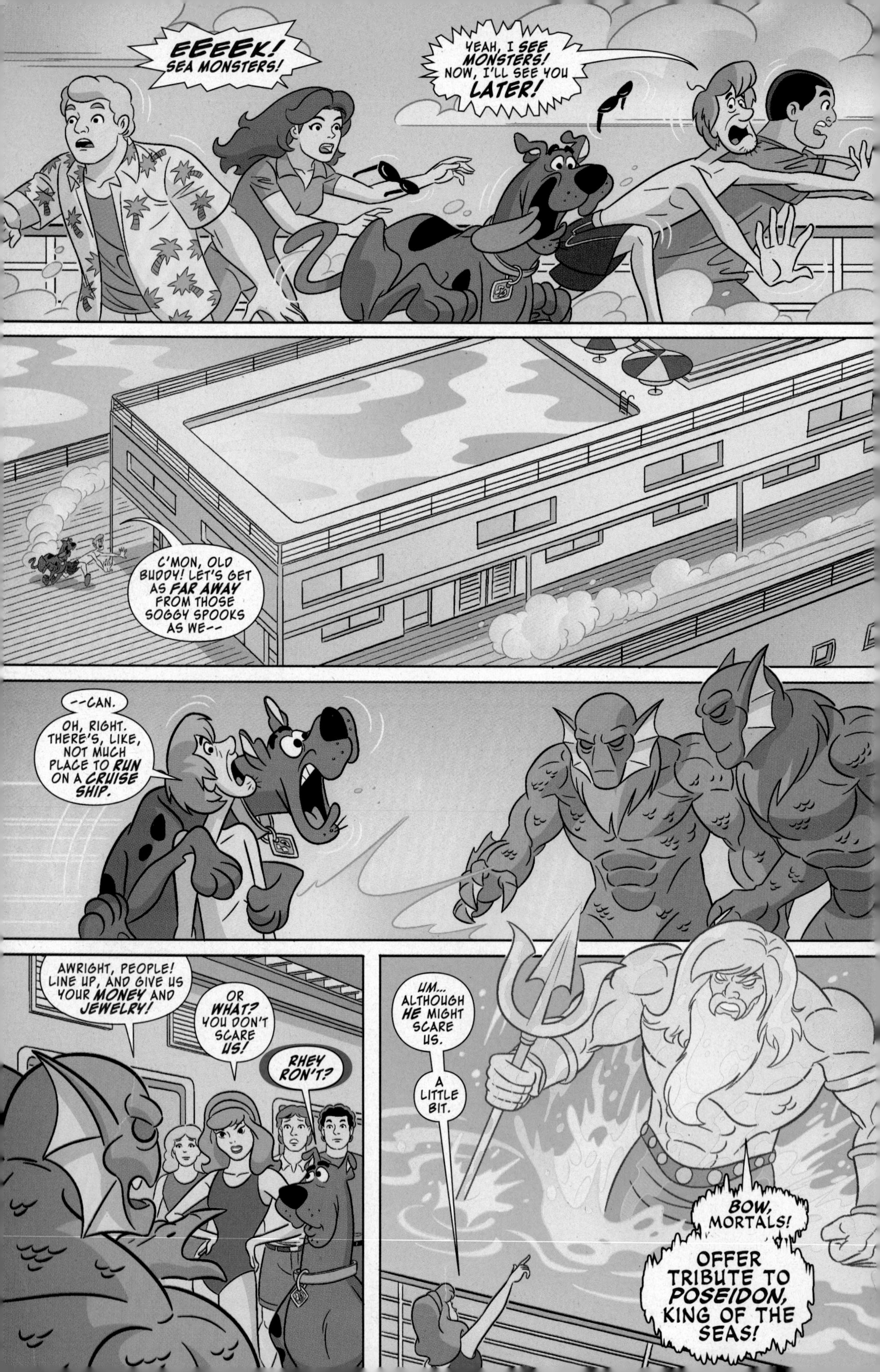
EEEEK! SEA MONSTERS!
YEAH, I SEE MONSTERS! NOW, I'LL SEE YOU LATER!
C'MON, OLD BUDDY! LET'S GET AS FAR AWAY FROM THOSE SOGGY SPOOKS AS WE--
--CAN.
OH, RIGHT. THERE'S, LIKE, NOT MUCH PLACE TO RUN ON A CRUISE SHIP.
AWRIGHT, PEOPLE! LINE UP, AND GIVE US YOUR MONEY AND JEWELRY!
OR WHAT? YOU DON'T SCARE US!
RHEY RON'T?
UM... ALTHOUGH HE MIGHT SCARE US.
A LITTLE BIT.
BOW, MORTALS!
OFFER TRIBUTE TO POSEIDON, KING OF THE SEAS!

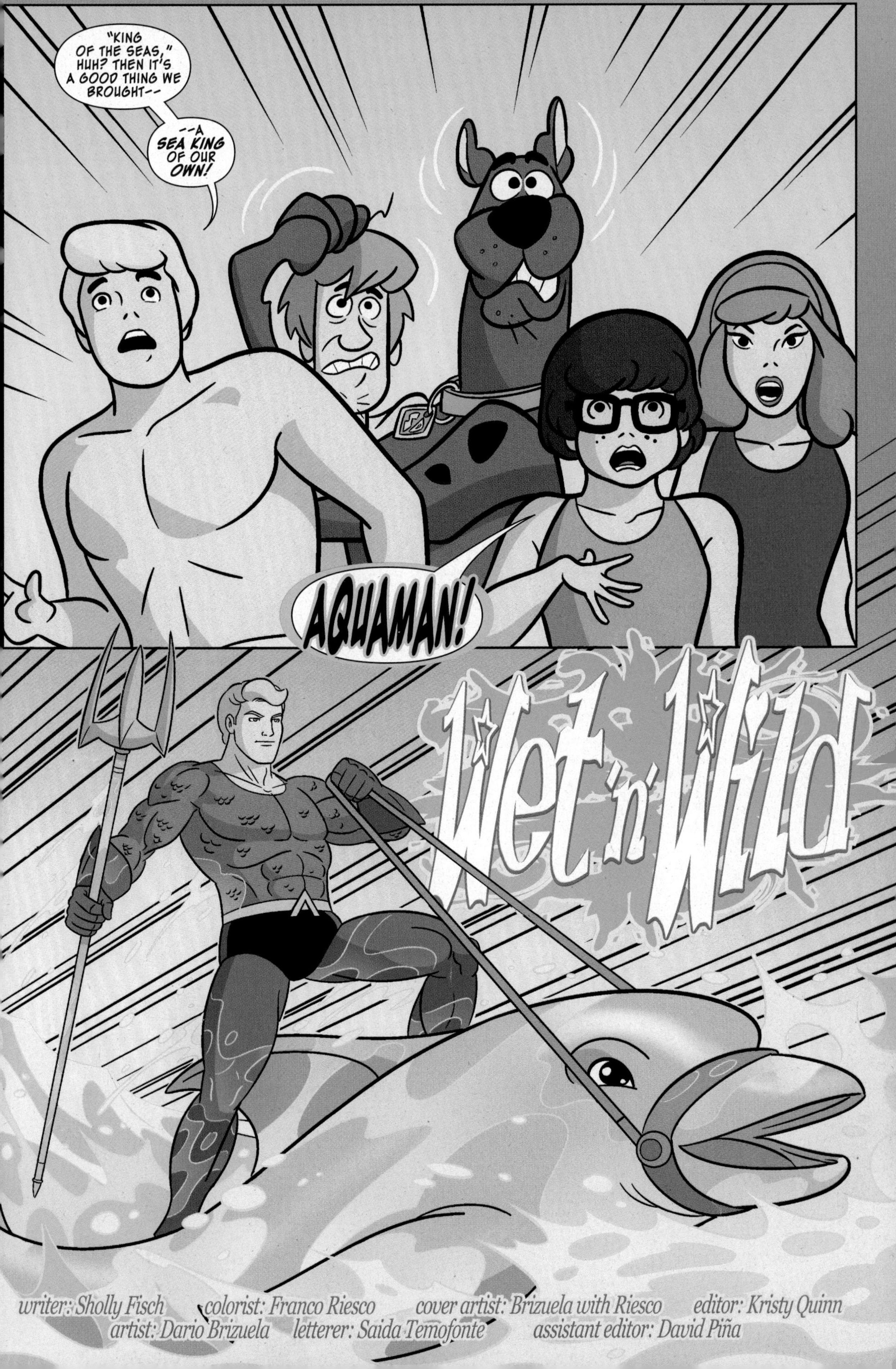
"KING OF THE SEAS," HUH? THEN IT'S A GOOD THING WE BROUGHT--
--A SEA KING OF OUR OWN!
AQUAMAN!
Wet 'n' Wild
writer: Sholly Fisch
artist: Dario Brizuela
colorist: Franco Riesco
letterer: Saida Temofonte
cover artist: Brizuela with Riesco
assistant editor: David Piña
editor: Kristy Quinn

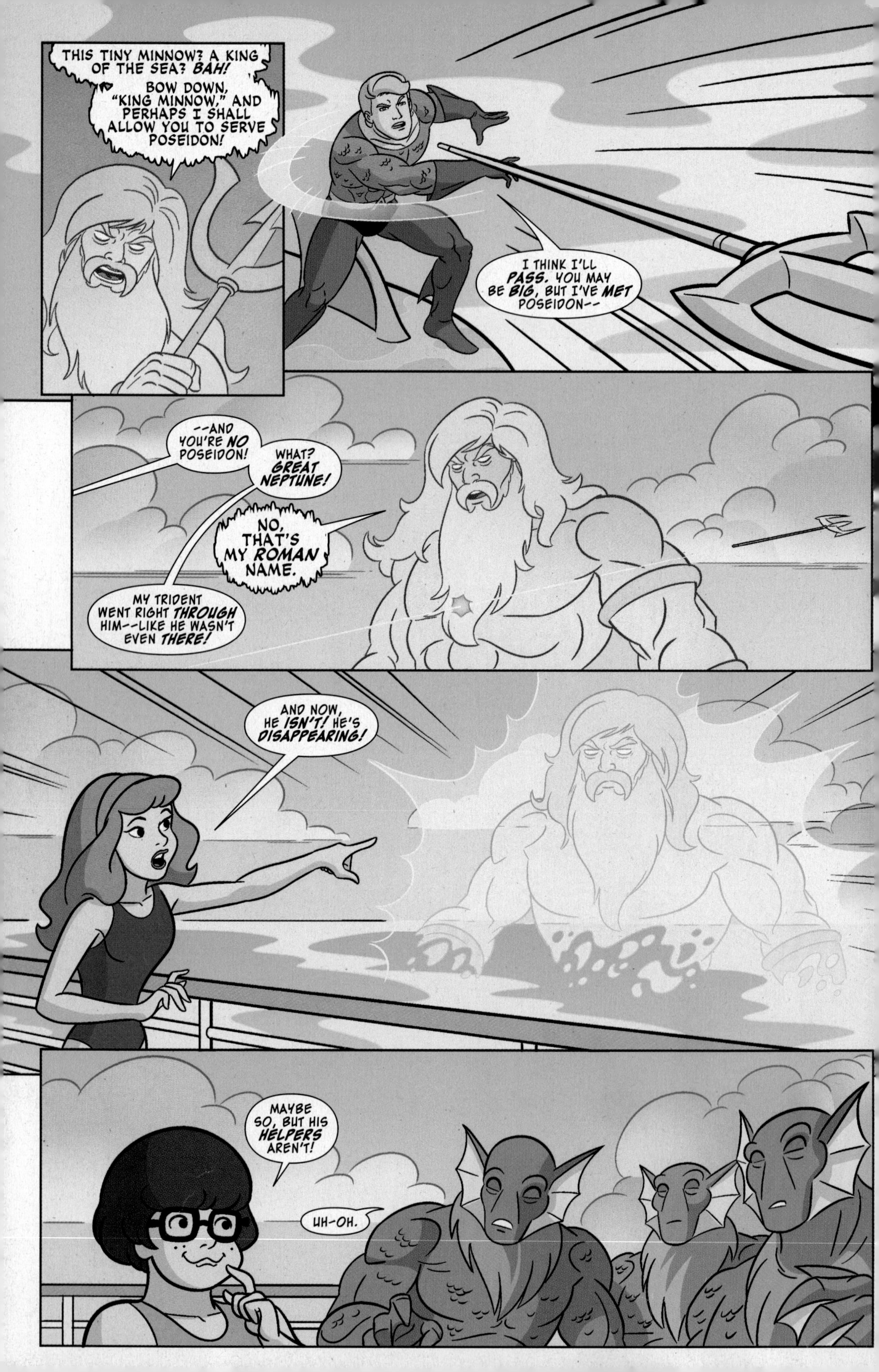
THIS TINY MINNOW? A KING OF THE SEA? BAH!
BOW DOWN, "KING MINNOW," AND PERHAPS I SHALL ALLOW YOU TO SERVE POSEIDON!
I THINK I'LL PASS. YOU MAY BE BIG, BUT I'VE MET POSEIDON--
--AND YOU'RE NO POSEIDON!
WHAT? GREAT NEPTUNE!
NO, THAT'S MY ROMAN NAME.
MY TRIDENT WENT RIGHT THROUGH HIM--LIKE HE WASN'T EVEN THERE!
AND NOW, HE ISN'T! HE'S DISAPPEARING!
MAYBE SO, BUT HIS HELPERS AREN'T!
UH-OH.

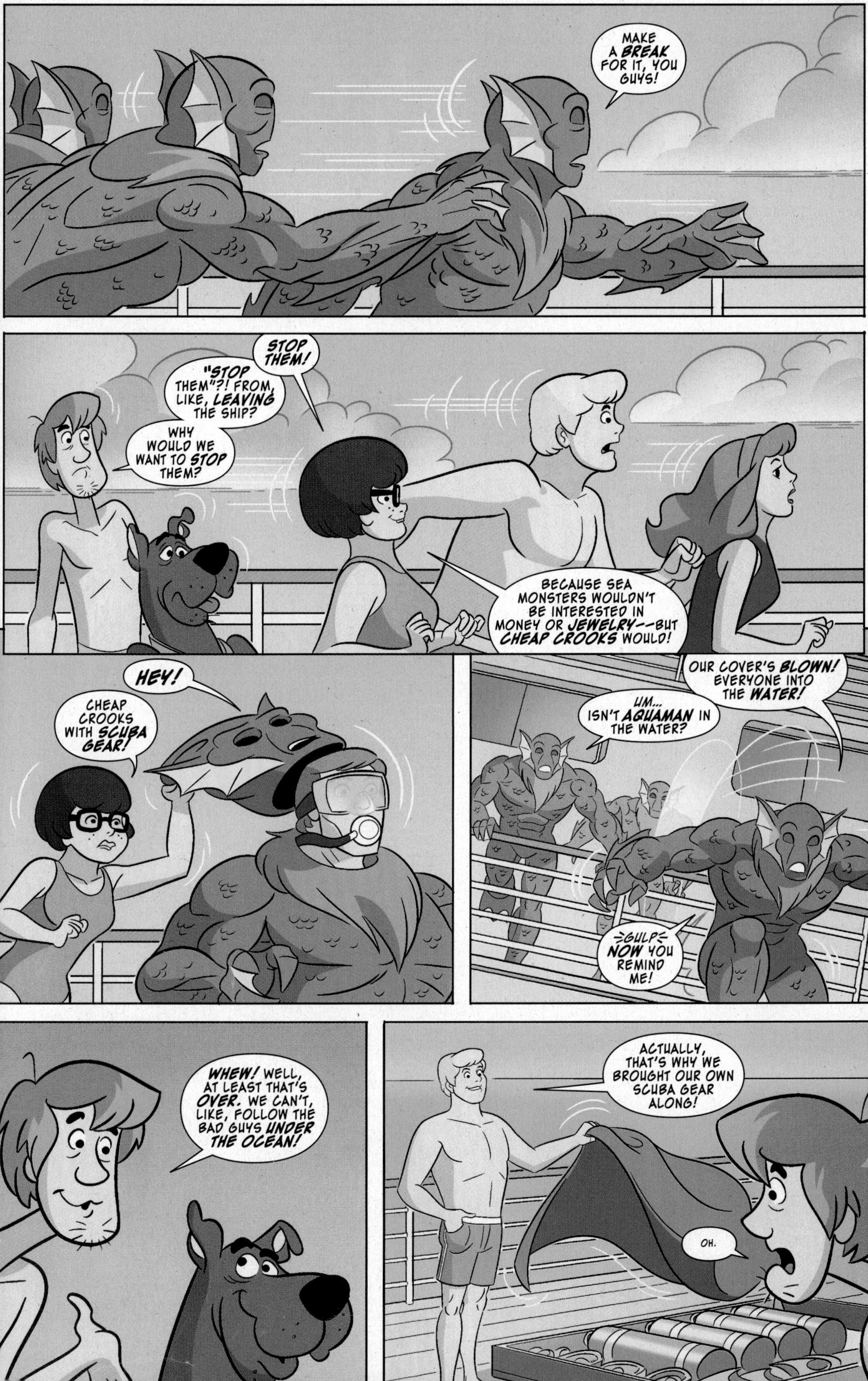
MAKE A BREAK FOR IT, YOU GUYS!
STOP THEM!
"STOP THEM"?! FROM, LIKE, LEAVING THE SHIP?
WHY WOULD WE WANT TO STOP THEM?
BECAUSE SEA MONSTERS WOULDN'T BE INTERESTED IN MONEY OR JEWELRY--BUT CHEAP CROOKS WOULD!
HEY!
CHEAP CROOKS WITH SCUBA GEAR!
OUR COVER'S BLOWN! EVERYONE INTO THE WATER!
UM... ISN'T AQUAMAN IN THE WATER?
GULP NOW YOU REMIND ME!
WHEW! WELL, AT LEAST THAT'S OVER. WE CAN'T, LIKE, FOLLOW THE BAD GUYS UNDER THE OCEAN!
ACTUALLY, THAT'S WHY WE BROUGHT OUR OWN SCUBA GEAR ALONG!
OH.

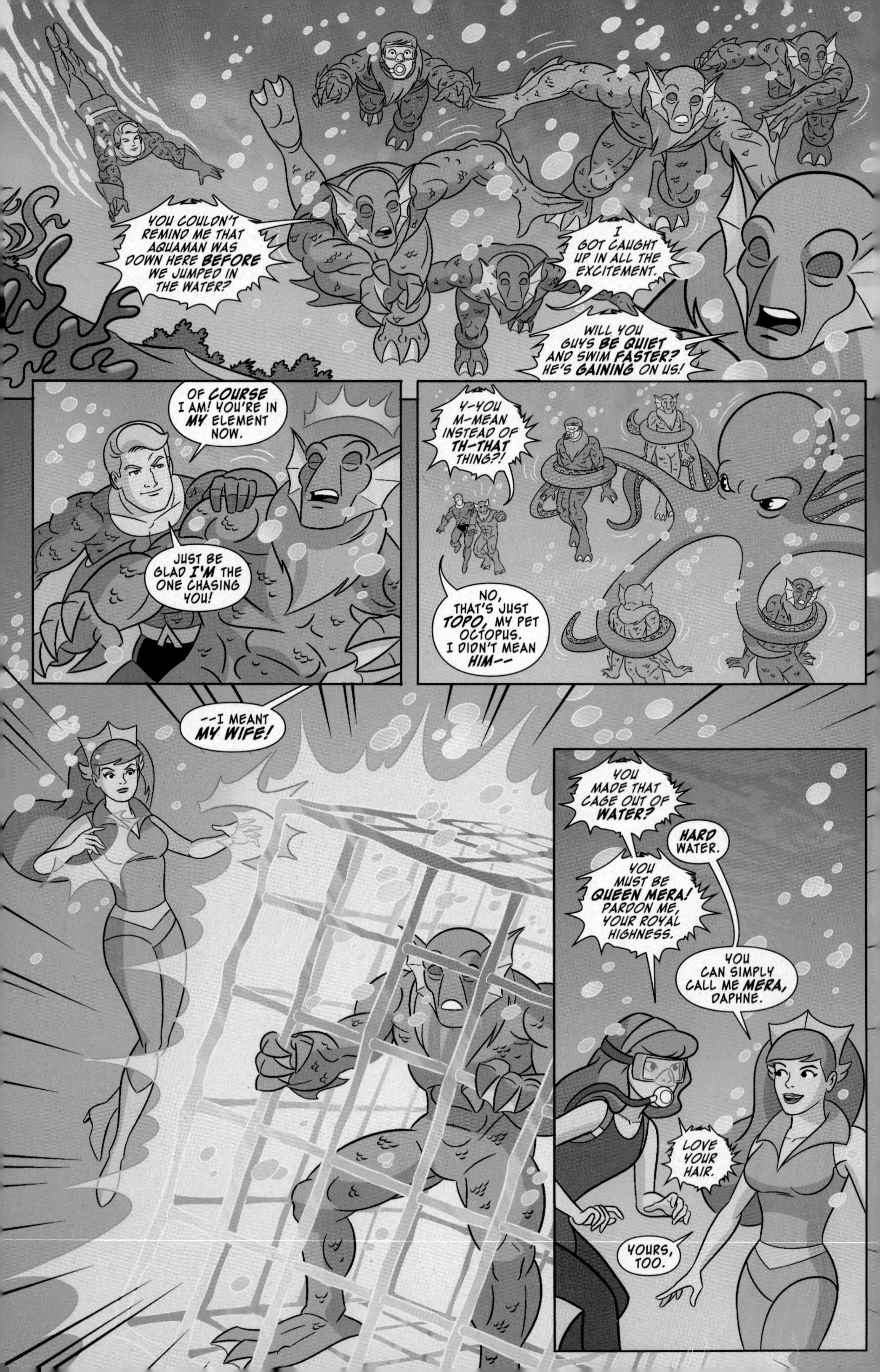

YOU COULDN'T REMIND ME THAT AQUAMAN WAS DOWN HERE BEFORE WE JUMPED IN THE WATER?
I GOT CAUGHT UP IN ALL THE EXCITEMENT.
WILL YOU GUYS BE QUIET AND SWIM FASTER? HE'S GAINING ON US!
OF COURSE I AM! YOU'RE IN MY ELEMENT NOW.
JUST BE GLAD I'M THE ONE CHASING YOU!
Y-YOU M-MEAN INSTEAD OF TH-THAT THING?!
NO, THAT'S JUST TOPO, MY PET OCTOPUS. I DIDN'T MEAN HIM--
--I MEANT MY WIFE!
YOU MADE THAT CAGE OUT OF WATER?
HARD WATER.
YOU MUST BE QUEEN MERA! PARDON ME, YOUR ROYAL HIGHNESS.
YOU CAN SIMPLY CALL ME MERA, DAPHNE.
LOVE YOUR HAIR.
YOURS, TOO.

THANKS FOR HELPING US CATCH THIS GANG. I'M SORRY WE HAD TO TAKE YOU AWAY FROM YOUR RESPONSIBILITIES IN **ATLANTIS**.

NO PROBLEM, VELMA. AS KING OF **ALL** SEVEN SEAS, **ANY** CRIME IN THE WATER IS MY RESPONSIBILITY.

I AM PLEASED WE COULD HELP YOU **SOLVE** YOUR CASE.

I'M PLEASED WE CAN GET **FAR AWAY** FROM THOSE CREEPY CROOKS!

NOT SO FAST, SHAGGY. THE CASE **ISN'T** SOLVED YET!

WHERE DID "POSEIDON" COME FROM? AND HOW DID HE **DISAPPEAR**?

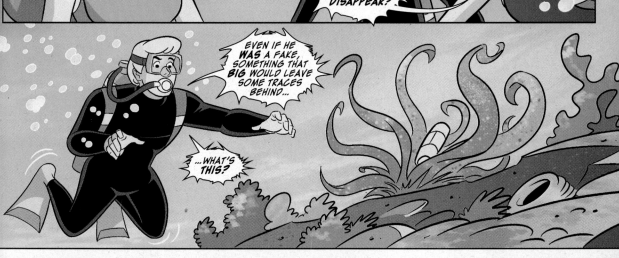

EVEN IF HE **WAS** A FAKE, SOMETHING THAT **BIG** WOULD LEAVE SOME TRACES BEHIND...

...WHAT'S **THIS**?

A HOLOGRAM PROJECTOR!

KLIK

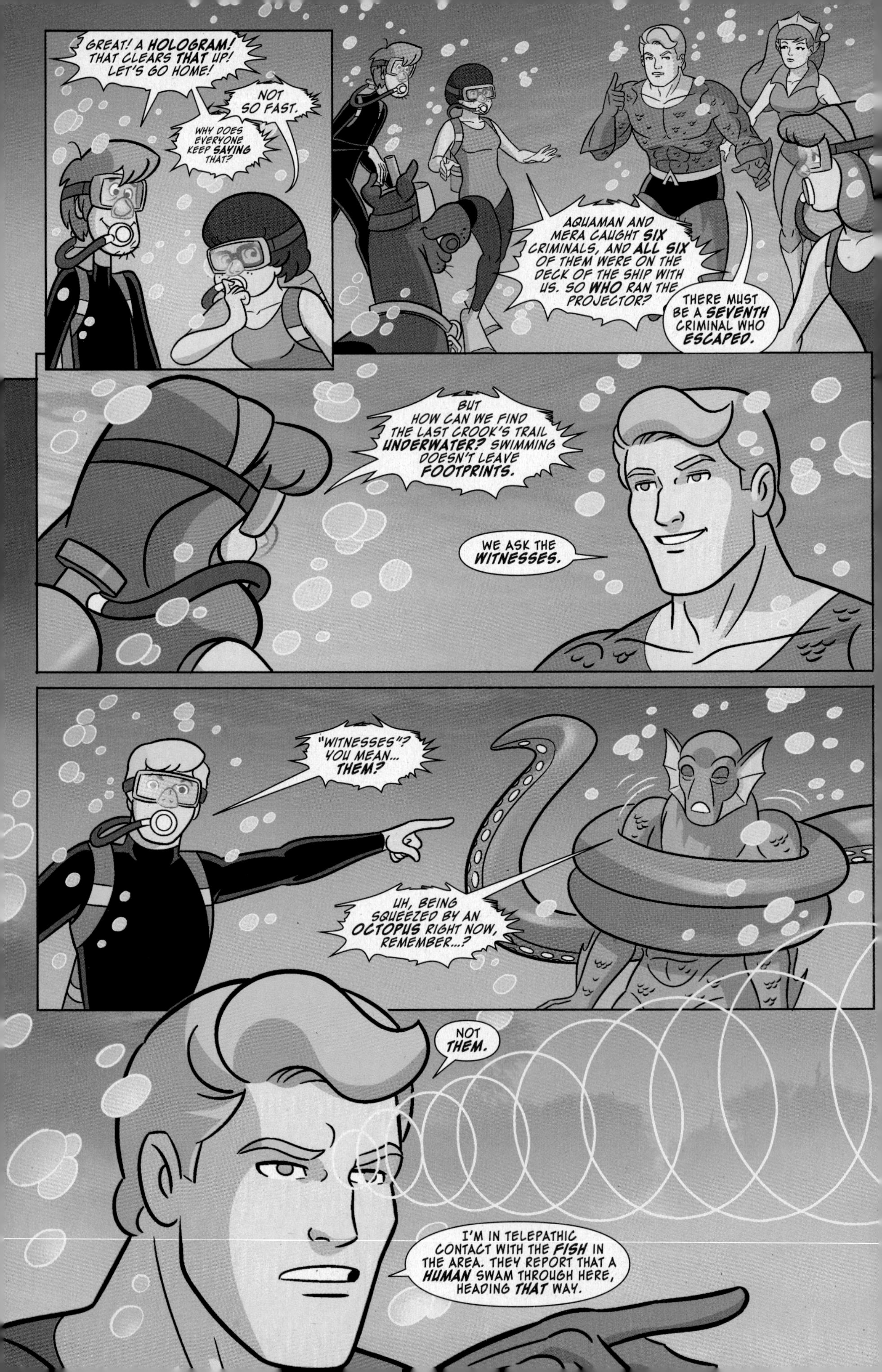
GREAT! A HOLOGRAM! THAT CLEARS THAT UP! LET'S GO HOME!
NOT SO FAST.
WHY DOES EVERYONE KEEP SAYING THAT?
AQUAMAN AND MERA CAUGHT SIX CRIMINALS, AND ALL SIX OF THEM WERE ON THE DECK OF THE SHIP WITH US. SO WHO RAN THE PROJECTOR?
THERE MUST BE A SEVENTH CRIMINAL WHO ESCAPED.
BUT HOW CAN WE FIND THE LAST CROOK'S TRAIL UNDERWATER? SWIMMING DOESN'T LEAVE FOOTPRINTS.
WE ASK THE WITNESSES.
"WITNESSES"? YOU MEAN... THEM?
UH, BEING SQUEEZED BY AN OCTOPUS RIGHT NOW, REMEMBER...?
NOT THEM.
I'M IN TELEPATHIC CONTACT WITH THE FISH IN THE AREA. THEY REPORT THAT A HUMAN SWAM THROUGH HERE, HEADING THAT WAY.

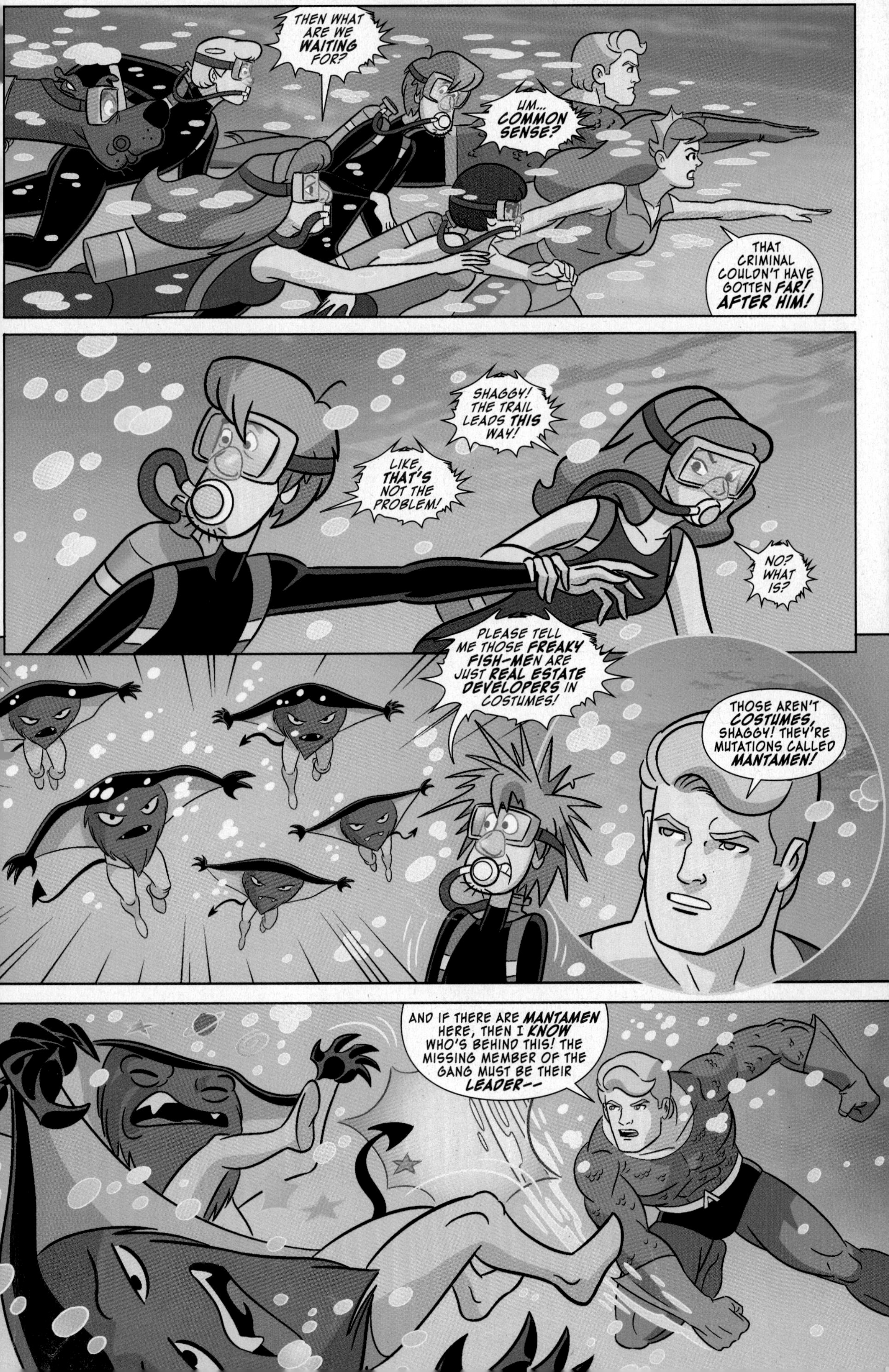
THEN WHAT ARE WE WAITING FOR?
UM... COMMON SENSE?
THAT CRIMINAL COULDN'T HAVE GOTTEN FAR! AFTER HIM!
SHAGGY! THE TRAIL LEADS THIS WAY!
LIKE, THAT'S NOT THE PROBLEM!
NO? WHAT IS?
PLEASE TELL ME THOSE FREAKY FISH-MEN ARE JUST REAL ESTATE DEVELOPERS IN COSTUMES!
THOSE AREN'T COSTUMES, SHAGGY! THEY'RE MUTATIONS CALLED MANTAMEN!
AND IF THERE ARE MANTAMEN HERE, THEN I KNOW WHO'S BEHIND THIS! THE MISSING MEMBER OF THE GANG MUST BE THEIR LEADER--

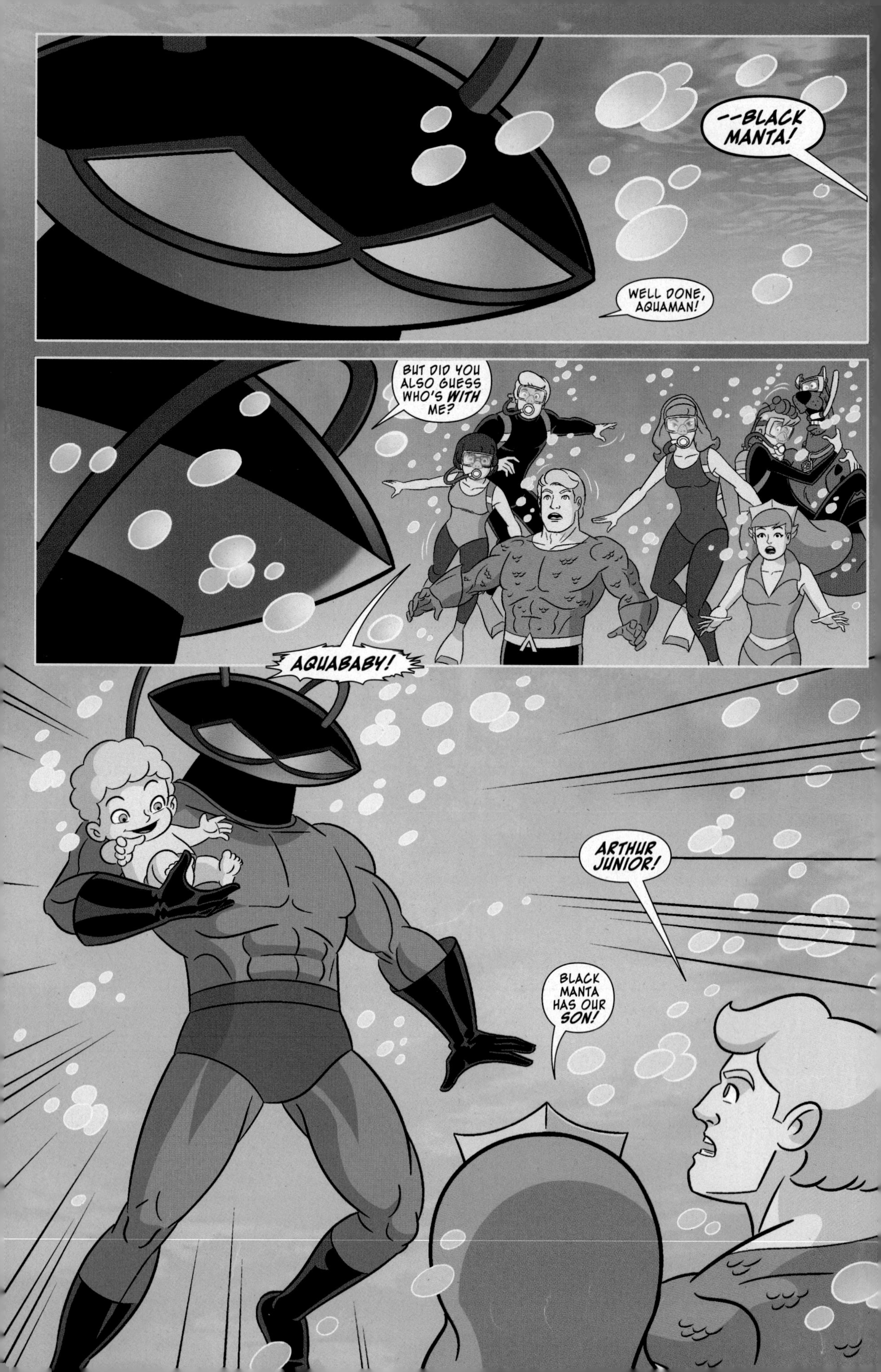
--BLACK MANTA!
WELL DONE, AQUAMAN!
BUT DID YOU ALSO GUESS WHO'S WITH ME?
AQUABABY!
ARTHUR JUNIOR!
BLACK MANTA HAS OUR SON!

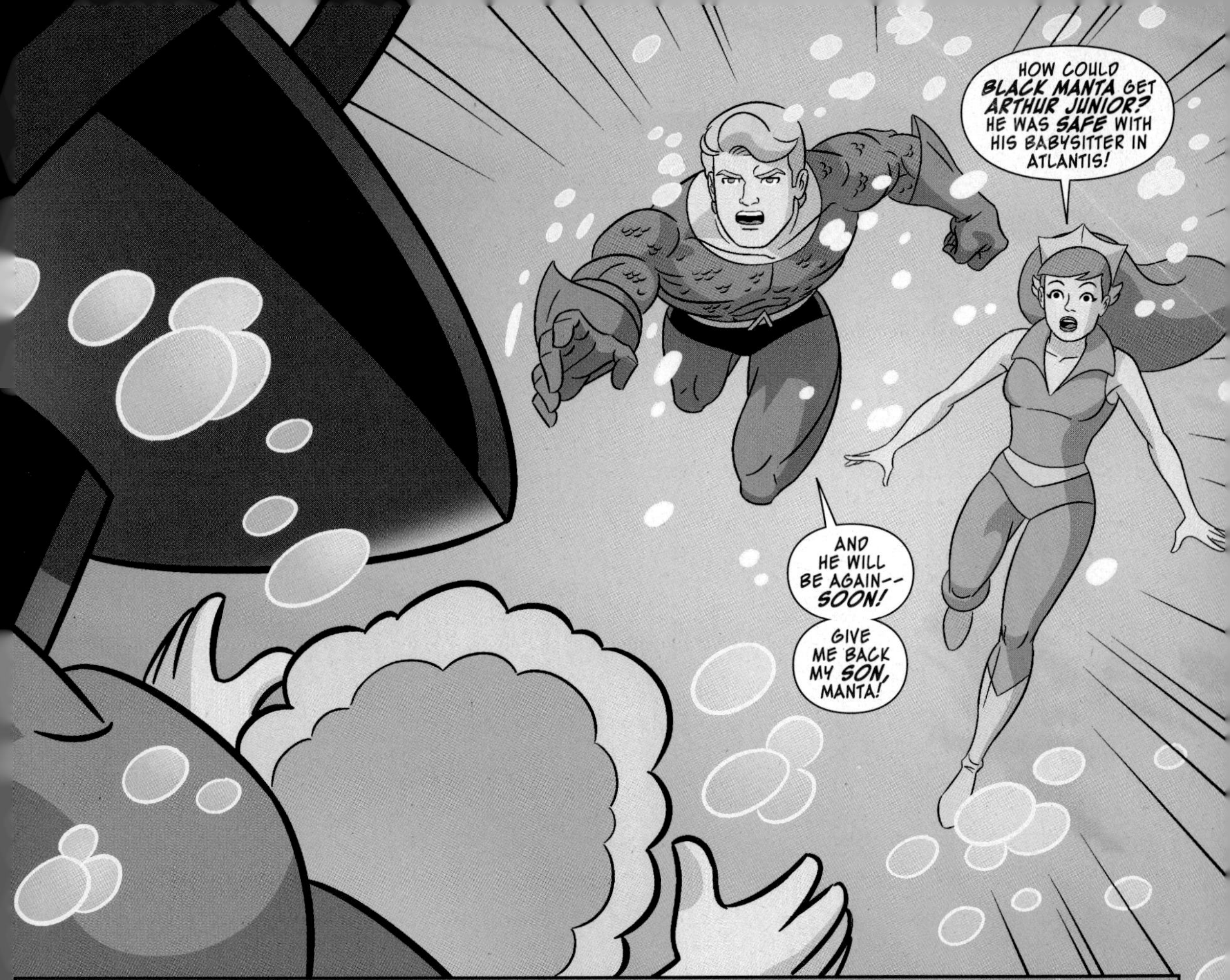
HOW COULD BLACK MANTA GET ARTHUR JUNIOR? HE WAS SAFE WITH HIS BABYSITTER IN ATLANTIS!
AND HE WILL BE AGAIN-- SOON!
GIVE ME BACK MY SON, MANTA!

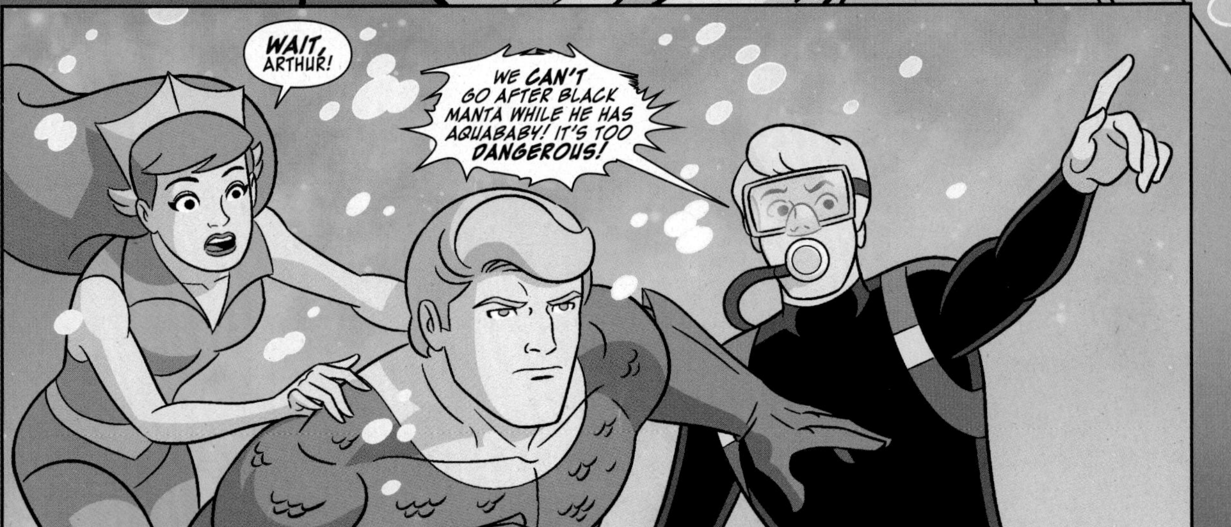
WAIT, ARTHUR!
WE CAN'T GO AFTER BLACK MANTA WHILE HE HAS AQUABABY! IT'S TOO DANGEROUS!

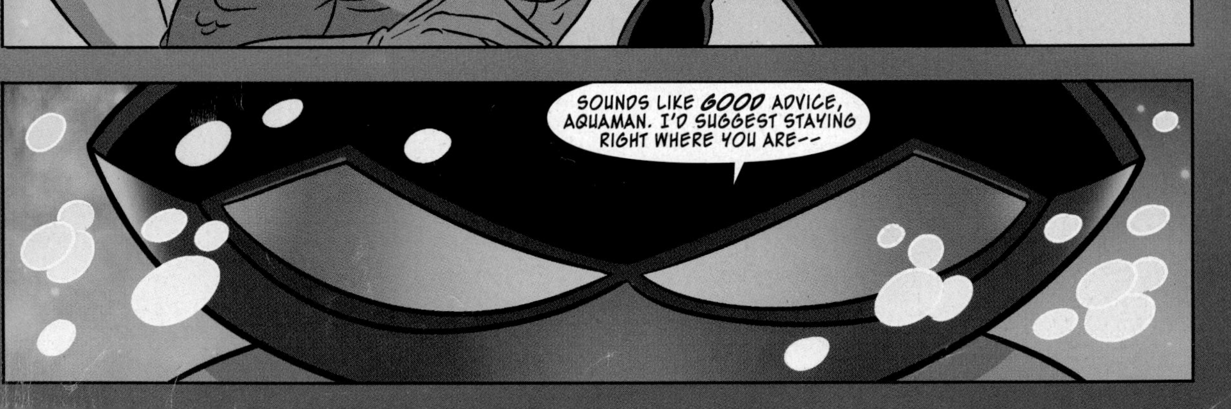
SOUNDS LIKE GOOD ADVICE, AQUAMAN. I'D SUGGEST STAYING RIGHT WHERE YOU ARE--

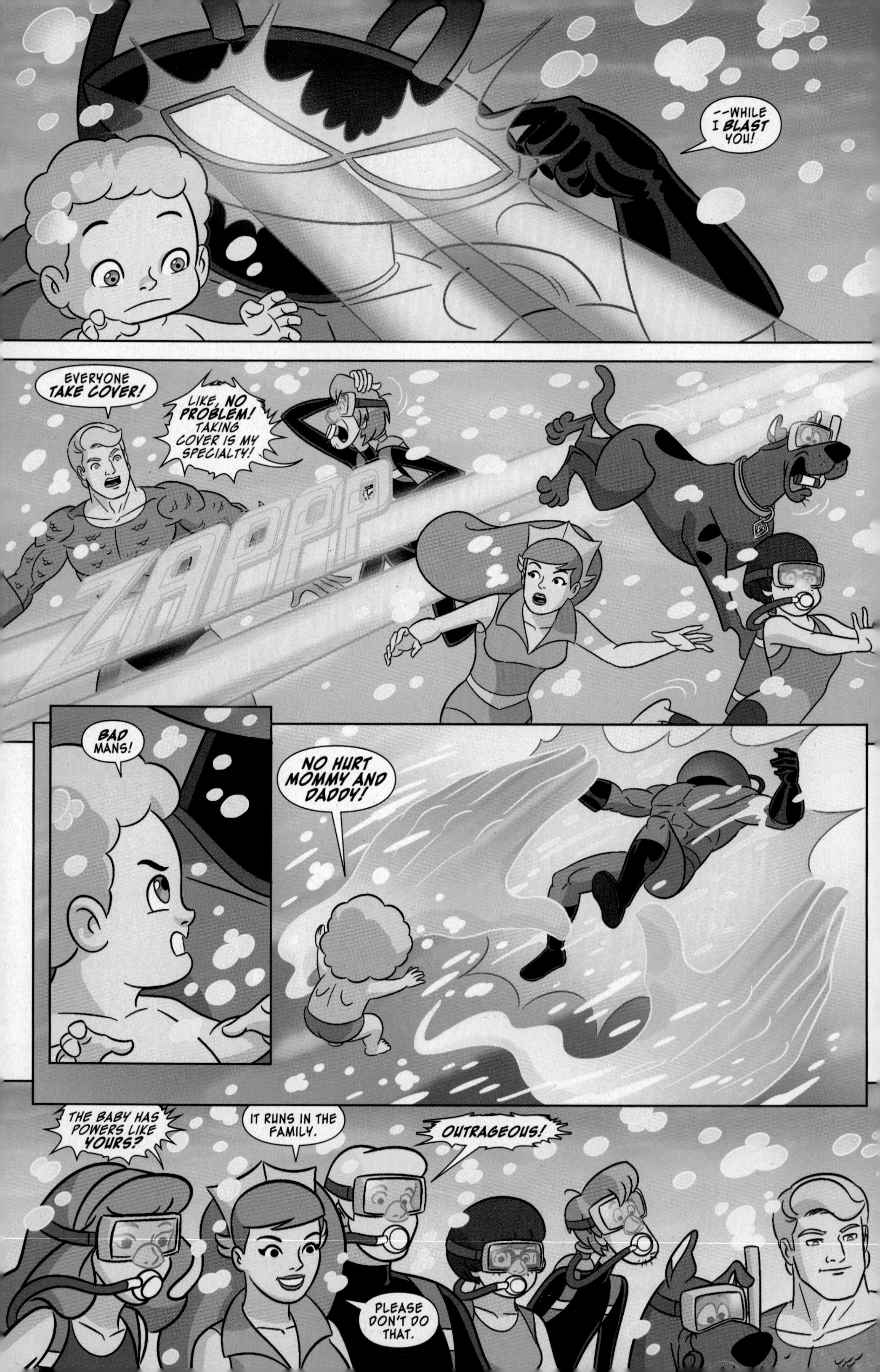
--WHILE I BLAST YOU!
EVERYONE TAKE COVER!
LIKE, NO PROBLEM! TAKING COVER IS MY SPECIALTY!
ZAPPP
BAD MANS!
NO HURT MOMMY AND DADDY!
THE BABY HAS POWERS LIKE YOURS?
IT RUNS IN THE FAMILY.
OUTRAGEOUS!
PLEASE DON'T DO THAT.

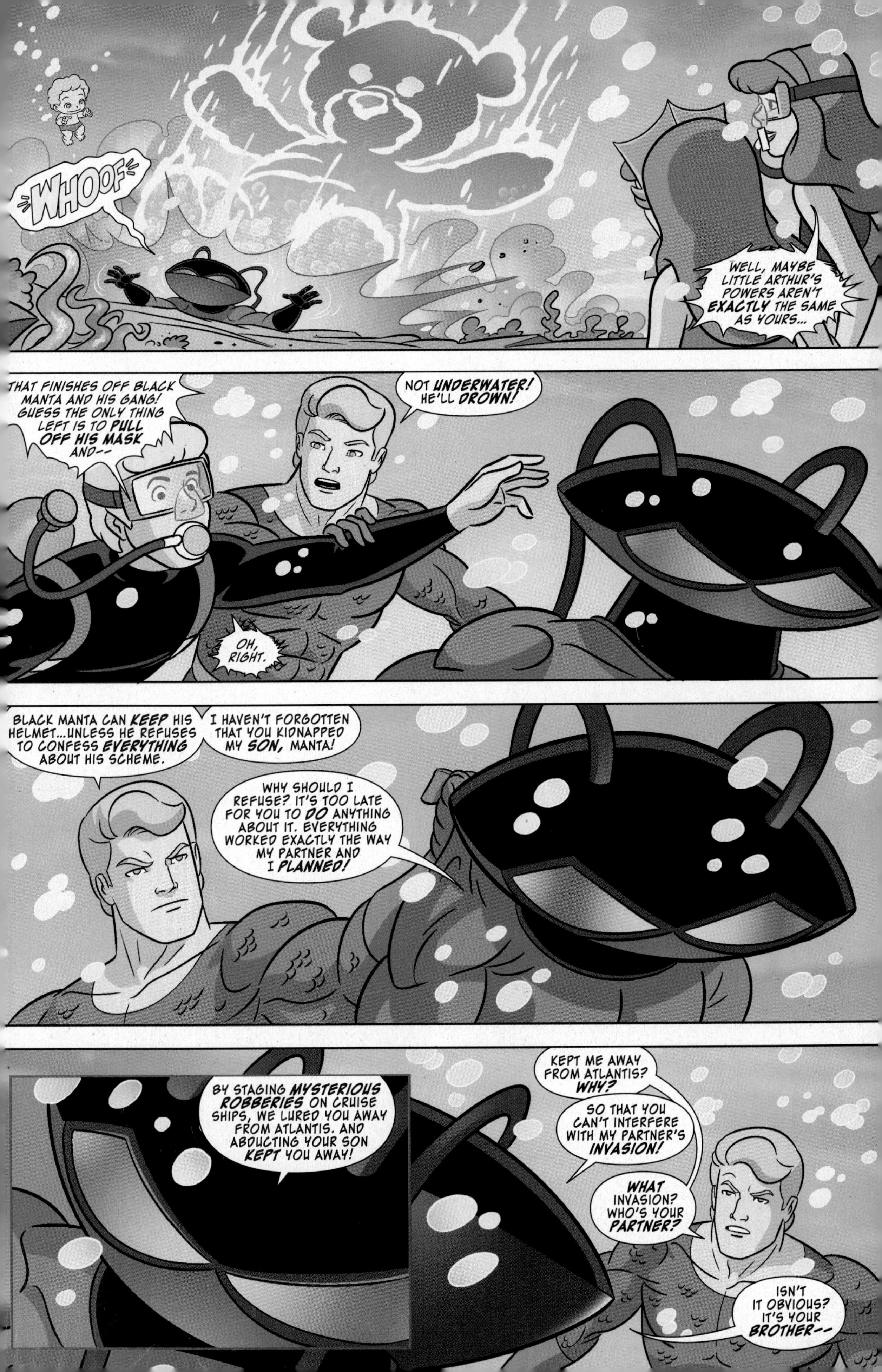

WHOOF
WELL, MAYBE LITTLE ARTHUR'S POWERS AREN'T EXACTLY THE SAME AS YOURS...
THAT FINISHES OFF BLACK MANTA AND HIS GANG! GUESS THE ONLY THING LEFT IS TO PULL OFF HIS MASK AND--
NOT UNDERWATER! HE'LL DROWN!
OH, RIGHT.
BLACK MANTA CAN KEEP HIS HELMET...UNLESS HE REFUSES TO CONFESS EVERYTHING ABOUT HIS SCHEME.
I HAVEN'T FORGOTTEN THAT YOU KIDNAPPED MY SON, MANTA!
WHY SHOULD I REFUSE? IT'S TOO LATE FOR YOU TO DO ANYTHING ABOUT IT. EVERYTHING WORKED EXACTLY THE WAY MY PARTNER AND I PLANNED!
BY STAGING MYSTERIOUS ROBBERIES ON CRUISE SHIPS, WE LURED YOU AWAY FROM ATLANTIS. AND ABDUCTING YOUR SON KEPT YOU AWAY!
KEPT ME AWAY FROM ATLANTIS? WHY?
SO THAT YOU CAN'T INTERFERE WITH MY PARTNER'S INVASION!
WHAT INVASION? WHO'S YOUR PARTNER?
ISN'T IT OBVIOUS? IT'S YOUR BROTHER--

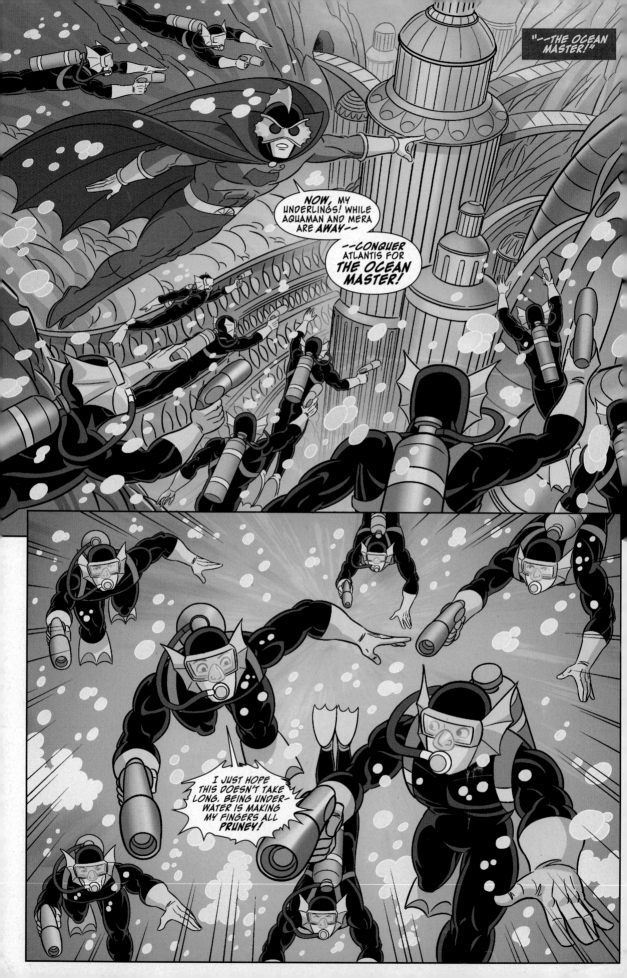

NOW, MY UNDERLINGS! WHILE AQUAMAN AND MERA ARE *AWAY*--

--CONQUER ATLANTIS FOR *THE OCEAN MASTER!*

I JUST HOPE THIS DOESN'T TAKE LONG. BEING UNDER-WATER IS MAKING MY FINGERS ALL *PRUNEY!*

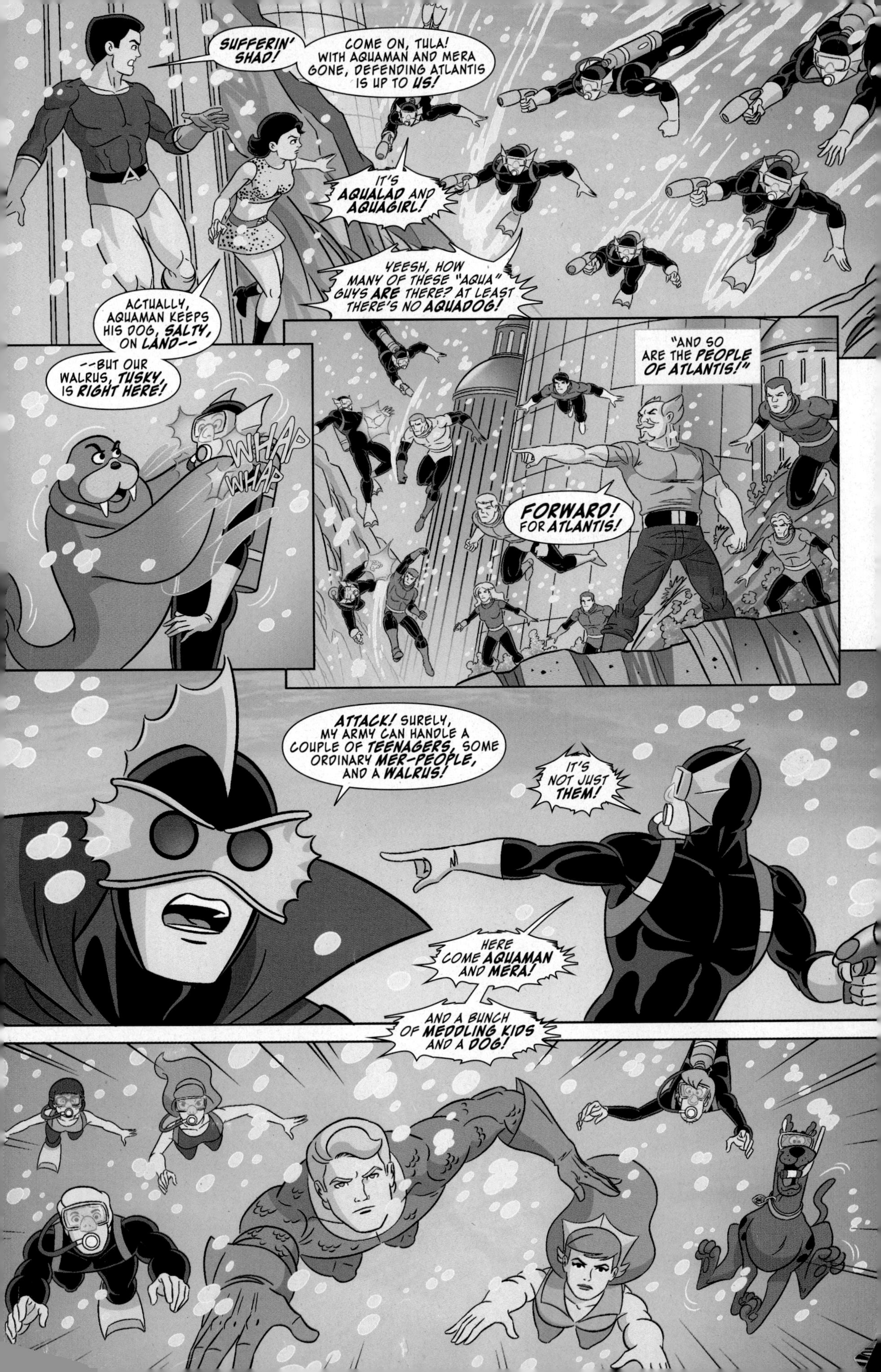
SUFFERIN' SHAD!
COME ON, TULA! WITH AQUAMAN AND MERA GONE, DEFENDING ATLANTIS IS UP TO US!
IT'S AQUALAD AND AQUAGIRL!
YEESH, HOW MANY OF THESE "AQUA" GUYS ARE THERE? AT LEAST THERE'S NO AQUADOG!
ACTUALLY, AQUAMAN KEEPS HIS DOG, SALTY, ON LAND--
--BUT OUR WALRUS, TUSKY, IS RIGHT HERE!
WHAP
WHAP
"AND SO ARE THE PEOPLE OF ATLANTIS!"
FORWARD! FOR ATLANTIS!
ATTACK! SURELY, MY ARMY CAN HANDLE A COUPLE OF TEENAGERS, SOME ORDINARY MER-PEOPLE, AND A WALRUS!
IT'S NOT JUST THEM!
HERE COME AQUAMAN AND MERA!
AND A BUNCH OF MEDDLING KIDS AND A DOG!

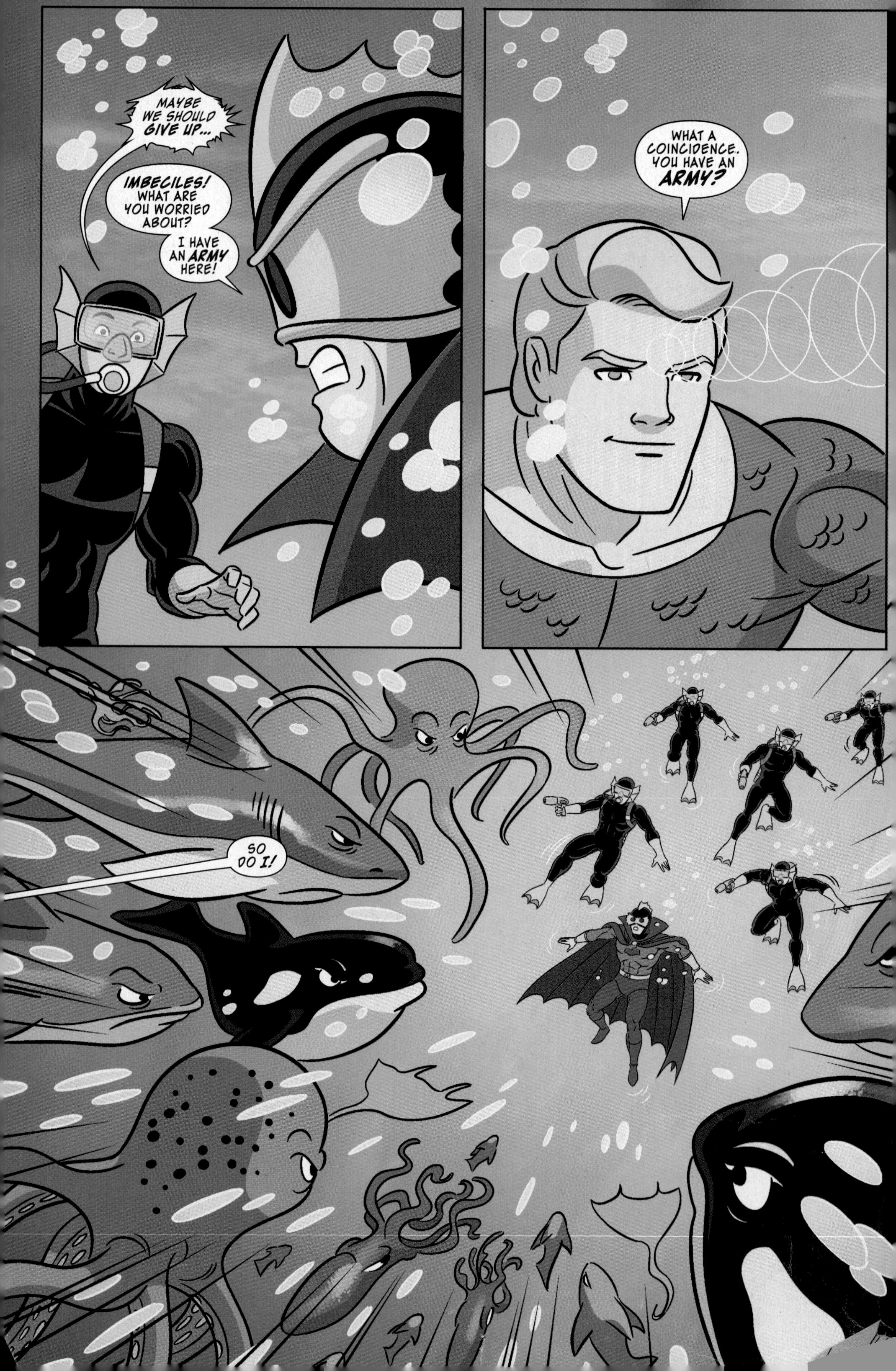
MAYBE WE SHOULD GIVE UP...
IMBECILES! WHAT ARE YOU WORRIED ABOUT?
I HAVE AN ARMY HERE!
WHAT A COINCIDENCE. YOU HAVE AN ARMY?
SO DO I!

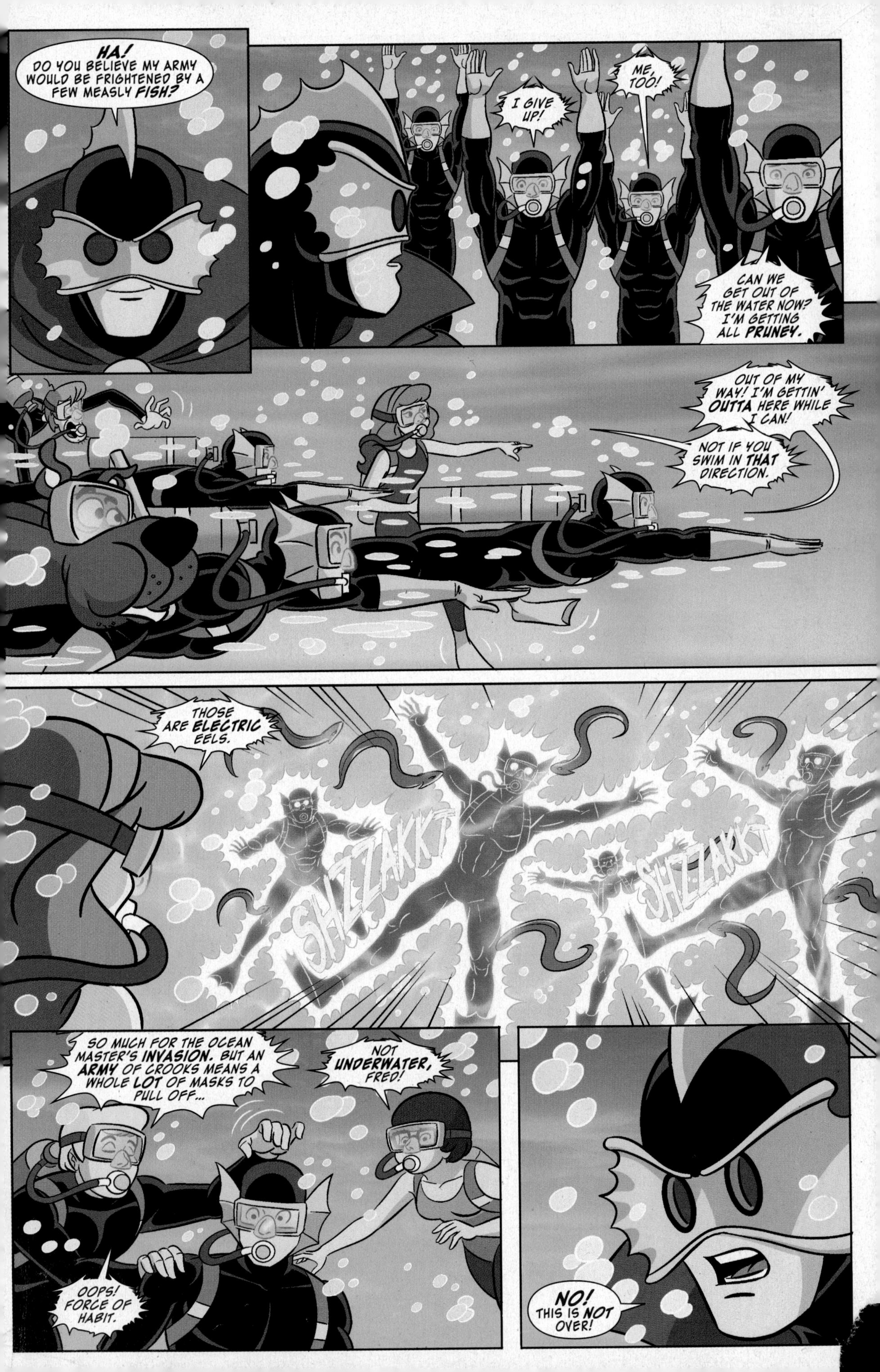
HA! DO YOU BELIEVE MY ARMY WOULD BE FRIGHTENED BY A FEW MEASLY FISH?
I GIVE UP!
ME, TOO!
CAN WE GET OUT OF THE WATER NOW? I'M GETTING ALL PRUNEY.
OUT OF MY WAY! I'M GETTIN' OUTTA HERE WHILE I CAN!
NOT IF YOU SWIM IN THAT DIRECTION.
THOSE ARE ELECTRIC EELS.
SHZZAKKT
SHZZAKKT
SO MUCH FOR THE OCEAN MASTER'S INVASION. BUT AN ARMY OF CROOKS MEANS A WHOLE LOT OF MASKS TO PULL OFF...
NOT UNDERWATER, FRED!
OOPS! FORCE OF HABIT.
NO! THIS IS NOT OVER!

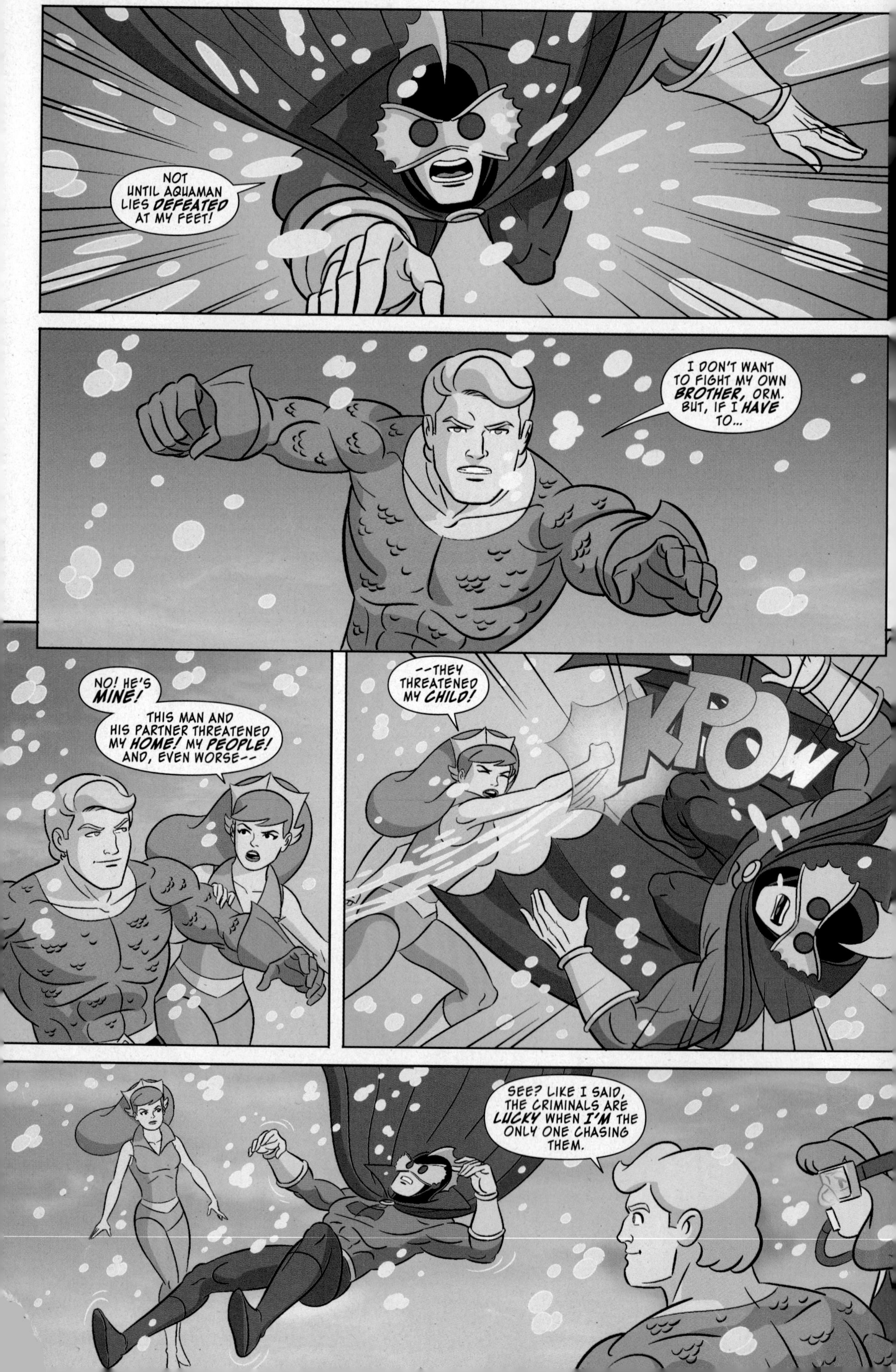
NOT UNTIL AQUAMAN LIES DEFEATED AT MY FEET!
I DON'T WANT TO FIGHT MY OWN BROTHER, ORM. BUT, IF I HAVE TO...
NO! HE'S MINE!
THIS MAN AND HIS PARTNER THREATENED MY HOME! MY PEOPLE! AND, EVEN WORSE--
--THEY THREATENED MY CHILD!
KPOW
SEE? LIKE I SAID, THE CRIMINALS ARE LUCKY WHEN I'M THE ONLY ONE CHASING THEM.

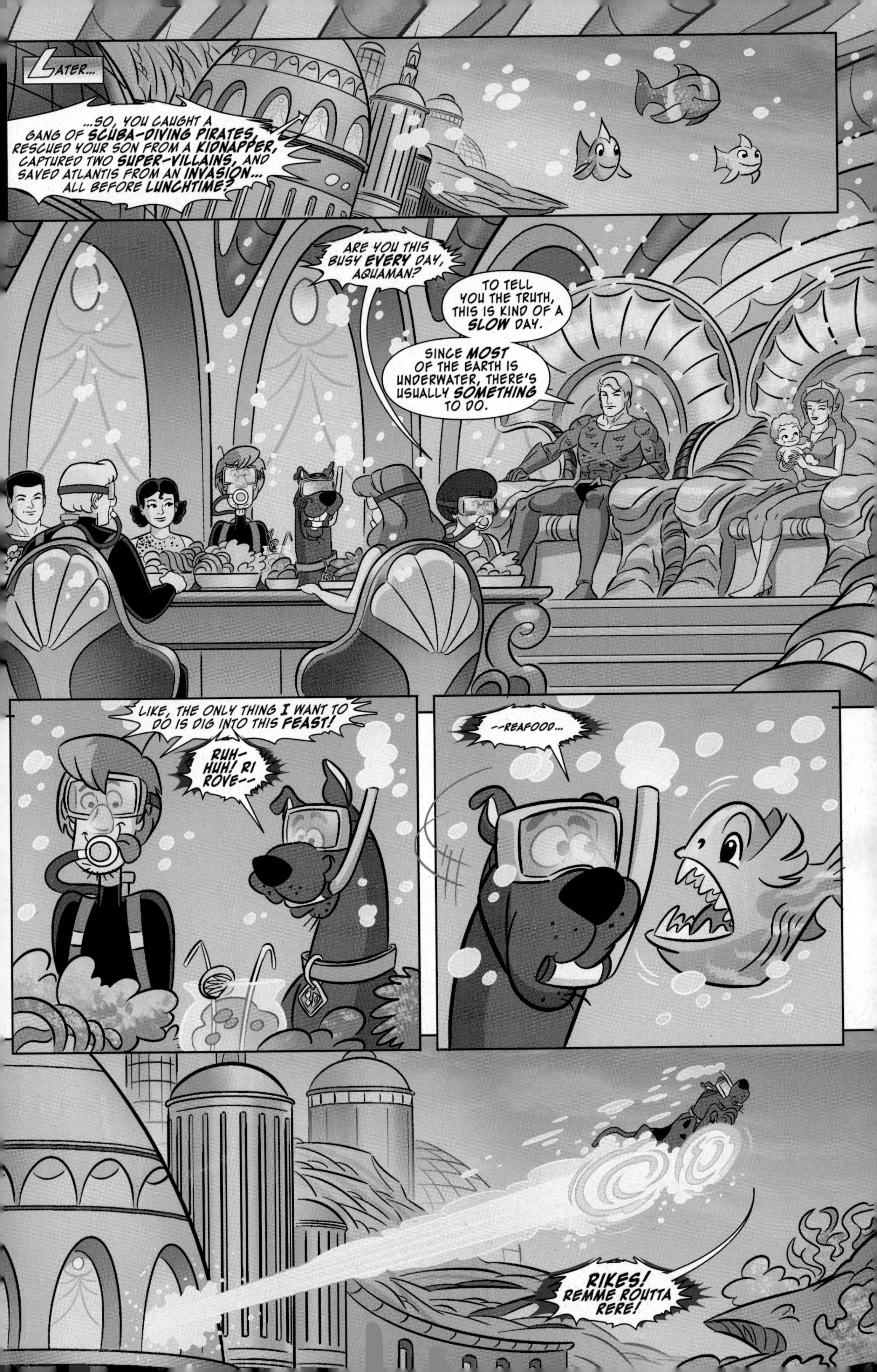
LATER...
...SO, YOU CAUGHT A GANG OF SCUBA-DIVING PIRATES, RESCUED YOUR SON FROM A KIDNAPPER, CAPTURED TWO SUPER-VILLAINS, AND SAVED ATLANTIS FROM AN INVASION... ALL BEFORE LUNCHTIME?
ARE YOU THIS BUSY EVERY DAY, AQUAMAN?
TO TELL YOU THE TRUTH, THIS IS KIND OF A SLOW DAY.
SINCE MOST OF THE EARTH IS UNDERWATER, THERE'S USUALLY SOMETHING TO DO.
LIKE, THE ONLY THING I WANT TO DO IS DIG INTO THIS FEAST!
RUH-HUH! RI ROVE--
--REAFOOD...
RIKES! REMME ROUTTA RERE!

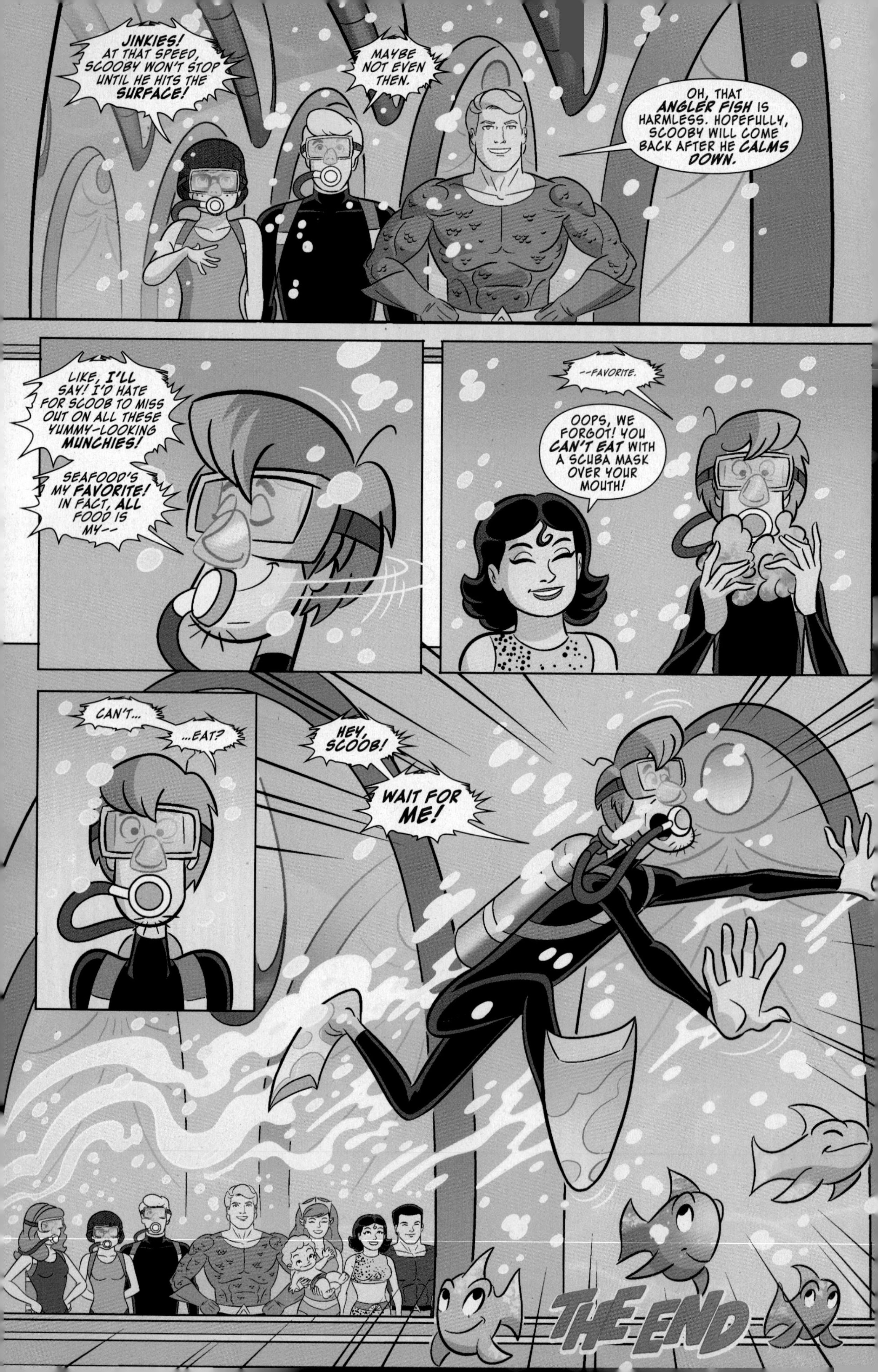
JINKIES! AT THAT SPEED, SCOOBY WON'T STOP UNTIL HE HITS THE SURFACE!
MAYBE NOT EVEN THEN.
OH, THAT ANGLER FISH IS HARMLESS. HOPEFULLY, SCOOBY WILL COME BACK AFTER HE CALMS DOWN.
LIKE, I'LL SAY! I'D HATE FOR SCOOB TO MISS OUT ON ALL THESE YUMMY-LOOKING MUNCHIES!
SEAFOOD'S MY FAVORITE! IN FACT, ALL FOOD IS MY--
--FAVORITE.
OOPS, WE FORGOT! YOU CAN'T EAT WITH A SCUBA MASK OVER YOUR MOUTH!
CAN'T...
...EAT?
HEY, SCOOB!
WAIT FOR ME!
THE END

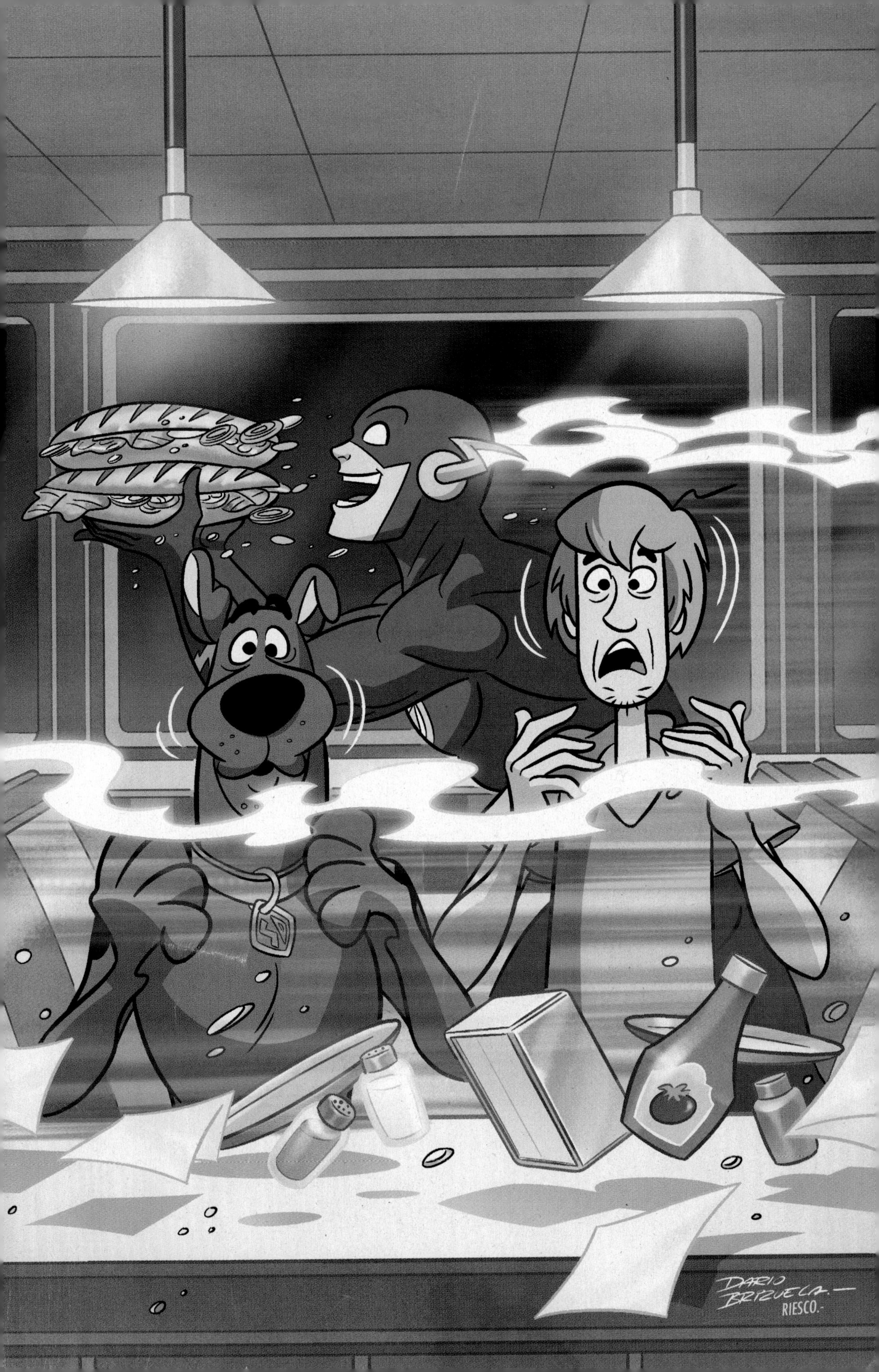
DARIO BRIZUELA—
RIESCO.-

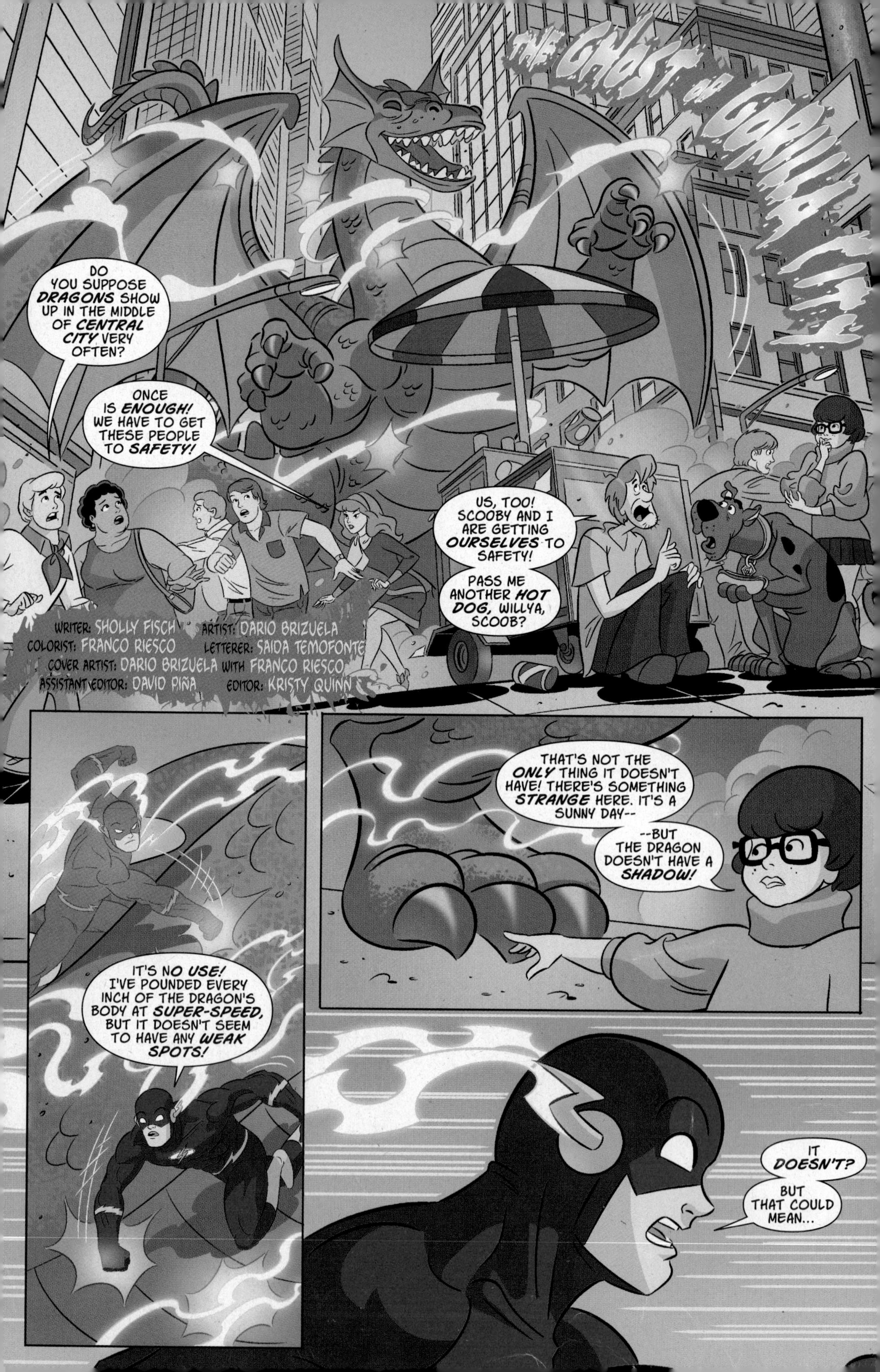
THE GHOST OF GORILLA CITY
DO YOU SUPPOSE DRAGONS SHOW UP IN THE MIDDLE OF CENTRAL CITY VERY OFTEN?
ONCE IS ENOUGH! WE HAVE TO GET THESE PEOPLE TO SAFETY!
US, TOO! SCOOBY AND I ARE GETTING OURSELVES TO SAFETY!
PASS ME ANOTHER HOT DOG, WILLYA, SCOOB?
WRITER: SHOLLY FISCH ARTIST: DARIO BRIZUELA
COLORIST: FRANCO RIESCO LETTERER: SAIDA TEMOFONTE
COVER ARTIST: DARIO BRIZUELA WITH FRANCO RIESCO
ASSISTANT EDITOR: DAVID PIÑA EDITOR: KRISTY QUINN
IT'S NO USE! I'VE POUNDED EVERY INCH OF THE DRAGON'S BODY AT SUPER-SPEED, BUT IT DOESN'T SEEM TO HAVE ANY WEAK SPOTS!
THAT'S NOT THE ONLY THING IT DOESN'T HAVE! THERE'S SOMETHING STRANGE HERE. IT'S A SUNNY DAY--
--BUT THE DRAGON DOESN'T HAVE A SHADOW!
IT DOESN'T?
BUT THAT COULD MEAN...

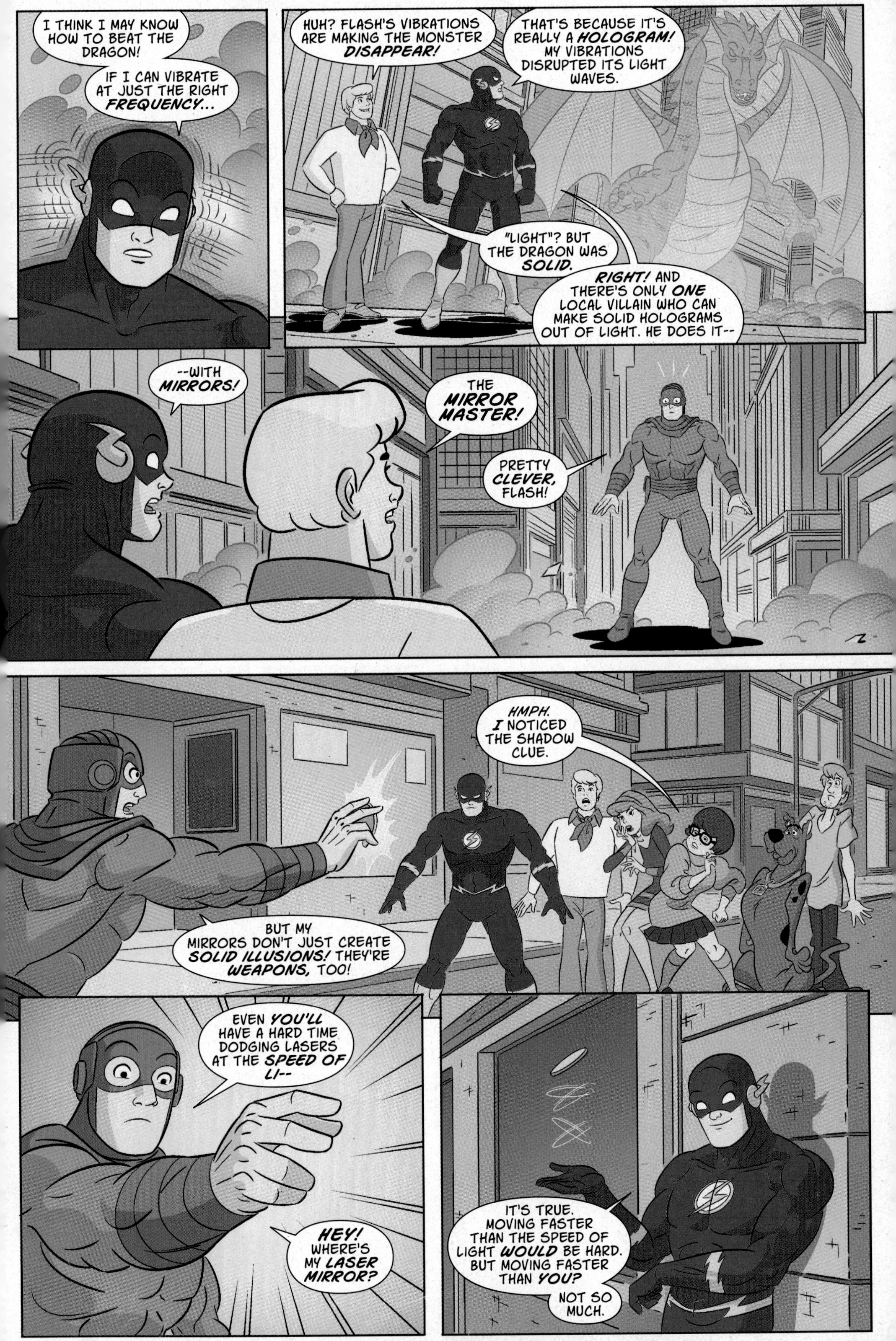
I THINK I MAY KNOW HOW TO BEAT THE DRAGON!
IF I CAN VIBRATE AT JUST THE RIGHT FREQUENCY...
HUH? FLASH'S VIBRATIONS ARE MAKING THE MONSTER DISAPPEAR!
THAT'S BECAUSE IT'S REALLY A HOLOGRAM! MY VIBRATIONS DISRUPTED ITS LIGHT WAVES.
"LIGHT"? BUT THE DRAGON WAS SOLID.
RIGHT! AND THERE'S ONLY ONE LOCAL VILLAIN WHO CAN MAKE SOLID HOLOGRAMS OUT OF LIGHT. HE DOES IT--
--WITH MIRRORS!
THE MIRROR MASTER!
PRETTY CLEVER, FLASH!
HMPH. I NOTICED THE SHADOW CLUE.
BUT MY MIRRORS DON'T JUST CREATE SOLID ILLUSIONS! THEY'RE WEAPONS, TOO!
EVEN YOU'LL HAVE A HARD TIME DODGING LASERS AT THE SPEED OF LI--
HEY! WHERE'S MY LASER MIRROR?
IT'S TRUE. MOVING FASTER THAN THE SPEED OF LIGHT WOULD BE HARD. BUT MOVING FASTER THAN YOU?
NOT SO MUCH.

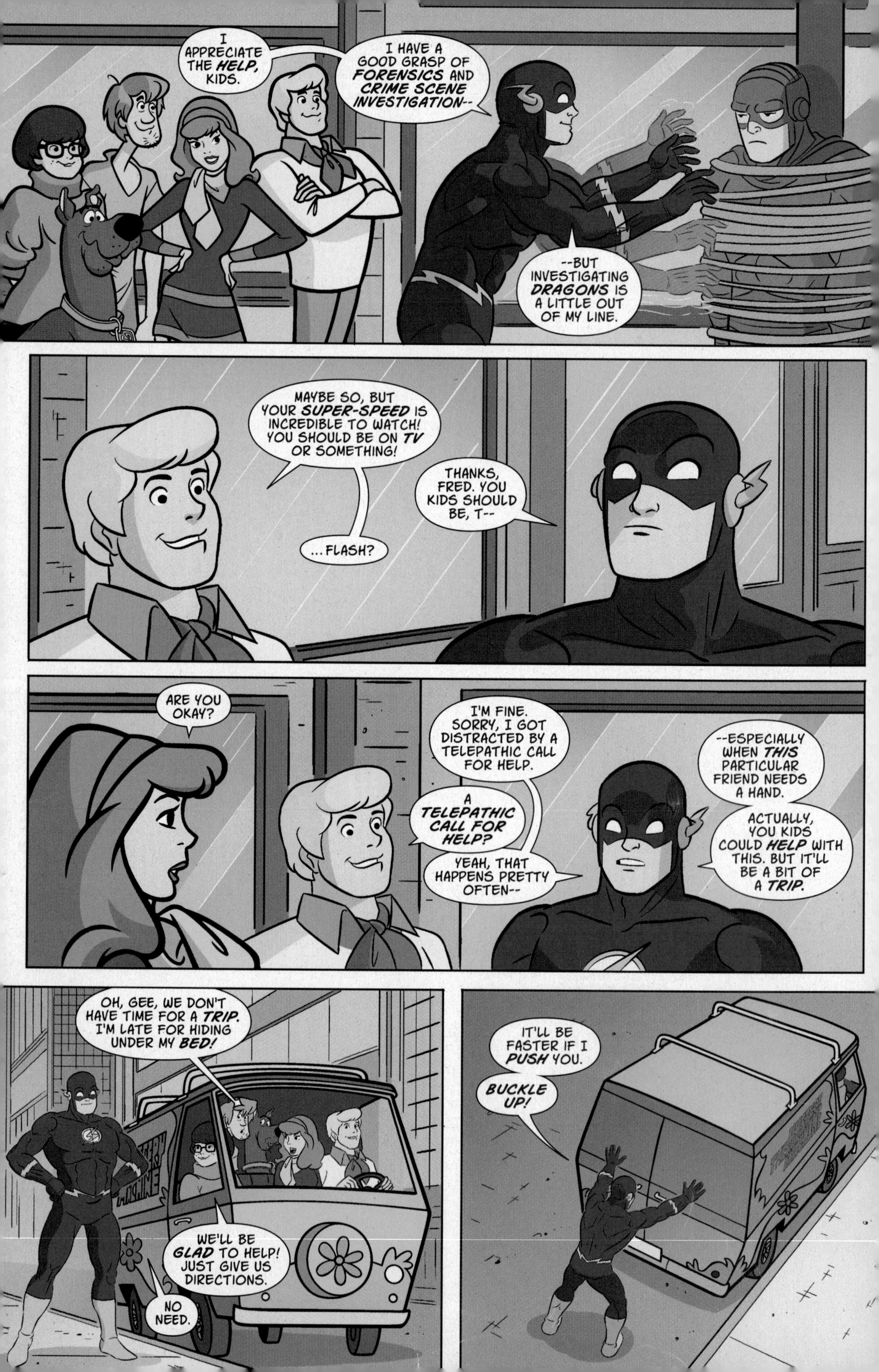

I APPRECIATE THE *HELP*, KIDS.
I HAVE A GOOD GRASP OF *FORENSICS* AND *CRIME SCENE INVESTIGATION*--
--BUT INVESTIGATING *DRAGONS* IS A LITTLE OUT OF MY LINE.
MAYBE SO, BUT YOUR *SUPER-SPEED* IS INCREDIBLE TO WATCH! YOU SHOULD BE ON *TV* OR SOMETHING!
THANKS, FRED. YOU KIDS SHOULD BE, T--
...FLASH?
ARE YOU OKAY?
I'M FINE. SORRY, I GOT DISTRACTED BY A TELEPATHIC CALL FOR HELP.
A *TELEPATHIC CALL FOR HELP?*
YEAH, THAT HAPPENS PRETTY OFTEN--
--ESPECIALLY WHEN *THIS* PARTICULAR FRIEND NEEDS A HAND.
ACTUALLY, YOU KIDS COULD *HELP* WITH THIS. BUT IT'LL BE A BIT OF A *TRIP*.
OH, GEE, WE DON'T HAVE TIME FOR A *TRIP*. I'M LATE FOR HIDING UNDER MY *BED!*
WE'LL BE *GLAD* TO HELP! JUST GIVE US DIRECTIONS.
NO NEED.
IT'LL BE FASTER IF I *PUSH* YOU.
BUCKLE UP!

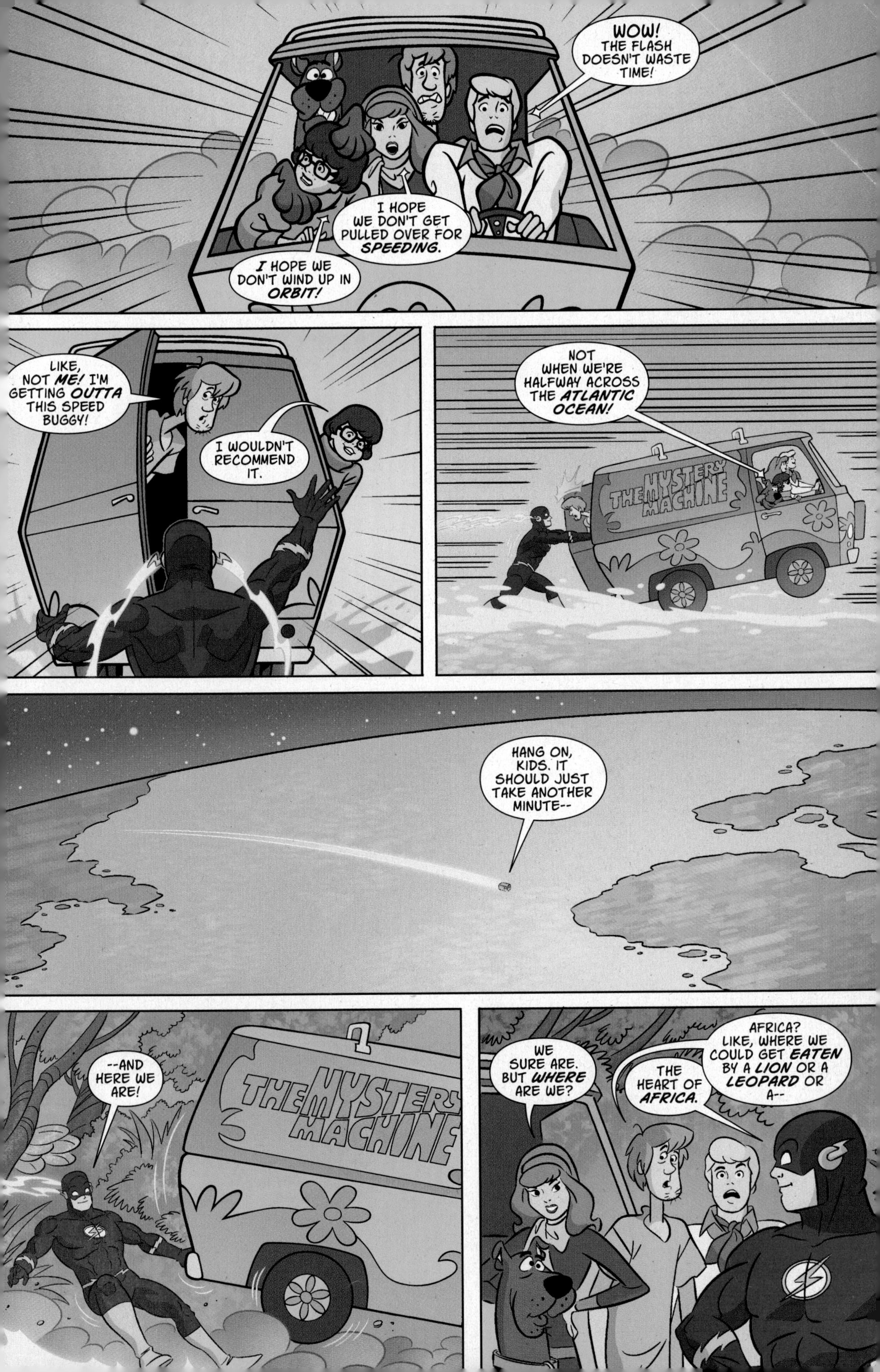
WOW! THE FLASH DOESN'T WASTE TIME!
I HOPE WE DON'T GET PULLED OVER FOR SPEEDING.
I HOPE WE DON'T WIND UP IN ORBIT!
LIKE, NOT ME! I'M GETTING OUTTA THIS SPEED BUGGY!
I WOULDN'T RECOMMEND IT.
NOT WHEN WE'RE HALFWAY ACROSS THE ATLANTIC OCEAN!
THE MYSTERY MACHINE
HANG ON, KIDS. IT SHOULD JUST TAKE ANOTHER MINUTE--
--AND HERE WE ARE!
THE MYSTERY MACHINE
WE SURE ARE. BUT WHERE ARE WE?
THE HEART OF AFRICA.
AFRICA? LIKE, WHERE WE COULD GET EATEN BY A LION OR A LEOPARD OR A--

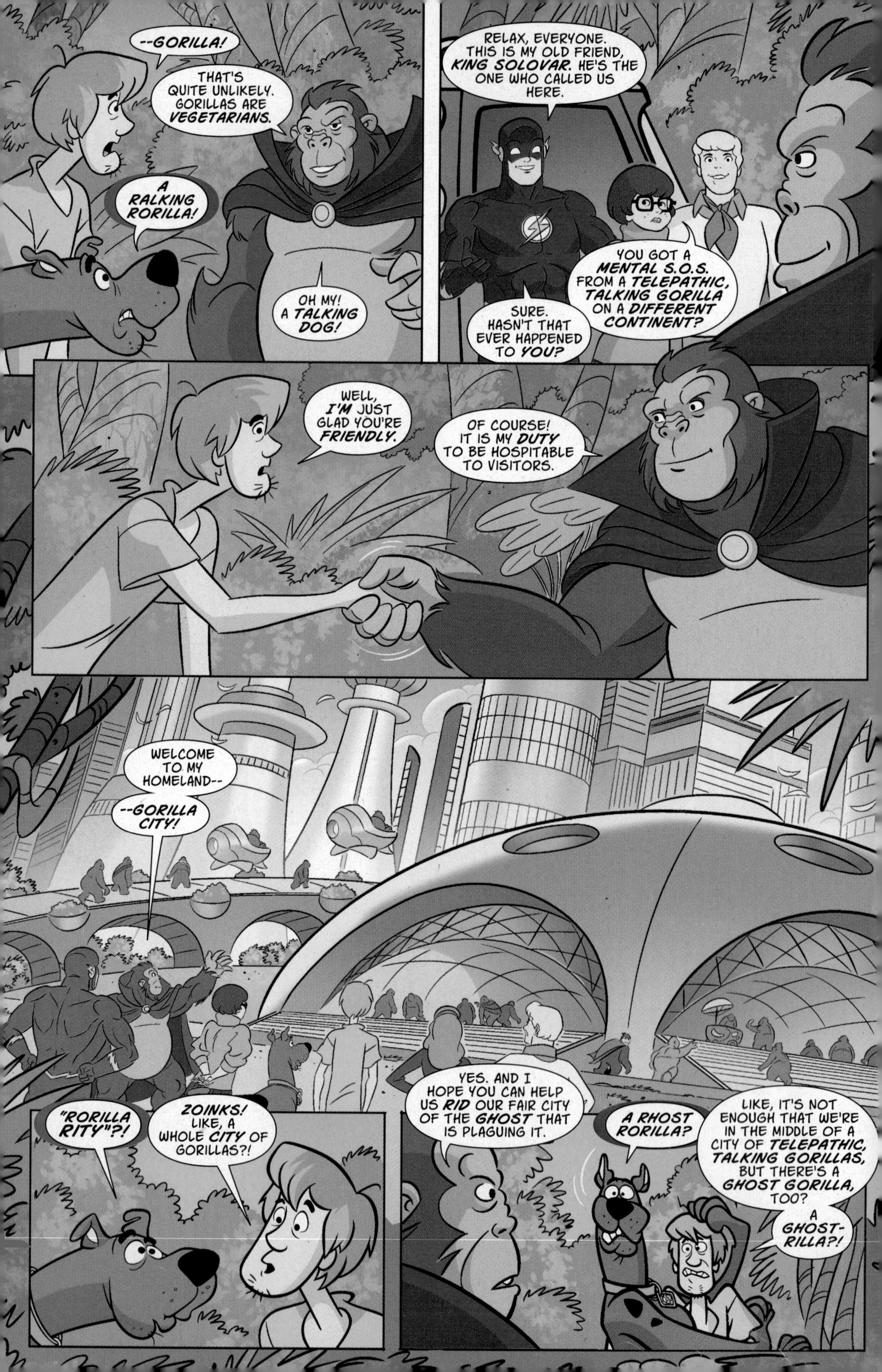
--GORILLA!
THAT'S QUITE UNLIKELY. GORILLAS ARE VEGETARIANS.
A RALKING RORILLA!
OH MY! A TALKING DOG!
RELAX, EVERYONE. THIS IS MY OLD FRIEND, KING SOLOVAR. HE'S THE ONE WHO CALLED US HERE.
YOU GOT A MENTAL S.O.S. FROM A TELEPATHIC, TALKING GORILLA ON A DIFFERENT CONTINENT?
SURE. HASN'T THAT EVER HAPPENED TO YOU?
WELL, I'M JUST GLAD YOU'RE FRIENDLY.
OF COURSE! IT IS MY DUTY TO BE HOSPITABLE TO VISITORS.
WELCOME TO MY HOMELAND--
--GORILLA CITY!
"RORILLA RITY"?!
ZOINKS! LIKE, A WHOLE CITY OF GORILLAS?!
YES. AND I HOPE YOU CAN HELP US RID OUR FAIR CITY OF THE GHOST THAT IS PLAGUING IT.
A RHOST RORILLA?
LIKE, IT'S NOT ENOUGH THAT WE'RE IN THE MIDDLE OF A CITY OF TELEPATHIC, TALKING GORILLAS, BUT THERE'S A GHOST GORILLA, TOO?
A GHOST-RILLA?!

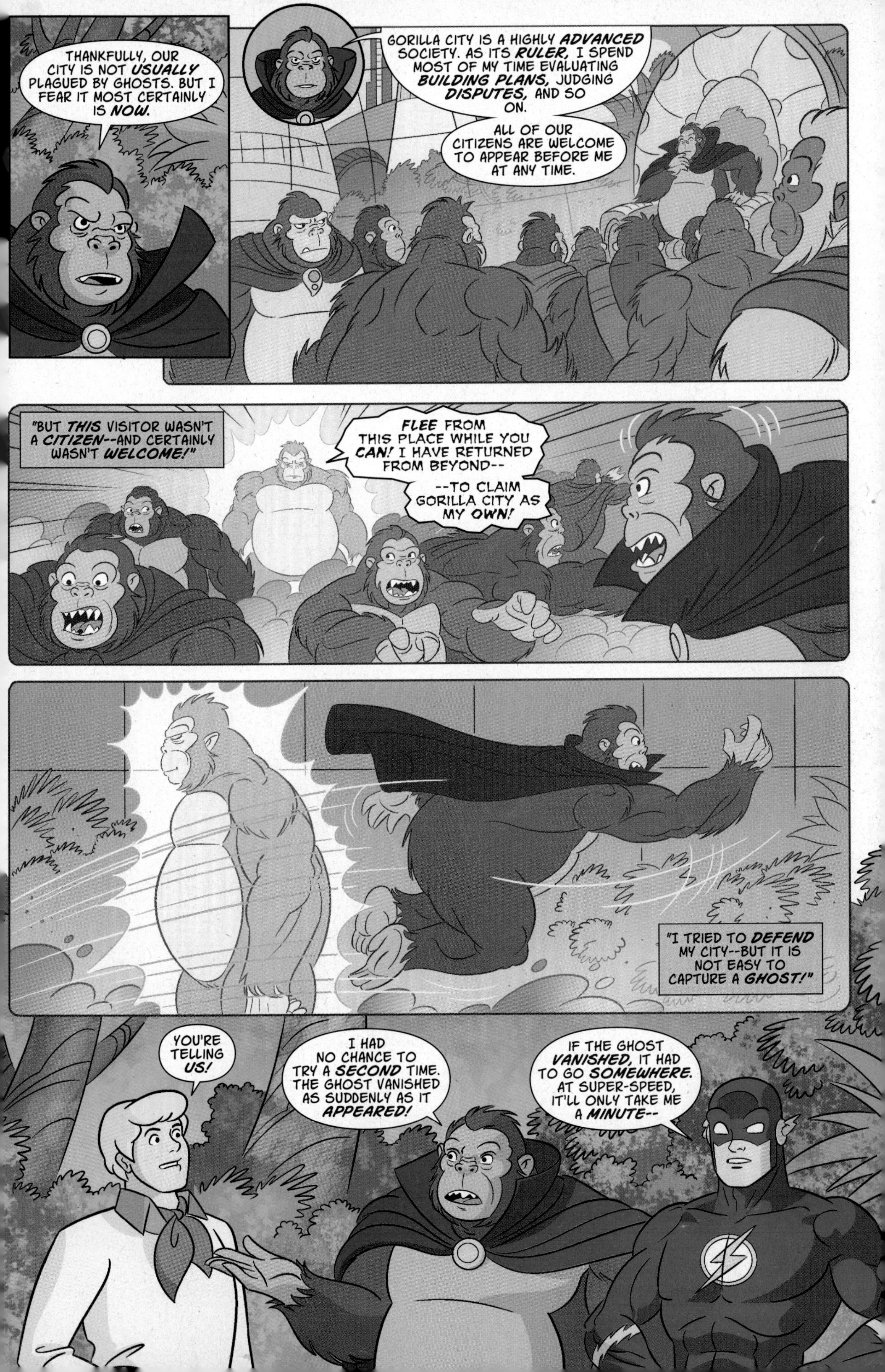
THANKFULLY, OUR CITY IS NOT USUALLY PLAGUED BY GHOSTS. BUT I FEAR IT MOST CERTAINLY IS NOW.
GORILLA CITY IS A HIGHLY ADVANCED SOCIETY. AS ITS RULER, I SPEND MOST OF MY TIME EVALUATING BUILDING PLANS, JUDGING DISPUTES, AND SO ON.
ALL OF OUR CITIZENS ARE WELCOME TO APPEAR BEFORE ME AT ANY TIME.
"BUT THIS VISITOR WASN'T A CITIZEN--AND CERTAINLY WASN'T WELCOME!"
FLEE FROM THIS PLACE WHILE YOU CAN! I HAVE RETURNED FROM BEYOND--
--TO CLAIM GORILLA CITY AS MY OWN!
"I TRIED TO DEFEND MY CITY--BUT IT IS NOT EASY TO CAPTURE A GHOST!"
YOU'RE TELLING US!
I HAD NO CHANCE TO TRY A SECOND TIME. THE GHOST VANISHED AS SUDDENLY AS IT APPEARED!
IF THE GHOST VANISHED, IT HAD TO GO SOMEWHERE. AT SUPER-SPEED, IT'LL ONLY TAKE ME A MINUTE--

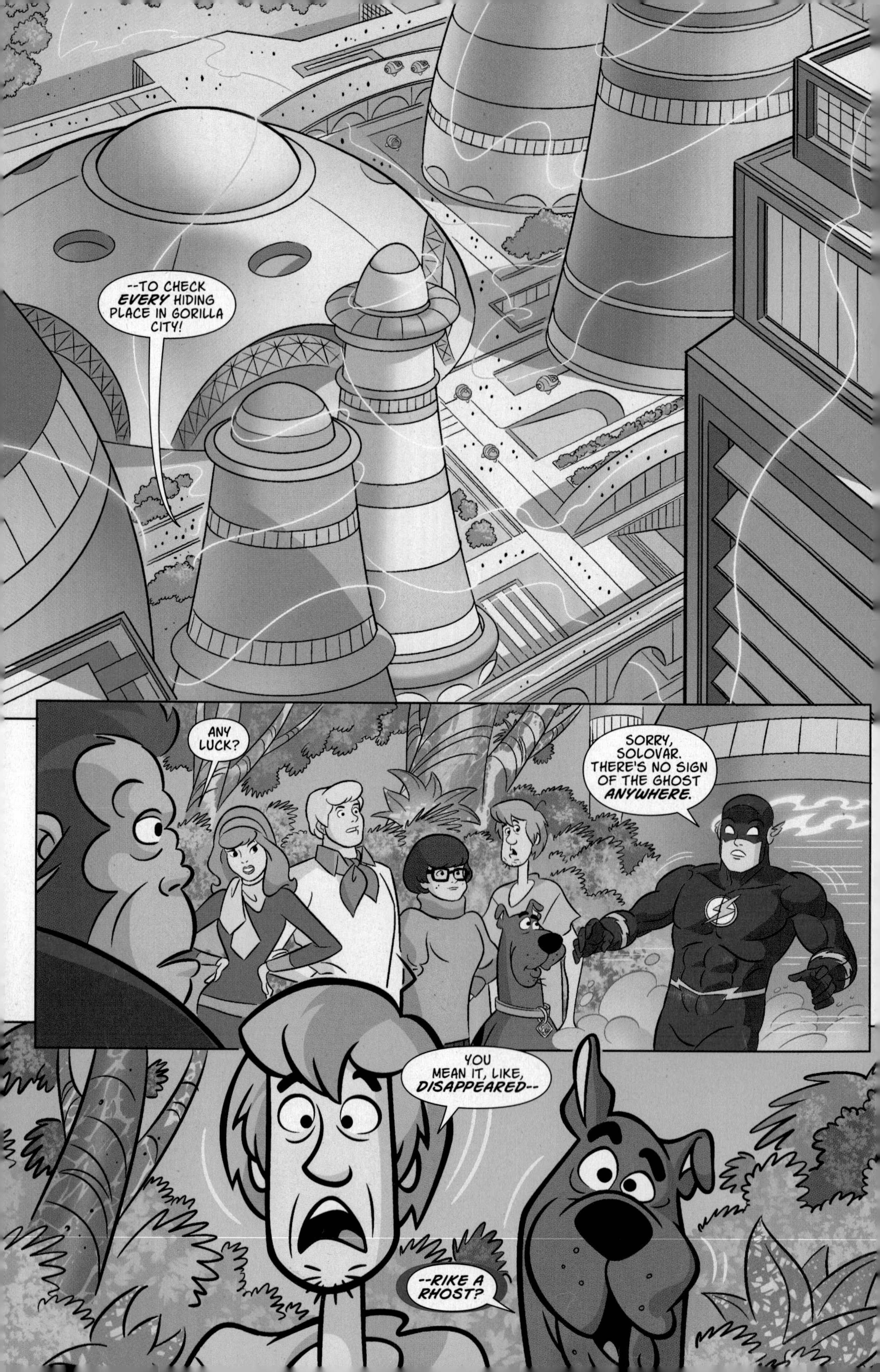
--TO CHECK EVERY HIDING PLACE IN GORILLA CITY!
ANY LUCK?
SORRY, SOLOVAR. THERE'S NO SIGN OF THE GHOST ANYWHERE.
YOU MEAN IT, LIKE, DISAPPEARED--
--RIKE A RHOST?

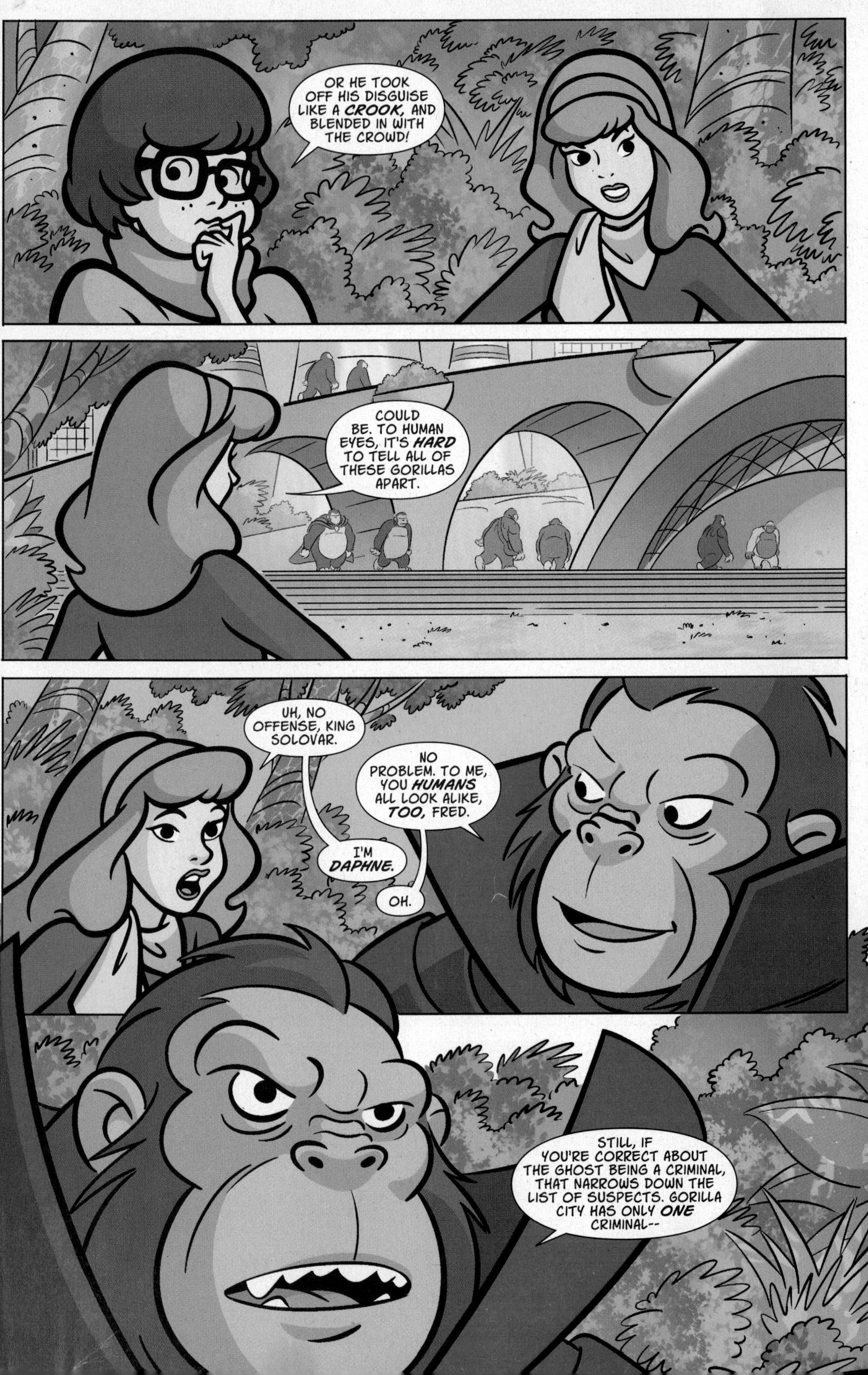
OR HE TOOK OFF HIS DISGUISE LIKE A CROOK, AND BLENDED IN WITH THE CROWD!
COULD BE. TO HUMAN EYES, IT'S HARD TO TELL ALL OF THESE GORILLAS APART.
UH, NO OFFENSE, KING SOLOVAR.
NO PROBLEM. TO ME, YOU HUMANS ALL LOOK ALIKE, TOO, FRED.
I'M DAPHNE.
OH.
STILL, IF YOU'RE CORRECT ABOUT THE GHOST BEING A CRIMINAL, THAT NARROWS DOWN THE LIST OF SUSPECTS. GORILLA CITY HAS ONLY ONE CRIMINAL--

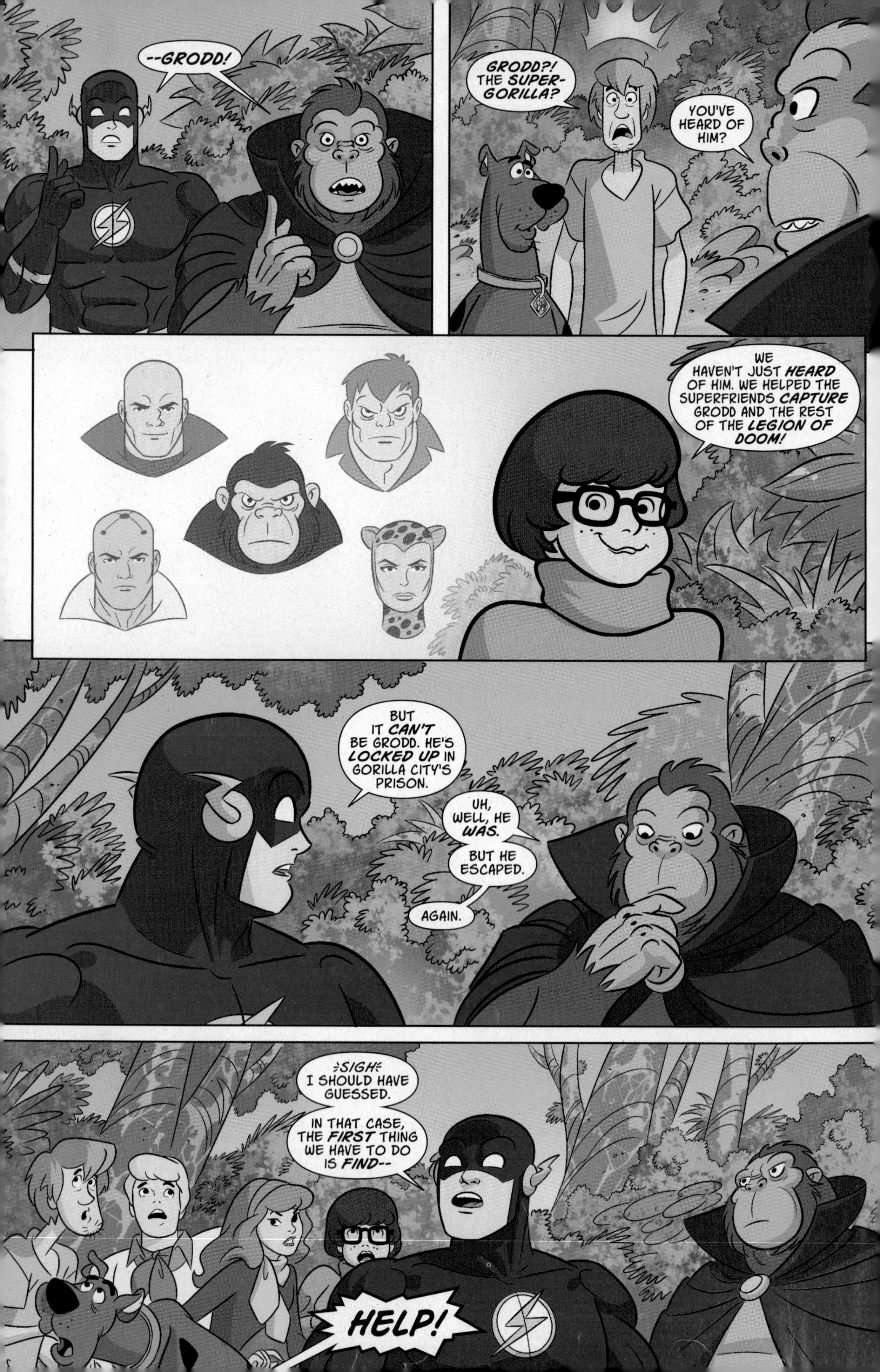
--GRODD!
GRODD?! THE SUPER-GORILLA?
YOU'VE HEARD OF HIM?
WE HAVEN'T JUST HEARD OF HIM. WE HELPED THE SUPERFRIENDS CAPTURE GRODD AND THE REST OF THE LEGION OF DOOM!
BUT IT CAN'T BE GRODD. HE'S LOCKED UP IN GORILLA CITY'S PRISON.
UH, WELL, HE WAS.
BUT HE ESCAPED.
AGAIN.
SIGH I SHOULD HAVE GUESSED.
IN THAT CASE, THE FIRST THING WE HAVE TO DO IS FIND--
HELP!

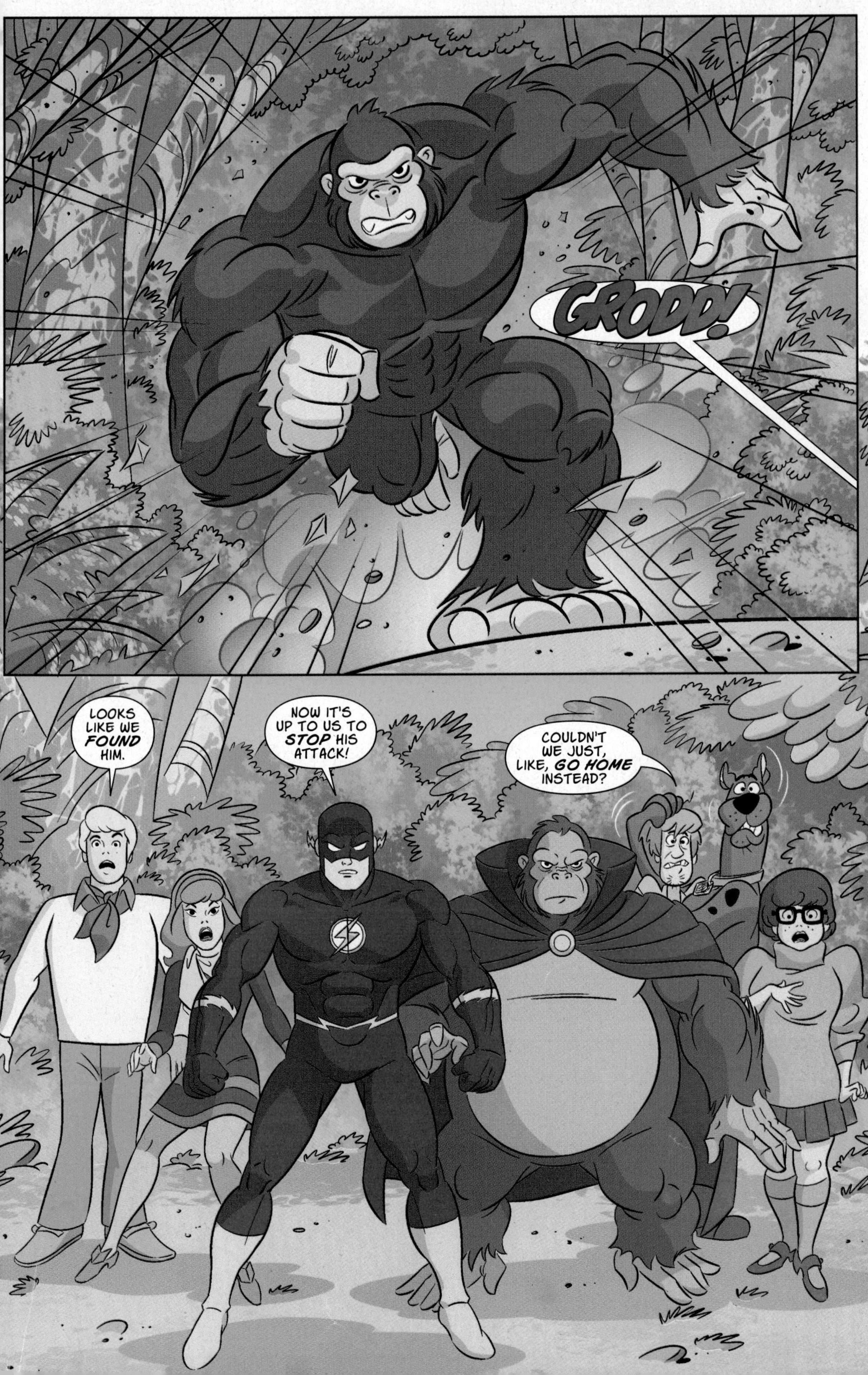
GRODD!
LOOKS LIKE WE FOUND HIM.
NOW IT'S UP TO US TO STOP HIS ATTACK!
COULDN'T WE JUST, LIKE, GO HOME INSTEAD?

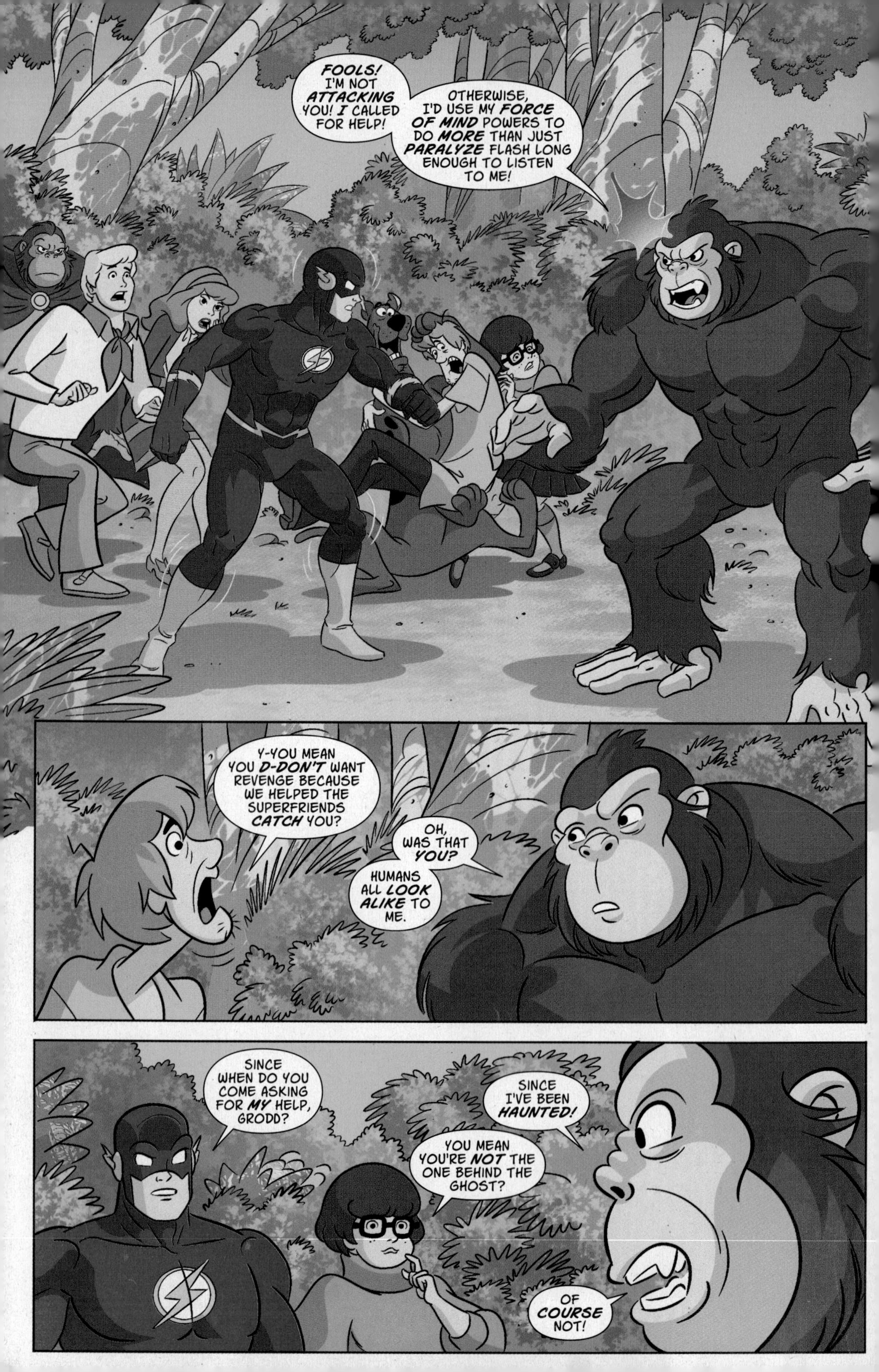

FOOLS! I'M NOT ATTACKING YOU! I CALLED FOR HELP!
OTHERWISE, I'D USE MY FORCE OF MIND POWERS TO DO MORE THAN JUST PARALYZE FLASH LONG ENOUGH TO LISTEN TO ME!
Y-YOU MEAN YOU D-DON'T WANT REVENGE BECAUSE WE HELPED THE SUPERFRIENDS CATCH YOU?
OH, WAS THAT YOU?
HUMANS ALL LOOK ALIKE TO ME.
SINCE WHEN DO YOU COME ASKING FOR MY HELP, GRODD?
SINCE I'VE BEEN HAUNTED!
YOU MEAN YOU'RE NOT THE ONE BEHIND THE GHOST?
OF COURSE NOT!

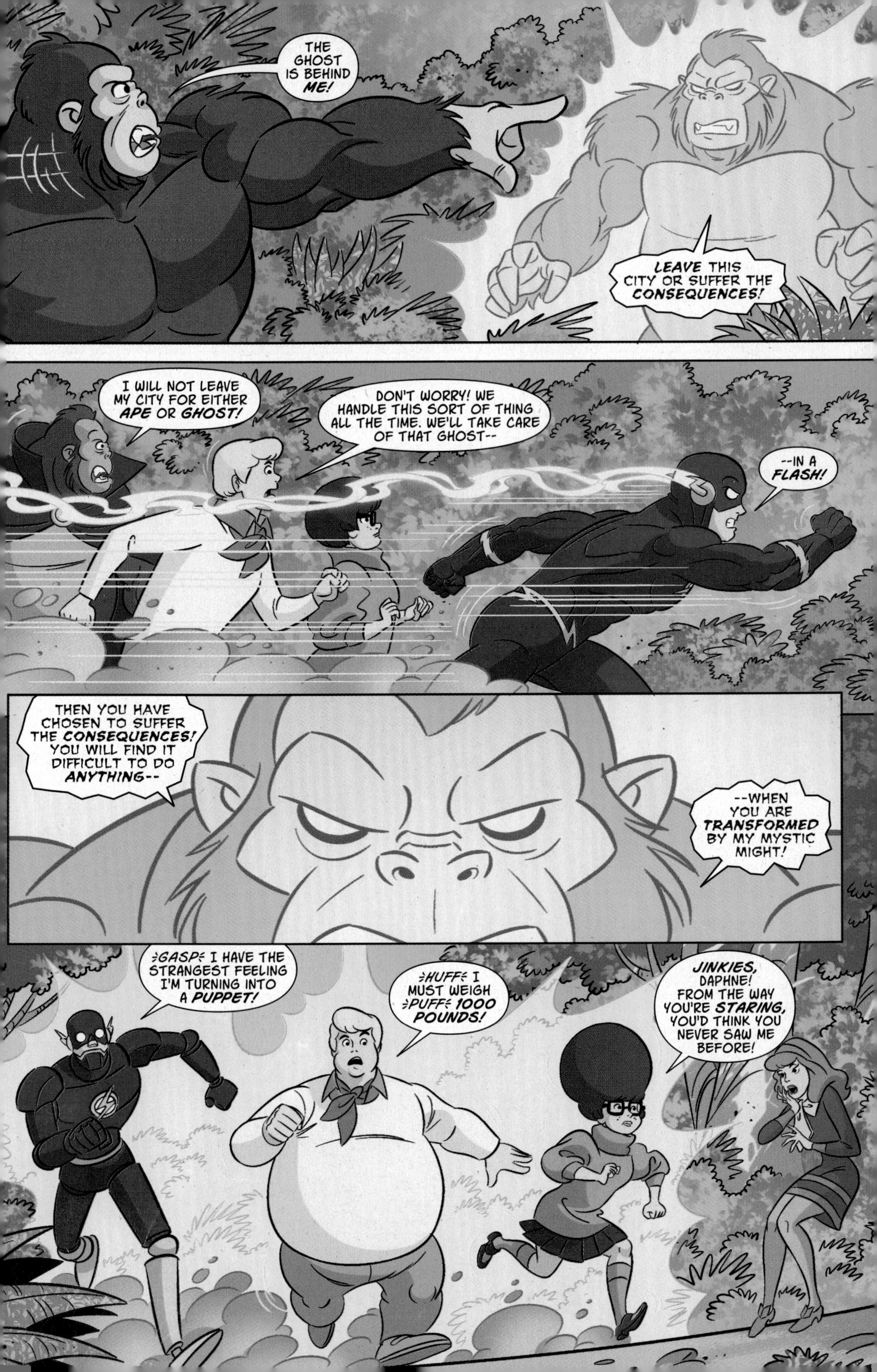
THE GHOST IS BEHIND ME!
LEAVE THIS CITY OR SUFFER THE CONSEQUENCES!
I WILL NOT LEAVE MY CITY FOR EITHER APE OR GHOST!
DON'T WORRY! WE HANDLE THIS SORT OF THING ALL THE TIME. WE'LL TAKE CARE OF THAT GHOST--
--IN A FLASH!
THEN YOU HAVE CHOSEN TO SUFFER THE CONSEQUENCES! YOU WILL FIND IT DIFFICULT TO DO ANYTHING--
--WHEN YOU ARE TRANSFORMED BY MY MYSTIC MIGHT!
GASP I HAVE THE STRANGEST FEELING I'M TURNING INTO A PUPPET!
HUFF I MUST WEIGH PUFF 1000 POUNDS!
JINKIES, DAPHNE! FROM THE WAY YOU'RE STARING, YOU'D THINK YOU NEVER SAW ME BEFORE!

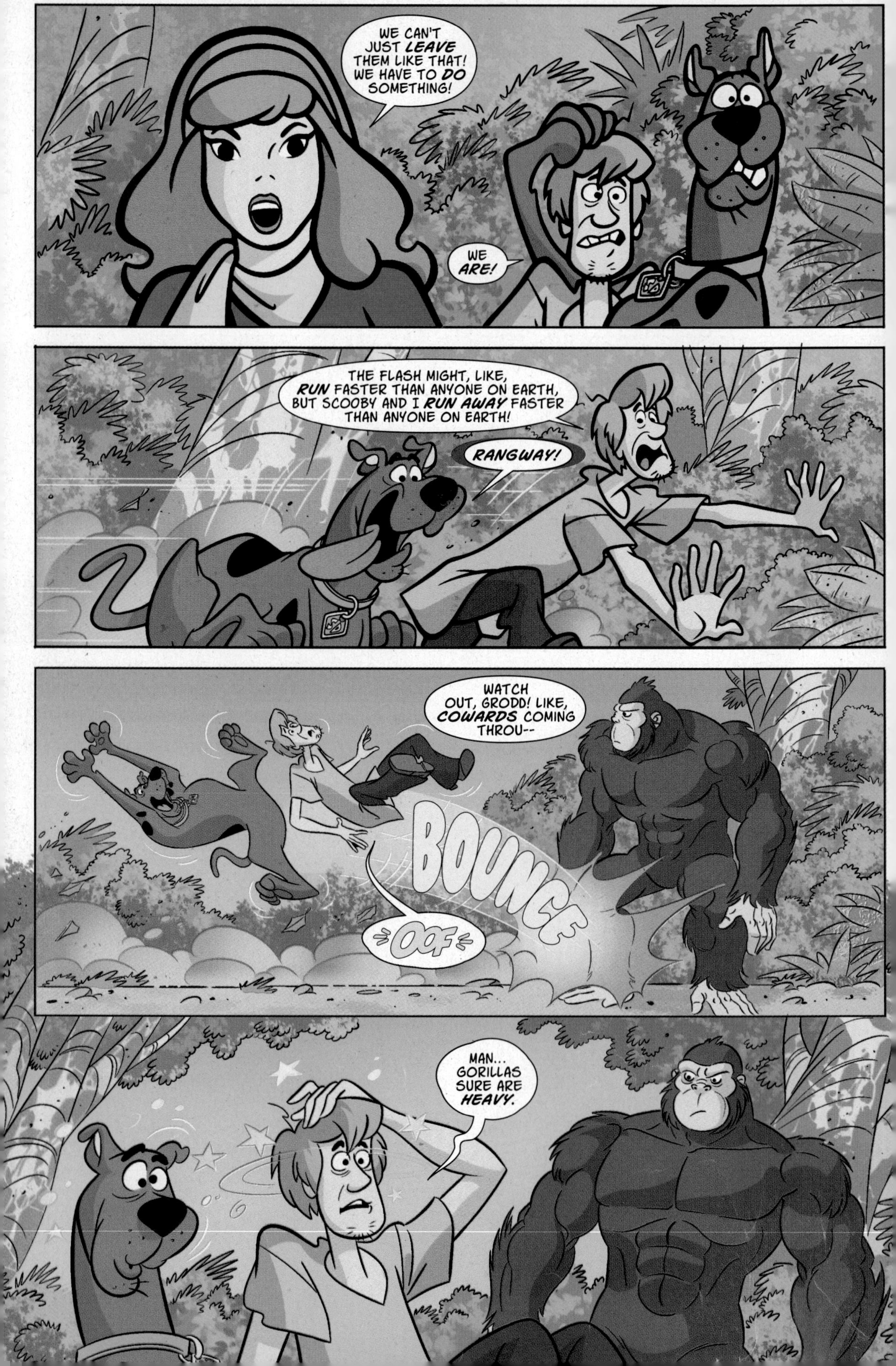
WE CAN'T JUST LEAVE THEM LIKE THAT! WE HAVE TO DO SOMETHING!
WE ARE!
THE FLASH MIGHT, LIKE, RUN FASTER THAN ANYONE ON EARTH, BUT SCOOBY AND I RUN AWAY FASTER THAN ANYONE ON EARTH!
RANGWAY!
WATCH OUT, GRODD! LIKE, COWARDS COMING THROU--
BOUNCE
OOF
MAN... GORILLAS SURE ARE HEAVY.

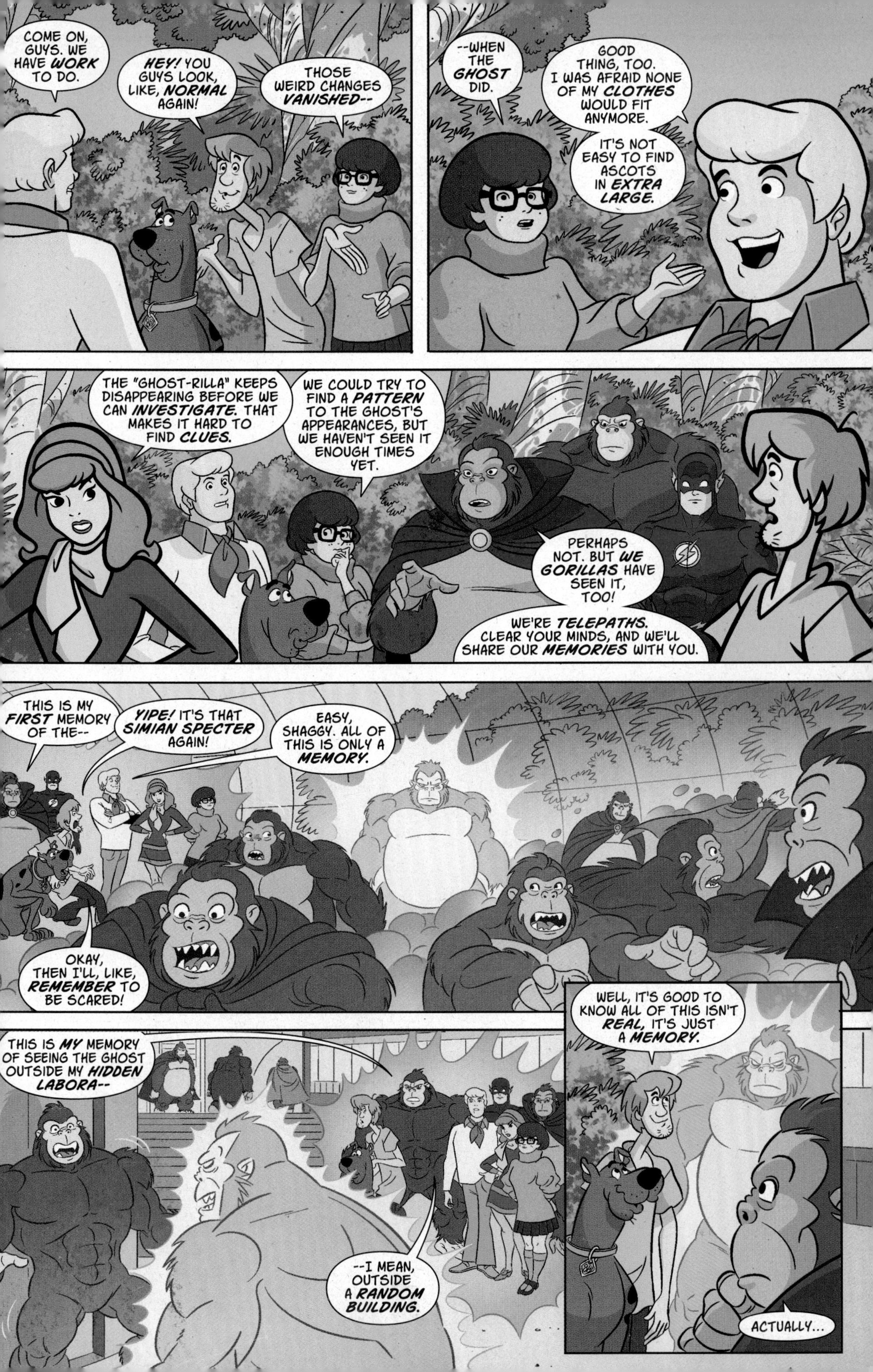
COME ON, GUYS. WE HAVE WORK TO DO.
HEY! YOU GUYS LOOK, LIKE, NORMAL AGAIN!
THOSE WEIRD CHANGES VANISHED--
--WHEN THE GHOST DID.
GOOD THING, TOO. I WAS AFRAID NONE OF MY CLOTHES WOULD FIT ANYMORE.
IT'S NOT EASY TO FIND ASCOTS IN EXTRA LARGE.
THE "GHOST-RILLA" KEEPS DISAPPEARING BEFORE WE CAN INVESTIGATE. THAT MAKES IT HARD TO FIND CLUES.
WE COULD TRY TO FIND A PATTERN TO THE GHOST'S APPEARANCES, BUT WE HAVEN'T SEEN IT ENOUGH TIMES YET.
PERHAPS NOT. BUT WE GORILLAS HAVE SEEN IT, TOO!
WE'RE TELEPATHS. CLEAR YOUR MINDS, AND WE'LL SHARE OUR MEMORIES WITH YOU.
THIS IS MY FIRST MEMORY OF THE--
YIPE! IT'S THAT SIMIAN SPECTER AGAIN!
EASY, SHAGGY. ALL OF THIS IS ONLY A MEMORY.
OKAY, THEN I'LL, LIKE, REMEMBER TO BE SCARED!
THIS IS MY MEMORY OF SEEING THE GHOST OUTSIDE MY HIDDEN LABORA--
--I MEAN, OUTSIDE A RANDOM BUILDING.
WELL, IT'S GOOD TO KNOW ALL OF THIS ISN'T REAL, IT'S JUST A MEMORY.
ACTUALLY...

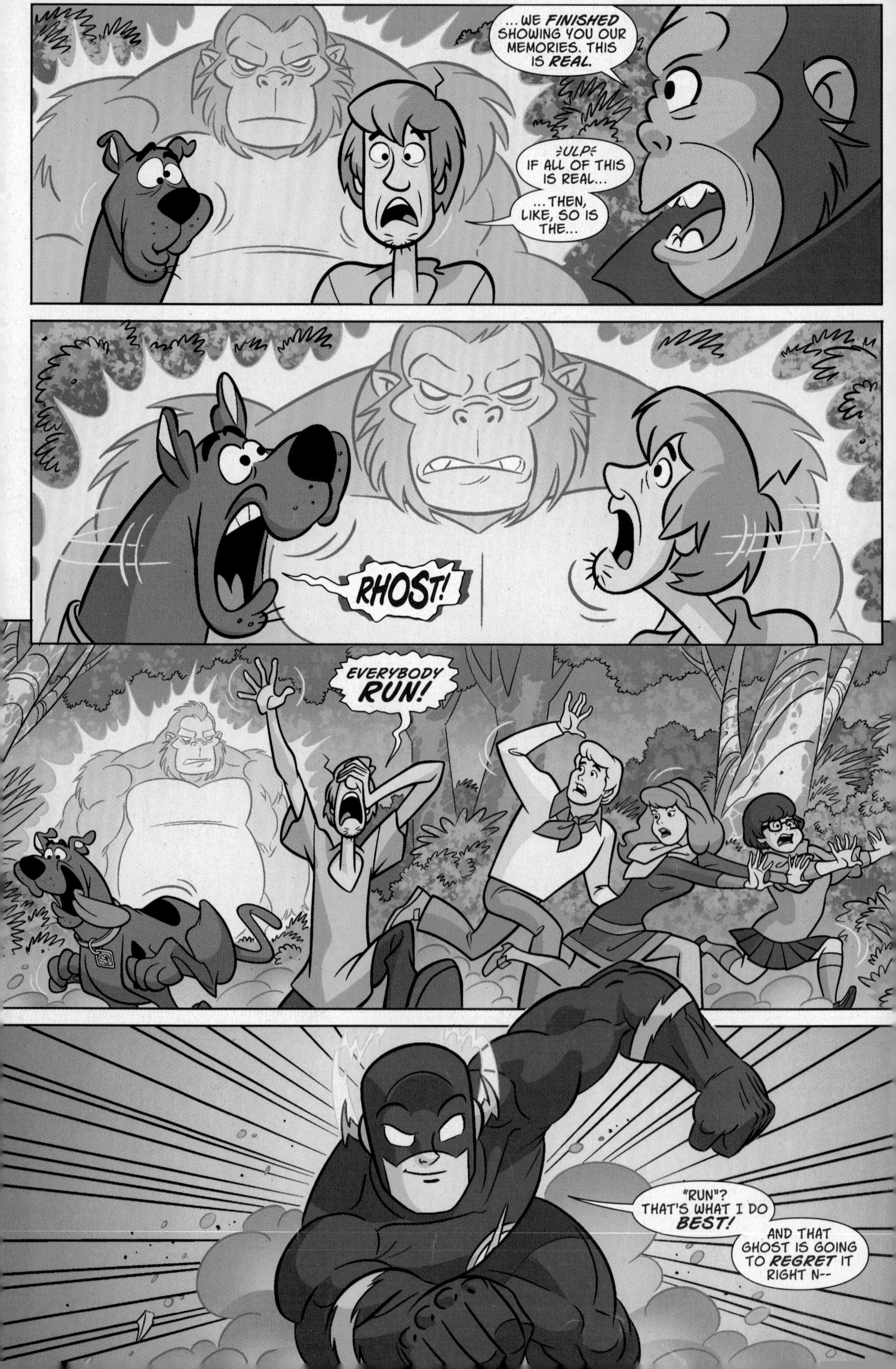
...WE FINISHED SHOWING YOU OUR MEMORIES. THIS IS REAL.
≑ULP≑ IF ALL OF THIS IS REAL...
...THEN, LIKE, SO IS THE...
RHOST!
EVERYBODY RUN!
"RUN"? THAT'S WHAT I DO BEST!
AND THAT GHOST IS GOING TO REGRET IT RIGHT N--

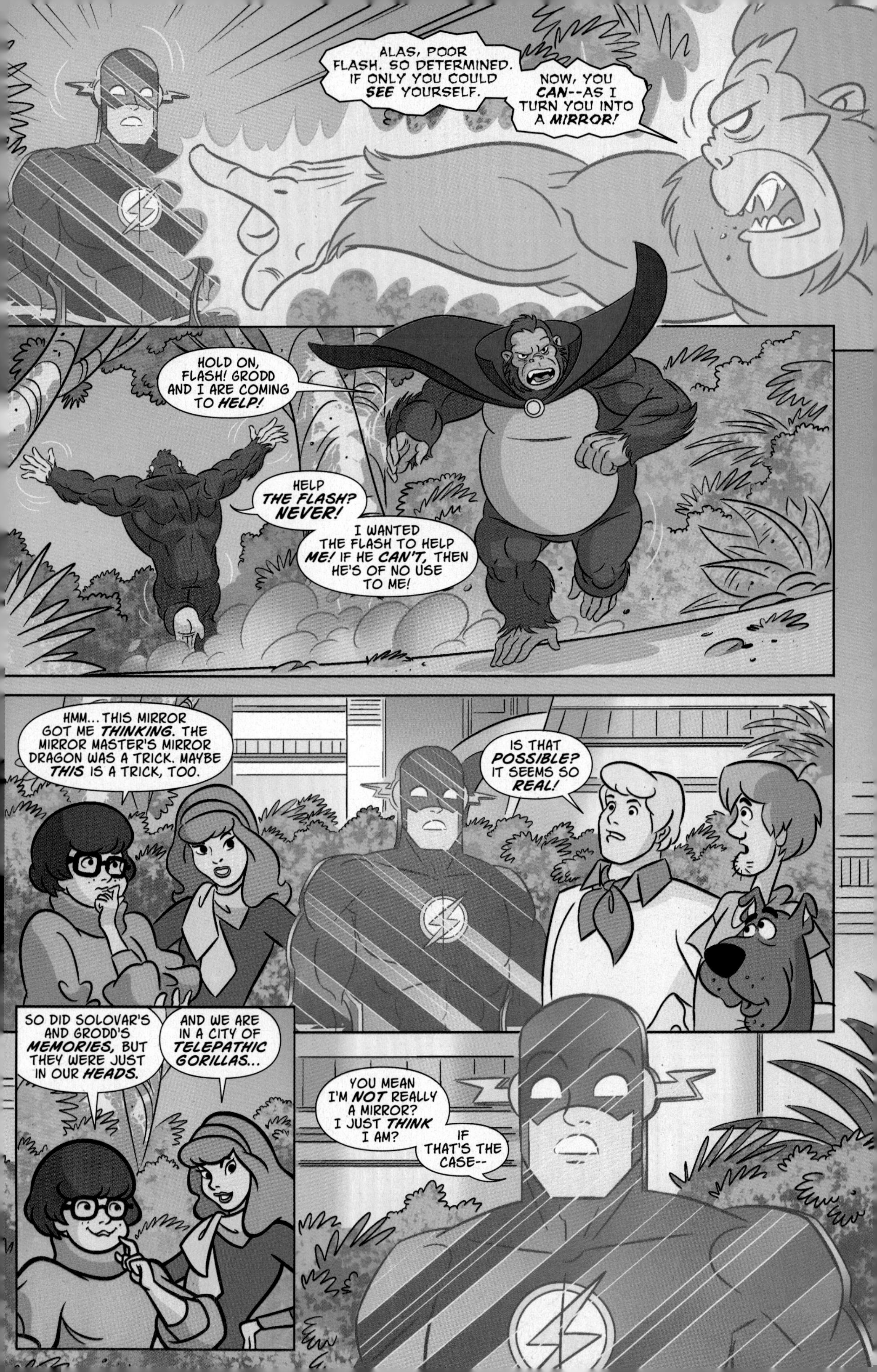
ALAS, POOR FLASH. SO DETERMINED. IF ONLY YOU COULD SEE YOURSELF.
NOW, YOU CAN--AS I TURN YOU INTO A MIRROR!
HOLD ON, FLASH! GRODD AND I ARE COMING TO HELP!
HELP THE FLASH? NEVER!
I WANTED THE FLASH TO HELP ME! IF HE CAN'T, THEN HE'S OF NO USE TO ME!
HMM... THIS MIRROR GOT ME THINKING. THE MIRROR MASTER'S MIRROR DRAGON WAS A TRICK. MAYBE THIS IS A TRICK, TOO.
IS THAT POSSIBLE? IT SEEMS SO REAL!
SO DID SOLOVAR'S AND GRODD'S MEMORIES, BUT THEY WERE JUST IN OUR HEADS.
AND WE ARE IN A CITY OF TELEPATHIC GORILLAS...
YOU MEAN I'M NOT REALLY A MIRROR? I JUST THINK I AM?
IF THAT'S THE CASE--

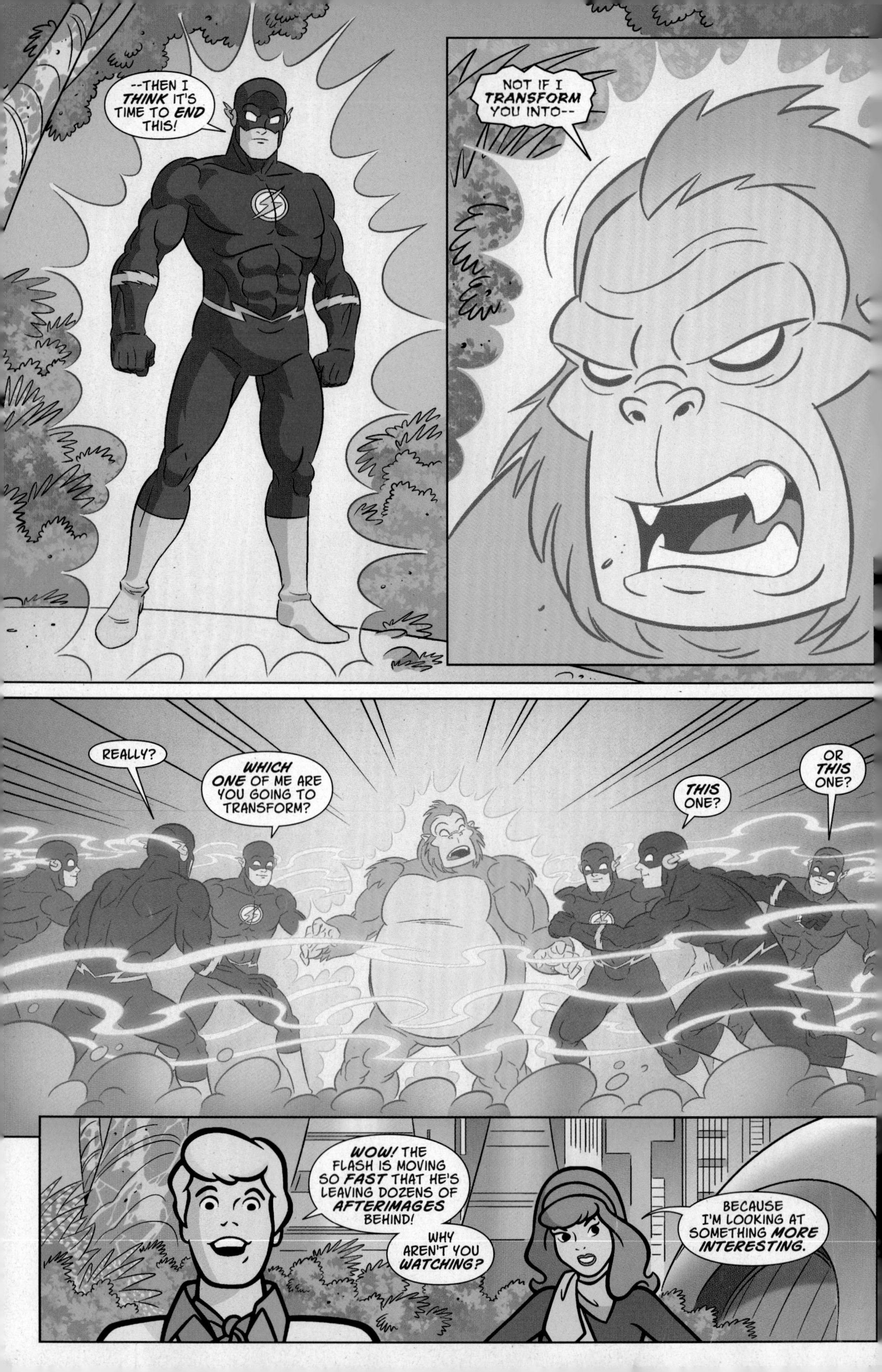
--THEN I THINK IT'S TIME TO END THIS!
NOT IF I TRANSFORM YOU INTO--
REALLY?
WHICH ONE OF ME ARE YOU GOING TO TRANSFORM?
THIS ONE?
OR THIS ONE?
WOW! THE FLASH IS MOVING SO FAST THAT HE'S LEAVING DOZENS OF AFTERIMAGES BEHIND!
WHY AREN'T YOU WATCHING?
BECAUSE I'M LOOKING AT SOMETHING MORE INTERESTING.

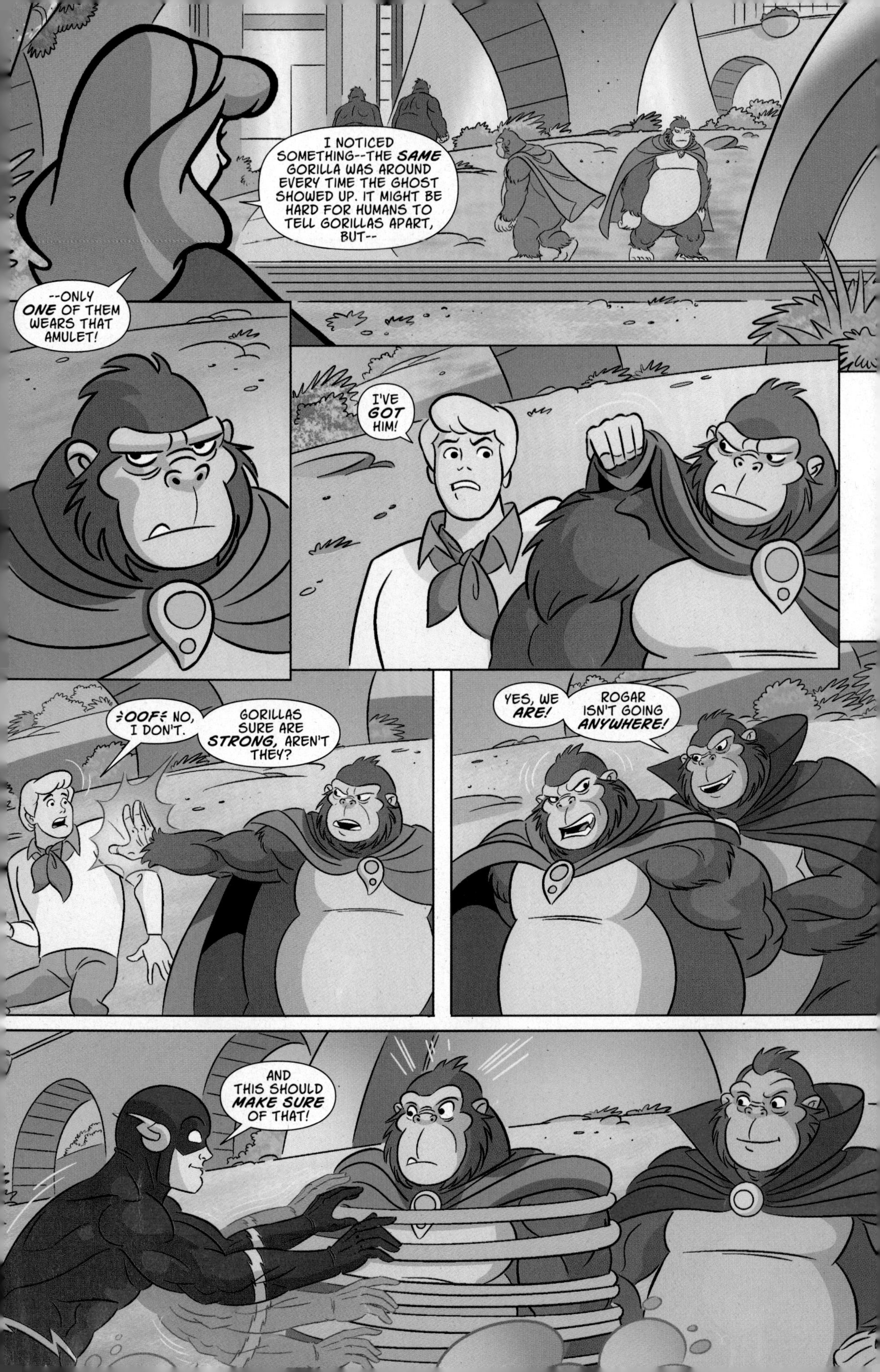

I NOTICED SOMETHING--THE SAME GORILLA WAS AROUND EVERY TIME THE GHOST SHOWED UP. IT MIGHT BE HARD FOR HUMANS TO TELL GORILLAS APART, BUT--
--ONLY ONE OF THEM WEARS THAT AMULET!
I'VE GOT HIM!
OOF NO, I DON'T.
GORILLAS SURE ARE STRONG, AREN'T THEY?
YES, WE ARE!
ROGAR ISN'T GOING ANYWHERE!
AND THIS SHOULD MAKE SURE OF THAT!

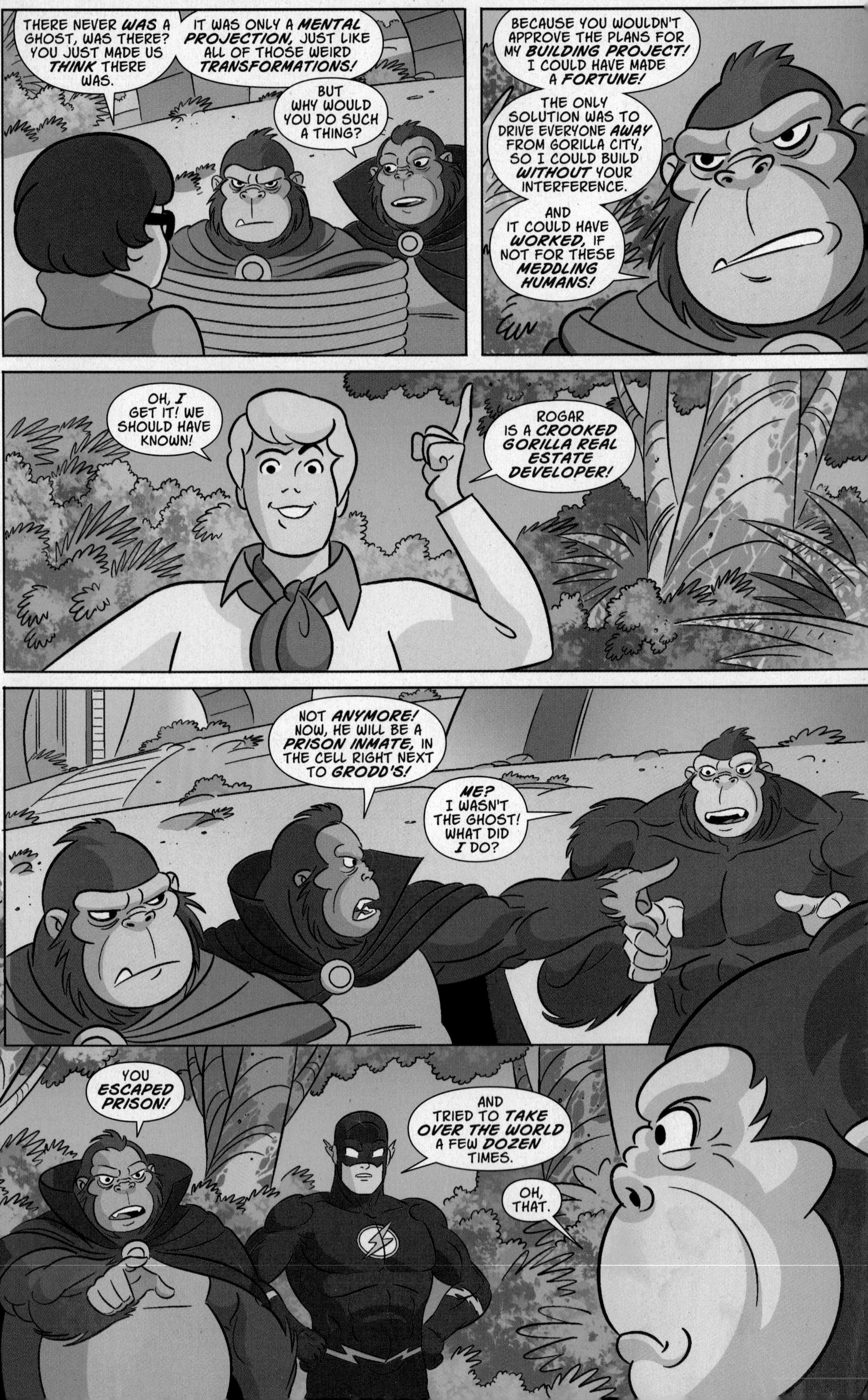
THERE NEVER WAS A GHOST, WAS THERE? YOU JUST MADE US THINK THERE WAS.
IT WAS ONLY A MENTAL PROJECTION, JUST LIKE ALL OF THOSE WEIRD TRANSFORMATIONS!
BUT WHY WOULD YOU DO SUCH A THING?
BECAUSE YOU WOULDN'T APPROVE THE PLANS FOR MY BUILDING PROJECT! I COULD HAVE MADE A FORTUNE!
THE ONLY SOLUTION WAS TO DRIVE EVERYONE AWAY FROM GORILLA CITY, SO I COULD BUILD WITHOUT YOUR INTERFERENCE.
AND IT COULD HAVE WORKED, IF NOT FOR THESE MEDDLING HUMANS!
OH, I GET IT! WE SHOULD HAVE KNOWN!
ROGAR IS A CROOKED GORILLA REAL ESTATE DEVELOPER!
NOT ANYMORE! NOW, HE WILL BE A PRISON INMATE, IN THE CELL RIGHT NEXT TO GRODD'S!
ME? I WASN'T THE GHOST! WHAT DID I DO?
YOU ESCAPED PRISON!
AND TRIED TO TAKE OVER THE WORLD A FEW DOZEN TIMES.
OH, THAT.

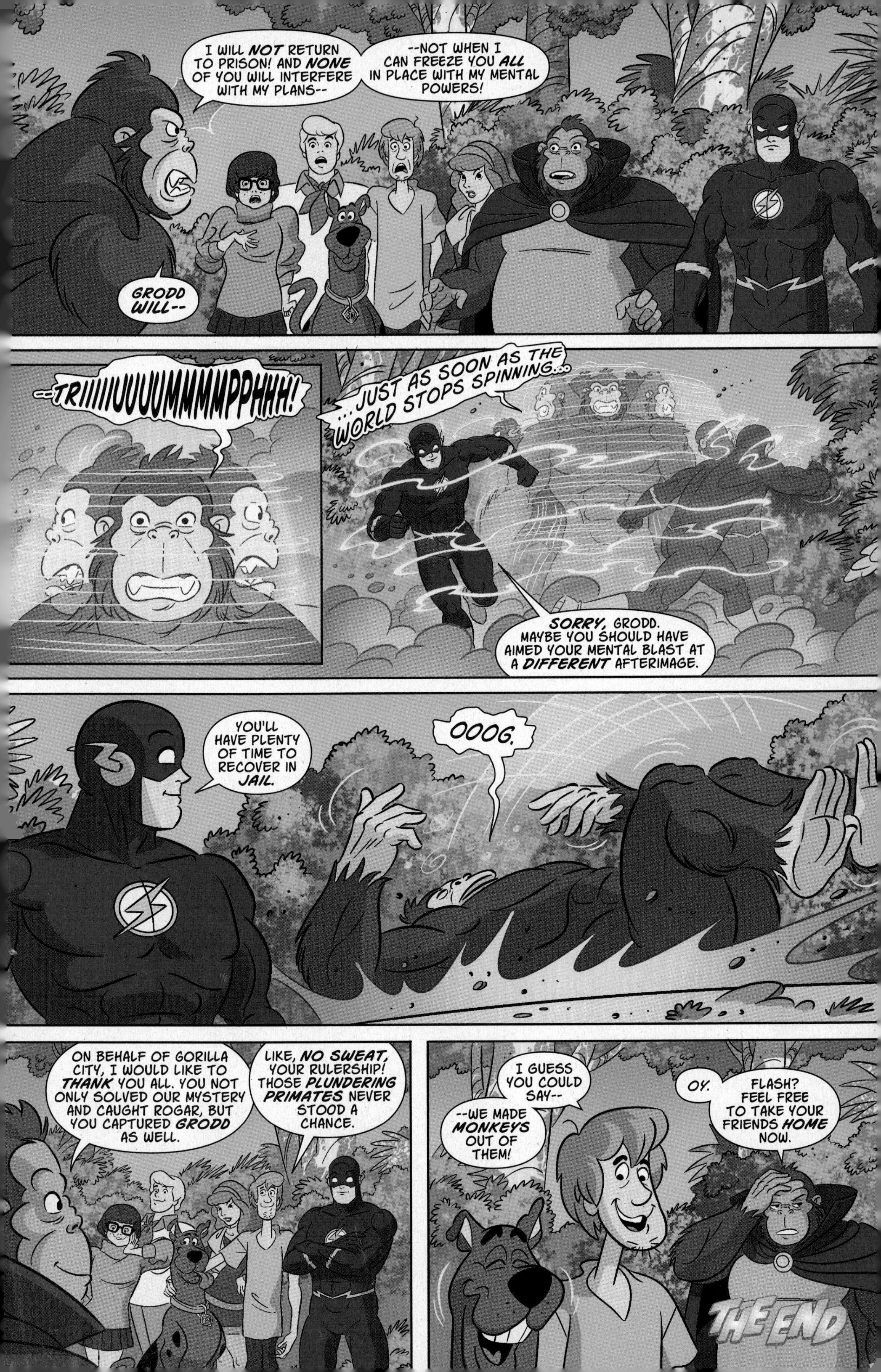
I WILL NOT RETURN TO PRISON! AND NONE OF YOU WILL INTERFERE WITH MY PLANS--
--NOT WHEN I CAN FREEZE YOU ALL IN PLACE WITH MY MENTAL POWERS!
GRODD WILL--
--TRIIIIIUUUUMMMMPPHHH!
...JUST AS SOON AS THE WORLD STOPS SPINNING...
SORRY, GRODD. MAYBE YOU SHOULD HAVE AIMED YOUR MENTAL BLAST AT A DIFFERENT AFTERIMAGE.
YOU'LL HAVE PLENTY OF TIME TO RECOVER IN JAIL.
OOOG.
ON BEHALF OF GORILLA CITY, I WOULD LIKE TO THANK YOU ALL. YOU NOT ONLY SOLVED OUR MYSTERY AND CAUGHT ROGAR, BUT YOU CAPTURED GRODD AS WELL.
LIKE, NO SWEAT, YOUR RULERSHIP! THOSE PLUNDERING PRIMATES NEVER STOOD A CHANCE.
I GUESS YOU COULD SAY--
--WE MADE MONKEYS OUT OF THEM!
OY.
FLASH? FEEL FREE TO TAKE YOUR FRIENDS HOME NOW.
THE END

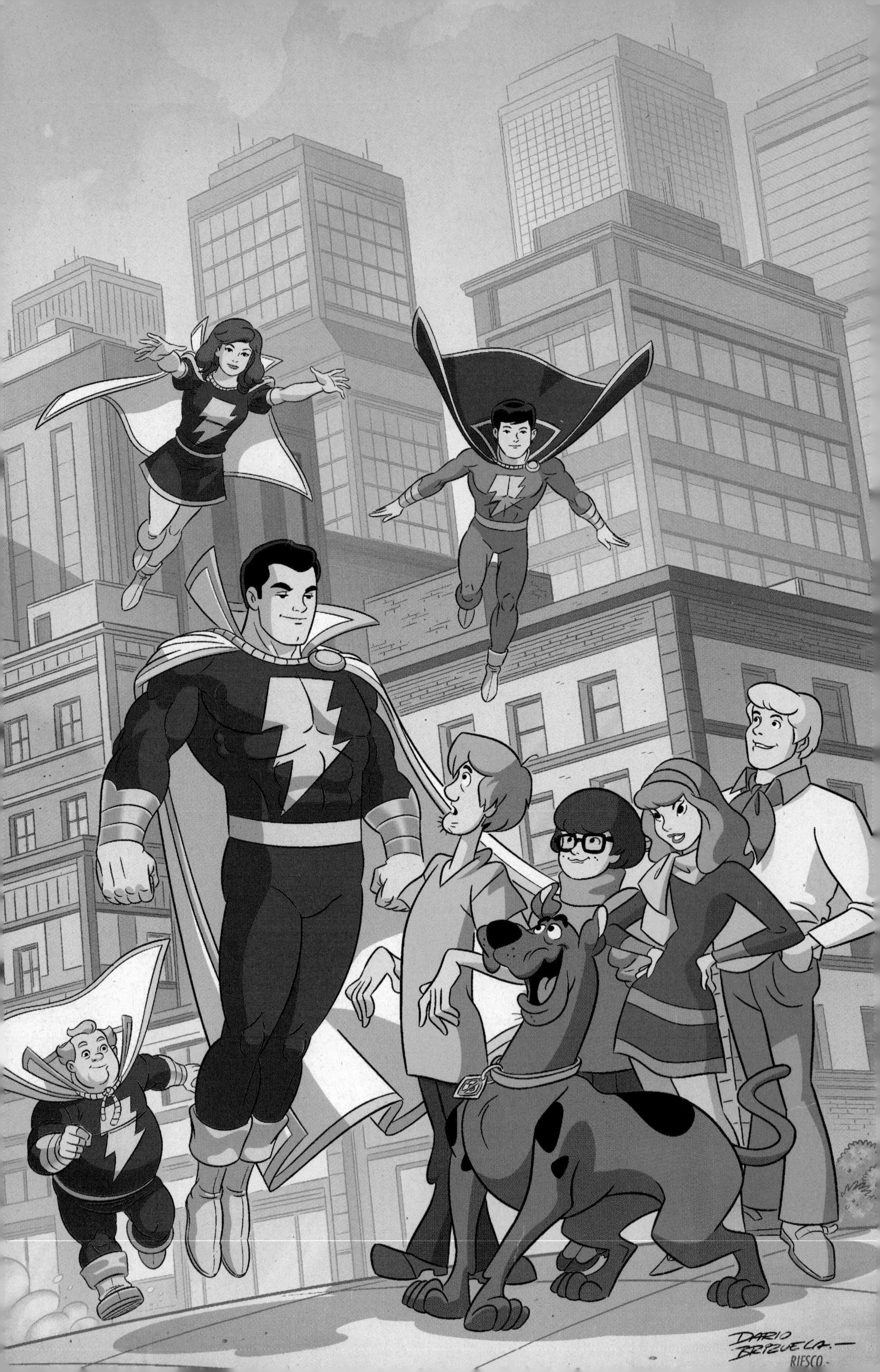
DARIO BRIZUELA.
RIFSCO.-

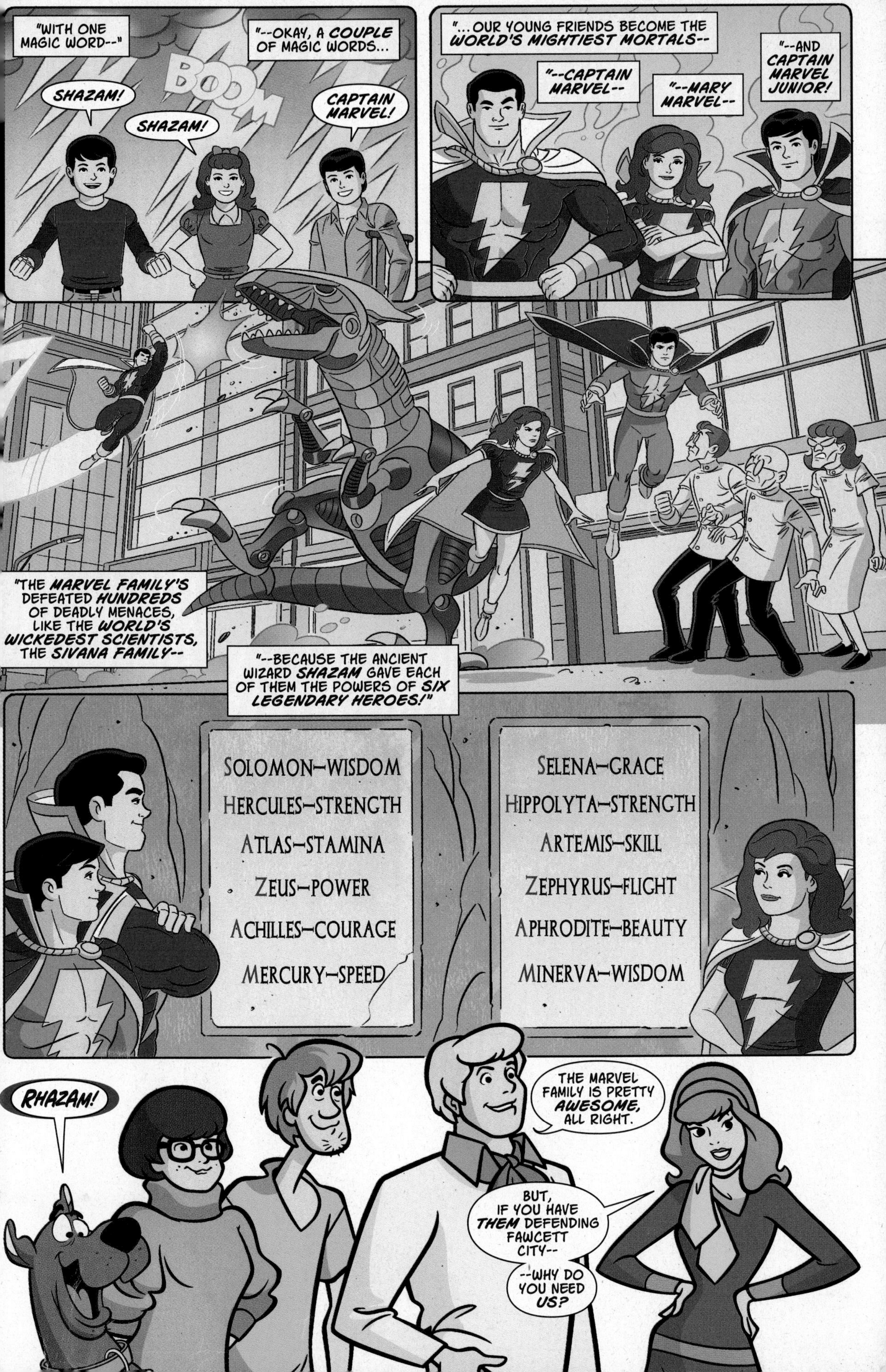

"WITH ONE MAGIC WORD--"
SHAZAM!
SHAZAM!
"--OKAY, A COUPLE OF MAGIC WORDS...
BOOM
CAPTAIN MARVEL!
"...OUR YOUNG FRIENDS BECOME THE WORLD'S MIGHTIEST MORTALS--
"--CAPTAIN MARVEL--
"--MARY MARVEL--
"--AND CAPTAIN MARVEL JUNIOR!
"THE MARVEL FAMILY'S DEFEATED HUNDREDS OF DEADLY MENACES, LIKE THE WORLD'S WICKEDEST SCIENTISTS, THE SIVANA FAMILY--
"--BECAUSE THE ANCIENT WIZARD SHAZAM GAVE EACH OF THEM THE POWERS OF SIX LEGENDARY HEROES!"
SOLOMON–WISDOM
HERCULES–STRENGTH
ATLAS–STAMINA
ZEUS–POWER
ACHILLES–COURAGE
MERCURY–SPEED
SELENA–GRACE
HIPPOLYTA–STRENGTH
ARTEMIS–SKILL
ZEPHYRUS–FLIGHT
APHRODITE–BEAUTY
MINERVA–WISDOM
RHAZAM!
THE MARVEL FAMILY IS PRETTY AWESOME, ALL RIGHT.
BUT, IF YOU HAVE THEM DEFENDING FAWCETT CITY--
--WHY DO YOU NEED US?

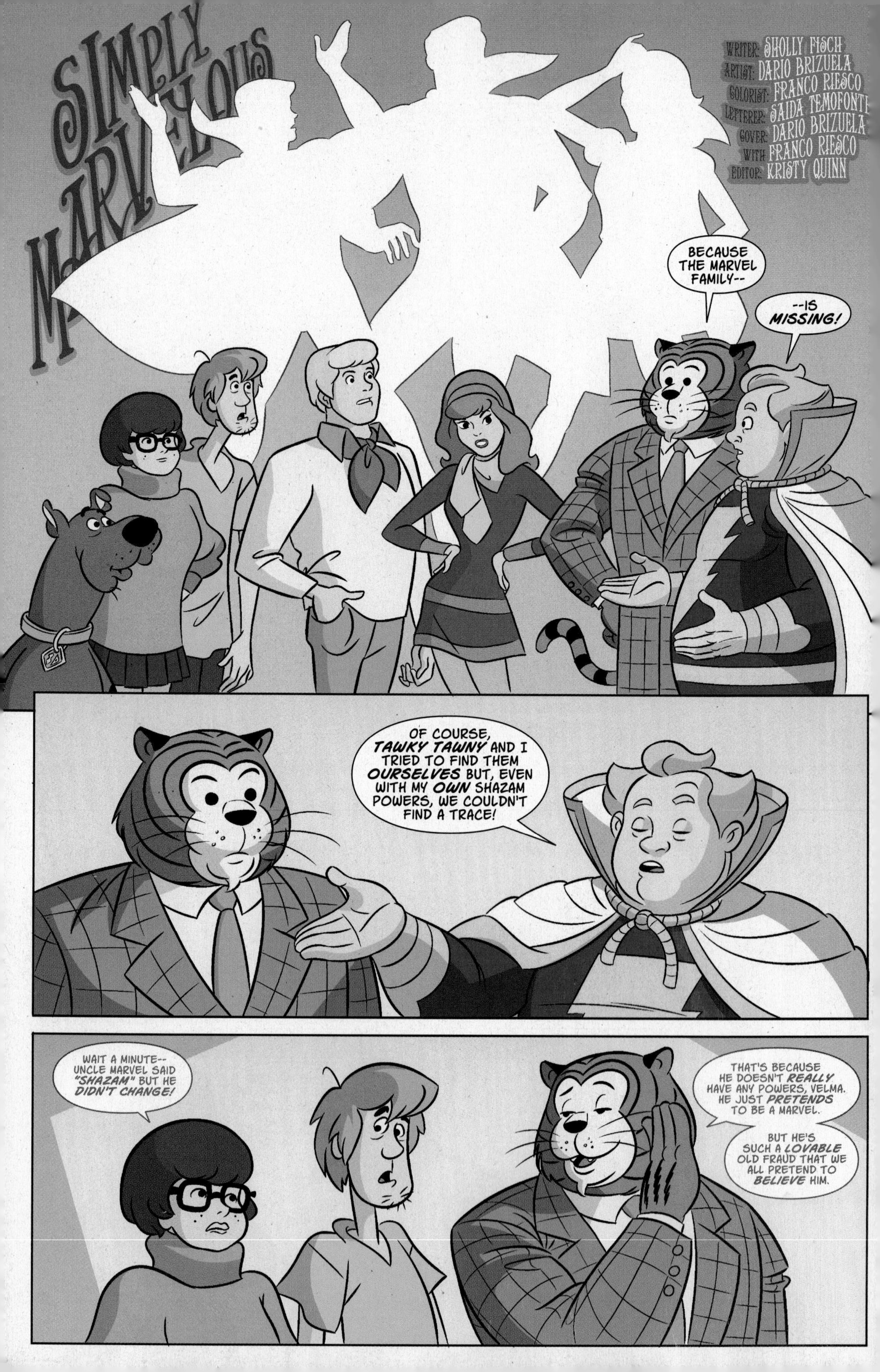
SIMPLY MARVELOUS
WRITER: SHOLLY FISCH
ARTIST: DARIO BRIZUELA
COLORIST: FRANCO RIESCO
LETTERER: SAIDA TEMOFONTE
COVER: DARIO BRIZUELA WITH FRANCO RIESCO
EDITOR: KRISTY QUINN
BECAUSE THE MARVEL FAMILY--
--IS MISSING!
OF COURSE, TAWKY TAWNY AND I TRIED TO FIND THEM OURSELVES BUT, EVEN WITH MY OWN SHAZAM POWERS, WE COULDN'T FIND A TRACE!
WAIT A MINUTE-- UNCLE MARVEL SAID "SHAZAM" BUT HE DIDN'T CHANGE!
THAT'S BECAUSE HE DOESN'T REALLY HAVE ANY POWERS, VELMA. HE JUST PRETENDS TO BE A MARVEL.
BUT HE'S SUCH A LOVABLE OLD FRAUD THAT WE ALL PRETEND TO BELIEVE HIM.

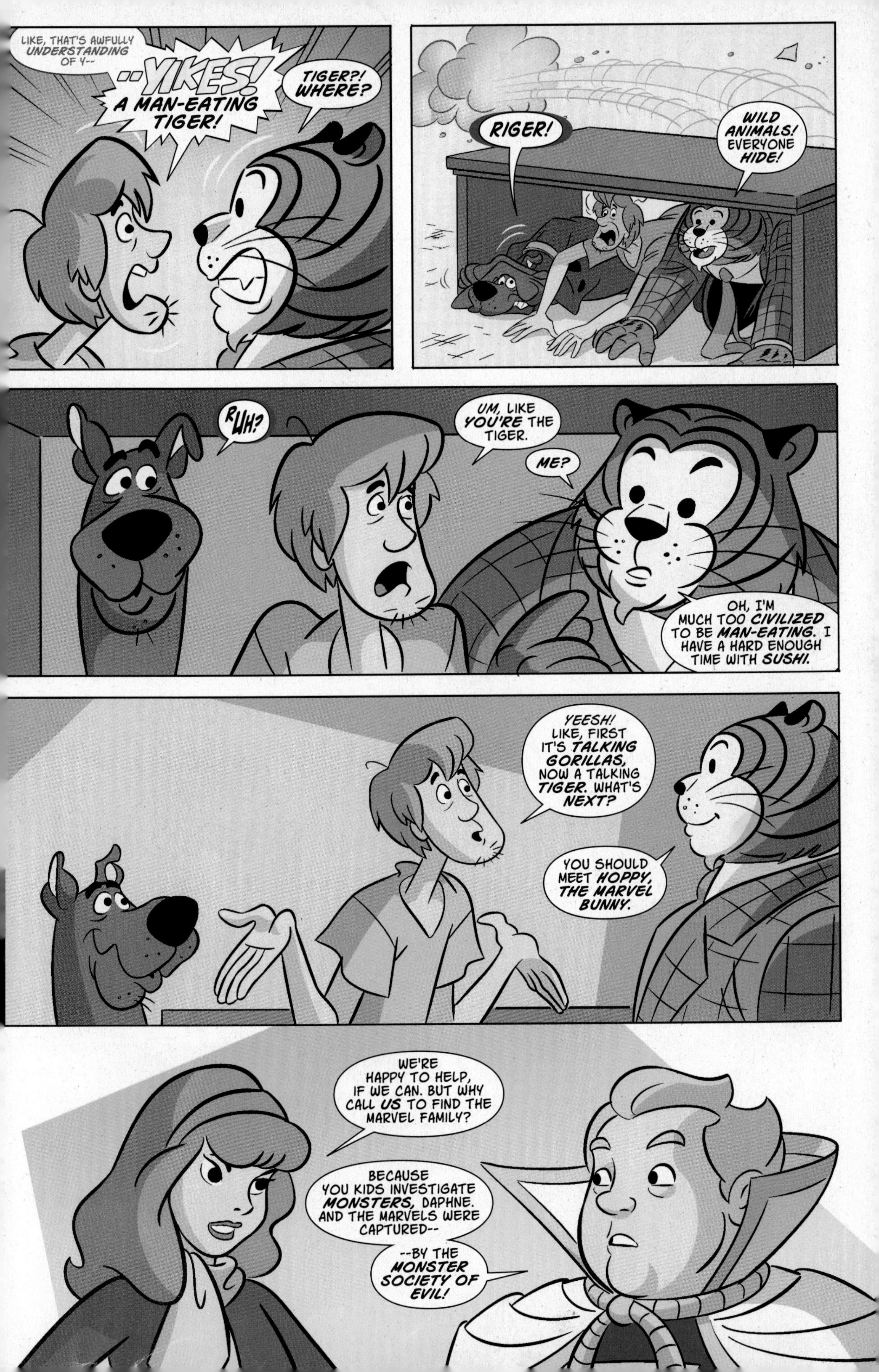
LIKE, THAT'S AWFULLY UNDERSTANDING OF Y--
--YIKES! A MAN-EATING TIGER!
TIGER?! WHERE?
RIGER!
WILD ANIMALS! EVERYONE HIDE!
RUH?
UM, LIKE YOU'RE THE TIGER.
ME?
OH, I'M MUCH TOO CIVILIZED TO BE MAN-EATING. I HAVE A HARD ENOUGH TIME WITH SUSHI.
YEESH! LIKE, FIRST IT'S TALKING GORILLAS, NOW A TALKING TIGER. WHAT'S NEXT?
YOU SHOULD MEET HOPPY, THE MARVEL BUNNY.
WE'RE HAPPY TO HELP, IF WE CAN. BUT WHY CALL US TO FIND THE MARVEL FAMILY?
BECAUSE YOU KIDS INVESTIGATE MONSTERS, DAPHNE. AND THE MARVELS WERE CAPTURED--
--BY THE MONSTER SOCIETY OF EVIL!

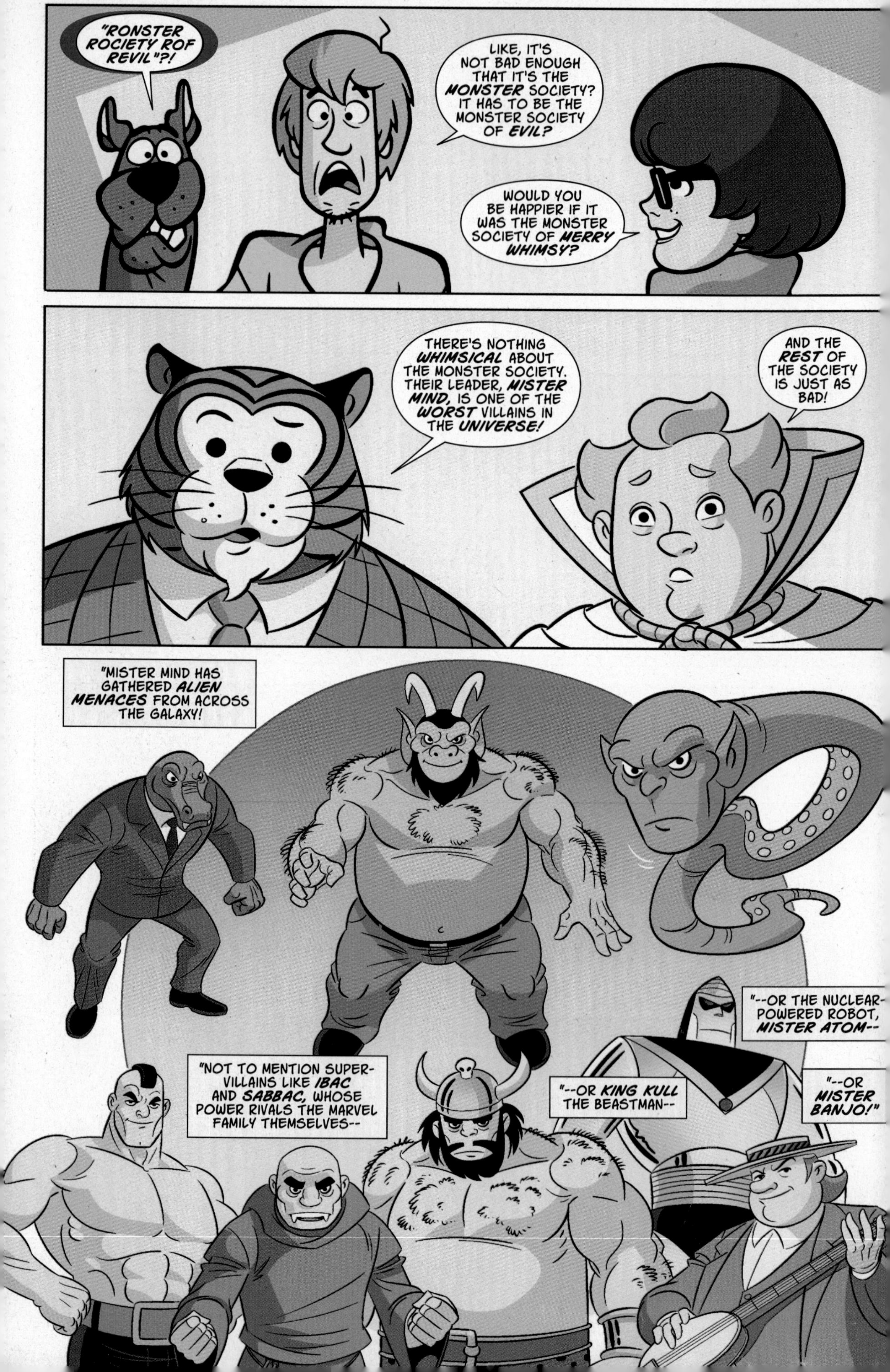
"RONSTER ROCIETY ROF REVIL"?!
LIKE, IT'S NOT BAD ENOUGH THAT IT'S THE MONSTER SOCIETY? IT HAS TO BE THE MONSTER SOCIETY OF EVIL?
WOULD YOU BE HAPPIER IF IT WAS THE MONSTER SOCIETY OF MERRY WHIMSY?
THERE'S NOTHING WHIMSICAL ABOUT THE MONSTER SOCIETY. THEIR LEADER, MISTER MIND, IS ONE OF THE WORST VILLAINS IN THE UNIVERSE!
AND THE REST OF THE SOCIETY IS JUST AS BAD!
"MISTER MIND HAS GATHERED ALIEN MENACES FROM ACROSS THE GALAXY!
"NOT TO MENTION SUPER-VILLAINS LIKE IBAC AND SABBAC, WHOSE POWER RIVALS THE MARVEL FAMILY THEMSELVES--
"--OR KING KULL THE BEASTMAN--
"--OR THE NUCLEAR-POWERED ROBOT, MISTER ATOM--
"--OR MISTER BANJO!"

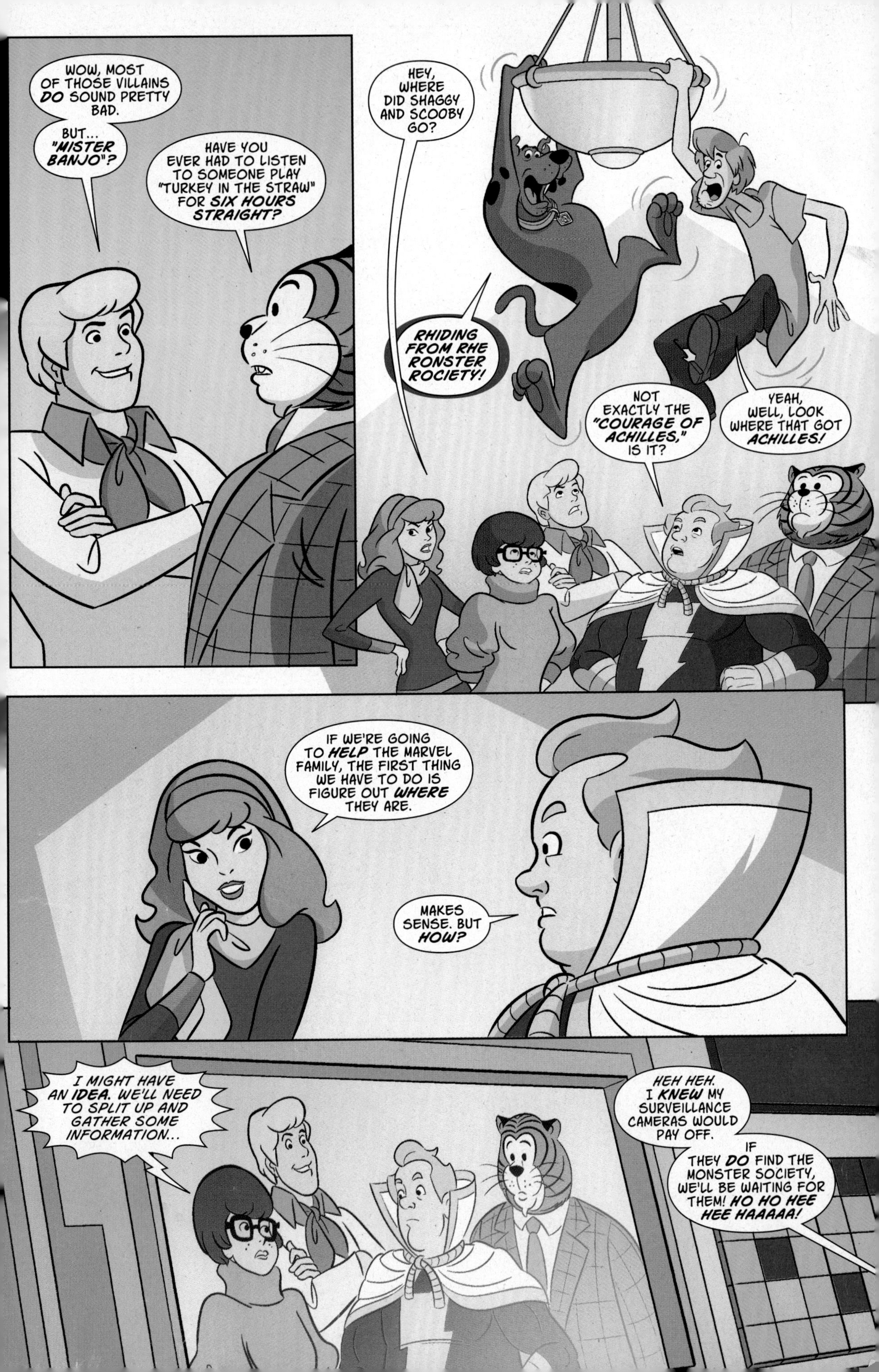

WOW, MOST OF THOSE VILLAINS DO SOUND PRETTY BAD.
BUT... "MISTER BANJO"?
HAVE YOU EVER HAD TO LISTEN TO SOMEONE PLAY "TURKEY IN THE STRAW" FOR SIX HOURS STRAIGHT?
HEY, WHERE DID SHAGGY AND SCOOBY GO?
RHIDING FROM RHE RONSTER ROCIETY!
NOT EXACTLY THE "COURAGE OF ACHILLES," IS IT?
YEAH, WELL, LOOK WHERE THAT GOT ACHILLES!
IF WE'RE GOING TO HELP THE MARVEL FAMILY, THE FIRST THING WE HAVE TO DO IS FIGURE OUT WHERE THEY ARE.
MAKES SENSE. BUT HOW?
I MIGHT HAVE AN IDEA. WE'LL NEED TO SPLIT UP AND GATHER SOME INFORMATION...
HEH HEH. I KNEW MY SURVEILLANCE CAMERAS WOULD PAY OFF.
IF THEY DO FIND THE MONSTER SOCIETY, WE'LL BE WAITING FOR THEM! HO HO HEE HEE HAAAAA!

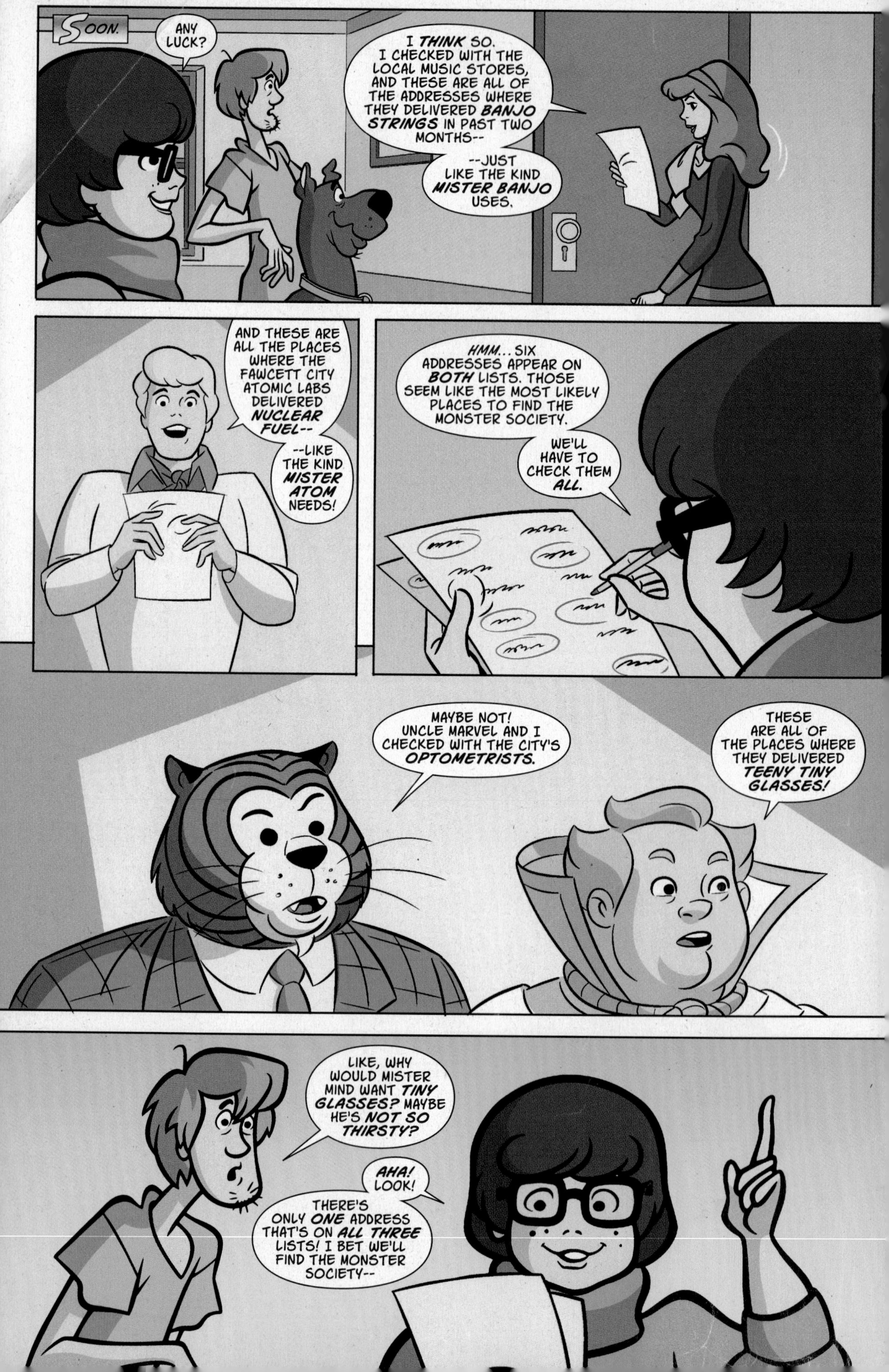
SOON.
ANY LUCK?
I THINK SO. I CHECKED WITH THE LOCAL MUSIC STORES, AND THESE ARE ALL OF THE ADDRESSES WHERE THEY DELIVERED BANJO STRINGS IN PAST TWO MONTHS--
--JUST LIKE THE KIND MISTER BANJO USES.
AND THESE ARE ALL THE PLACES WHERE THE FAWCETT CITY ATOMIC LABS DELIVERED NUCLEAR FUEL--
--LIKE THE KIND MISTER ATOM NEEDS!
HMM... SIX ADDRESSES APPEAR ON BOTH LISTS. THOSE SEEM LIKE THE MOST LIKELY PLACES TO FIND THE MONSTER SOCIETY.
WE'LL HAVE TO CHECK THEM ALL.
MAYBE NOT! UNCLE MARVEL AND I CHECKED WITH THE CITY'S OPTOMETRISTS.
THESE ARE ALL OF THE PLACES WHERE THEY DELIVERED TEENY TINY GLASSES!
LIKE, WHY WOULD MISTER MIND WANT TINY GLASSES? MAYBE HE'S NOT SO THIRSTY?
AHA! LOOK!
THERE'S ONLY ONE ADDRESS THAT'S ON ALL THREE LISTS! I BET WE'LL FIND THE MONSTER SOCIETY--

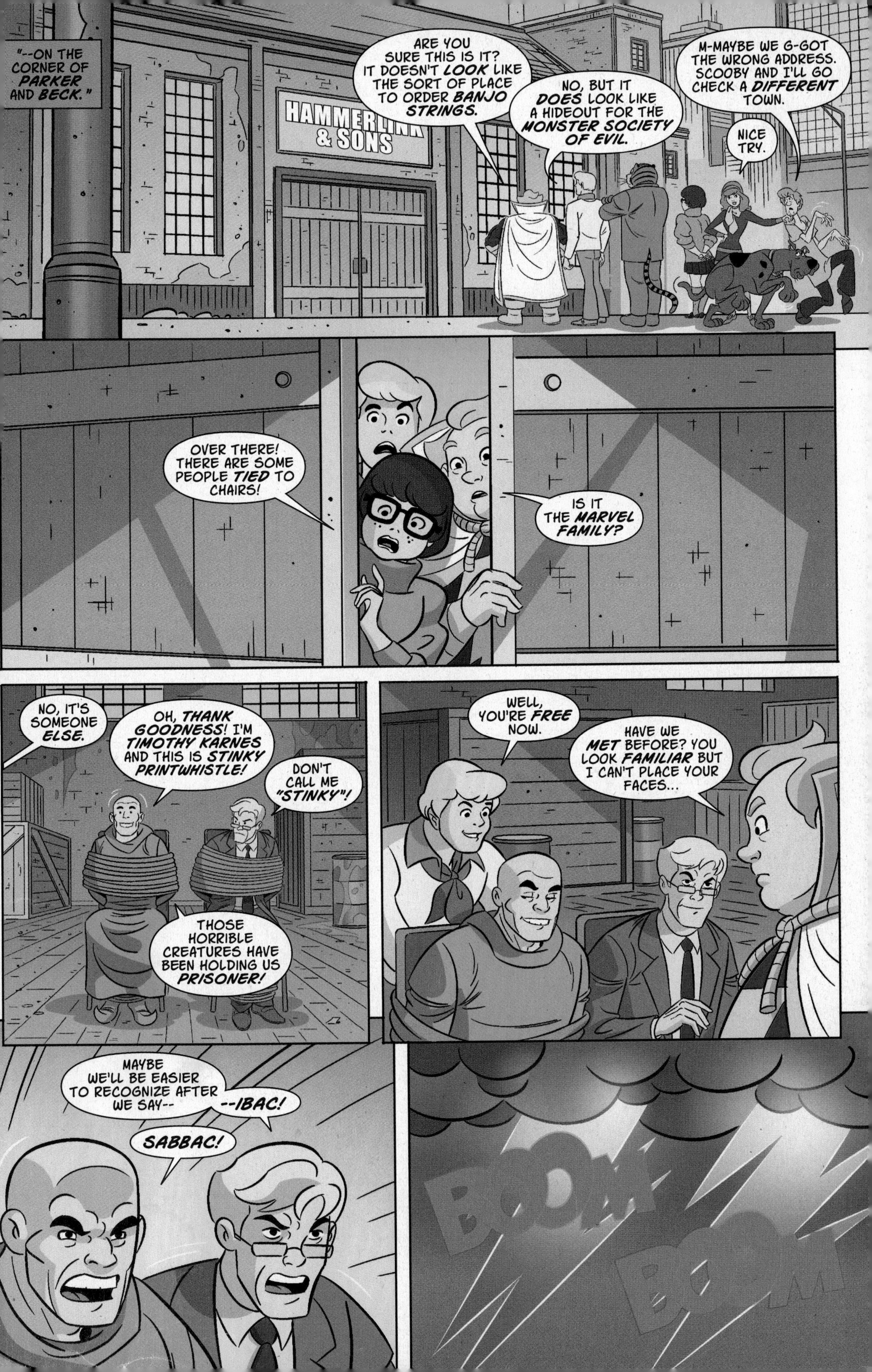
"--ON THE CORNER OF PARKER AND BECK."
HAMMERLINK & SONS
ARE YOU SURE THIS IS IT? IT DOESN'T LOOK LIKE THE SORT OF PLACE TO ORDER BANJO STRINGS.
NO, BUT IT DOES LOOK LIKE A HIDEOUT FOR THE MONSTER SOCIETY OF EVIL.
M-MAYBE WE G-GOT THE WRONG ADDRESS. SCOOBY AND I'LL GO CHECK A DIFFERENT TOWN.
NICE TRY.
OVER THERE! THERE ARE SOME PEOPLE TIED TO CHAIRS!
IS IT THE MARVEL FAMILY?
NO, IT'S SOMEONE ELSE.
OH, THANK GOODNESS! I'M TIMOTHY KARNES AND THIS IS STINKY PRINTWHISTLE!
DON'T CALL ME "STINKY"!
THOSE HORRIBLE CREATURES HAVE BEEN HOLDING US PRISONER!
WELL, YOU'RE FREE NOW.
HAVE WE MET BEFORE? YOU LOOK FAMILIAR BUT I CAN'T PLACE YOUR FACES...
MAYBE WE'LL BE EASIER TO RECOGNIZE AFTER WE SAY--
--IBAC!
SABBAC!
BOOM
BOOM

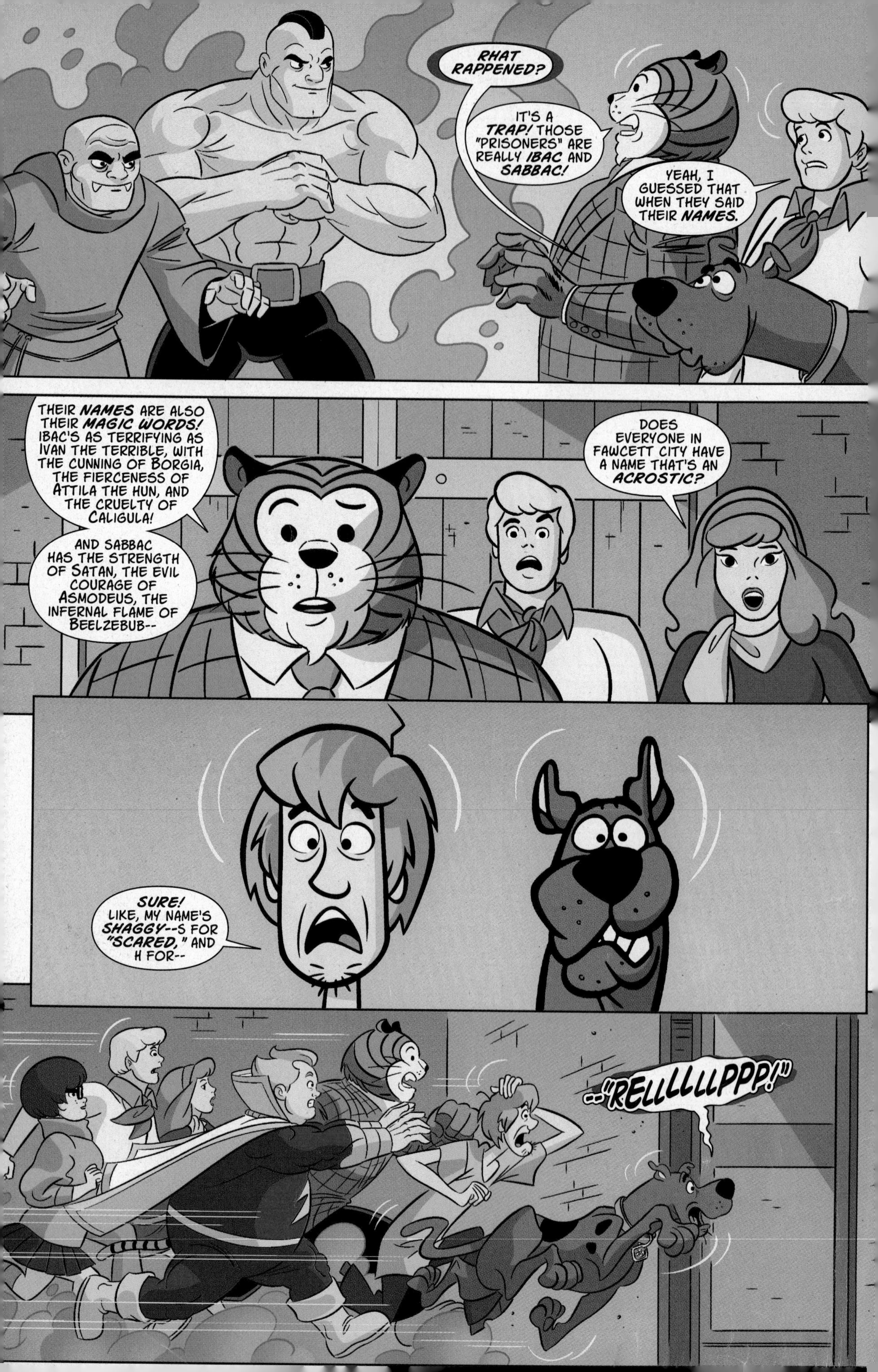
RHAT RAPPENED?
IT'S A TRAP! THOSE "PRISONERS" ARE REALLY IBAC AND SABBAC!
YEAH, I GUESSED THAT WHEN THEY SAID THEIR NAMES.
THEIR NAMES ARE ALSO THEIR MAGIC WORDS! IBAC'S AS TERRIFYING AS IVAN THE TERRIBLE, WITH THE CUNNING OF BORGIA, THE FIERCENESS OF ATTILA THE HUN, AND THE CRUELTY OF CALIGULA!
AND SABBAC HAS THE STRENGTH OF SATAN, THE EVIL COURAGE OF ASMODEUS, THE INFERNAL FLAME OF BEELZEBUB--
DOES EVERYONE IN FAWCETT CITY HAVE A NAME THAT'S AN ACROSTIC?
SURE! LIKE, MY NAME'S SHAGGY--S FOR "SCARED," AND H FOR--
--"RELLLLLLPPP!"

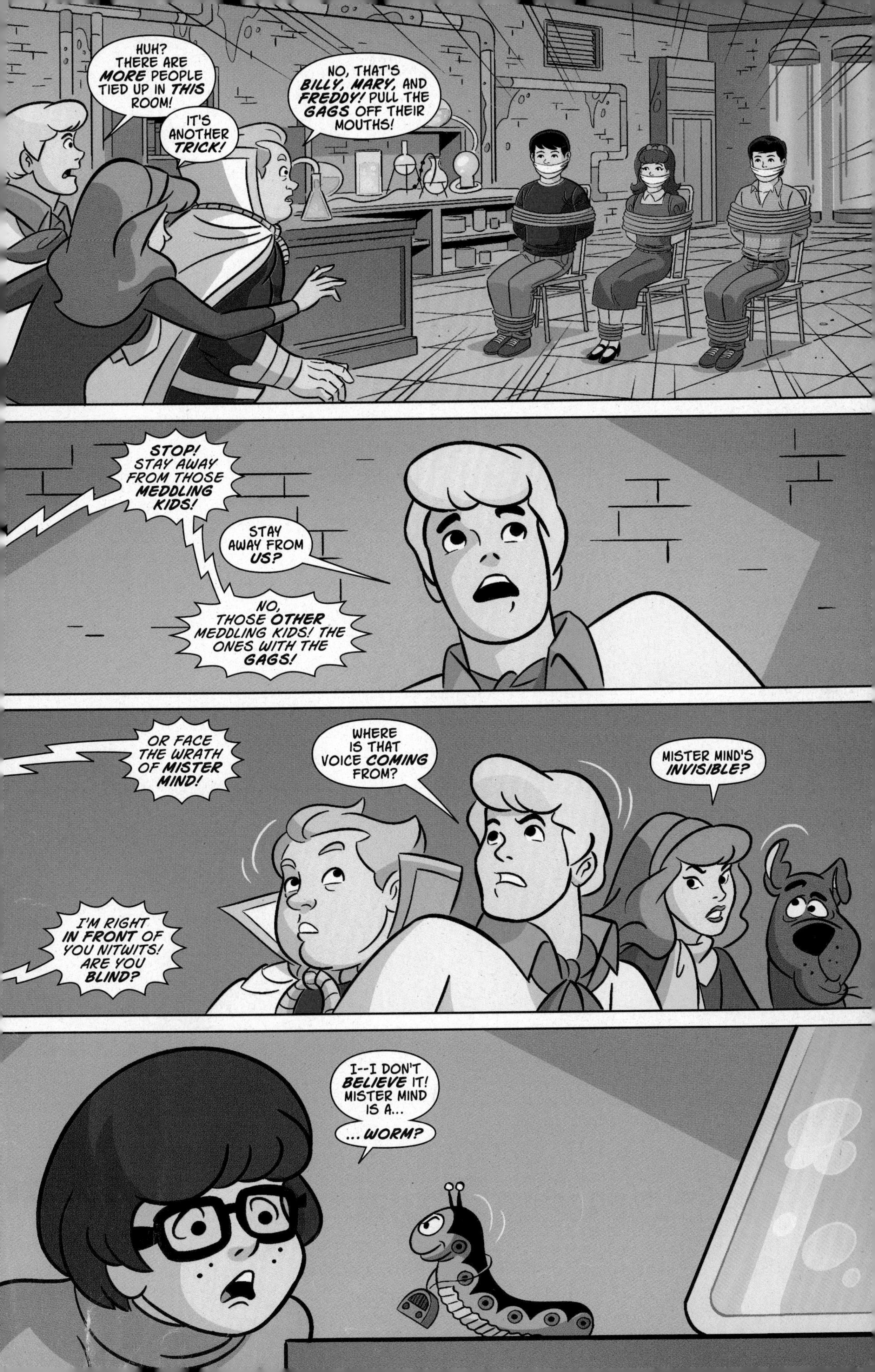
HUH? THERE ARE MORE PEOPLE TIED UP IN THIS ROOM!
IT'S ANOTHER TRICK!
NO, THAT'S BILLY, MARY, AND FREDDY! PULL THE GAGS OFF THEIR MOUTHS!
STOP! STAY AWAY FROM THOSE MEDDLING KIDS!
STAY AWAY FROM US?
NO, THOSE OTHER MEDDLING KIDS! THE ONES WITH THE GAGS!
OR FACE THE WRATH OF MISTER MIND!
WHERE IS THAT VOICE COMING FROM?
MISTER MIND'S INVISIBLE?
I'M RIGHT IN FRONT OF YOU NITWITS! ARE YOU BLIND?
I--I DON'T BELIEVE IT! MISTER MIND IS A...
...WORM?

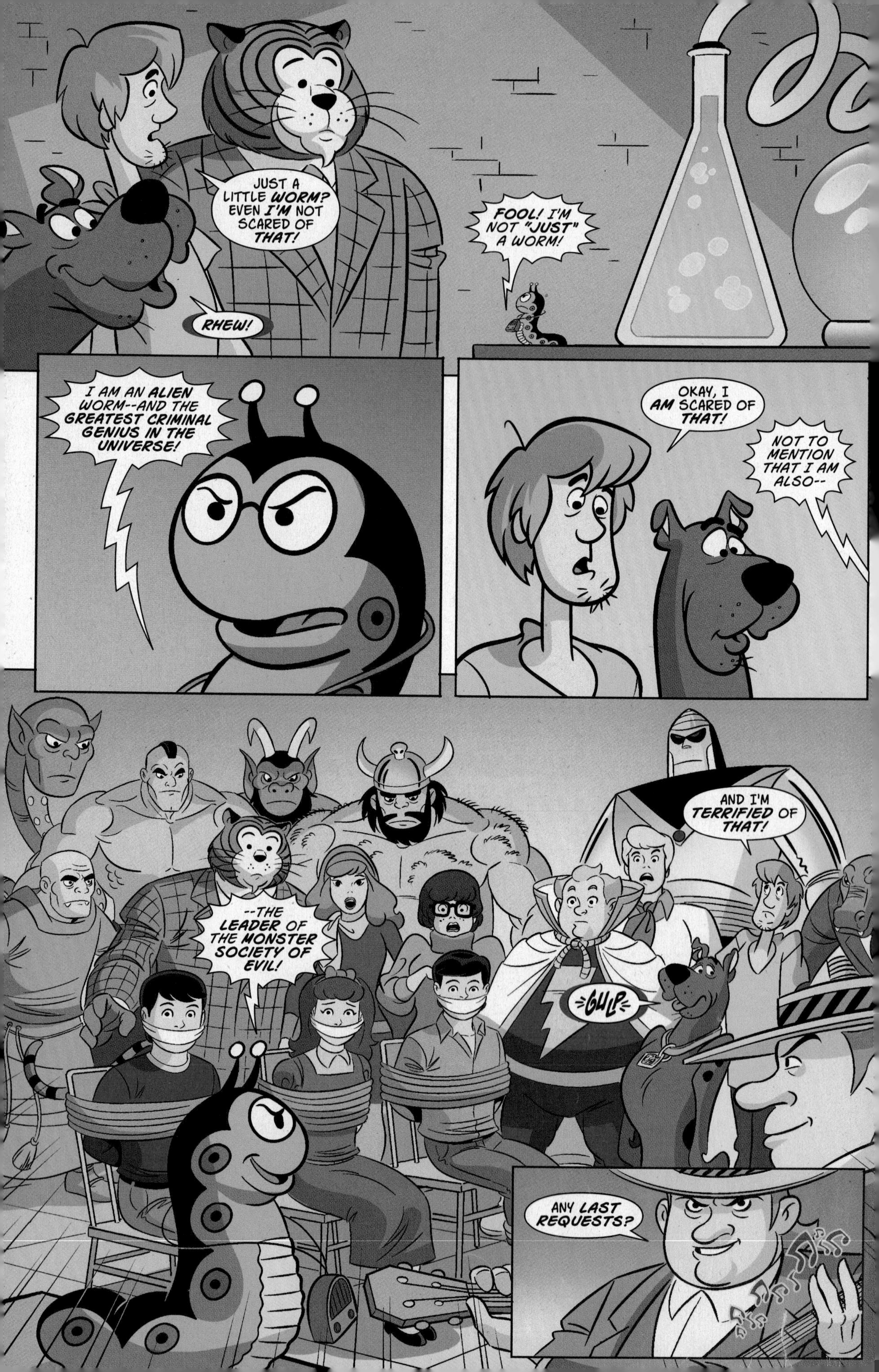
JUST A LITTLE WORM? EVEN I'M NOT SCARED OF THAT!
RHEW!
FOOL! I'M NOT "JUST" A WORM!
I AM AN ALIEN WORM--AND THE GREATEST CRIMINAL GENIUS IN THE UNIVERSE!
OKAY, I AM SCARED OF THAT!
NOT TO MENTION THAT I AM ALSO--
--THE LEADER OF THE MONSTER SOCIETY OF EVIL!
AND I'M TERRIFIED OF THAT!
GULP
ANY LAST REQUESTS?

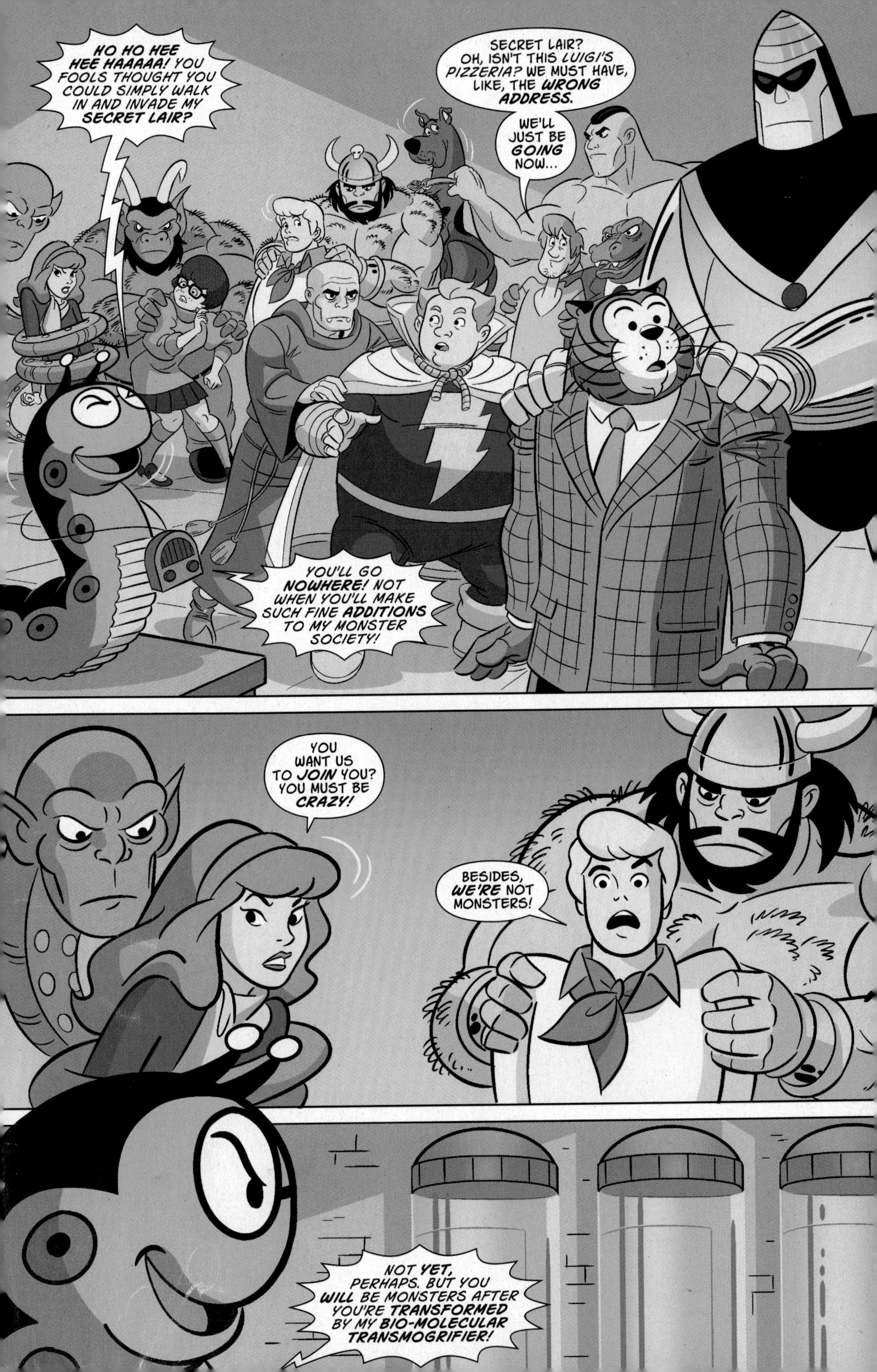
HO HO HEE HEE HAAAAA! YOU FOOLS THOUGHT YOU COULD SIMPLY WALK IN AND INVADE MY SECRET LAIR?
SECRET LAIR? OH, ISN'T THIS LUIGI'S PIZZERIA? WE MUST HAVE, LIKE, THE WRONG ADDRESS.
WE'LL JUST BE GOING NOW...
YOU'LL GO NOWHERE! NOT WHEN YOU'LL MAKE SUCH FINE ADDITIONS TO MY MONSTER SOCIETY!
YOU WANT US TO JOIN YOU? YOU MUST BE CRAZY!
BESIDES, WE'RE NOT MONSTERS!
NOT YET, PERHAPS. BUT YOU WILL BE MONSTERS AFTER YOU'RE TRANSFORMED BY MY BIO-MOLECULAR TRANSMOGRIFIER!

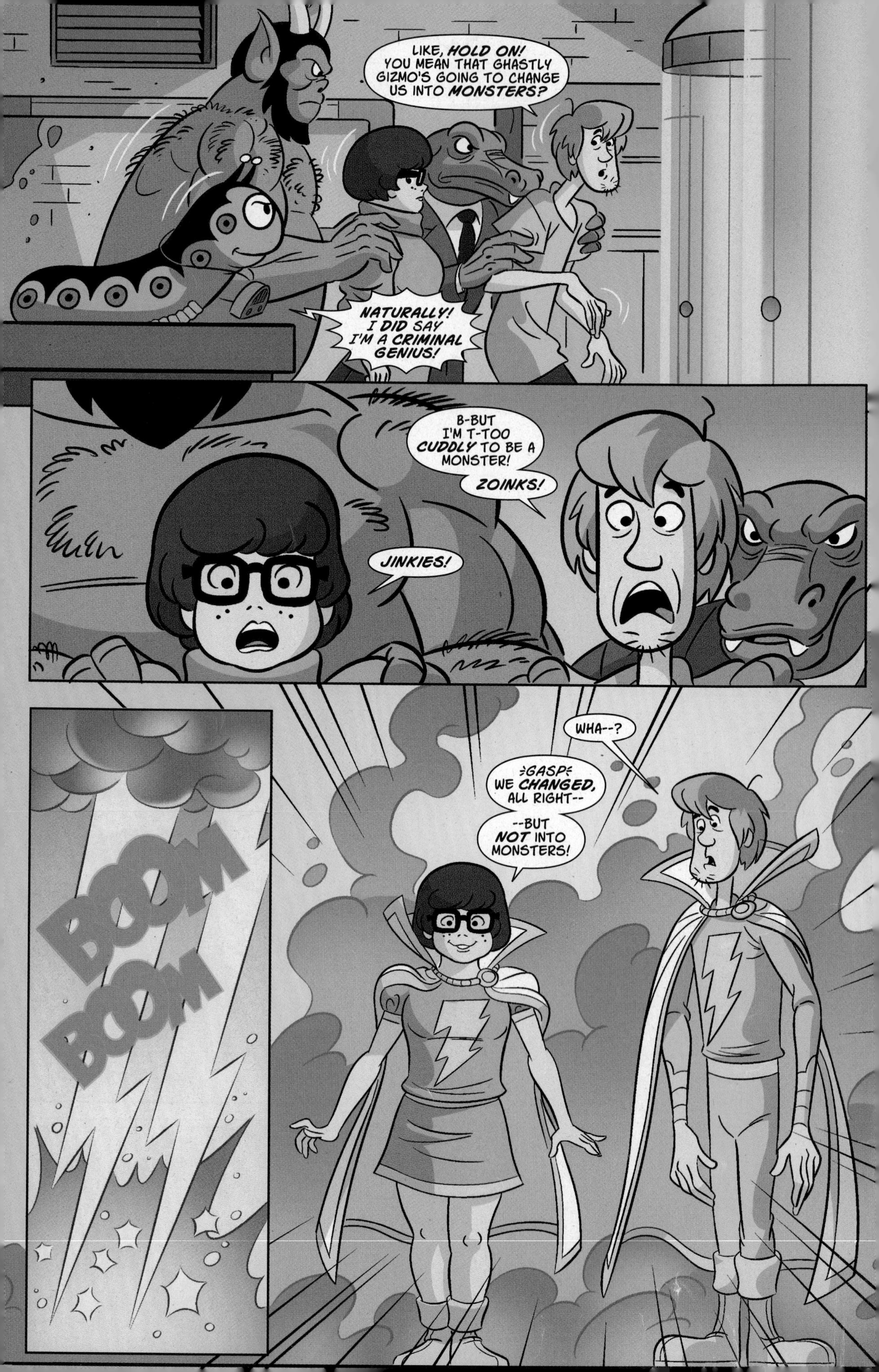
LIKE, HOLD ON! YOU MEAN THAT GHASTLY GIZMO'S GOING TO CHANGE US INTO MONSTERS?
NATURALLY! I DID SAY I'M A CRIMINAL GENIUS!
B-BUT I'M T-TOO CUDDLY TO BE A MONSTER!
ZOINKS!
JINKIES!
BOOM
BOOM
WHA--?
GASP WE CHANGED, ALL RIGHT--
--BUT NOT INTO MONSTERS!

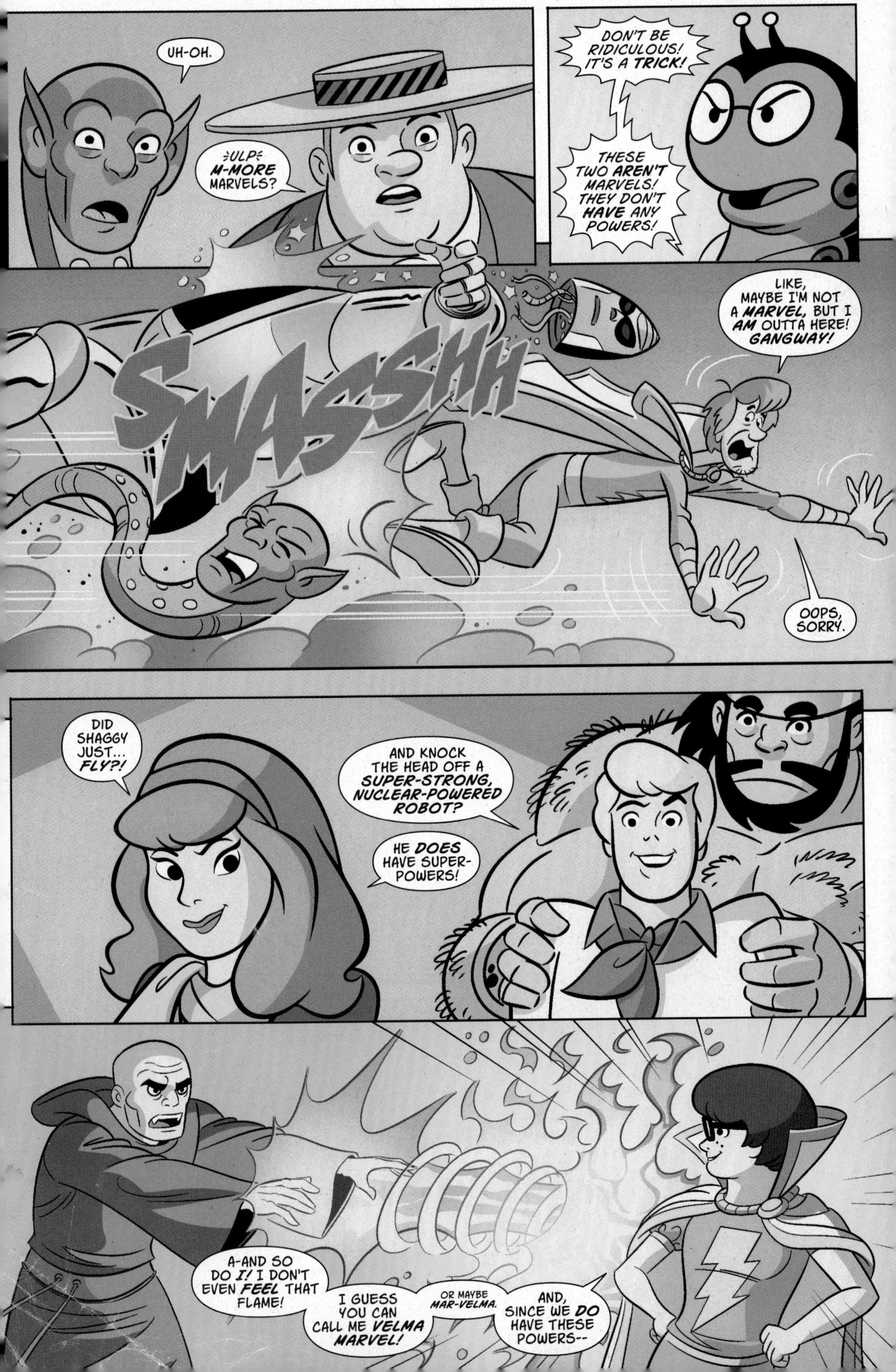
UH-OH.
ULP M-MORE MARVELS?
DON'T BE RIDICULOUS! IT'S A TRICK!
THESE TWO AREN'T MARVELS! THEY DON'T HAVE ANY POWERS!
SMASSHH
LIKE, MAYBE I'M NOT A MARVEL, BUT I AM OUTTA HERE! GANGWAY!
OOPS, SORRY.
DID SHAGGY JUST... FLY?!
AND KNOCK THE HEAD OFF A SUPER-STRONG, NUCLEAR-POWERED ROBOT?
HE DOES HAVE SUPER-POWERS!
A-AND SO DO I! I DON'T EVEN FEEL THAT FLAME!
I GUESS YOU CAN CALL ME VELMA MARVEL!
OR MAYBE MAR-VELMA.
AND, SINCE WE DO HAVE THESE POWERS--

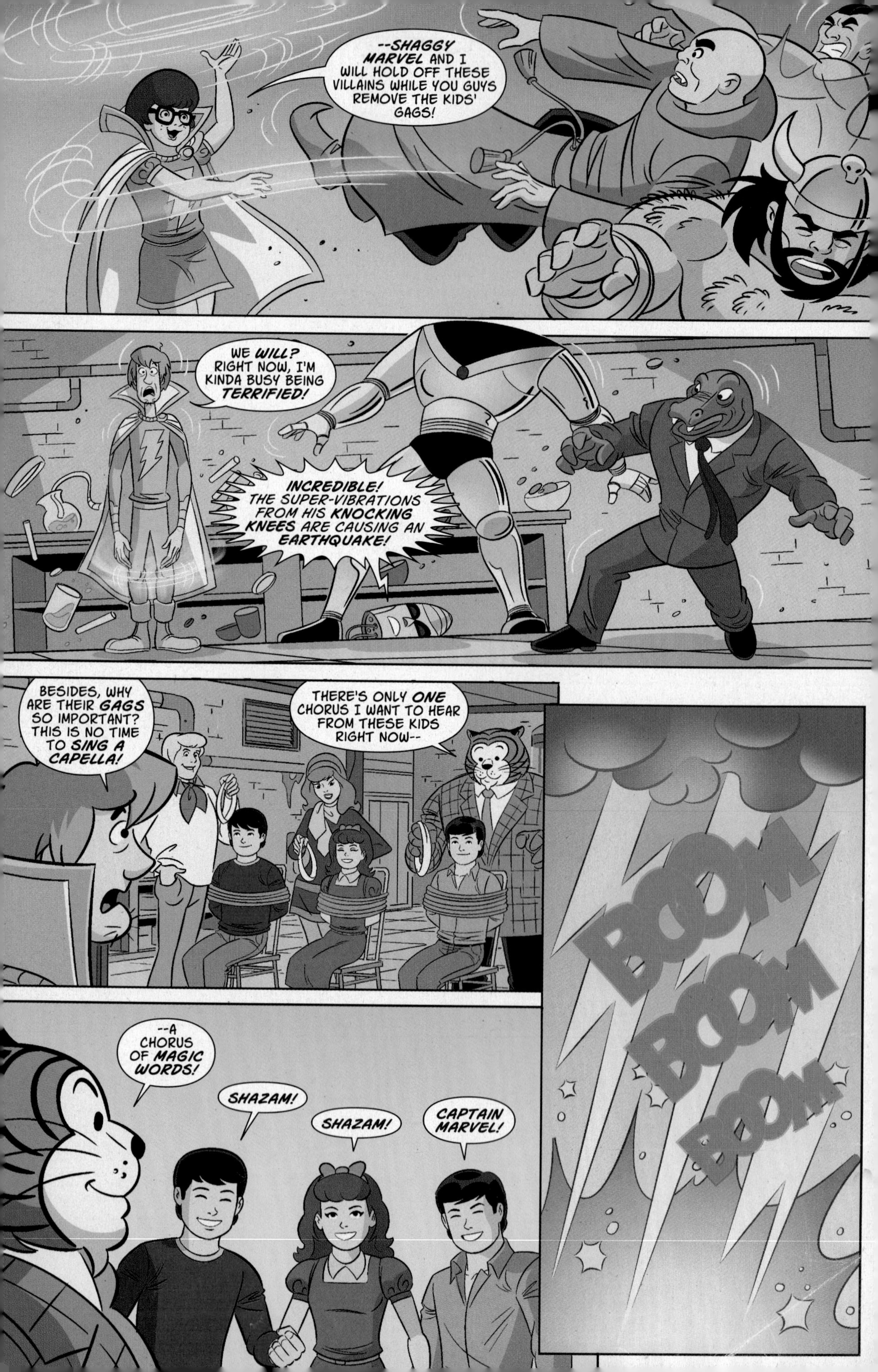
--SHAGGY MARVEL AND I WILL HOLD OFF THESE VILLAINS WHILE YOU GUYS REMOVE THE KIDS' GAGS!
WE WILL? RIGHT NOW, I'M KINDA BUSY BEING TERRIFIED!
INCREDIBLE! THE SUPER-VIBRATIONS FROM HIS KNOCKING KNEES ARE CAUSING AN EARTHQUAKE!
BESIDES, WHY ARE THEIR GAGS SO IMPORTANT? THIS IS NO TIME TO SING A CAPELLA!
THERE'S ONLY ONE CHORUS I WANT TO HEAR FROM THESE KIDS RIGHT NOW--
--A CHORUS OF MAGIC WORDS!
SHAZAM!
SHAZAM!
CAPTAIN MARVEL!
BOOM
BOOM
BOOM

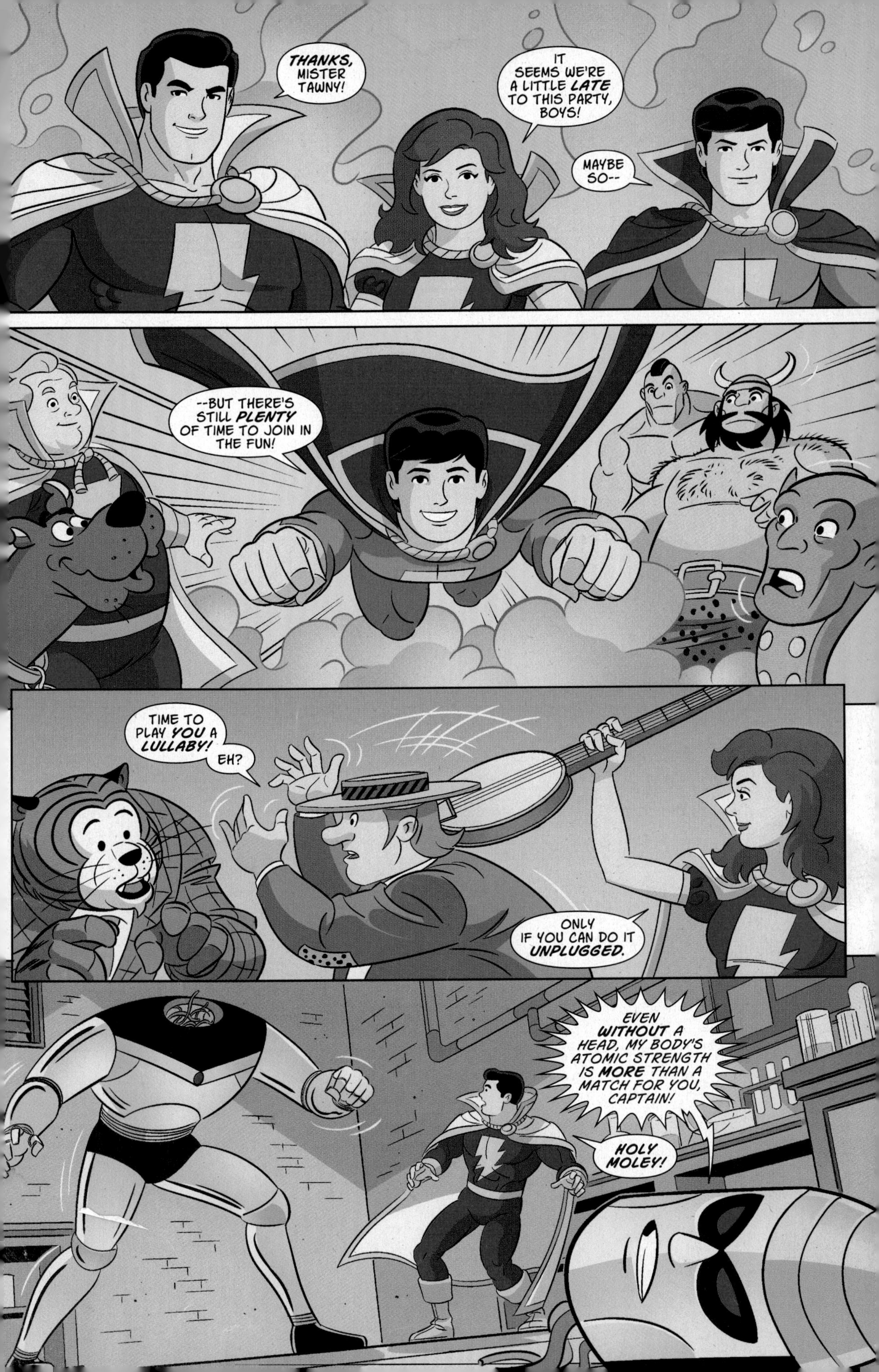
THANKS, MISTER TAWNY!
IT SEEMS WE'RE A LITTLE LATE TO THIS PARTY, BOYS!
MAYBE SO--
--BUT THERE'S STILL PLENTY OF TIME TO JOIN IN THE FUN!
TIME TO PLAY YOU A LULLABY!
EH?
ONLY IF YOU CAN DO IT UNPLUGGED.
EVEN WITHOUT A HEAD, MY BODY'S ATOMIC STRENGTH IS MORE THAN A MATCH FOR YOU, CAPTAIN!
HOLY MOLEY!

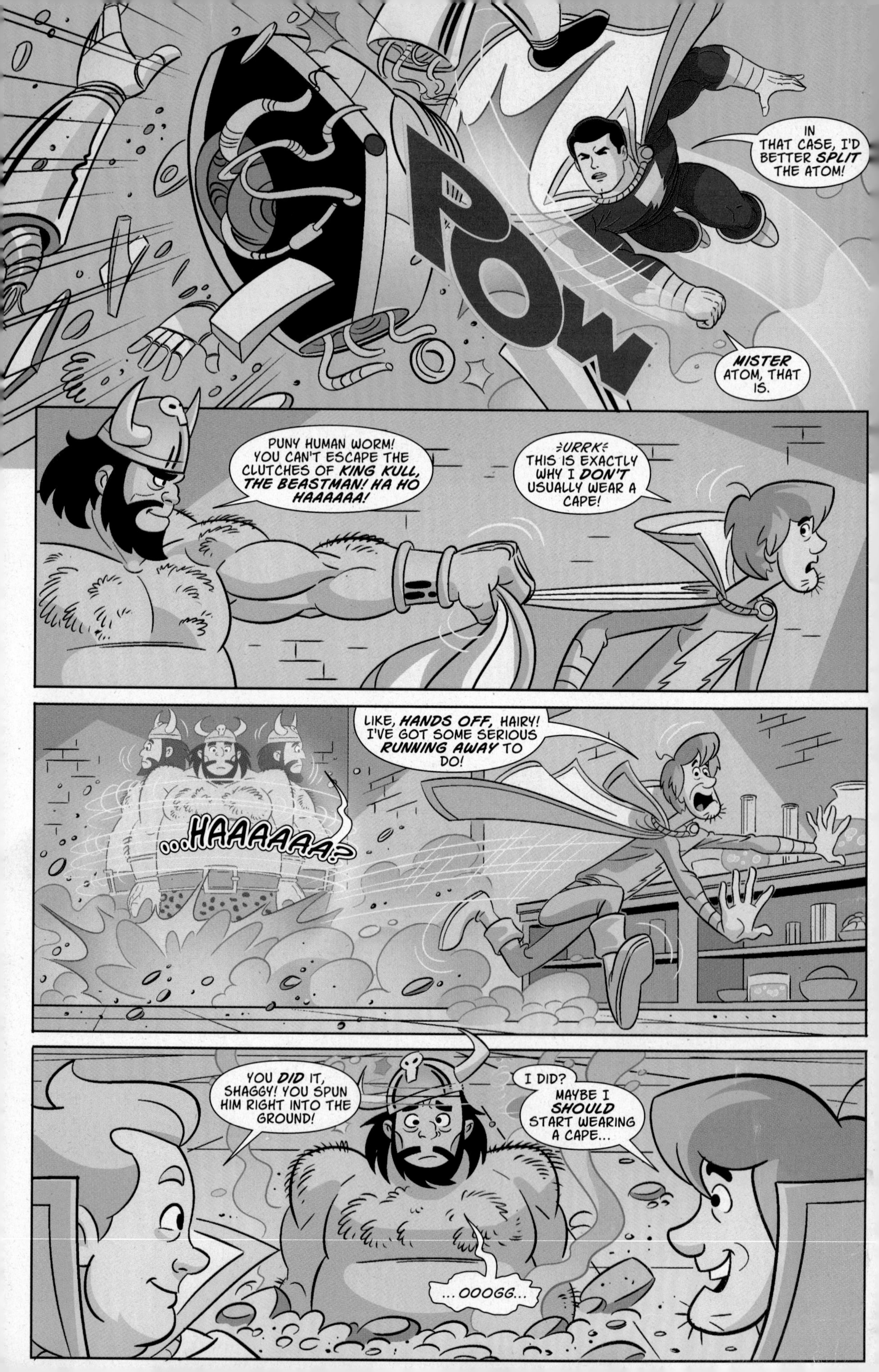
IN THAT CASE, I'D BETTER SPLIT THE ATOM!
POW
MISTER ATOM, THAT IS.
PUNY HUMAN WORM! YOU CAN'T ESCAPE THE CLUTCHES OF KING KULL, THE BEASTMAN! HA HO HAAAAAA!
URRK
THIS IS EXACTLY WHY I DON'T USUALLY WEAR A CAPE!
LIKE, HANDS OFF, HAIRY! I'VE GOT SOME SERIOUS RUNNING AWAY TO DO!
...HAAAAAA?
YOU DID IT, SHAGGY! YOU SPUN HIM RIGHT INTO THE GROUND!
I DID?
MAYBE I SHOULD START WEARING A CAPE...
...OOOGG...

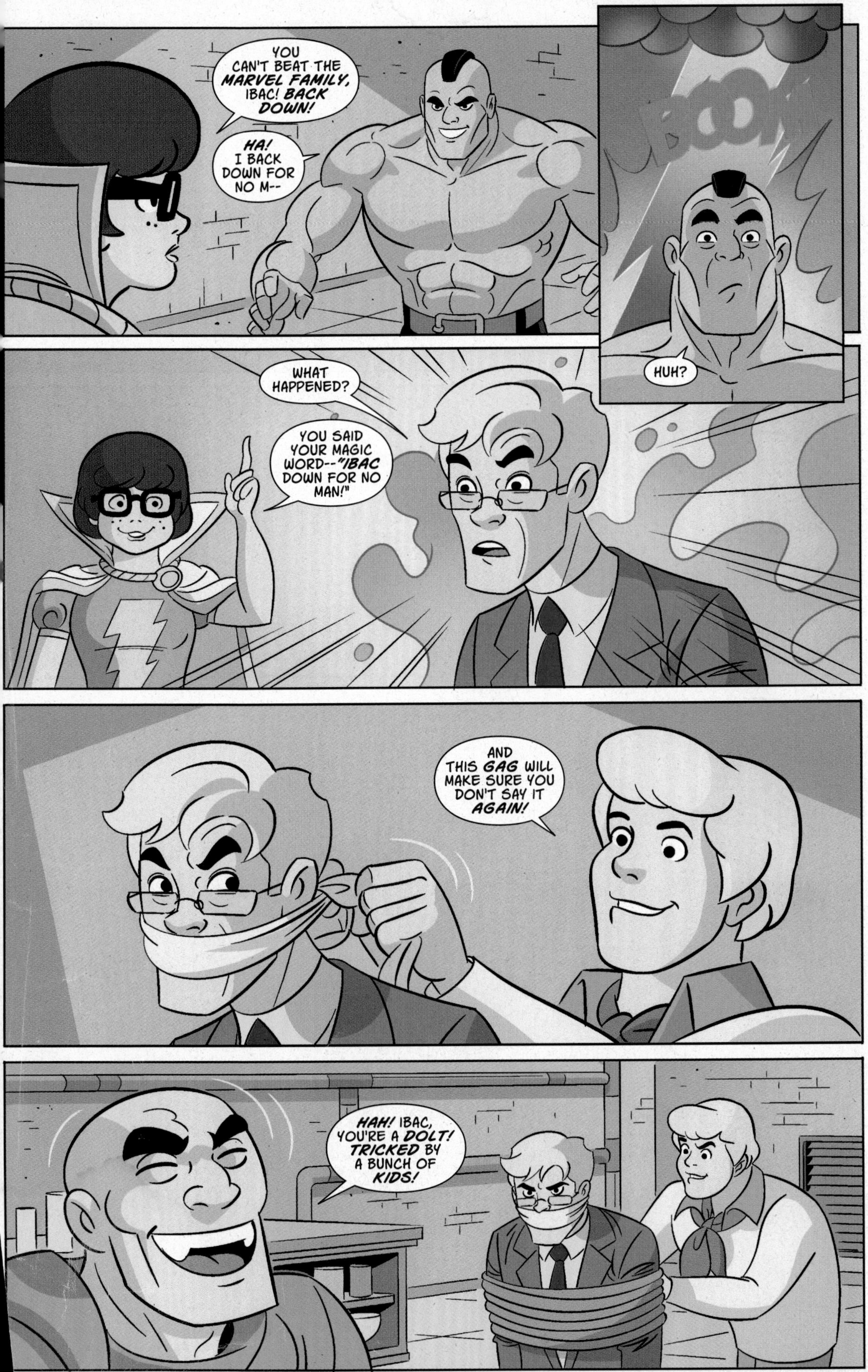
YOU CAN'T BEAT THE MARVEL FAMILY, IBAC! BACK DOWN!
HA! I BACK DOWN FOR NO M--
BOOM
HUH?
WHAT HAPPENED?
YOU SAID YOUR MAGIC WORD--"IBAC DOWN FOR NO MAN!"
AND THIS GAG WILL MAKE SURE YOU DON'T SAY IT AGAIN!
HAH! IBAC, YOU'RE A DOLT! TRICKED BY A BUNCH OF KIDS!

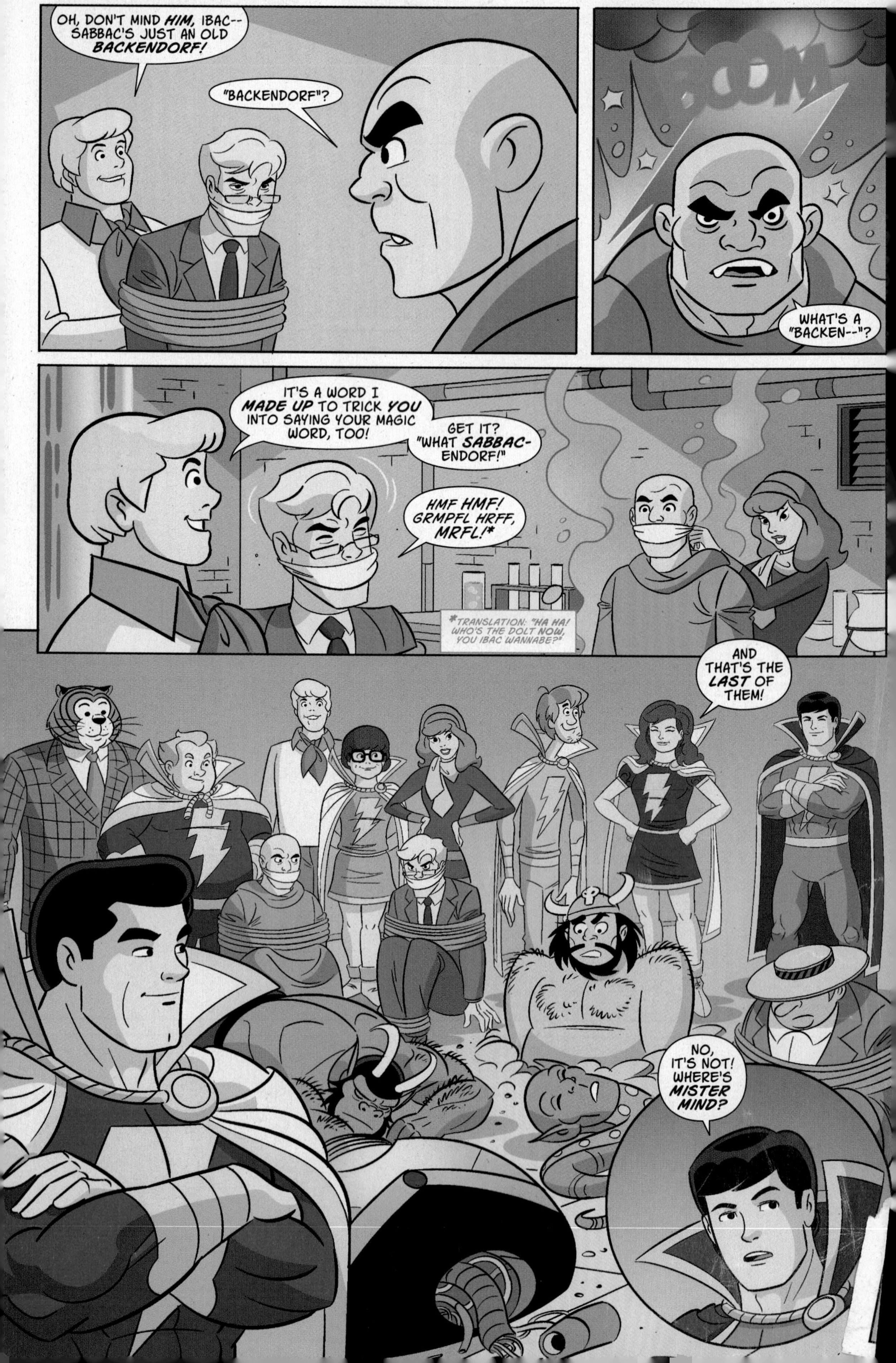
OH, DON'T MIND HIM, IBAC-- SABBAC'S JUST AN OLD BACKENDORF!
"BACKENDORF"?
BOOM
WHAT'S A "BACKEN--"?
IT'S A WORD I MADE UP TO TRICK YOU INTO SAYING YOUR MAGIC WORD, TOO!
GET IT? "WHAT SABBAC-ENDORF!"
HMF HMF! GRMPFL HRFF, MRFL!*
*TRANSLATION: "HA HA! WHO'S THE DOLT NOW, YOU IBAC WANNABE?"
AND THAT'S THE LAST OF THEM!
NO, IT'S NOT! WHERE'S MISTER MIND?

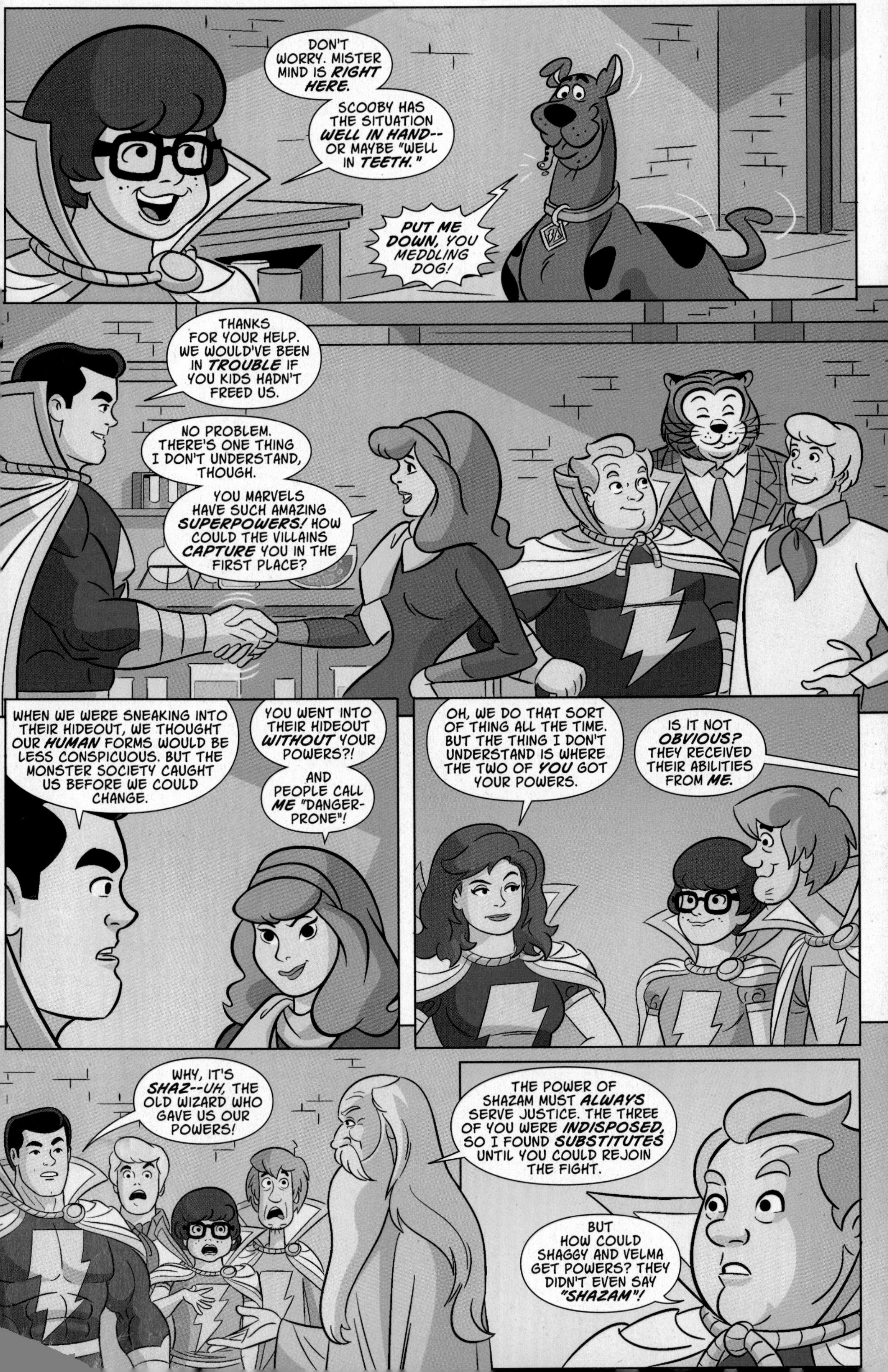

DON'T WORRY. MISTER MIND IS RIGHT HERE.
SCOOBY HAS THE SITUATION WELL IN HAND--OR MAYBE "WELL IN TEETH."
PUT ME DOWN, YOU MEDDLING DOG!
THANKS FOR YOUR HELP. WE WOULD'VE BEEN IN TROUBLE IF YOU KIDS HADN'T FREED US.
NO PROBLEM. THERE'S ONE THING I DON'T UNDERSTAND, THOUGH.
YOU MARVELS HAVE SUCH AMAZING SUPERPOWERS! HOW COULD THE VILLAINS CAPTURE YOU IN THE FIRST PLACE?
WHEN WE WERE SNEAKING INTO THEIR HIDEOUT, WE THOUGHT OUR HUMAN FORMS WOULD BE LESS CONSPICUOUS. BUT THE MONSTER SOCIETY CAUGHT US BEFORE WE COULD CHANGE.
YOU WENT INTO THEIR HIDEOUT WITHOUT YOUR POWERS?!
AND PEOPLE CALL ME "DANGER-PRONE"!
OH, WE DO THAT SORT OF THING ALL THE TIME. BUT THE THING I DON'T UNDERSTAND IS WHERE THE TWO OF YOU GOT YOUR POWERS.
IS IT NOT OBVIOUS? THEY RECEIVED THEIR ABILITIES FROM ME.
WHY, IT'S SHAZ--UH, THE OLD WIZARD WHO GAVE US OUR POWERS!
THE POWER OF SHAZAM MUST ALWAYS SERVE JUSTICE. THE THREE OF YOU WERE INDISPOSED, SO I FOUND SUBSTITUTES UNTIL YOU COULD REJOIN THE FIGHT.
BUT HOW COULD SHAGGY AND VELMA GET POWERS? THEY DIDN'T EVEN SAY "SHAZAM"!

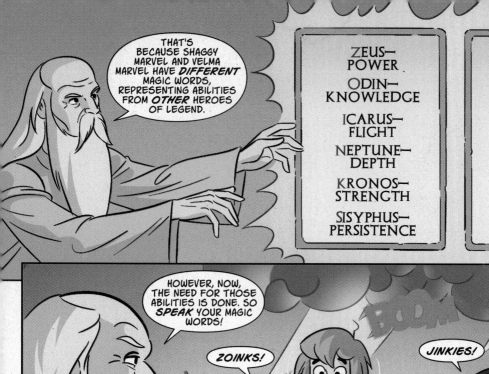

THAT'S BECAUSE SHAGGY MARVEL AND VELMA MARVEL HAVE *DIFFERENT* MAGIC WORDS, REPRESENTING ABILITIES FROM *OTHER* HEROES OF LEGEND.

ZEUS— POWER

ODIN— KNOWLEDGE

ICARUS— FLIGHT

NEPTUNE— DEPTH

KRONOS— STRENGTH

SISYPHUS— PERSISTENCE

JUNO— DOMINION

ISIS— MAGIC

NEMESIS— JUSTICE

KALI— STRENGTH

ISHTAR— LOVE

ELECTRA— COURAGE

SIBYL— FORESIGHT

HOWEVER, NOW, THE NEED FOR THOSE ABILITIES IS DONE. SO *SPEAK* YOUR MAGIC WORDS!

ZOINKS!

JINKIES!

BOOM

BOOM

LIKE, AM I GLAD TO BE BACK IN A *T-SHIRT* AGAIN. THAT SKIN-TIGHT OUTFIT WAS CUTTING OFF MY *CIRCULATION!*

⊰SIGH⊱ MAYBE SO, BUT HAVING SUPERPOWERS WAS *FUN!* USUALLY, *YOU AND SCOOBY* ARE THE ONLY ONES WHO GET THEM.

I'M GOING TO *MISS* HAVING MARVEL POWERS...

DON'T WORRY, VELMA. WITH OR WITHOUT POWERS, YOU'RE *ALL* PART OF THE FAMILY NOW--

--THE *MARVEL FAMILY!*

ABSOLUTELY!

AFTER ALL, YOU'RE ALL PRETTY *MARVEL-OUS* TO ME!

THE END

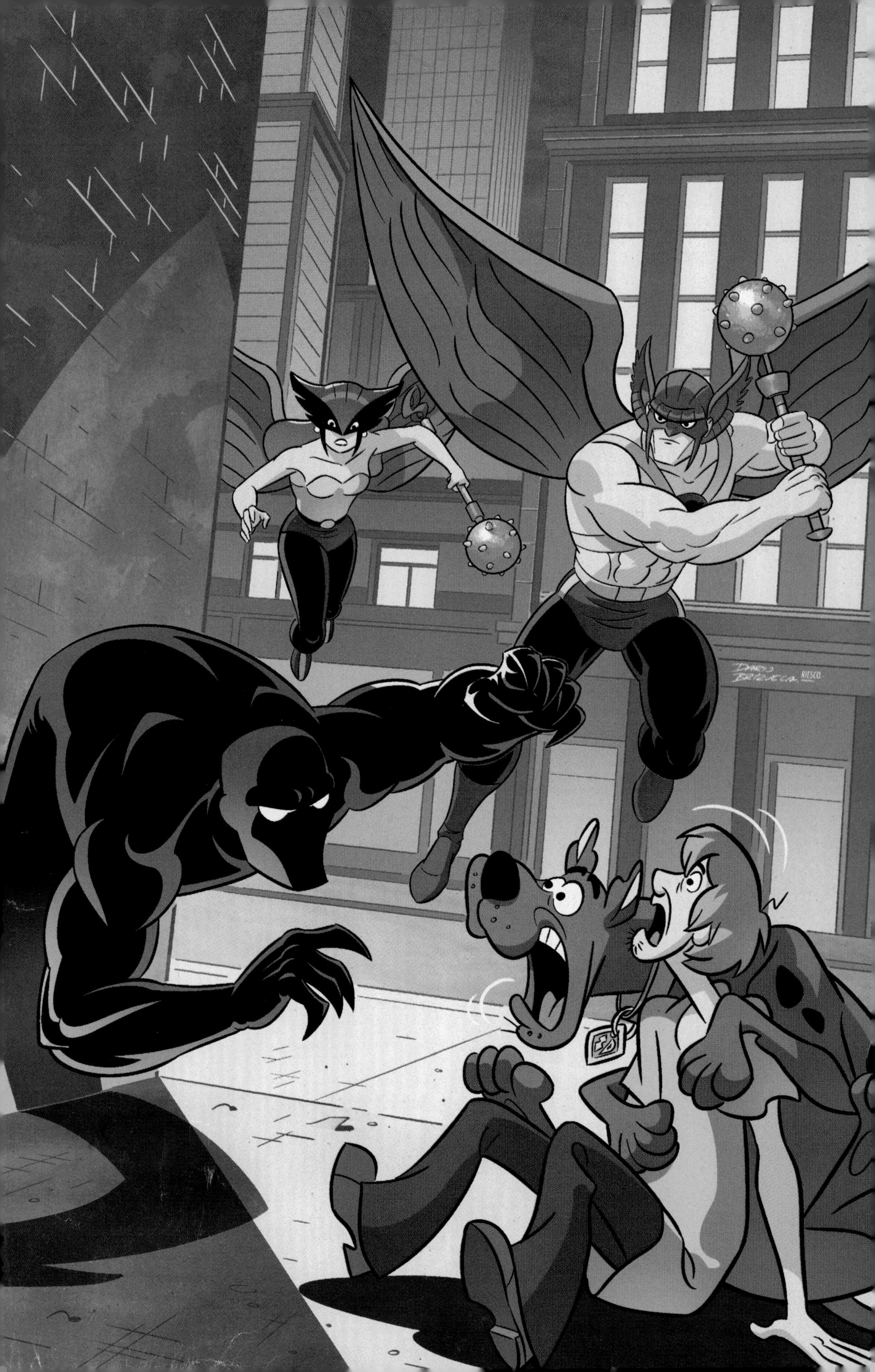

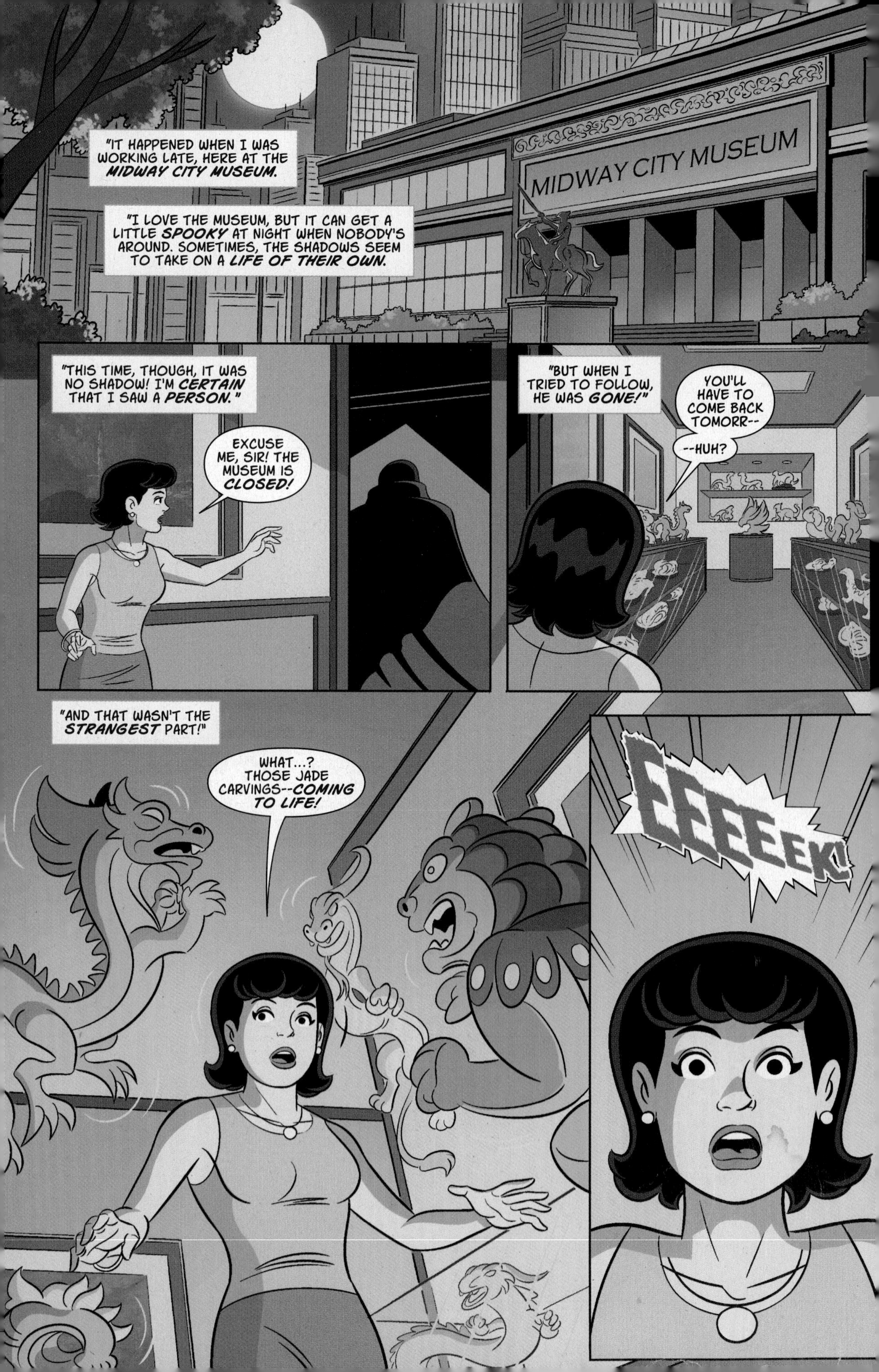

"IT HAPPENED WHEN I WAS WORKING LATE, HERE AT THE MIDWAY CITY MUSEUM.
MIDWAY CITY MUSEUM
"I LOVE THE MUSEUM, BUT IT CAN GET A LITTLE SPOOKY AT NIGHT WHEN NOBODY'S AROUND. SOMETIMES, THE SHADOWS SEEM TO TAKE ON A LIFE OF THEIR OWN.
"THIS TIME, THOUGH, IT WAS NO SHADOW! I'M CERTAIN THAT I SAW A PERSON."
EXCUSE ME, SIR! THE MUSEUM IS CLOSED!
"BUT WHEN I TRIED TO FOLLOW, HE WAS GONE!"
YOU'LL HAVE TO COME BACK TOMORR--
--HUH?
"AND THAT WASN'T THE STRANGEST PART!"
WHAT...? THOSE JADE CARVINGS--COMING TO LIFE!
EEEEEK!

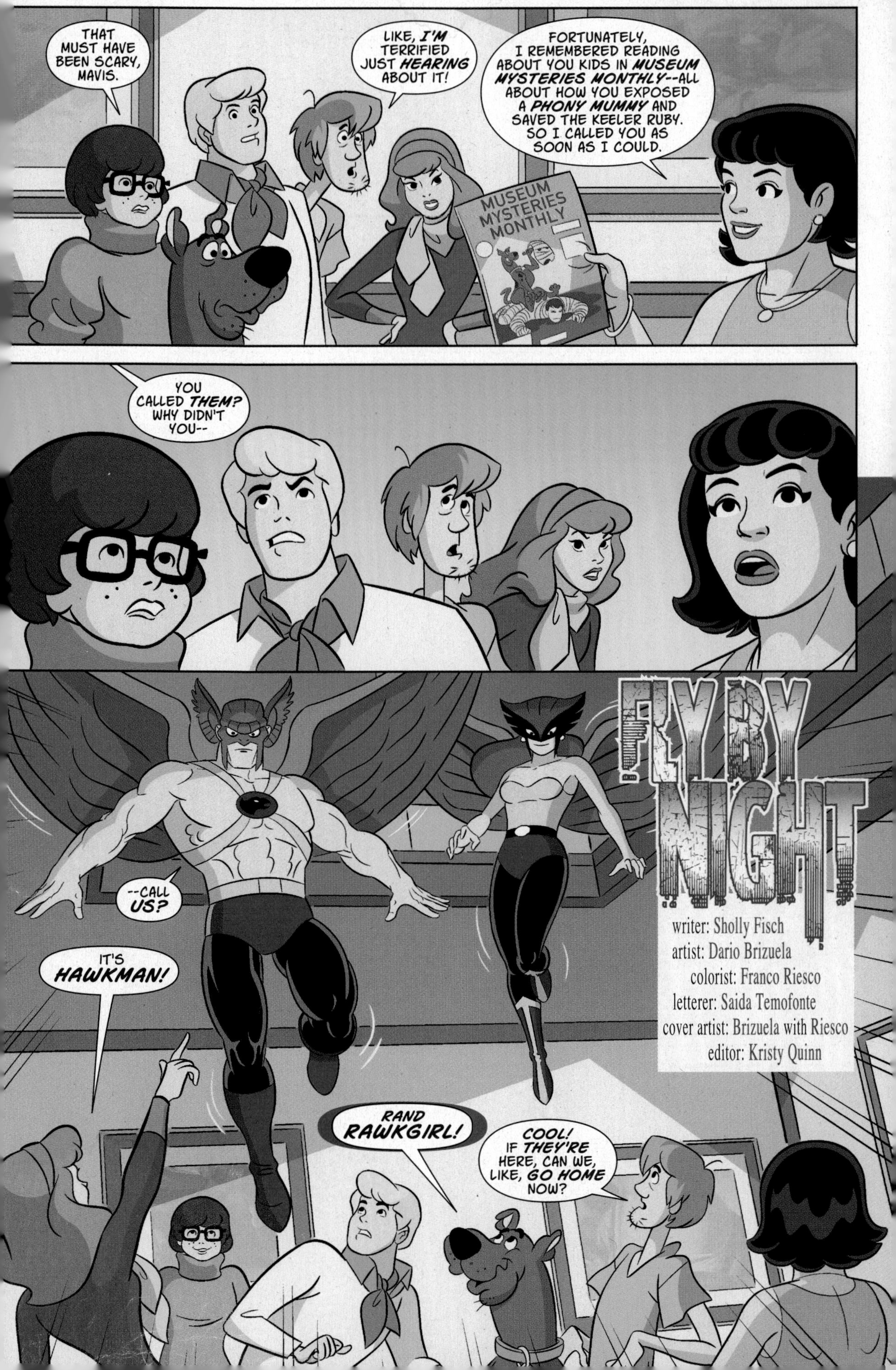
THAT MUST HAVE BEEN SCARY, MAVIS.
LIKE, I'M TERRIFIED JUST HEARING ABOUT IT!
FORTUNATELY, I REMEMBERED READING ABOUT YOU KIDS IN MUSEUM MYSTERIES MONTHLY--ALL ABOUT HOW YOU EXPOSED A PHONY MUMMY AND SAVED THE KEELER RUBY. SO I CALLED YOU AS SOON AS I COULD.
MUSEUM MYSTERIES MONTHLY
YOU CALLED THEM? WHY DIDN'T YOU--
--CALL US?
FLY BY NIGHT
writer: Sholly Fisch
artist: Dario Brizuela
colorist: Franco Riesco
letterer: Saida Temofonte
cover artist: Brizuela with Riesco
editor: Kristy Quinn
IT'S HAWKMAN!
RAND RAWKGIRL!
COOL! IF THEY'RE HERE, CAN WE, LIKE, GO HOME NOW?

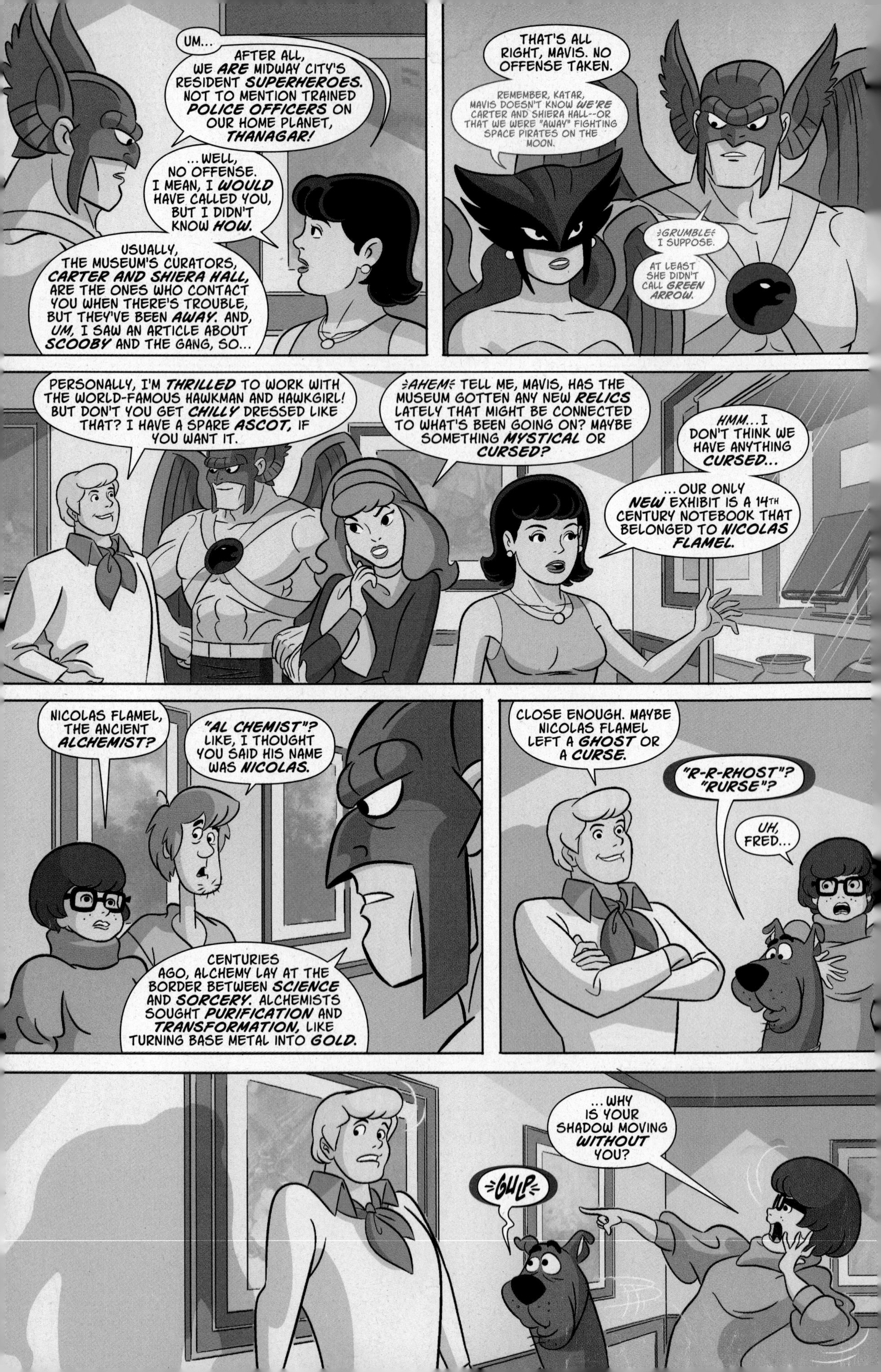
UM...
AFTER ALL, WE ARE MIDWAY CITY'S RESIDENT SUPERHEROES. NOT TO MENTION TRAINED POLICE OFFICERS ON OUR HOME PLANET, THANAGAR!
...WELL, NO OFFENSE. I MEAN, I WOULD HAVE CALLED YOU, BUT I DIDN'T KNOW HOW.
USUALLY, THE MUSEUM'S CURATORS, CARTER AND SHIERA HALL, ARE THE ONES WHO CONTACT YOU WHEN THERE'S TROUBLE, BUT THEY'VE BEEN AWAY. AND, UM, I SAW AN ARTICLE ABOUT SCOOBY AND THE GANG, SO...
THAT'S ALL RIGHT, MAVIS. NO OFFENSE TAKEN.
REMEMBER, KATAR, MAVIS DOESN'T KNOW WE'RE CARTER AND SHIERA HALL--OR THAT WE WERE "AWAY" FIGHTING SPACE PIRATES ON THE MOON.
GRUMBLE I SUPPOSE.
AT LEAST SHE DIDN'T CALL GREEN ARROW.
PERSONALLY, I'M THRILLED TO WORK WITH THE WORLD-FAMOUS HAWKMAN AND HAWKGIRL! BUT DON'T YOU GET CHILLY DRESSED LIKE THAT? I HAVE A SPARE ASCOT, IF YOU WANT IT.
AHEM TELL ME, MAVIS, HAS THE MUSEUM GOTTEN ANY NEW RELICS LATELY THAT MIGHT BE CONNECTED TO WHAT'S BEEN GOING ON? MAYBE SOMETHING MYSTICAL OR CURSED?
HMM...I DON'T THINK WE HAVE ANYTHING CURSED...
...OUR ONLY NEW EXHIBIT IS A 14TH CENTURY NOTEBOOK THAT BELONGED TO NICOLAS FLAMEL.
NICOLAS FLAMEL, THE ANCIENT ALCHEMIST?
"AL CHEMIST"? LIKE, I THOUGHT YOU SAID HIS NAME WAS NICOLAS.
CENTURIES AGO, ALCHEMY LAY AT THE BORDER BETWEEN SCIENCE AND SORCERY. ALCHEMISTS SOUGHT PURIFICATION AND TRANSFORMATION, LIKE TURNING BASE METAL INTO GOLD.
CLOSE ENOUGH. MAYBE NICOLAS FLAMEL LEFT A GHOST OR A CURSE.
"R-R-RHOST"? "RURSE"?
UH, FRED...
...WHY IS YOUR SHADOW MOVING WITHOUT YOU?
GULP

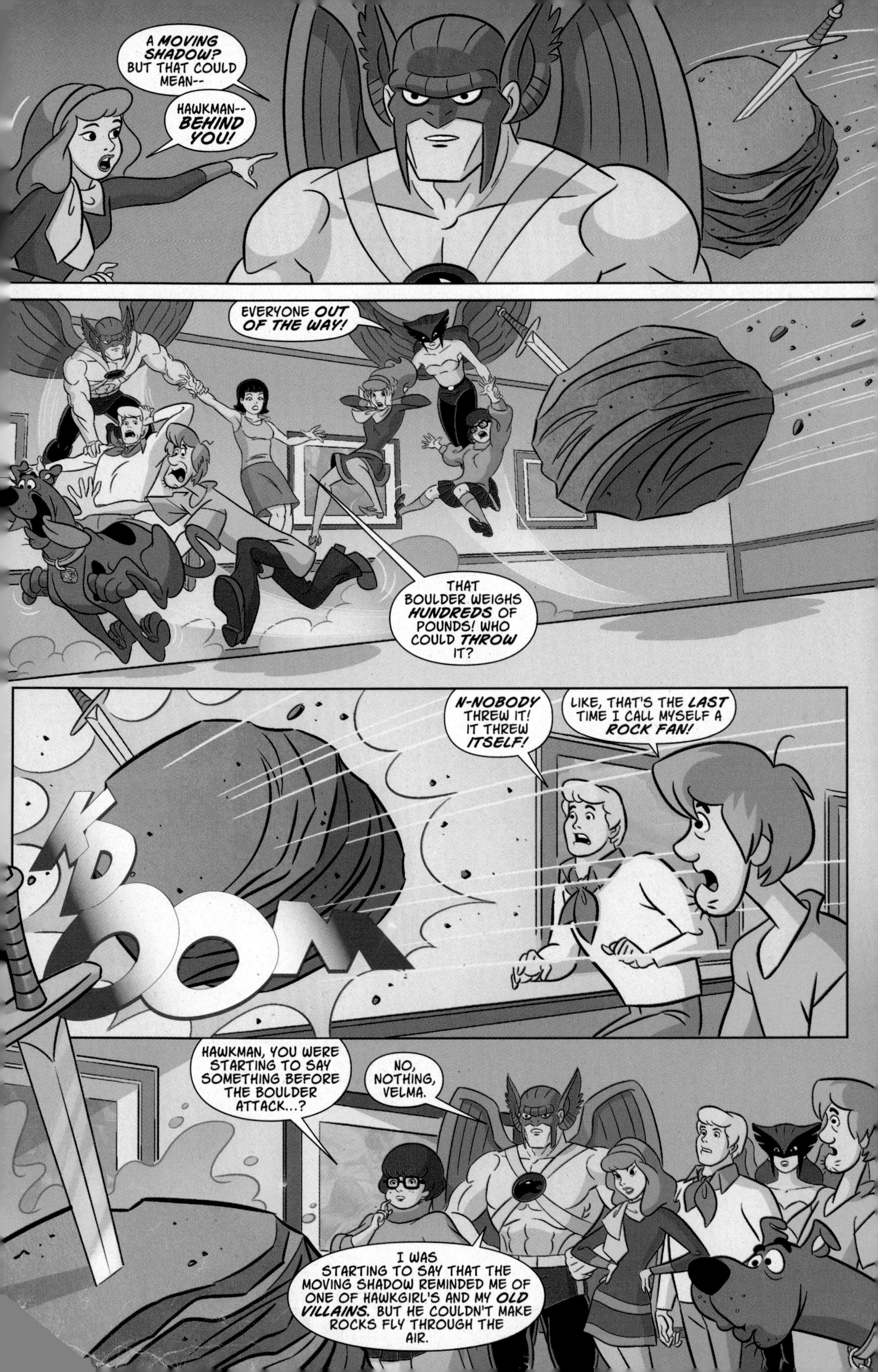
A MOVING SHADOW? BUT THAT COULD MEAN--
HAWKMAN-- BEHIND YOU!
EVERYONE OUT OF THE WAY!
THAT BOULDER WEIGHS HUNDREDS OF POUNDS! WHO COULD THROW IT?
N-NOBODY THREW IT! IT THREW ITSELF!
LIKE, THAT'S THE LAST TIME I CALL MYSELF A ROCK FAN!
KA DOOM
HAWKMAN, YOU WERE STARTING TO SAY SOMETHING BEFORE THE BOULDER ATTACK...?
NO, NOTHING, VELMA.
I WAS STARTING TO SAY THAT THE MOVING SHADOW REMINDED ME OF ONE OF HAWKGIRL'S AND MY OLD VILLAINS. BUT HE COULDN'T MAKE ROCKS FLY THROUGH THE AIR.

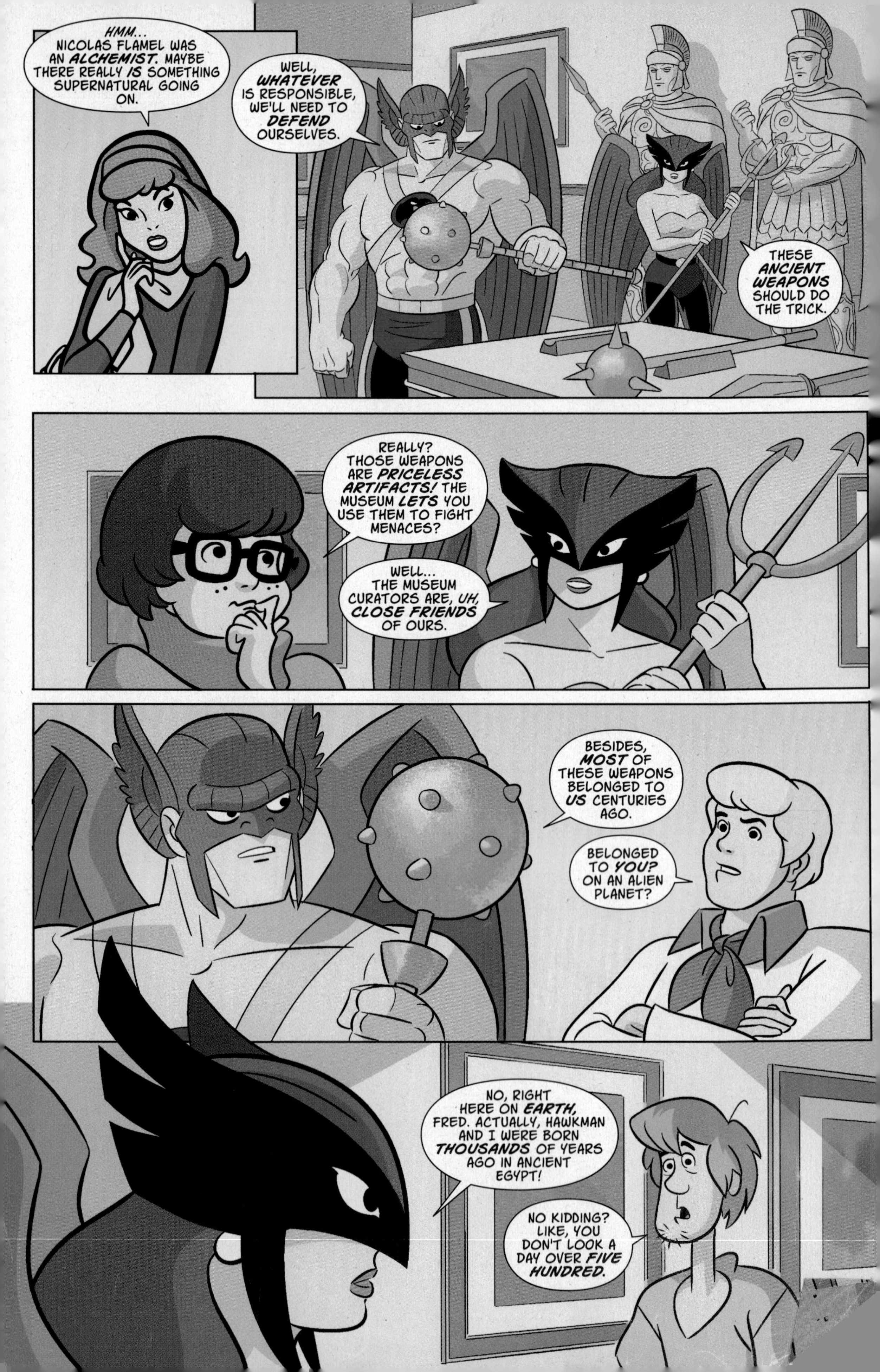
HMM... NICOLAS FLAMEL WAS AN ALCHEMIST. MAYBE THERE REALLY IS SOMETHING SUPERNATURAL GOING ON.
WELL, WHATEVER IS RESPONSIBLE, WE'LL NEED TO DEFEND OURSELVES.
THESE ANCIENT WEAPONS SHOULD DO THE TRICK.
REALLY? THOSE WEAPONS ARE PRICELESS ARTIFACTS! THE MUSEUM LETS YOU USE THEM TO FIGHT MENACES?
WELL... THE MUSEUM CURATORS ARE, UH, CLOSE FRIENDS OF OURS.
BESIDES, MOST OF THESE WEAPONS BELONGED TO US CENTURIES AGO.
BELONGED TO YOU? ON AN ALIEN PLANET?
NO, RIGHT HERE ON EARTH, FRED. ACTUALLY, HAWKMAN AND I WERE BORN THOUSANDS OF YEARS AGO IN ANCIENT EGYPT!
NO KIDDING? LIKE, YOU DON'T LOOK A DAY OVER FIVE HUNDRED.

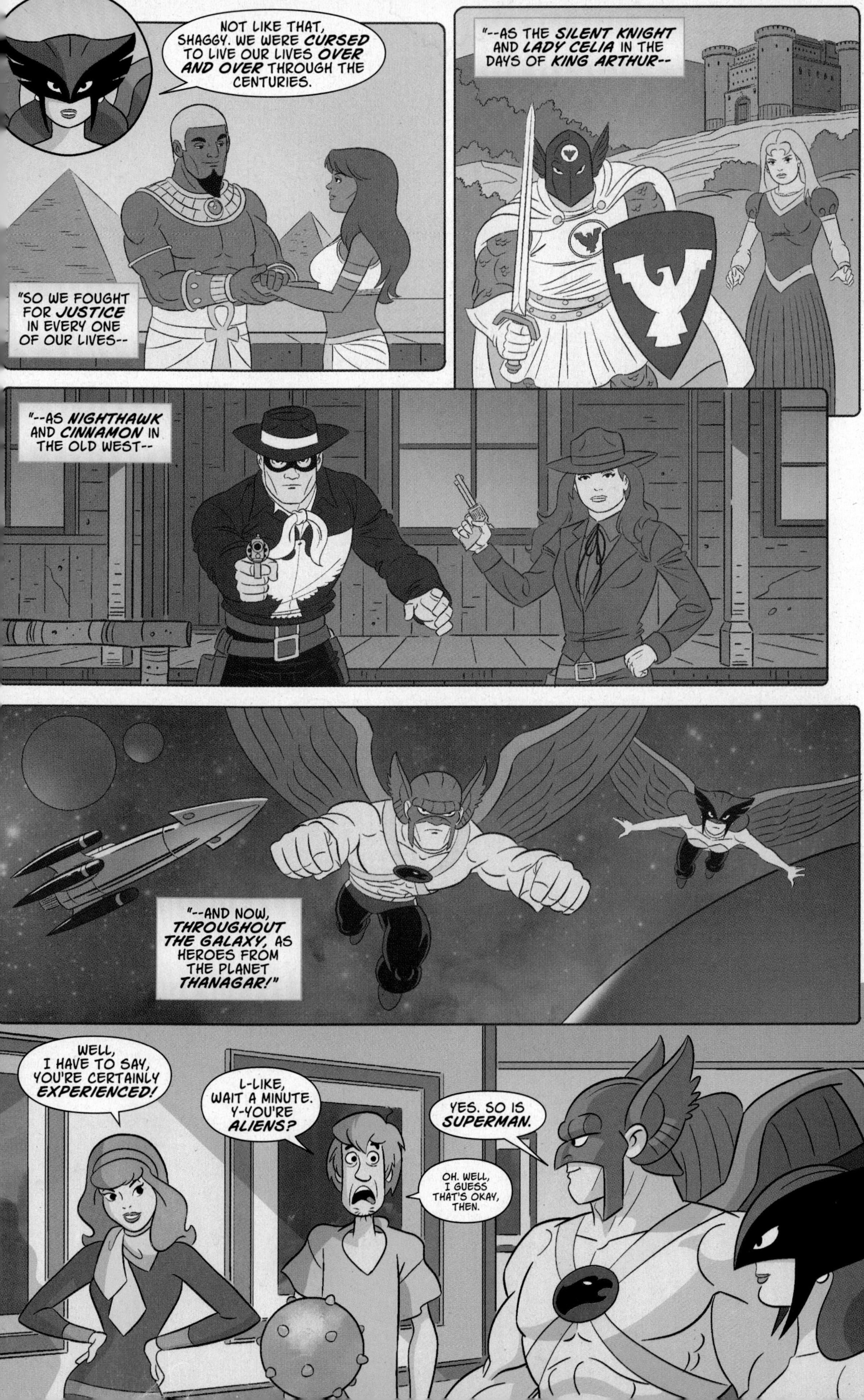
NOT LIKE THAT, SHAGGY. WE WERE CURSED TO LIVE OUR LIVES OVER AND OVER THROUGH THE CENTURIES.
"SO WE FOUGHT FOR JUSTICE IN EVERY ONE OF OUR LIVES--
"--AS THE SILENT KNIGHT AND LADY CELIA IN THE DAYS OF KING ARTHUR--
"--AS NIGHTHAWK AND CINNAMON IN THE OLD WEST--
"--AND NOW, THROUGHOUT THE GALAXY, AS HEROES FROM THE PLANET THANAGAR!"
WELL, I HAVE TO SAY, YOU'RE CERTAINLY EXPERIENCED!
L-LIKE, WAIT A MINUTE. Y-YOU'RE ALIENS?
YES. SO IS SUPERMAN.
OH. WELL, I GUESS THAT'S OKAY, THEN.

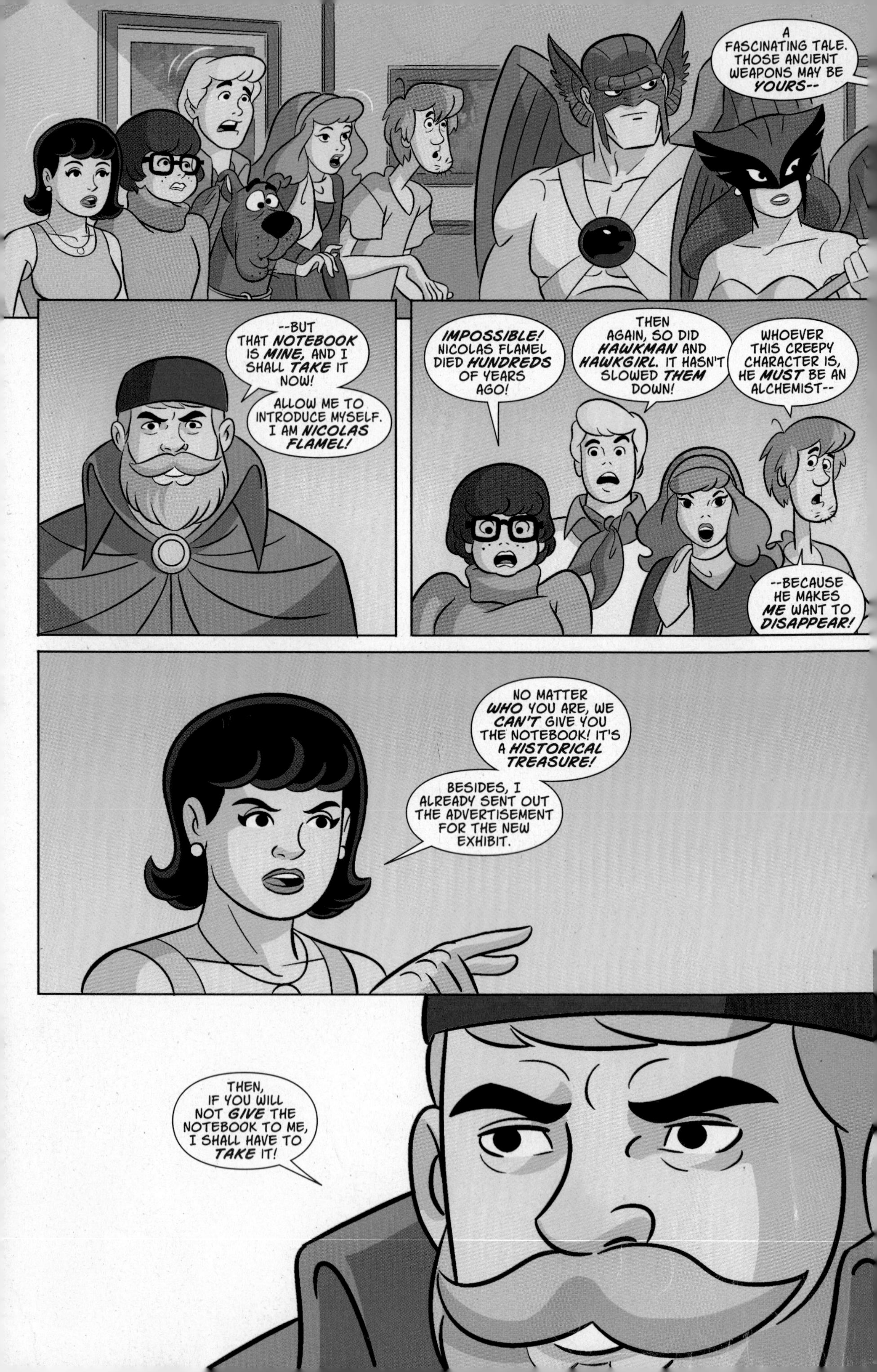
A FASCINATING TALE. THOSE ANCIENT WEAPONS MAY BE YOURS--
--BUT THAT NOTEBOOK IS MINE, AND I SHALL TAKE IT NOW!
ALLOW ME TO INTRODUCE MYSELF. I AM NICOLAS FLAMEL!
IMPOSSIBLE! NICOLAS FLAMEL DIED HUNDREDS OF YEARS AGO!
THEN AGAIN, SO DID HAWKMAN AND HAWKGIRL. IT HASN'T SLOWED THEM DOWN!
WHOEVER THIS CREEPY CHARACTER IS, HE MUST BE AN ALCHEMIST--
--BECAUSE HE MAKES ME WANT TO DISAPPEAR!
NO MATTER WHO YOU ARE, WE CAN'T GIVE YOU THE NOTEBOOK! IT'S A HISTORICAL TREASURE!
BESIDES, I ALREADY SENT OUT THE ADVERTISEMENT FOR THE NEW EXHIBIT.
THEN, IF YOU WILL NOT GIVE THE NOTEBOOK TO ME, I SHALL HAVE TO TAKE IT!

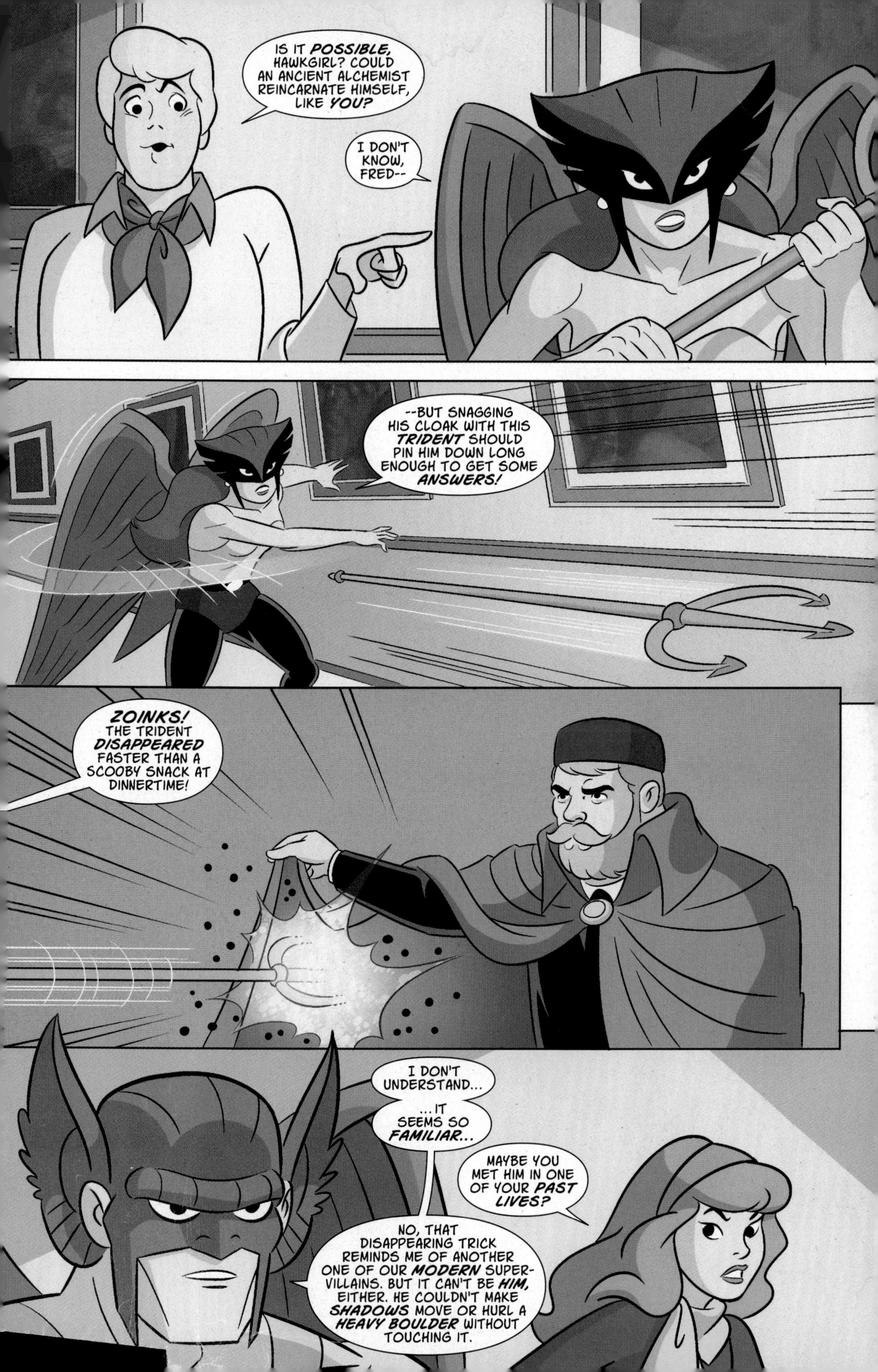
IS IT POSSIBLE, HAWKGIRL? COULD AN ANCIENT ALCHEMIST REINCARNATE HIMSELF, LIKE YOU?
I DON'T KNOW, FRED--
--BUT SNAGGING HIS CLOAK WITH THIS TRIDENT SHOULD PIN HIM DOWN LONG ENOUGH TO GET SOME ANSWERS!
ZOINKS! THE TRIDENT DISAPPEARED FASTER THAN A SCOOBY SNACK AT DINNERTIME!
I DON'T UNDERSTAND...
...IT SEEMS SO FAMILIAR...
MAYBE YOU MET HIM IN ONE OF YOUR PAST LIVES?
NO, THAT DISAPPEARING TRICK REMINDS ME OF ANOTHER ONE OF OUR MODERN SUPER-VILLAINS. BUT IT CAN'T BE HIM, EITHER. HE COULDN'T MAKE SHADOWS MOVE OR HURL A HEAVY BOULDER WITHOUT TOUCHING IT.

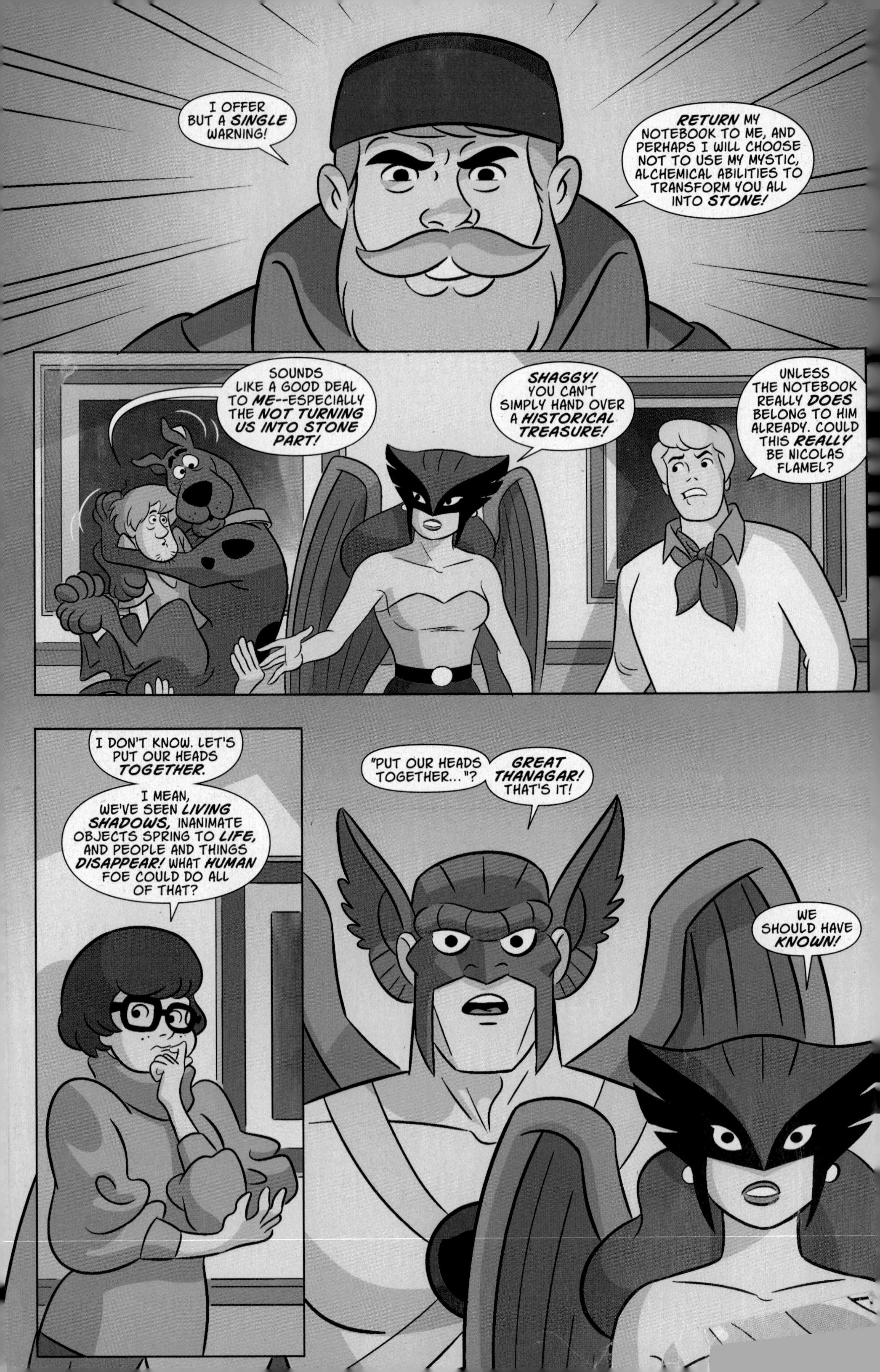
I OFFER BUT A SINGLE WARNING!
RETURN MY NOTEBOOK TO ME, AND PERHAPS I WILL CHOOSE NOT TO USE MY MYSTIC, ALCHEMICAL ABILITIES TO TRANSFORM YOU ALL INTO STONE!
SOUNDS LIKE A GOOD DEAL TO ME--ESPECIALLY THE NOT TURNING US INTO STONE PART!
SHAGGY! YOU CAN'T SIMPLY HAND OVER A HISTORICAL TREASURE!
UNLESS THE NOTEBOOK REALLY DOES BELONG TO HIM ALREADY. COULD THIS REALLY BE NICOLAS FLAMEL?
I DON'T KNOW. LET'S PUT OUR HEADS TOGETHER.
I MEAN, WE'VE SEEN LIVING SHADOWS, INANIMATE OBJECTS SPRING TO LIFE, AND PEOPLE AND THINGS DISAPPEAR! WHAT HUMAN FOE COULD DO ALL OF THAT?
"PUT OUR HEADS TOGETHER..."?
GREAT THANAGAR! THAT'S IT!
WE SHOULD HAVE KNOWN!

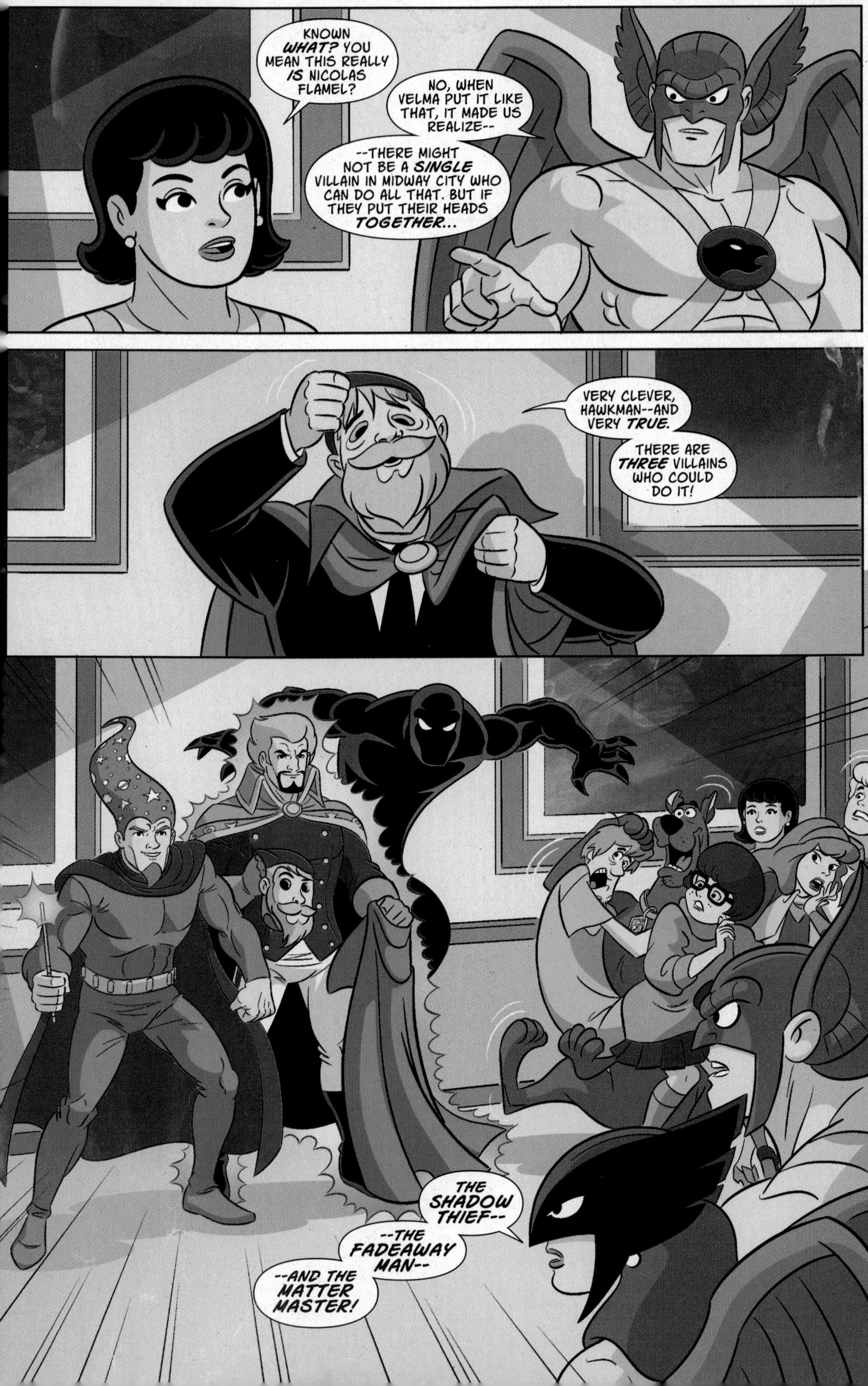

KNOWN WHAT? YOU MEAN THIS REALLY IS NICOLAS FLAMEL?
NO, WHEN VELMA PUT IT LIKE THAT, IT MADE US REALIZE--
--THERE MIGHT NOT BE A SINGLE VILLAIN IN MIDWAY CITY WHO CAN DO ALL THAT. BUT IF THEY PUT THEIR HEADS TOGETHER...
VERY CLEVER, HAWKMAN--AND VERY TRUE.
THERE ARE THREE VILLAINS WHO COULD DO IT!
THE SHADOW THIEF--
--THE FADEAWAY MAN--
--AND THE MATTER MASTER!

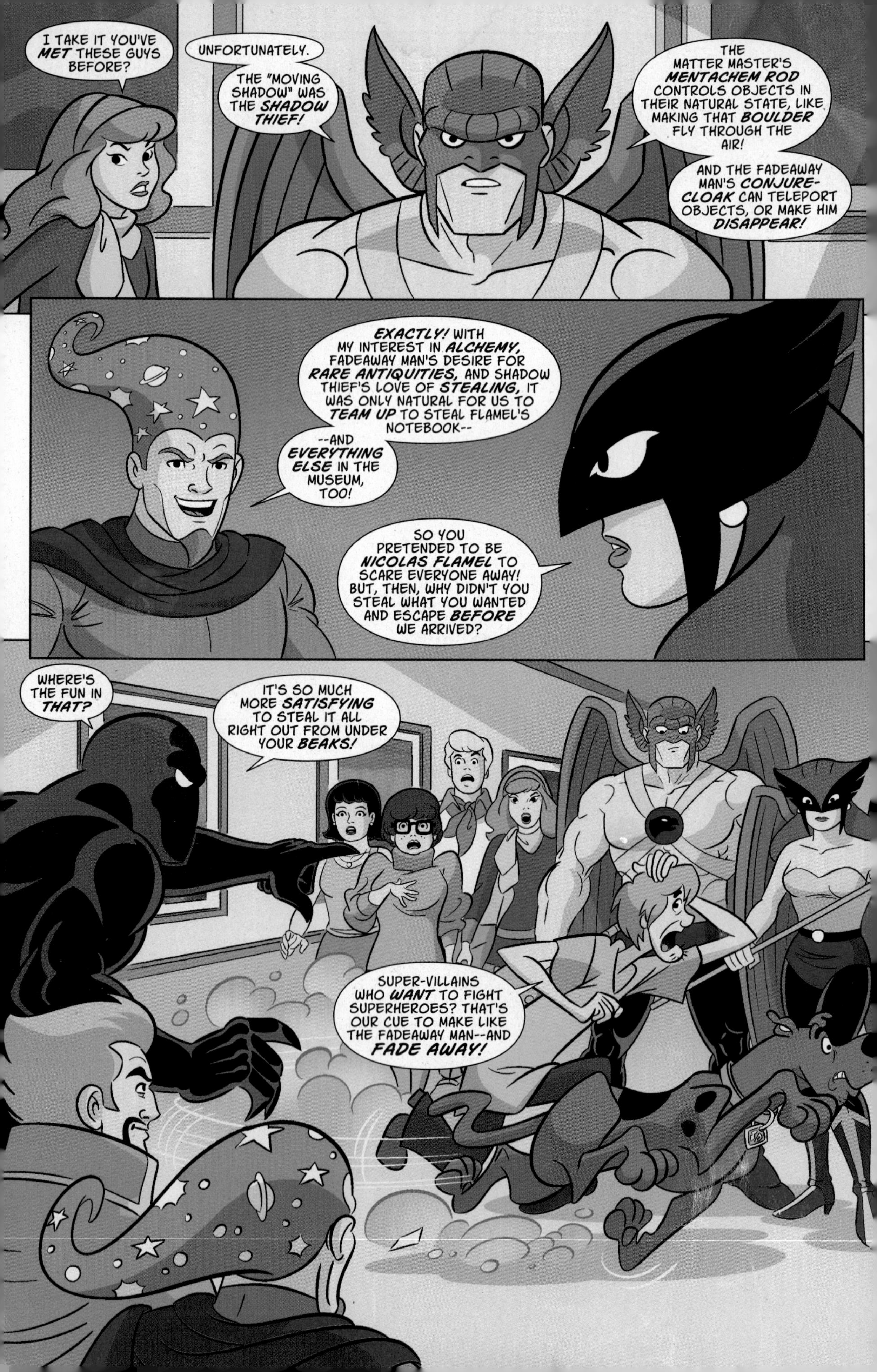
I TAKE IT YOU'VE MET THESE GUYS BEFORE?
UNFORTUNATELY.
THE "MOVING SHADOW" WAS THE SHADOW THIEF!
THE MATTER MASTER'S MENTACHEM ROD CONTROLS OBJECTS IN THEIR NATURAL STATE, LIKE MAKING THAT BOULDER FLY THROUGH THE AIR!
AND THE FADEAWAY MAN'S CONJURE-CLOAK CAN TELEPORT OBJECTS, OR MAKE HIM DISAPPEAR!
EXACTLY! WITH MY INTEREST IN ALCHEMY, FADEAWAY MAN'S DESIRE FOR RARE ANTIQUITIES, AND SHADOW THIEF'S LOVE OF STEALING, IT WAS ONLY NATURAL FOR US TO TEAM UP TO STEAL FLAMEL'S NOTEBOOK--
--AND EVERYTHING ELSE IN THE MUSEUM, TOO!
SO YOU PRETENDED TO BE NICOLAS FLAMEL TO SCARE EVERYONE AWAY! BUT, THEN, WHY DIDN'T YOU STEAL WHAT YOU WANTED AND ESCAPE BEFORE WE ARRIVED?
WHERE'S THE FUN IN THAT?
IT'S SO MUCH MORE SATISFYING TO STEAL IT ALL RIGHT OUT FROM UNDER YOUR BEAKS!
SUPER-VILLAINS WHO WANT TO FIGHT SUPERHEROES? THAT'S OUR CUE TO MAKE LIKE THE FADEAWAY MAN--AND FADE AWAY!

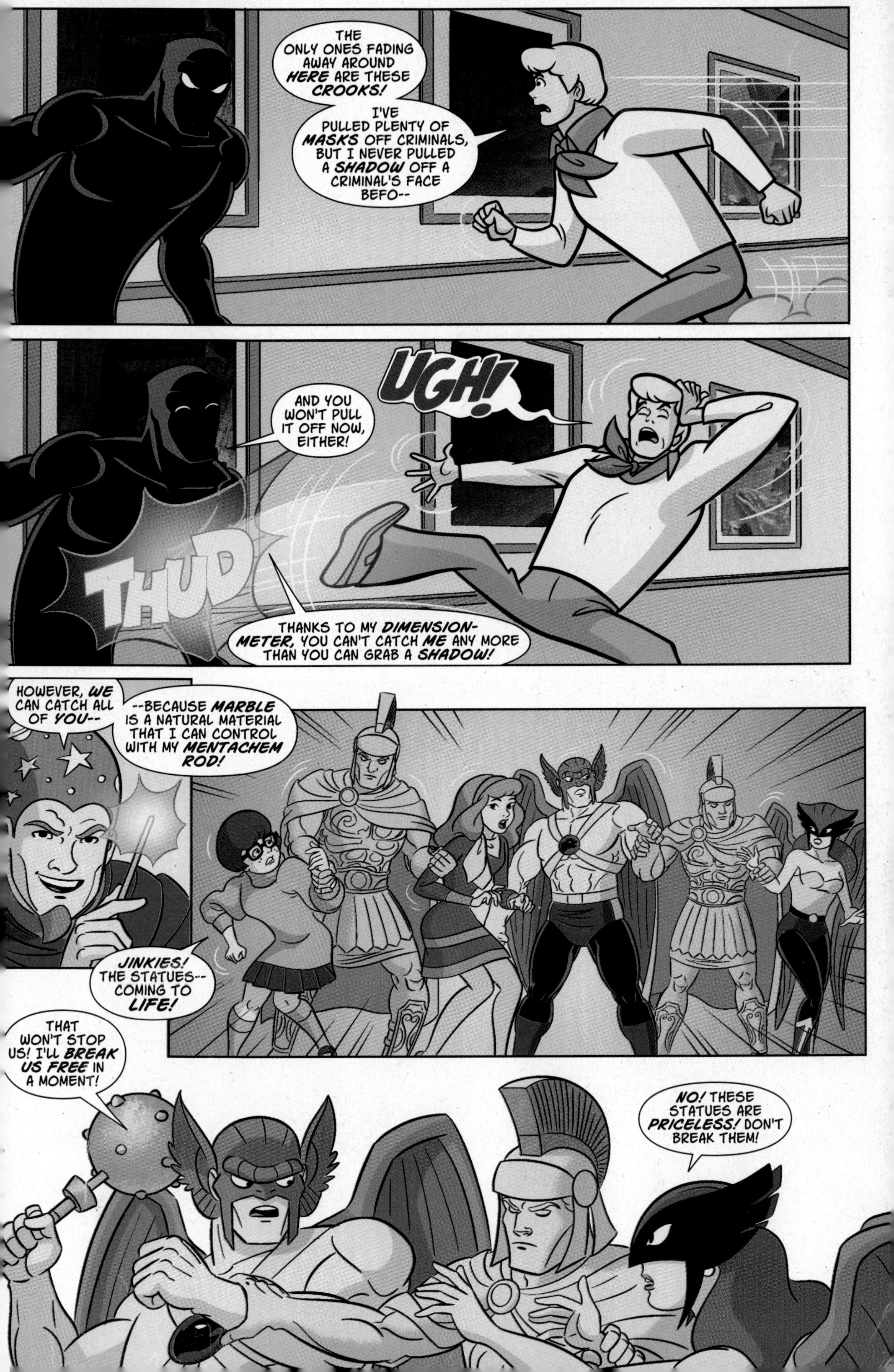
THE ONLY ONES FADING AWAY AROUND HERE ARE THESE CROOKS!
I'VE PULLED PLENTY OF MASKS OFF CRIMINALS, BUT I NEVER PULLED A SHADOW OFF A CRIMINAL'S FACE BEFO--
UGH!
AND YOU WON'T PULL IT OFF NOW, EITHER!
THUD
THANKS TO MY DIMENSION-METER, YOU CAN'T CATCH ME ANY MORE THAN YOU CAN GRAB A SHADOW!
HOWEVER, WE CAN CATCH ALL OF YOU--
--BECAUSE MARBLE IS A NATURAL MATERIAL THAT I CAN CONTROL WITH MY MENTACHEM ROD!
JINKIES! THE STATUES-- COMING TO LIFE!
THAT WON'T STOP US! I'LL BREAK US FREE IN A MOMENT!
NO! THESE STATUES ARE PRICELESS! DON'T BREAK THEM!

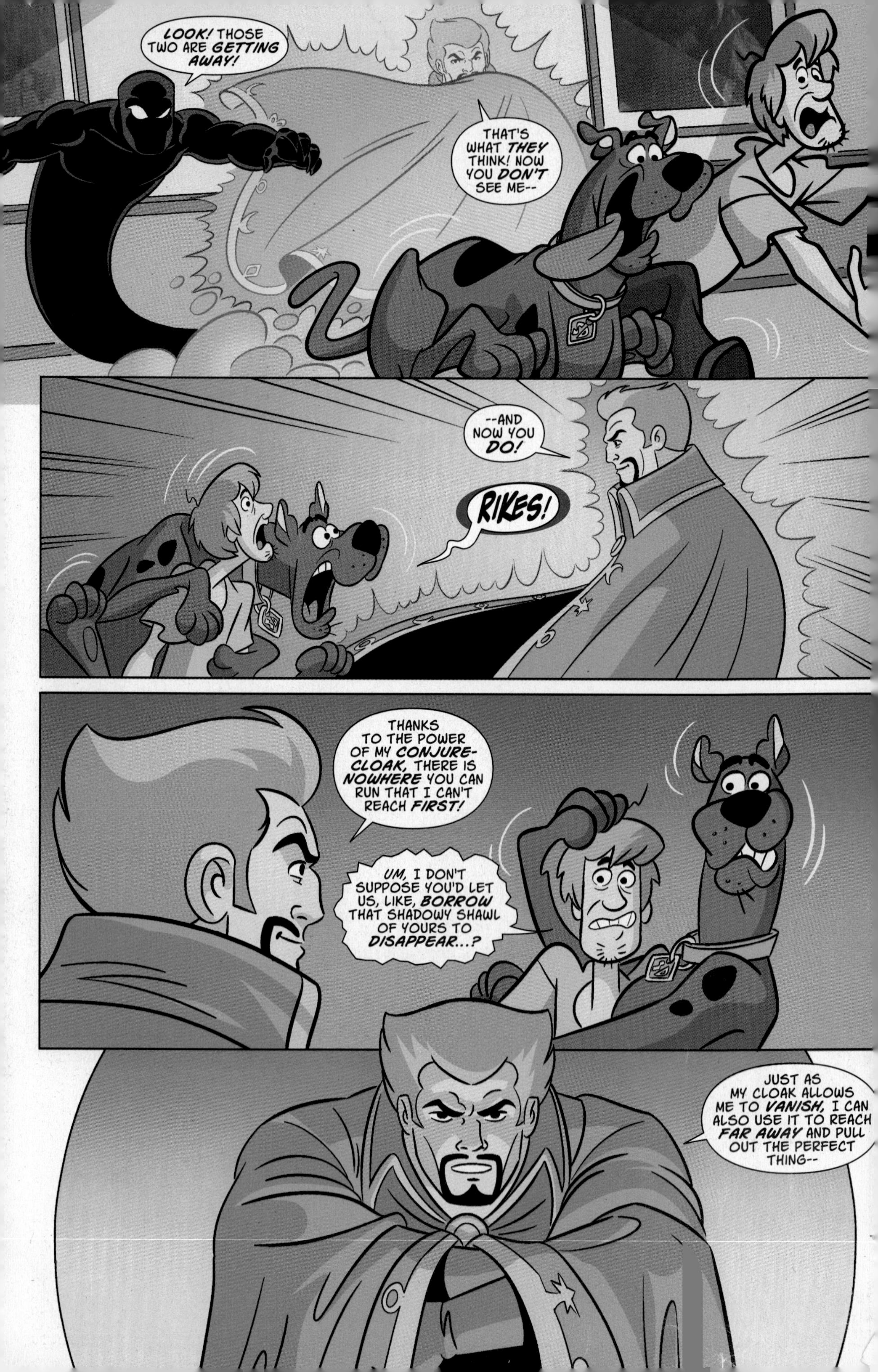
LOOK! THOSE TWO ARE GETTING AWAY!
THAT'S WHAT THEY THINK! NOW YOU DON'T SEE ME--
--AND NOW YOU DO!
RIKES!
THANKS TO THE POWER OF MY CONJURE-CLOAK, THERE IS NOWHERE YOU CAN RUN THAT I CAN'T REACH FIRST!
UM, I DON'T SUPPOSE YOU'D LET US, LIKE, BORROW THAT SHADOWY SHAWL OF YOURS TO DISAPPEAR...?
JUST AS MY CLOAK ALLOWS ME TO VANISH, I CAN ALSO USE IT TO REACH FAR AWAY AND PULL OUT THE PERFECT THING--

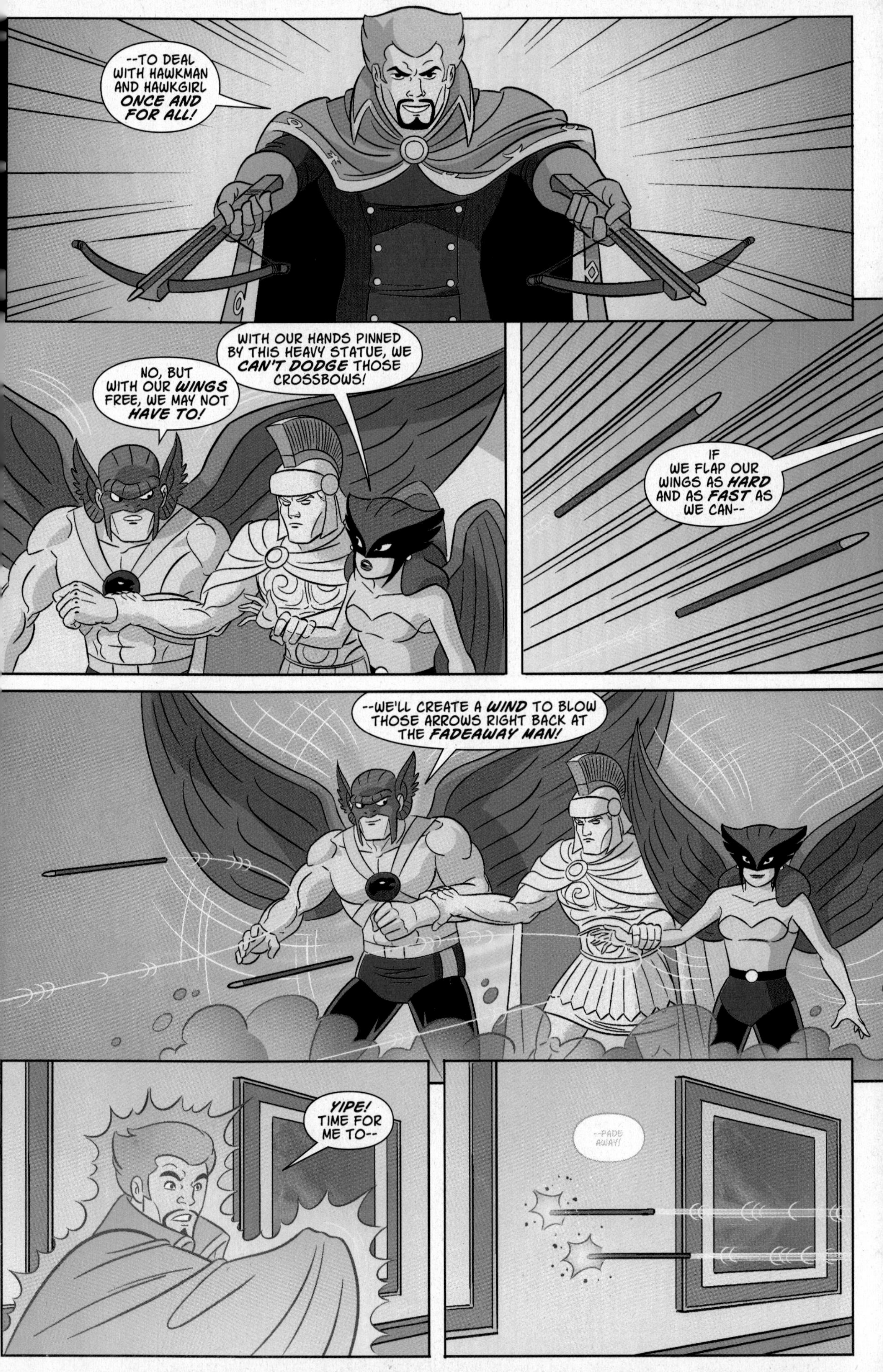
--TO DEAL WITH HAWKMAN AND HAWKGIRL *ONCE AND FOR ALL!*
WITH OUR HANDS PINNED BY THIS HEAVY STATUE, WE *CAN'T DODGE* THOSE CROSSBOWS!
NO, BUT WITH OUR *WINGS* FREE, WE MAY NOT *HAVE TO!*
IF WE FLAP OUR WINGS AS *HARD* AND AS *FAST* AS WE CAN--
--WE'LL CREATE A *WIND* TO BLOW THOSE ARROWS RIGHT BACK AT THE *FADEAWAY MAN!*
YIPE! TIME FOR ME TO--
--FADE AWAY!

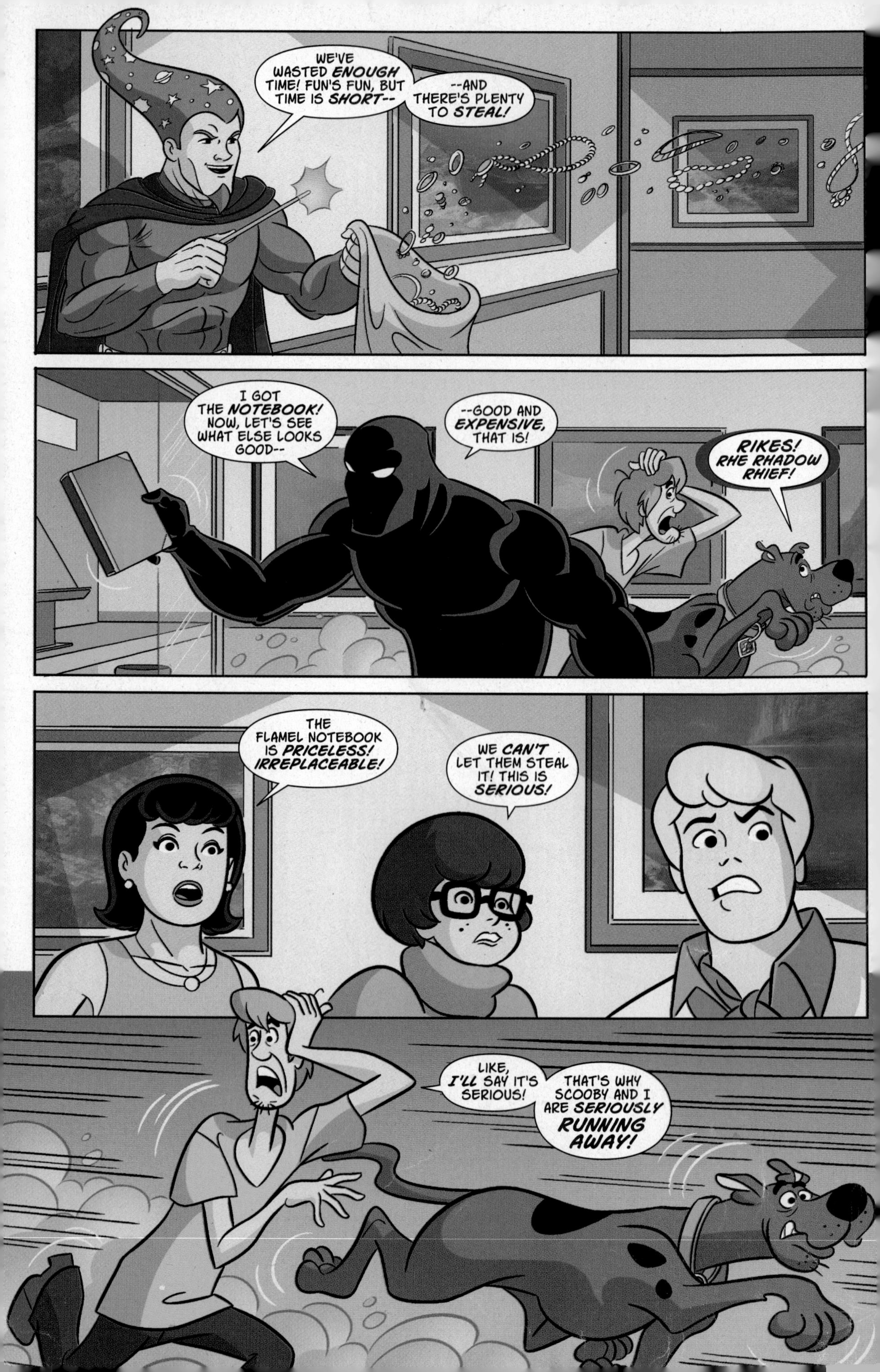
WE'VE WASTED ENOUGH TIME! FUN'S FUN, BUT TIME IS SHORT--
--AND THERE'S PLENTY TO STEAL!
I GOT THE NOTEBOOK! NOW, LET'S SEE WHAT ELSE LOOKS GOOD--
--GOOD AND EXPENSIVE, THAT IS!
RIKES! RHE RHADOW RHIEF!
THE FLAMEL NOTEBOOK IS PRICELESS! IRREPLACEABLE!
WE CAN'T LET THEM STEAL IT! THIS IS SERIOUS!
LIKE, I'LL SAY IT'S SERIOUS!
THAT'S WHY SCOOBY AND I ARE SERIOUSLY RUNNING AWAY!

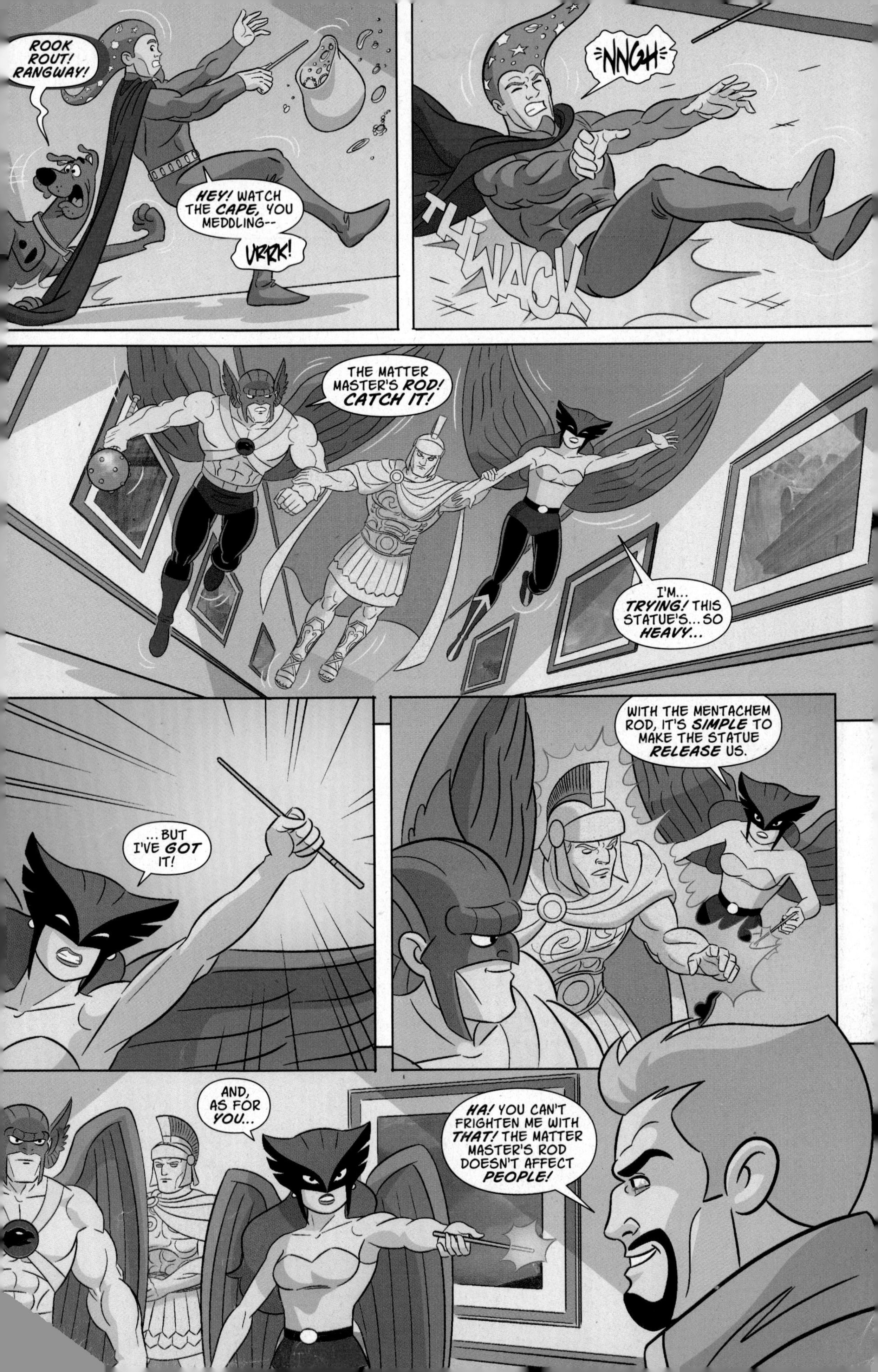
ROOK ROUT! RANGWAY!
HEY! WATCH THE CAPE, YOU MEDDLING--
URRK!
NNGH
THWACK
THE MATTER MASTER'S ROD! CATCH IT!
I'M... TRYING! THIS STATUE'S... SO HEAVY...
...BUT I'VE GOT IT!
WITH THE MENTACHEM ROD, IT'S SIMPLE TO MAKE THE STATUE RELEASE US.
AND, AS FOR YOU...
HA! YOU CAN'T FRIGHTEN ME WITH THAT! THE MATTER MASTER'S ROD DOESN'T AFFECT PEOPLE!

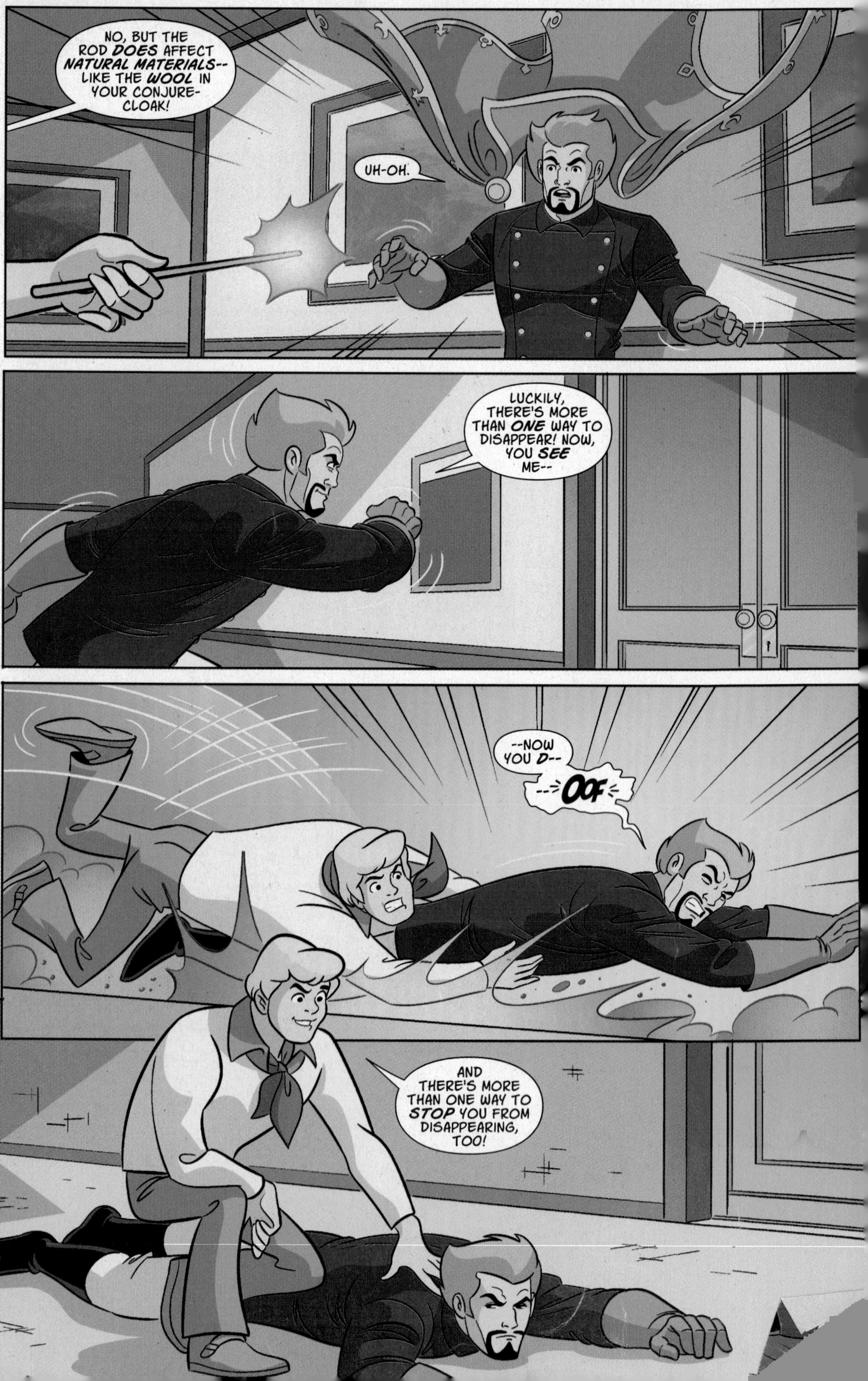
NO, BUT THE ROD DOES AFFECT NATURAL MATERIALS-- LIKE THE WOOL IN YOUR CONJURE-CLOAK!
UH-OH.
LUCKILY, THERE'S MORE THAN ONE WAY TO DISAPPEAR! NOW, YOU SEE ME--
--NOW YOU D--
--OOF
AND THERE'S MORE THAN ONE WAY TO STOP YOU FROM DISAPPEARING, TOO!

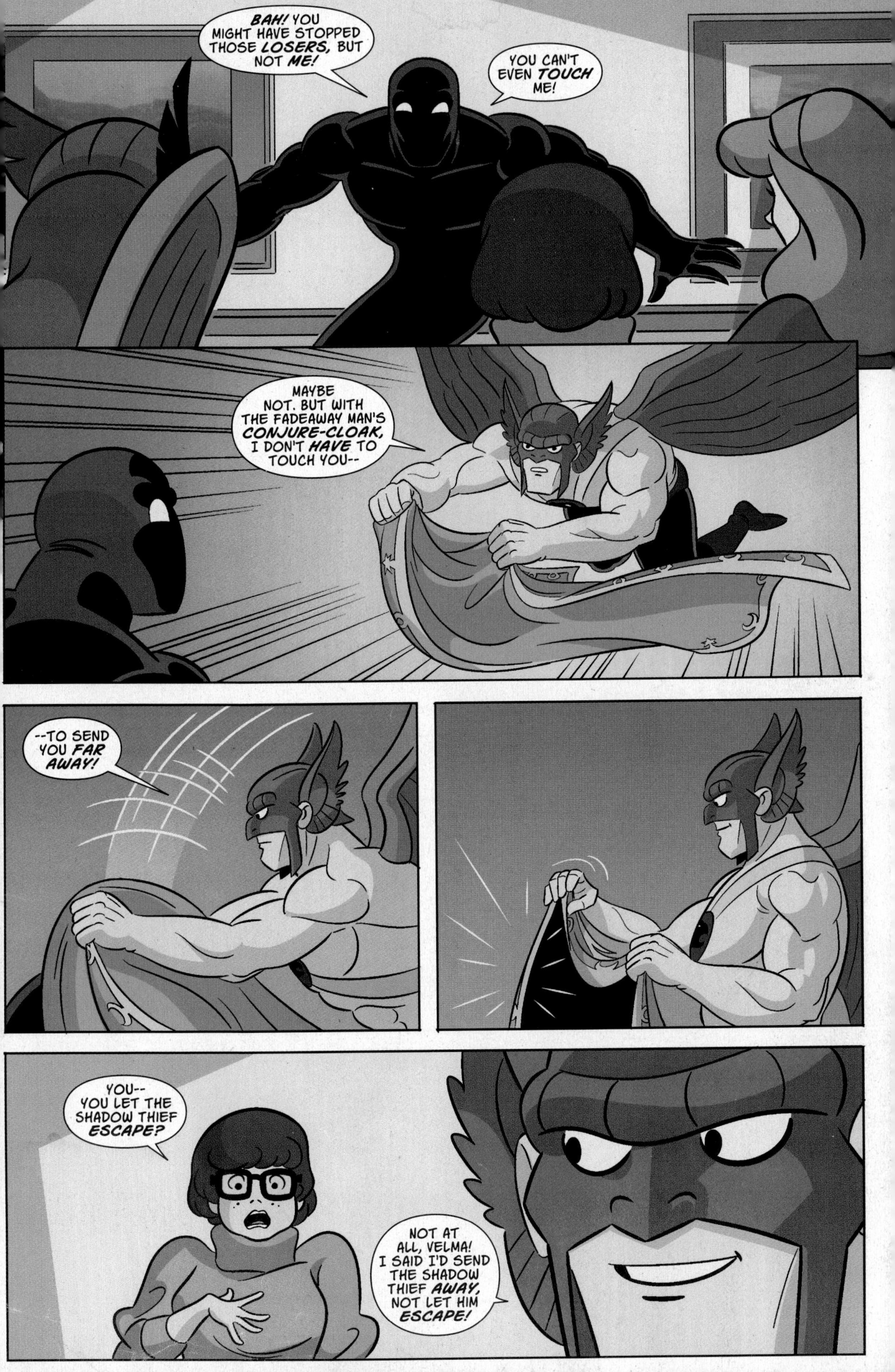
BAH! YOU MIGHT HAVE STOPPED THOSE LOSERS, BUT NOT ME!
YOU CAN'T EVEN TOUCH ME!
MAYBE NOT. BUT WITH THE FADEAWAY MAN'S CONJURE-CLOAK, I DON'T HAVE TO TOUCH YOU--
--TO SEND YOU FAR AWAY!
YOU-- YOU LET THE SHADOW THIEF ESCAPE?
NOT AT ALL, VELMA! I SAID I'D SEND THE SHADOW THIEF AWAY, NOT LET HIM ESCAPE!

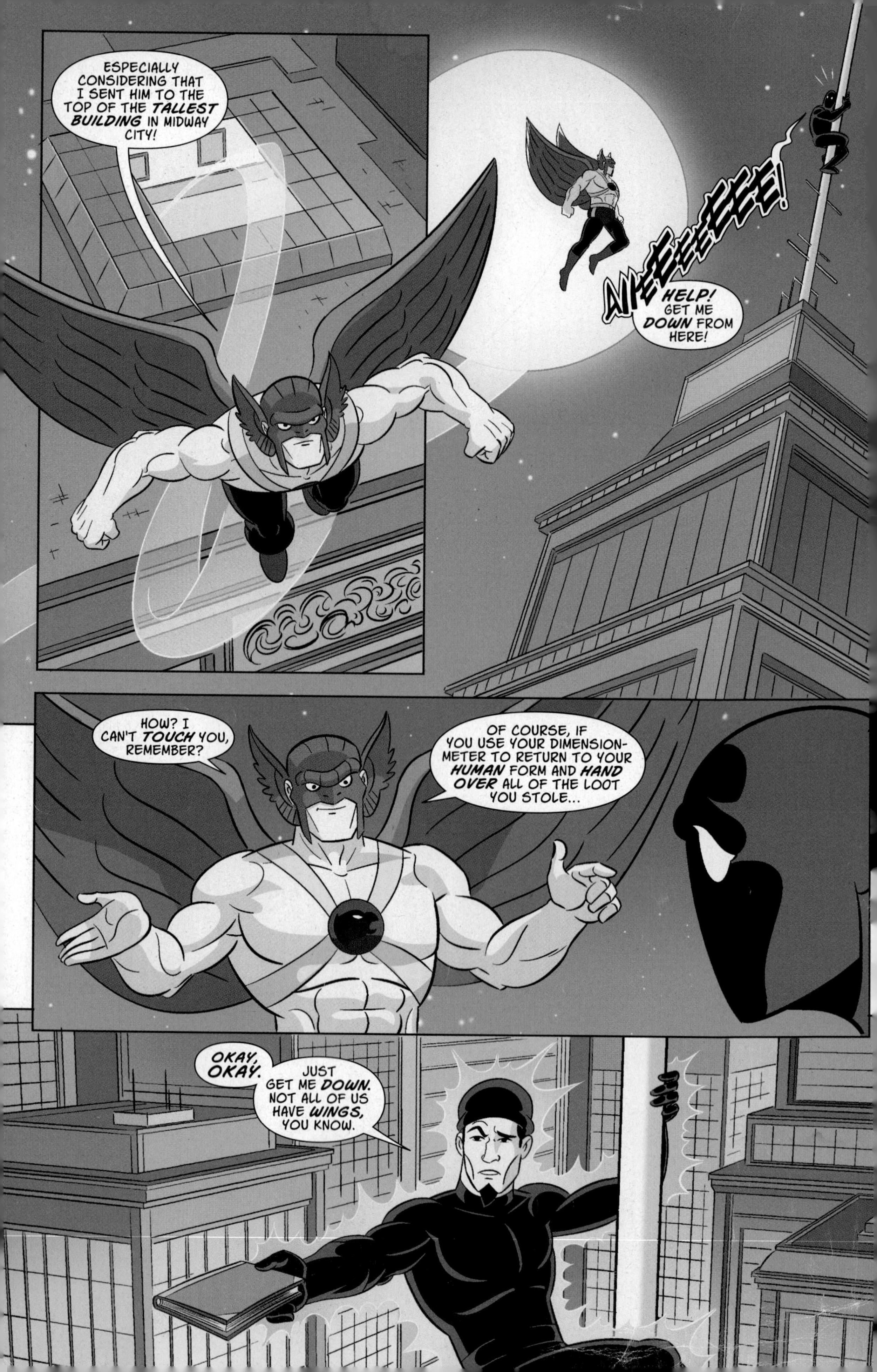
ESPECIALLY CONSIDERING THAT I SENT HIM TO THE TOP OF THE TALLEST BUILDING IN MIDWAY CITY!
AIIEEEEEEEE!
HELP! GET ME DOWN FROM HERE!
HOW? I CAN'T TOUCH YOU, REMEMBER?
OF COURSE, IF YOU USE YOUR DIMENSION-METER TO RETURN TO YOUR HUMAN FORM AND HAND OVER ALL OF THE LOOT YOU STOLE...
OKAY, OKAY.
JUST GET ME DOWN. NOT ALL OF US HAVE WINGS, YOU KNOW.

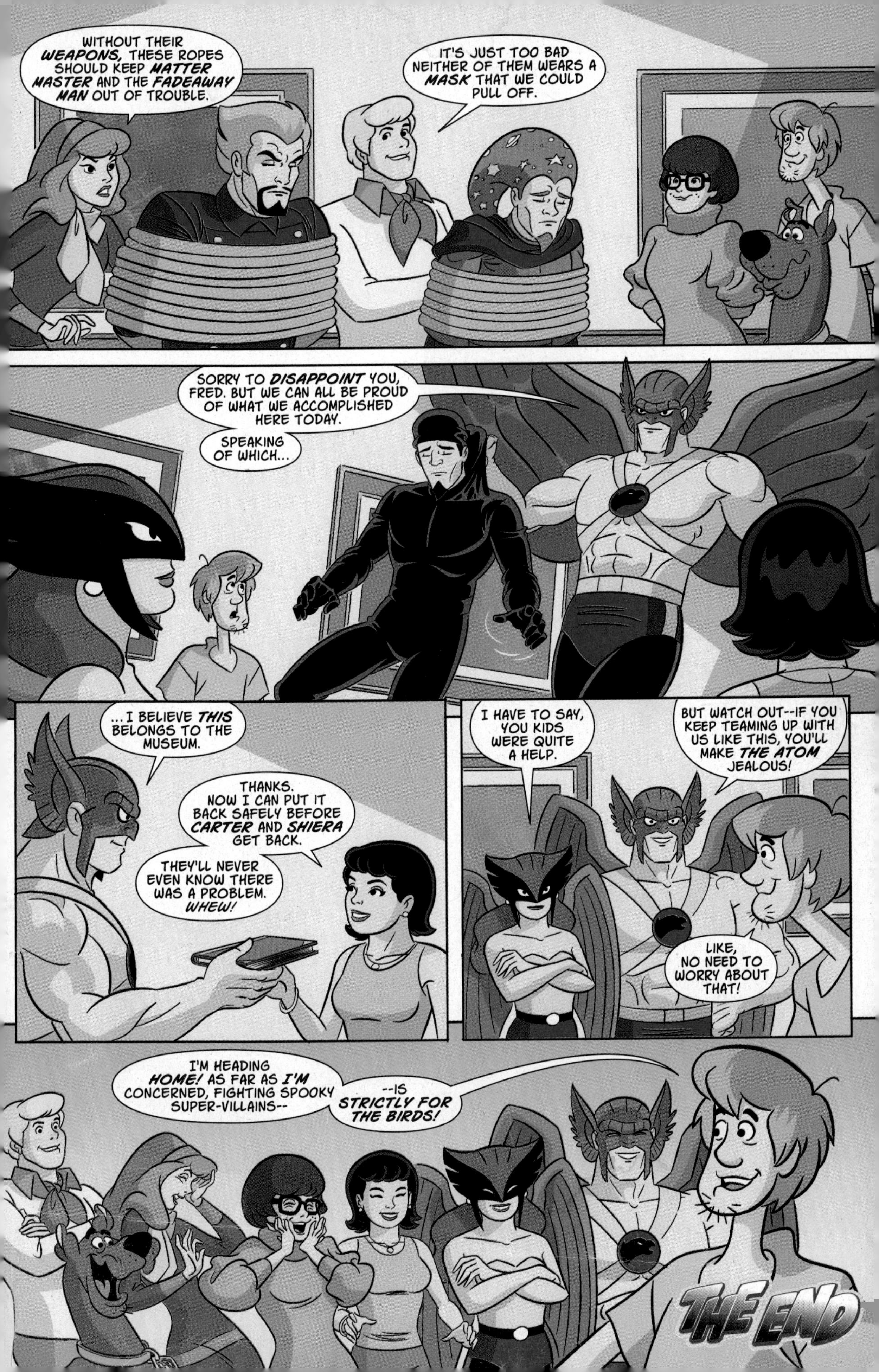
WITHOUT THEIR WEAPONS, THESE ROPES SHOULD KEEP MATTER MASTER AND THE FADEAWAY MAN OUT OF TROUBLE.
IT'S JUST TOO BAD NEITHER OF THEM WEARS A MASK THAT WE COULD PULL OFF.
SORRY TO DISAPPOINT YOU, FRED. BUT WE CAN ALL BE PROUD OF WHAT WE ACCOMPLISHED HERE TODAY.
SPEAKING OF WHICH...
...I BELIEVE THIS BELONGS TO THE MUSEUM.
THANKS. NOW I CAN PUT IT BACK SAFELY BEFORE CARTER AND SHIERA GET BACK.
THEY'LL NEVER EVEN KNOW THERE WAS A PROBLEM. WHEW!
I HAVE TO SAY, YOU KIDS WERE QUITE A HELP.
BUT WATCH OUT--IF YOU KEEP TEAMING UP WITH US LIKE THIS, YOU'LL MAKE THE ATOM JEALOUS!
LIKE, NO NEED TO WORRY ABOUT THAT!
I'M HEADING HOME! AS FAR AS I'M CONCERNED, FIGHTING SPOOKY SUPER-VILLAINS--
--IS STRICTLY FOR THE BIRDS!
THE END

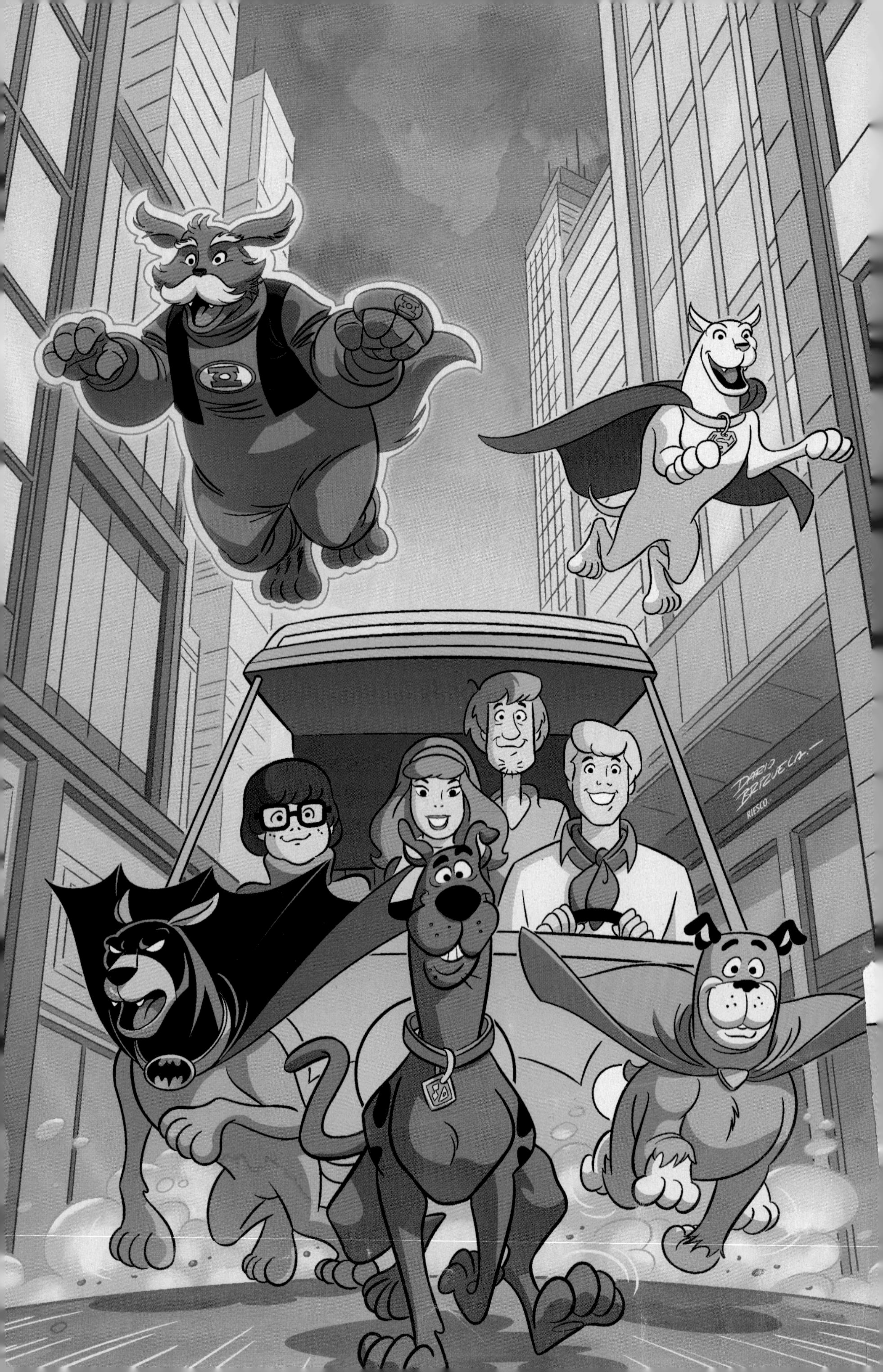
DARIO BRIZUELA
RIESCO

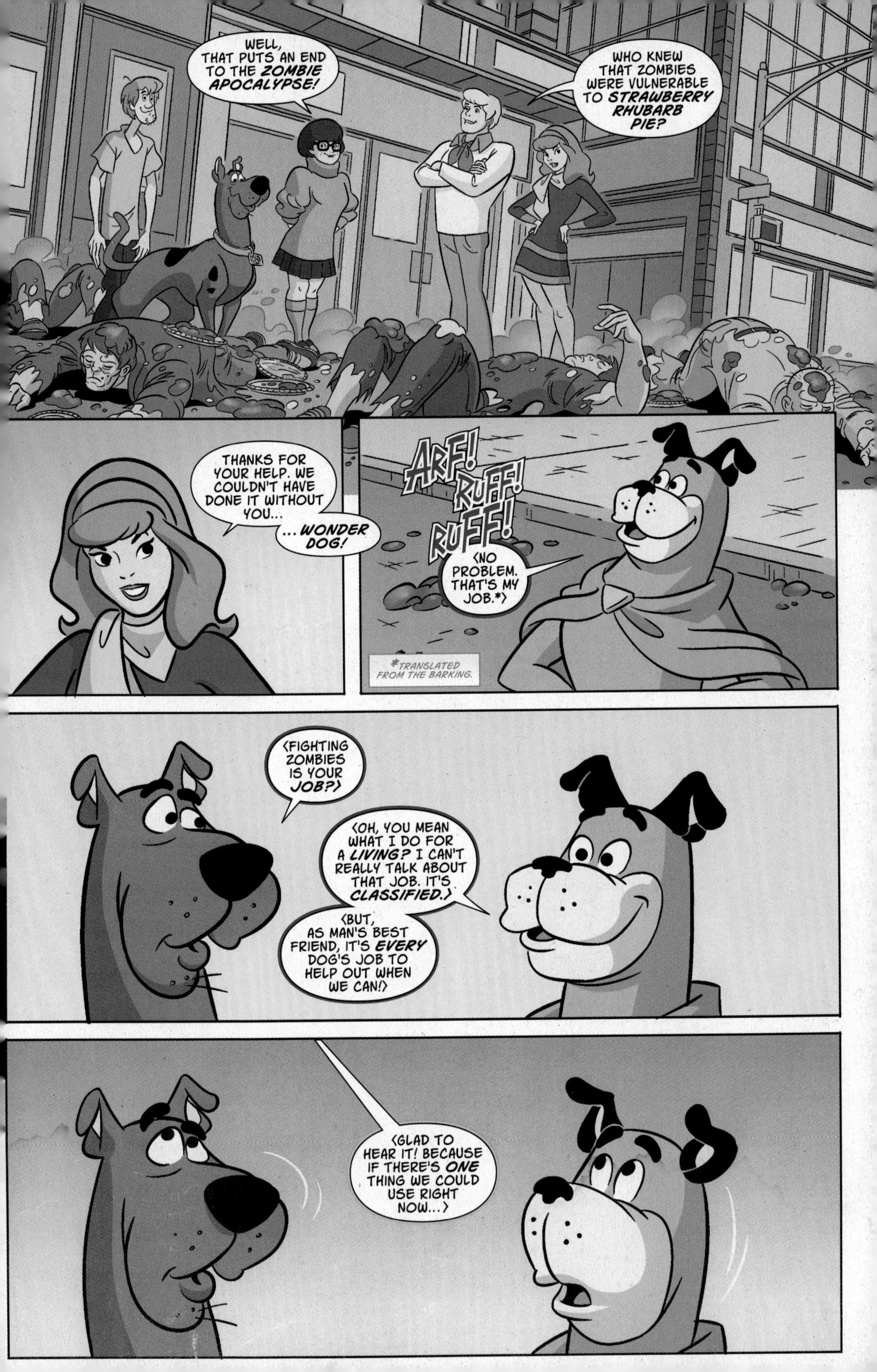
WELL, THAT PUTS AN END TO THE ZOMBIE APOCALYPSE!
WHO KNEW THAT ZOMBIES WERE VULNERABLE TO STRAWBERRY RHUBARB PIE?
THANKS FOR YOUR HELP. WE COULDN'T HAVE DONE IT WITHOUT YOU...
...WONDER DOG!
ARF! RUFF! RUFF!
<NO PROBLEM. THAT'S MY JOB.*>
*TRANSLATED FROM THE BARKING.
<FIGHTING ZOMBIES IS YOUR JOB?>
<OH, YOU MEAN WHAT I DO FOR A LIVING? I CAN'T REALLY TALK ABOUT THAT JOB. IT'S CLASSIFIED.>
<BUT, AS MAN'S BEST FRIEND, IT'S EVERY DOG'S JOB TO HELP OUT WHEN WE CAN!>
<GLAD TO HEAR IT! BECAUSE IF THERE'S ONE THING WE COULD USE RIGHT NOW...>

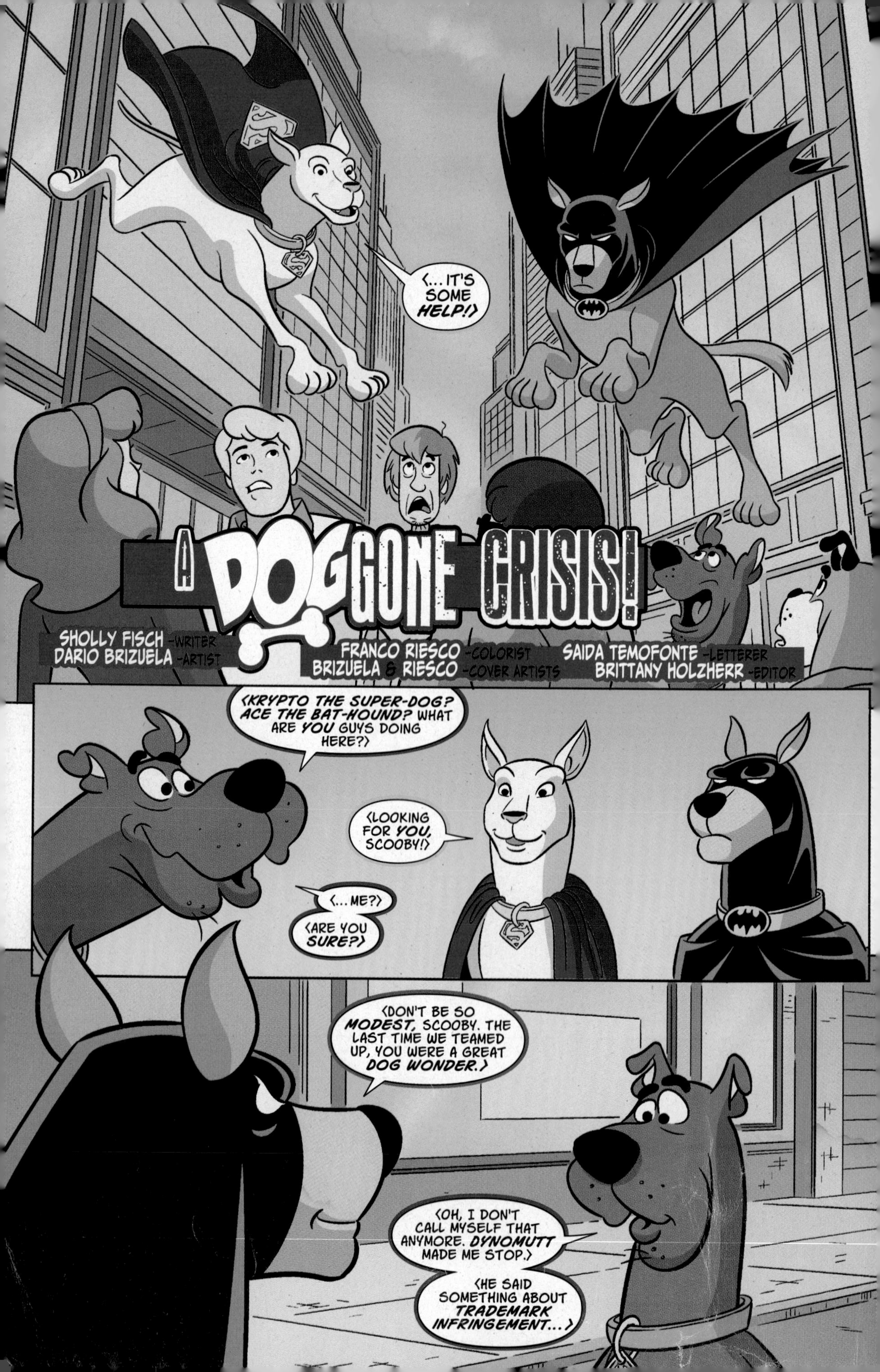
⟨... IT'S SOME HELP!⟩
A DOGGONE CRISIS!
SHOLLY FISCH -WRITER
DARIO BRIZUELA -ARTIST
FRANCO RIESCO -COLORIST
BRIZUELA & RIESCO -COVER ARTISTS
SAIDA TEMOFONTE -LETTERER
BRITTANY HOLZHERR -EDITOR
⟨KRYPTO THE SUPER-DOG? ACE THE BAT-HOUND? WHAT ARE YOU GUYS DOING HERE?⟩
⟨LOOKING FOR YOU, SCOOBY!⟩
⟨... ME?⟩
⟨ARE YOU SURE?⟩
⟨DON'T BE SO MODEST, SCOOBY. THE LAST TIME WE TEAMED UP, YOU WERE A GREAT DOG WONDER.⟩
⟨OH, I DON'T CALL MYSELF THAT ANYMORE. DYNOMUTT MADE ME STOP.⟩
⟨HE SAID SOMETHING ABOUT TRADEMARK INFRINGEMENT...⟩

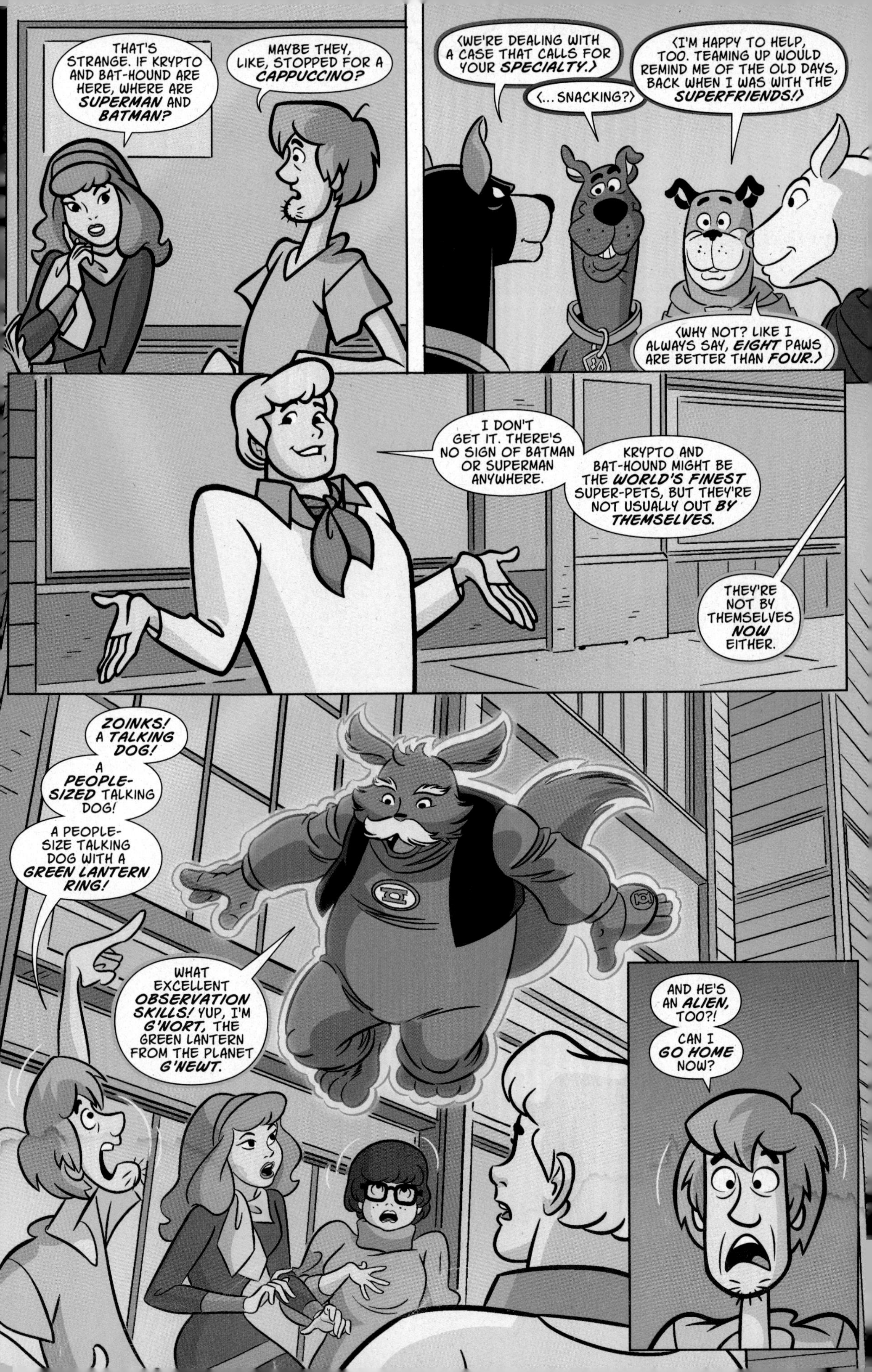
THAT'S STRANGE. IF KRYPTO AND BAT-HOUND ARE HERE, WHERE ARE SUPERMAN AND BATMAN?
MAYBE THEY, LIKE, STOPPED FOR A CAPPUCCINO?
⟨WE'RE DEALING WITH A CASE THAT CALLS FOR YOUR SPECIALTY.⟩
⟨...SNACKING?⟩
⟨I'M HAPPY TO HELP, TOO. TEAMING UP WOULD REMIND ME OF THE OLD DAYS, BACK WHEN I WAS WITH THE SUPERFRIENDS!⟩
⟨WHY NOT? LIKE I ALWAYS SAY, EIGHT PAWS ARE BETTER THAN FOUR.⟩
I DON'T GET IT. THERE'S NO SIGN OF BATMAN OR SUPERMAN ANYWHERE.
KRYPTO AND BAT-HOUND MIGHT BE THE WORLD'S FINEST SUPER-PETS, BUT THEY'RE NOT USUALLY OUT BY THEMSELVES.
THEY'RE NOT BY THEMSELVES NOW EITHER.
ZOINKS! A TALKING DOG!
A PEOPLE-SIZED TALKING DOG!
A PEOPLE-SIZE TALKING DOG WITH A GREEN LANTERN RING!
WHAT EXCELLENT OBSERVATION SKILLS! YUP, I'M G'NORT, THE GREEN LANTERN FROM THE PLANET G'NEWT.
AND HE'S AN ALIEN, TOO?!
CAN I GO HOME NOW?

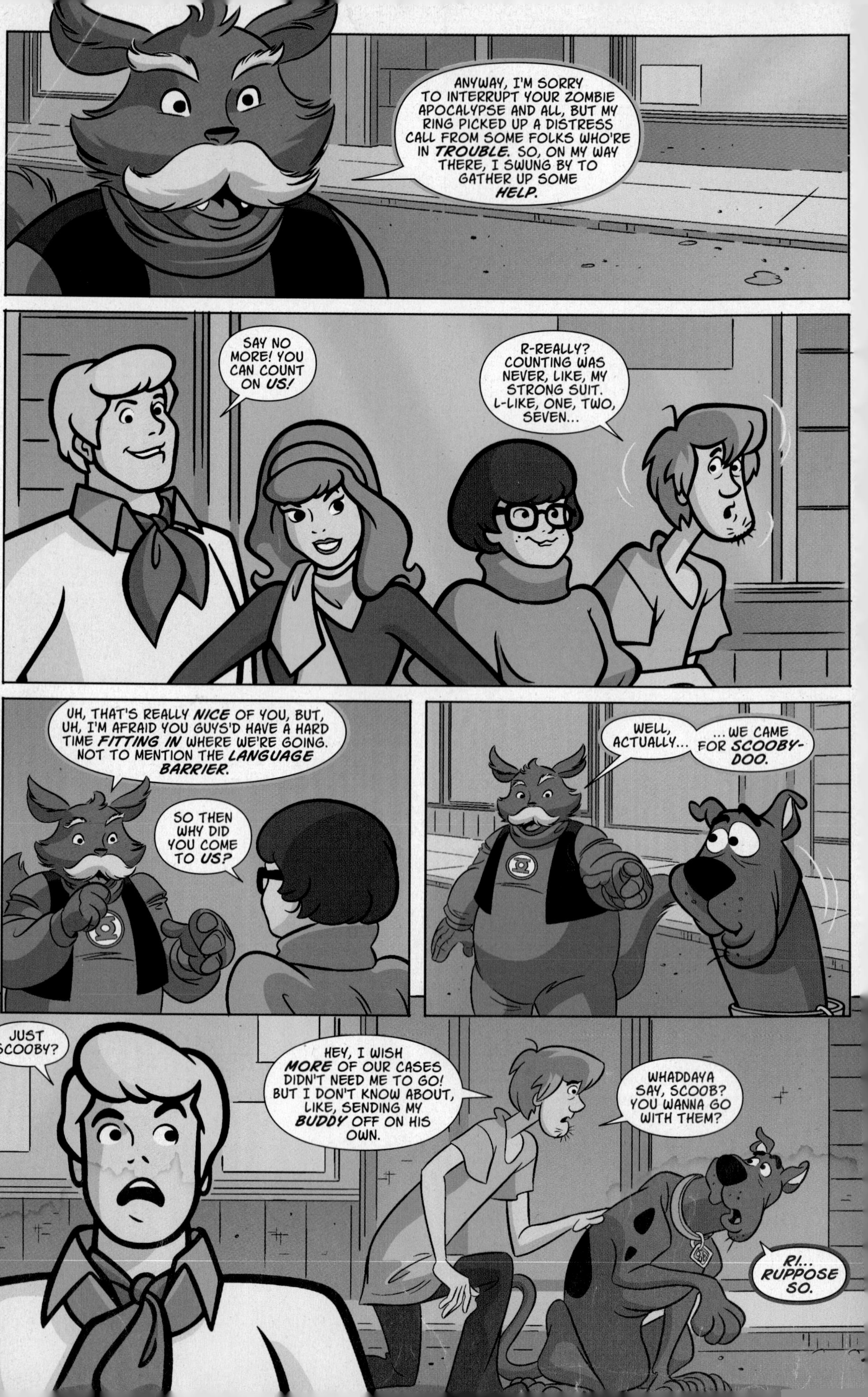
ANYWAY, I'M SORRY TO INTERRUPT YOUR ZOMBIE APOCALYPSE AND ALL, BUT MY RING PICKED UP A DISTRESS CALL FROM SOME FOLKS WHO'RE IN TROUBLE. SO, ON MY WAY THERE, I SWUNG BY TO GATHER UP SOME HELP.
SAY NO MORE! YOU CAN COUNT ON US!
R-REALLY? COUNTING WAS NEVER, LIKE, MY STRONG SUIT. L-LIKE, ONE, TWO, SEVEN...
UH, THAT'S REALLY NICE OF YOU, BUT, UH, I'M AFRAID YOU GUYS'D HAVE A HARD TIME FITTING IN WHERE WE'RE GOING. NOT TO MENTION THE LANGUAGE BARRIER.
SO THEN WHY DID YOU COME TO US?
WELL, ACTUALLY...
...WE CAME FOR SCOOBY-DOO.
JUST SCOOBY?
HEY, I WISH MORE OF OUR CASES DIDN'T NEED ME TO GO! BUT I DON'T KNOW ABOUT, LIKE, SENDING MY BUDDY OFF ON HIS OWN.
WHADDAYA SAY, SCOOB? YOU WANNA GO WITH THEM?
RI... RUPPOSE SO.

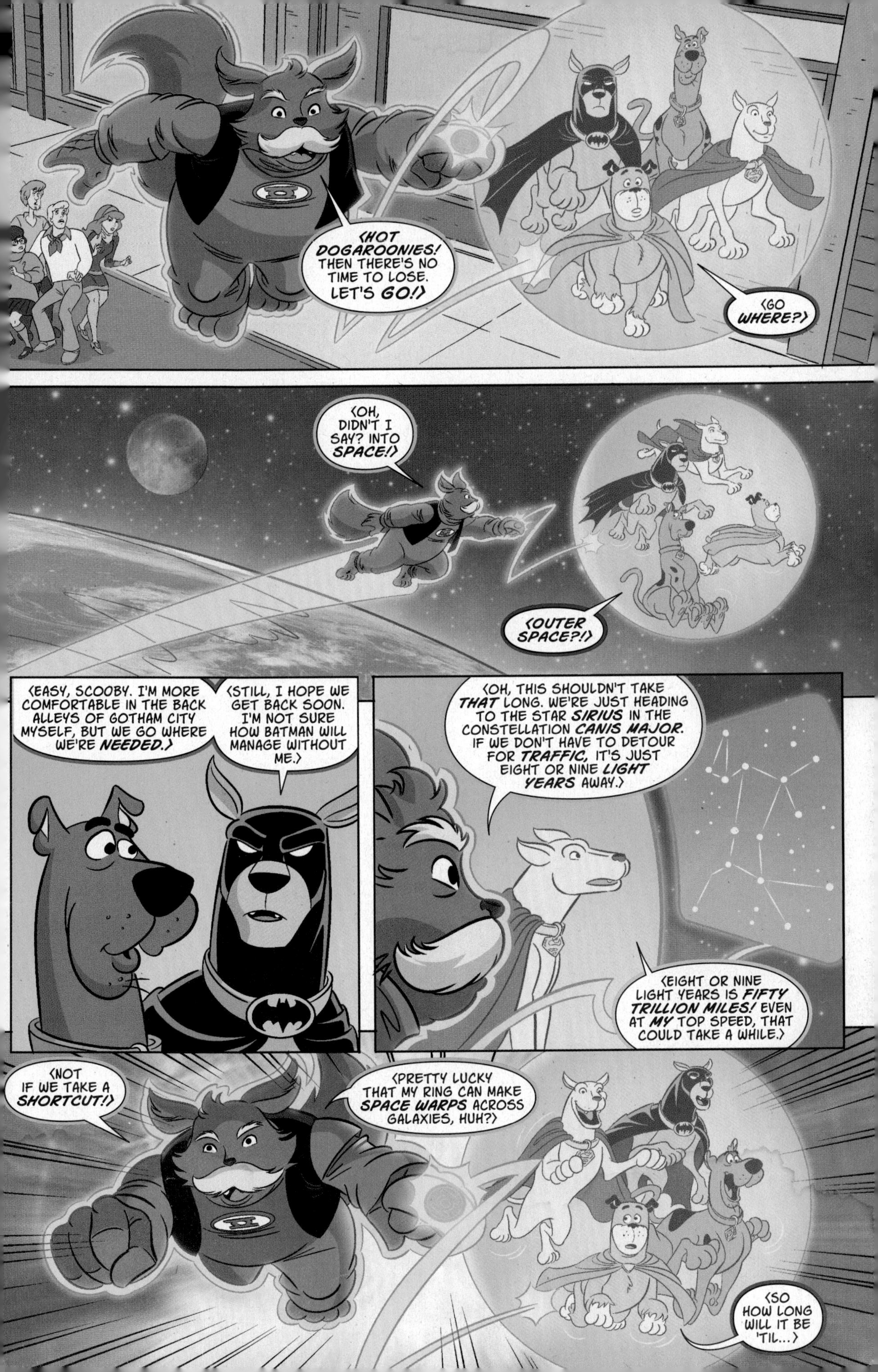
⟨HOT DOGAROONIES! THEN THERE'S NO TIME TO LOSE. LET'S GO!⟩
⟨GO WHERE?⟩
⟨OH, DIDN'T I SAY? INTO SPACE!⟩
⟨OUTER SPACE?!⟩
⟨EASY, SCOOBY. I'M MORE COMFORTABLE IN THE BACK ALLEYS OF GOTHAM CITY MYSELF, BUT WE GO WHERE WE'RE NEEDED.⟩
⟨STILL, I HOPE WE GET BACK SOON. I'M NOT SURE HOW BATMAN WILL MANAGE WITHOUT ME.⟩
⟨OH, THIS SHOULDN'T TAKE THAT LONG. WE'RE JUST HEADING TO THE STAR SIRIUS IN THE CONSTELLATION CANIS MAJOR. IF WE DON'T HAVE TO DETOUR FOR TRAFFIC, IT'S JUST EIGHT OR NINE LIGHT YEARS AWAY.⟩
⟨EIGHT OR NINE LIGHT YEARS IS FIFTY TRILLION MILES! EVEN AT MY TOP SPEED, THAT COULD TAKE A WHILE.⟩
⟨NOT IF WE TAKE A SHORTCUT!⟩
⟨PRETTY LUCKY THAT MY RING CAN MAKE SPACE WARPS ACROSS GALAXIES, HUH?⟩
⟨SO HOW LONG WILL IT BE 'TIL...⟩

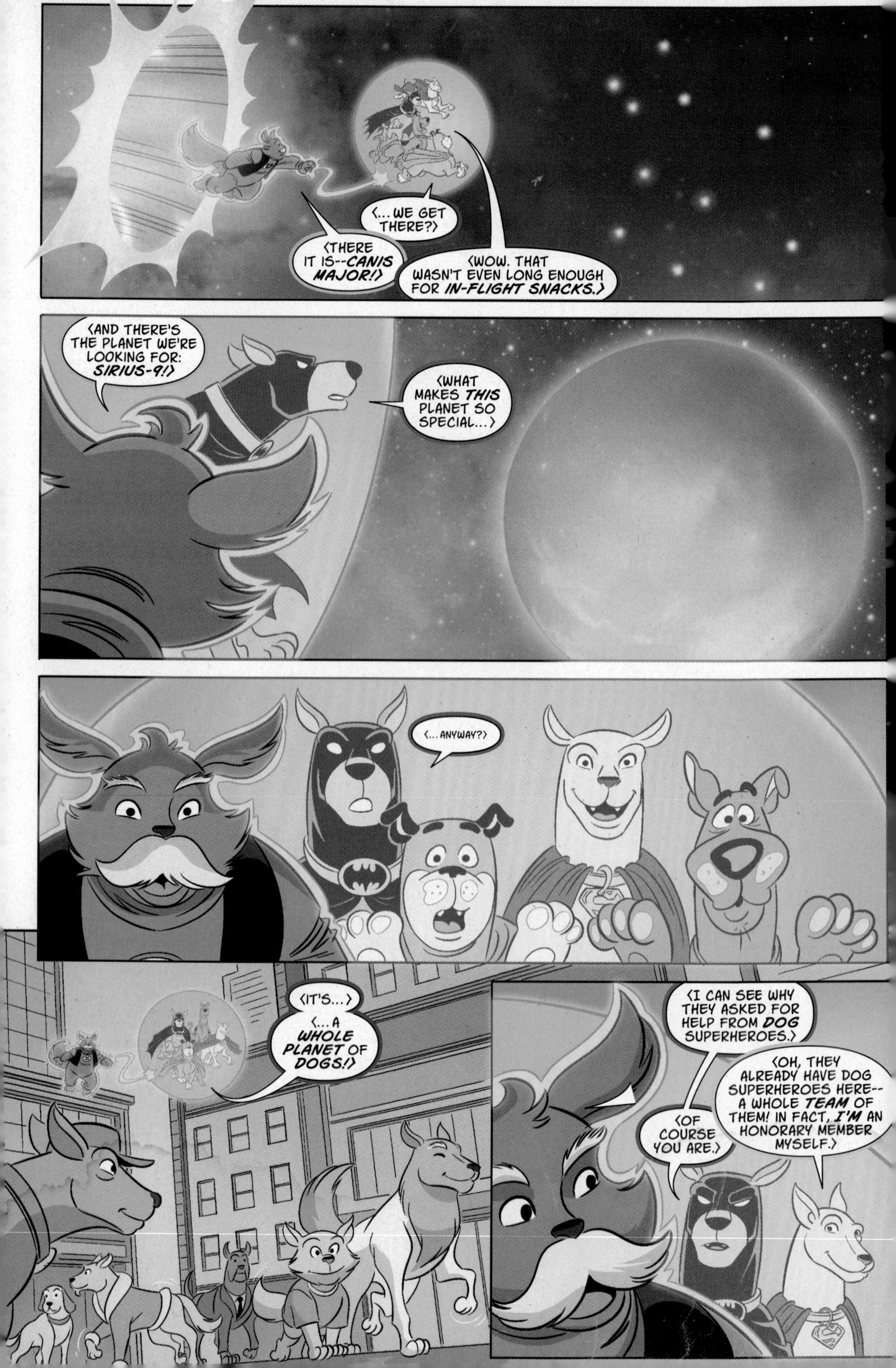

⟨...WE GET THERE?⟩
⟨THERE IT IS--CANIS MAJOR!⟩
⟨WOW. THAT WASN'T EVEN LONG ENOUGH FOR IN-FLIGHT SNACKS.⟩
⟨AND THERE'S THE PLANET WE'RE LOOKING FOR: SIRIUS-9!⟩
⟨WHAT MAKES THIS PLANET SO SPECIAL...⟩
⟨...ANYWAY?⟩
⟨IT'S...⟩
⟨...A WHOLE PLANET OF DOGS!⟩
⟨I CAN SEE WHY THEY ASKED FOR HELP FROM DOG SUPERHEROES.⟩
⟨OH, THEY ALREADY HAVE DOG SUPERHEROES HERE--A WHOLE TEAM OF THEM! IN FACT, I'M AN HONORARY MEMBER MYSELF.⟩
⟨OF COURSE YOU ARE.⟩

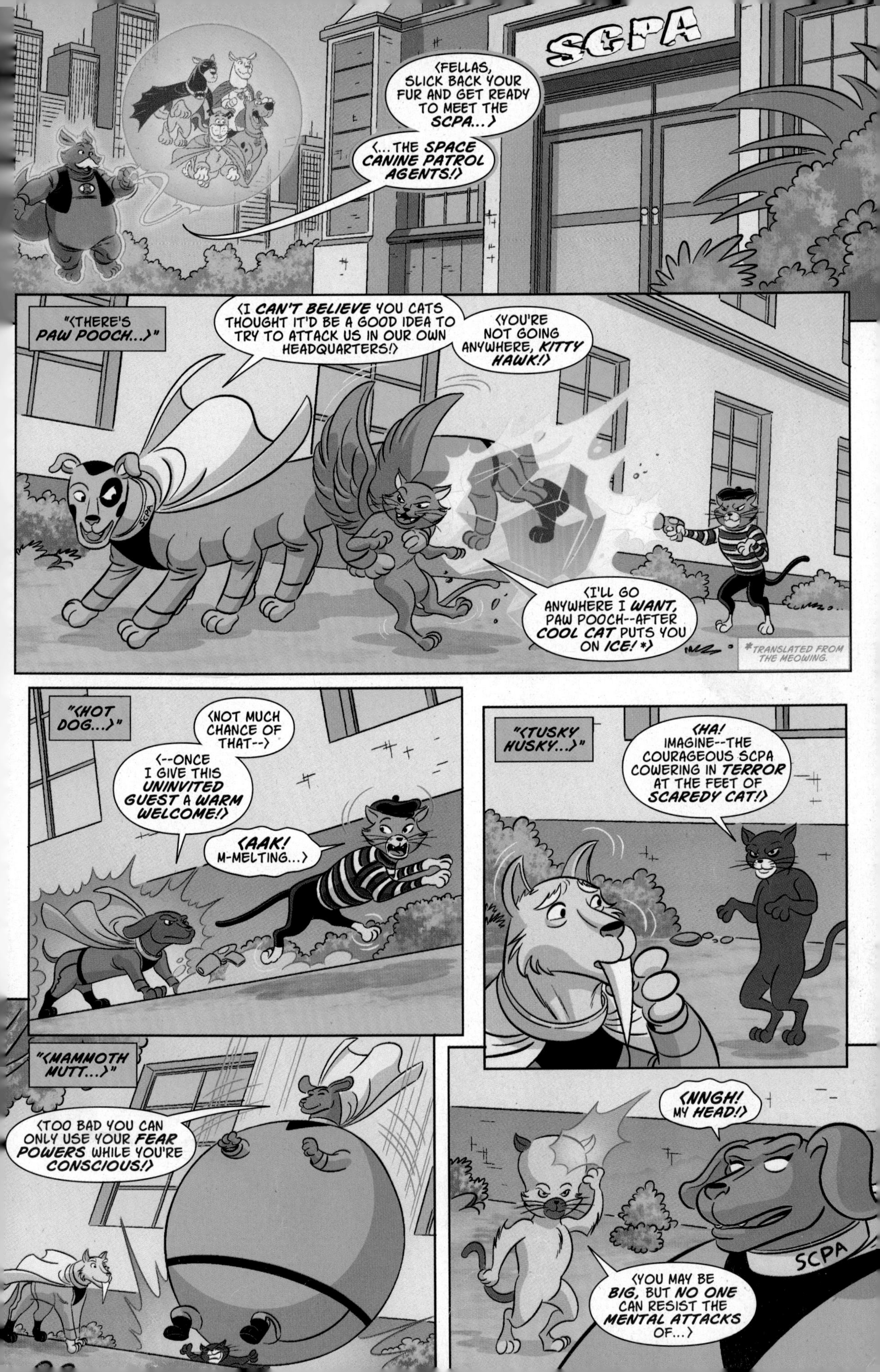
SCPA
‹FELLAS, SLICK BACK YOUR FUR AND GET READY TO MEET THE SCPA...›
‹...THE SPACE CANINE PATROL AGENTS!›
"‹THERE'S PAW POOCH...›"
‹I CAN'T BELIEVE YOU CATS THOUGHT IT'D BE A GOOD IDEA TO TRY TO ATTACK US IN OUR OWN HEADQUARTERS!›
‹YOU'RE NOT GOING ANYWHERE, KITTY HAWK!›
SCPA
‹I'LL GO ANYWHERE I WANT, PAW POOCH--AFTER COOL CAT PUTS YOU ON ICE! *›
*TRANSLATED FROM THE MEOWING.
"‹HOT DOG...›"
‹NOT MUCH CHANCE OF THAT--›
‹--ONCE I GIVE THIS UNINVITED GUEST A WARM WELCOME!›
‹AAK! M-MELTING...›
"‹TUSKY HUSKY...›"
‹HA! IMAGINE--THE COURAGEOUS SCPA COWERING IN TERROR AT THE FEET OF SCAREDY CAT!›
"‹MAMMOTH MUTT...›"
‹TOO BAD YOU CAN ONLY USE YOUR FEAR POWERS WHILE YOU'RE CONSCIOUS!›
‹NNGH! MY HEAD!›
SCPA
‹YOU MAY BE BIG, BUT NO ONE CAN RESIST THE MENTAL ATTACKS OF...›

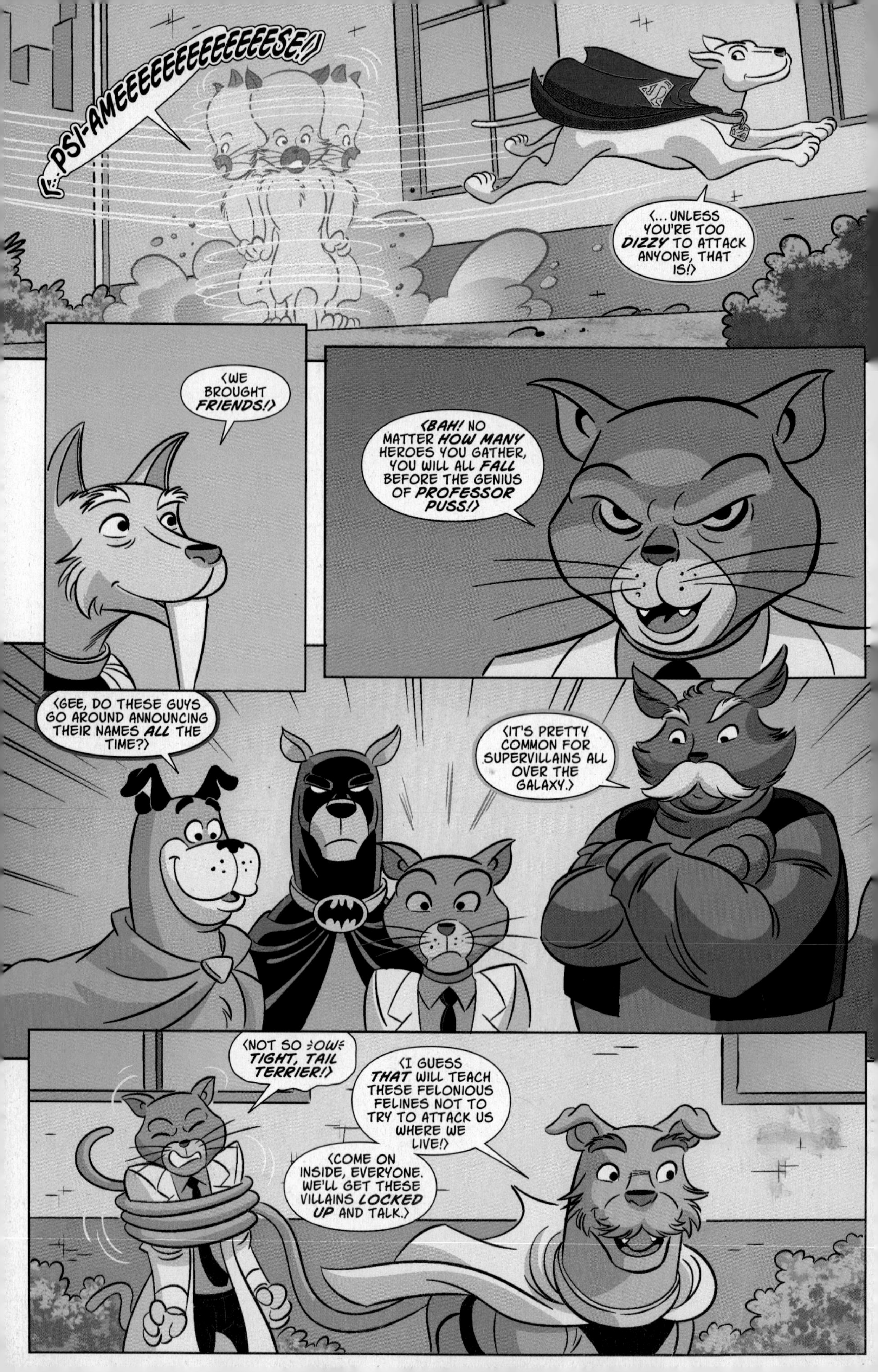
PSI-AMEEEEEEEEEEEEEEESE!!
⟨... UNLESS YOU'RE TOO DIZZY TO ATTACK ANYONE, THAT IS!⟩
⟨WE BROUGHT FRIENDS!⟩
⟨BAH! NO MATTER HOW MANY HEROES YOU GATHER, YOU WILL ALL FALL BEFORE THE GENIUS OF PROFESSOR PUSS!⟩
⟨GEE, DO THESE GUYS GO AROUND ANNOUNCING THEIR NAMES ALL THE TIME?⟩
⟨IT'S PRETTY COMMON FOR SUPERVILLAINS ALL OVER THE GALAXY.⟩
⟨NOT SO OW TIGHT, TAIL TERRIER!⟩
⟨I GUESS THAT WILL TEACH THESE FELONIOUS FELINES NOT TO TRY TO ATTACK US WHERE WE LIVE!⟩
⟨COME ON INSIDE, EVERYONE. WE'LL GET THESE VILLAINS LOCKED UP AND TALK.⟩

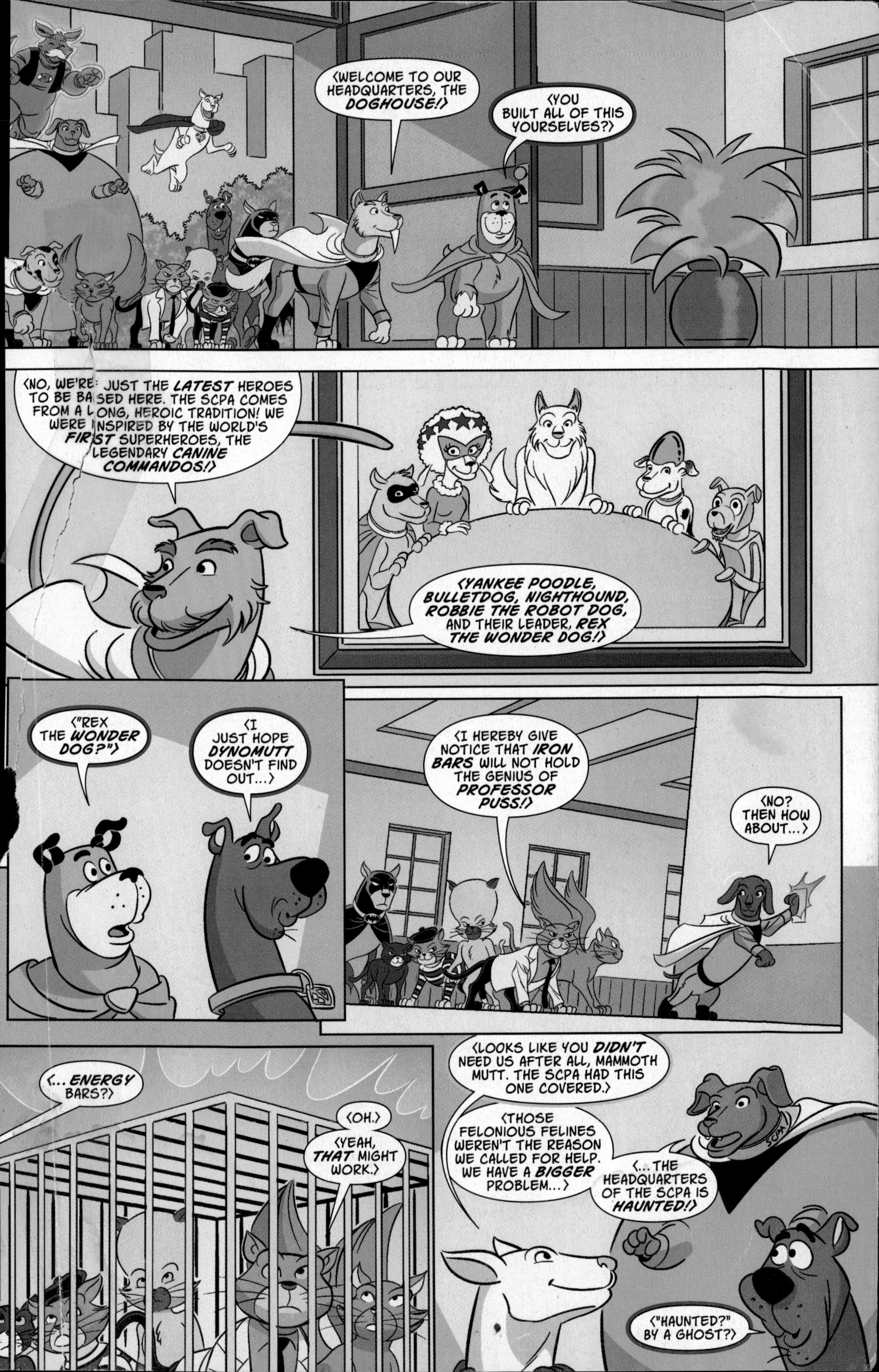
⟨WELCOME TO OUR HEADQUARTERS, THE *DOGHOUSE!*⟩
⟨YOU BUILT ALL OF THIS YOURSELVES?⟩
⟨NO, WE'RE JUST THE *LATEST* HEROES TO BE BASED HERE. THE SCPA COMES FROM A LONG, HEROIC TRADITION! WE WERE INSPIRED BY THE WORLD'S *FIRST* SUPERHEROES, THE LEGENDARY *CANINE COMMANDOS!*⟩
⟨*YANKEE POODLE, BULLETDOG, NIGHTHOUND, ROBBIE THE ROBOT DOG,* AND THEIR LEADER, *REX THE WONDER DOG!*⟩
⟨"REX THE *WONDER DOG?*"⟩
⟨I JUST HOPE *DYNOMUTT* DOESN'T FIND OUT...⟩
⟨I HEREBY GIVE NOTICE THAT *IRON BARS* WILL NOT HOLD THE GENIUS OF *PROFESSOR PUSS!*⟩
⟨NO? THEN HOW ABOUT...⟩
⟨... *ENERGY* BARS?⟩
⟨OH.⟩
⟨YEAH, *THAT* MIGHT WORK.⟩
⟨LOOKS LIKE YOU *DIDN'T* NEED US AFTER ALL, MAMMOTH MUTT. THE SCPA HAD THIS ONE COVERED.⟩
⟨THOSE FELONIOUS FELINES WEREN'T THE REASON WE CALLED FOR HELP. WE HAVE A *BIGGER* PROBLEM...⟩
⟨... THE HEADQUARTERS OF THE SCPA IS *HAUNTED!*⟩
⟨"HAUNTED?" BY A GHOST?⟩

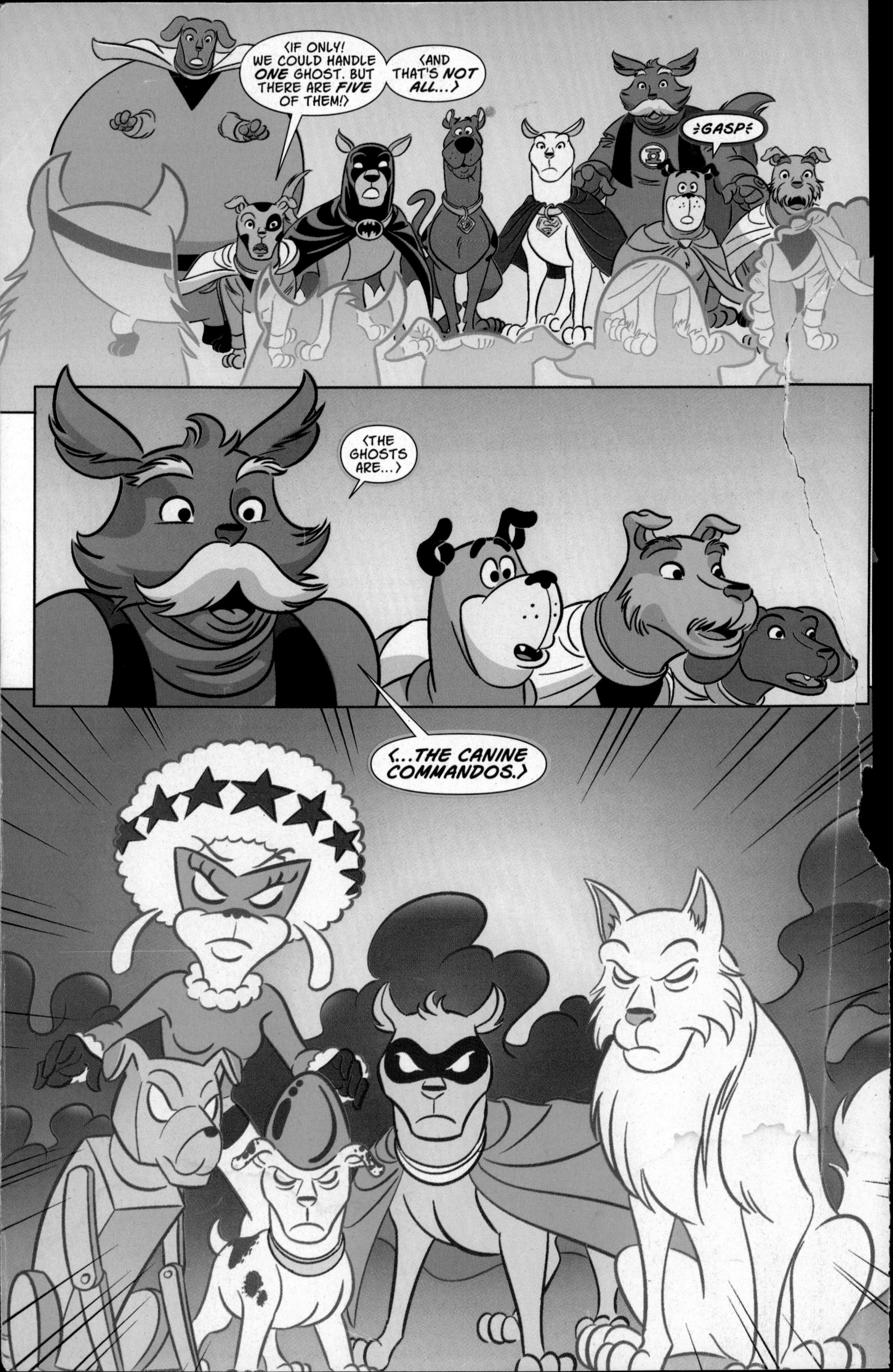

<IF ONLY! WE COULD HANDLE ONE GHOST. BUT THERE ARE FIVE OF THEM!>
<AND THAT'S NOT ALL...>
GASP
<THE GHOSTS ARE...>
<...THE CANINE COMMANDOS.>

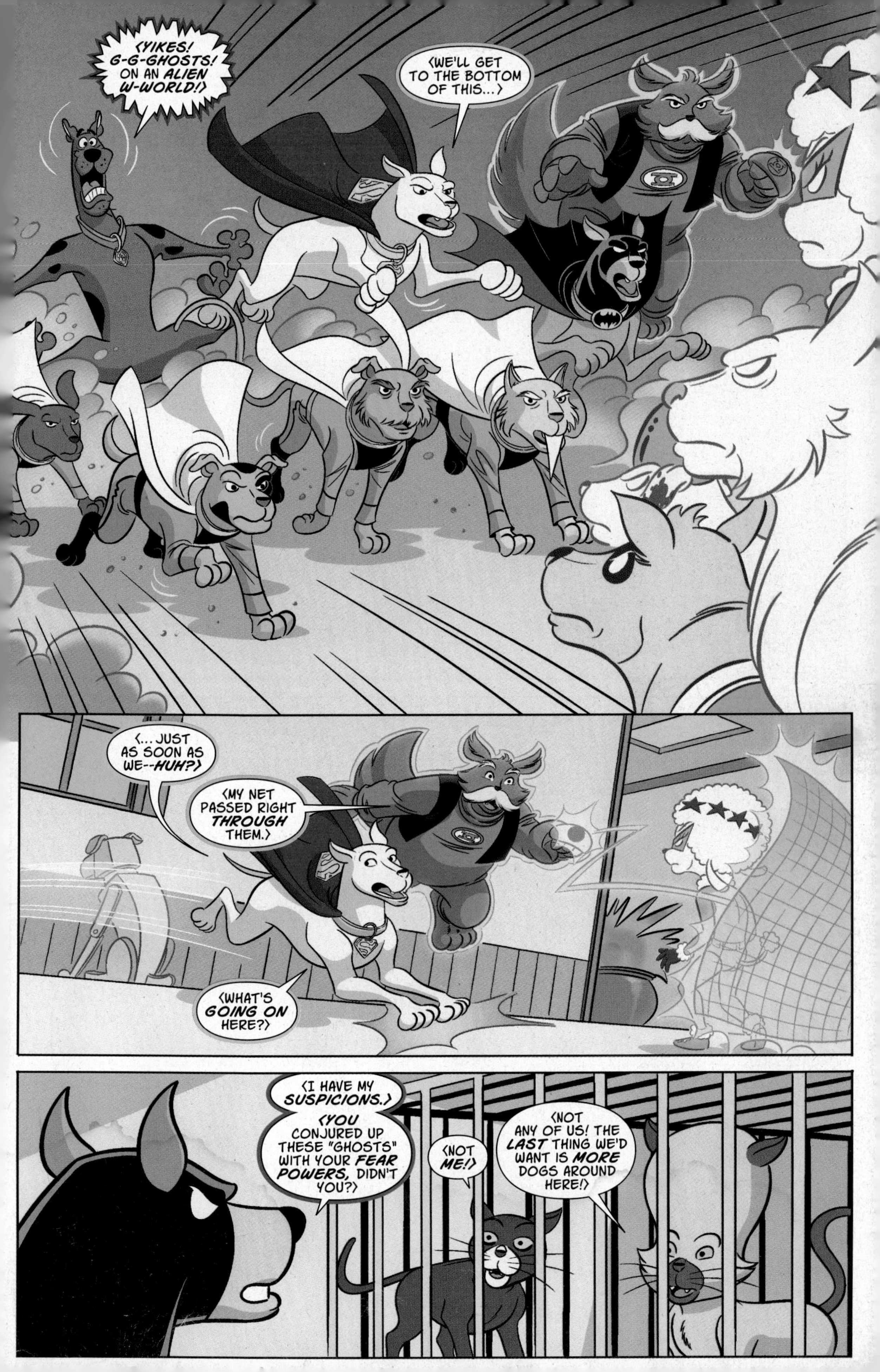

⟨YIKES! G-G-GHOSTS! ON AN ALIEN W-WORLD!⟩
⟨WE'LL GET TO THE BOTTOM OF THIS...⟩
⟨... JUST AS SOON AS WE--HUH?⟩
⟨MY NET PASSED RIGHT THROUGH THEM.⟩
⟨WHAT'S GOING ON HERE?⟩
⟨I HAVE MY SUSPICIONS.⟩
⟨YOU CONJURED UP THESE "GHOSTS" WITH YOUR FEAR POWERS, DIDN'T YOU?⟩
⟨NOT ME!⟩
⟨NOT ANY OF US! THE LAST THING WE'D WANT IS MORE DOGS AROUND HERE!⟩

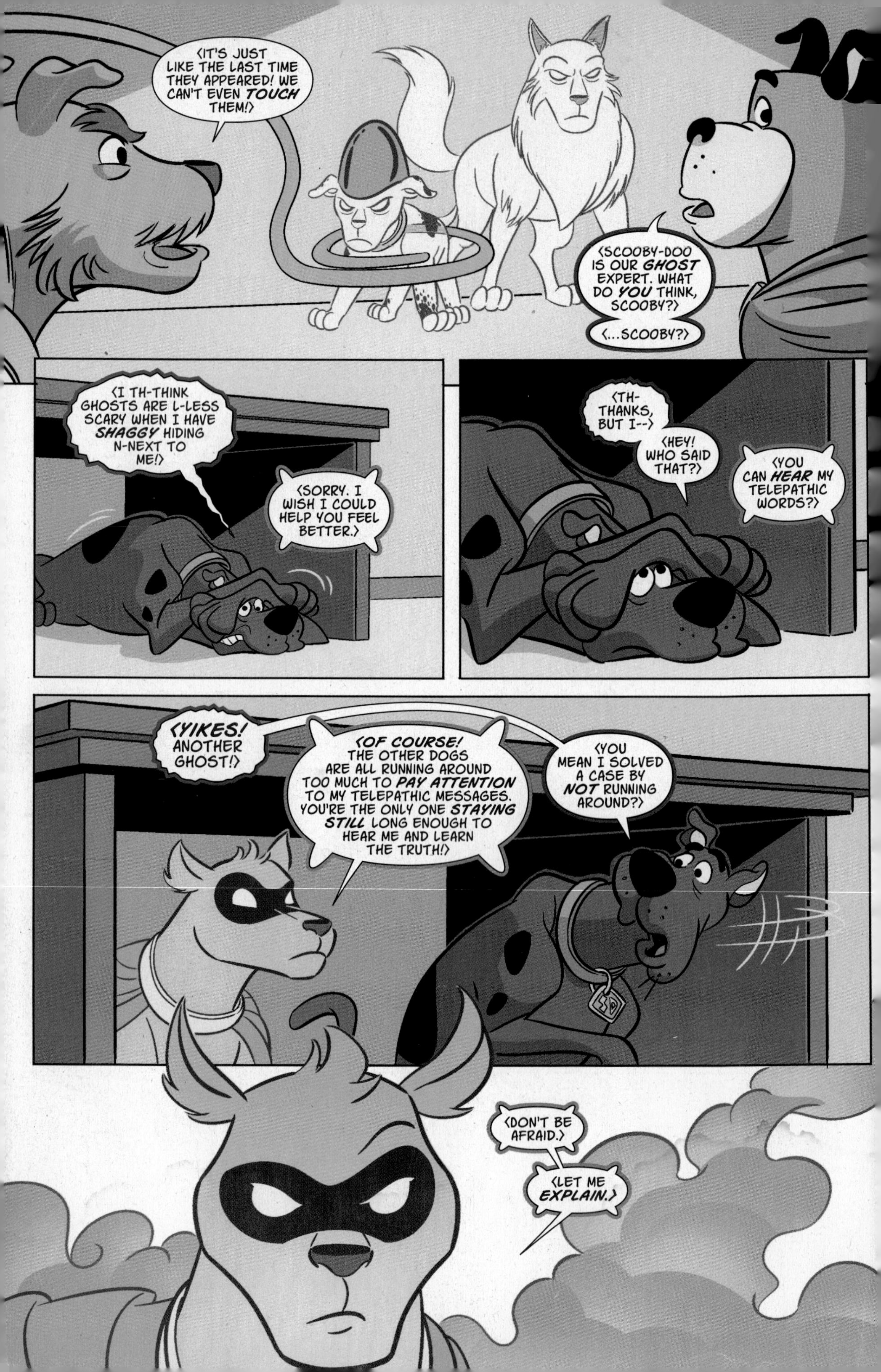
<IT'S JUST LIKE THE LAST TIME THEY APPEARED! WE CAN'T EVEN TOUCH THEM!>
<SCOOBY-DOO IS OUR GHOST EXPERT. WHAT DO YOU THINK, SCOOBY?>
<...SCOOBY?>
<I TH-THINK GHOSTS ARE L-LESS SCARY WHEN I HAVE SHAGGY HIDING N-NEXT TO ME!>
<SORRY. I WISH I COULD HELP YOU FEEL BETTER.>
<TH-THANKS, BUT I-->
<HEY! WHO SAID THAT?>
<YOU CAN HEAR MY TELEPATHIC WORDS?>
<YIKES! ANOTHER GHOST!>
<OF COURSE! THE OTHER DOGS ARE ALL RUNNING AROUND TOO MUCH TO PAY ATTENTION TO MY TELEPATHIC MESSAGES. YOU'RE THE ONLY ONE STAYING STILL LONG ENOUGH TO HEAR ME AND LEARN THE TRUTH!>
<YOU MEAN I SOLVED A CASE BY NOT RUNNING AROUND?>
<DON'T BE AFRAID.>
<LET ME EXPLAIN.>

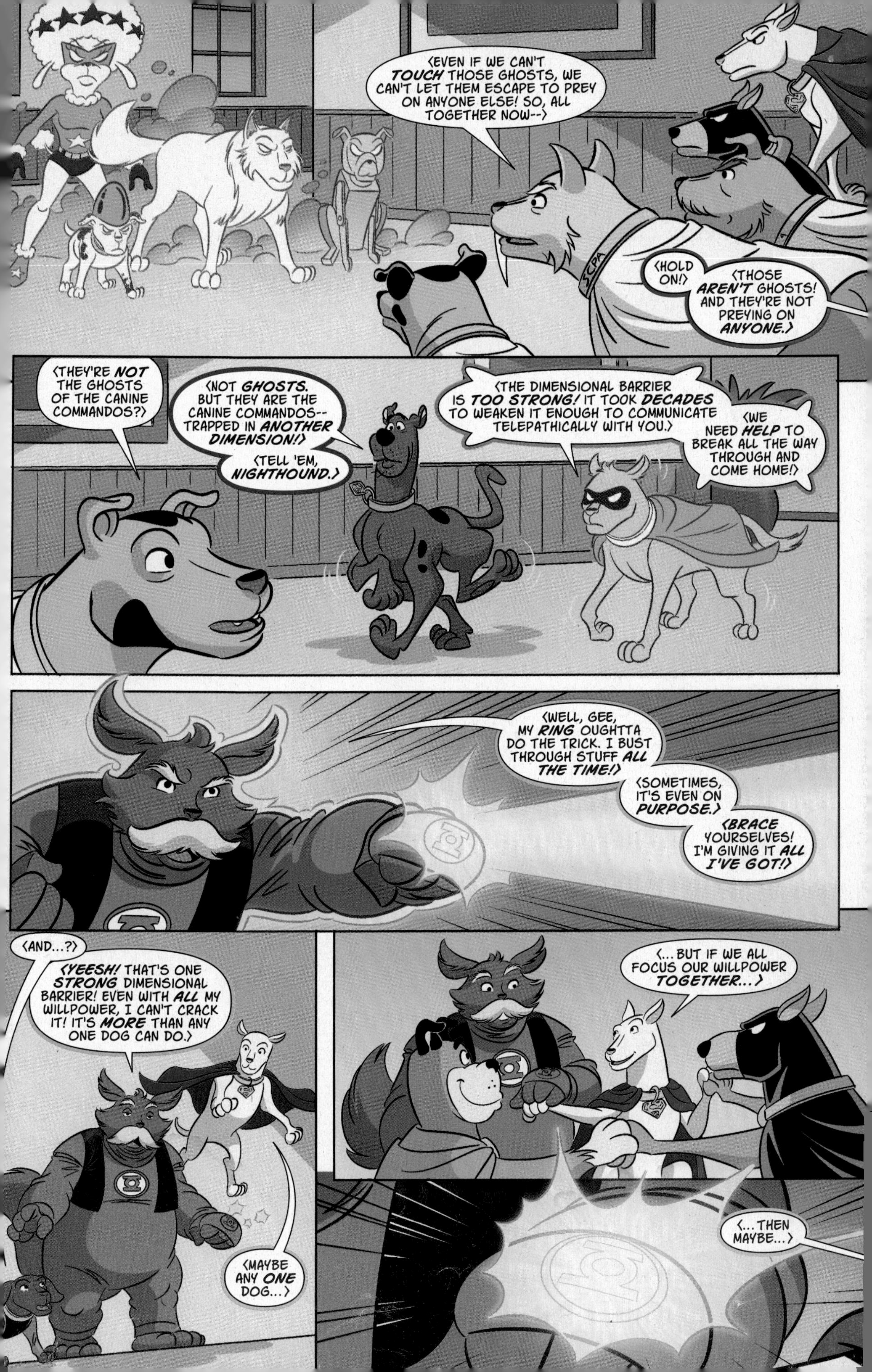

⟨EVEN IF WE CAN'T TOUCH THOSE GHOSTS, WE CAN'T LET THEM ESCAPE TO PREY ON ANYONE ELSE! SO, ALL TOGETHER NOW--⟩
⟨HOLD ON!⟩
⟨THOSE AREN'T GHOSTS! AND THEY'RE NOT PREYING ON ANYONE.⟩
⟨THEY'RE NOT THE GHOSTS OF THE CANINE COMMANDOS?⟩
⟨NOT GHOSTS. BUT THEY ARE THE CANINE COMMANDOS--TRAPPED IN ANOTHER DIMENSION!⟩
⟨TELL 'EM, NIGHTHOUND.⟩
⟨THE DIMENSIONAL BARRIER IS TOO STRONG! IT TOOK DECADES TO WEAKEN IT ENOUGH TO COMMUNICATE TELEPATHICALLY WITH YOU.⟩
⟨WE NEED HELP TO BREAK ALL THE WAY THROUGH AND COME HOME!⟩
⟨WELL, GEE, MY RING OUGHTTA DO THE TRICK. I BUST THROUGH STUFF ALL THE TIME!⟩
⟨SOMETIMES, IT'S EVEN ON PURPOSE.⟩
⟨BRACE YOURSELVES! I'M GIVING IT ALL I'VE GOT!⟩
⟨AND...?⟩
⟨YEESH! THAT'S ONE STRONG DIMENSIONAL BARRIER! EVEN WITH ALL MY WILLPOWER, I CAN'T CRACK IT! IT'S MORE THAN ANY ONE DOG CAN DO.⟩
⟨MAYBE ANY ONE DOG...⟩
⟨... BUT IF WE ALL FOCUS OUR WILLPOWER TOGETHER...⟩
⟨... THEN MAYBE...⟩

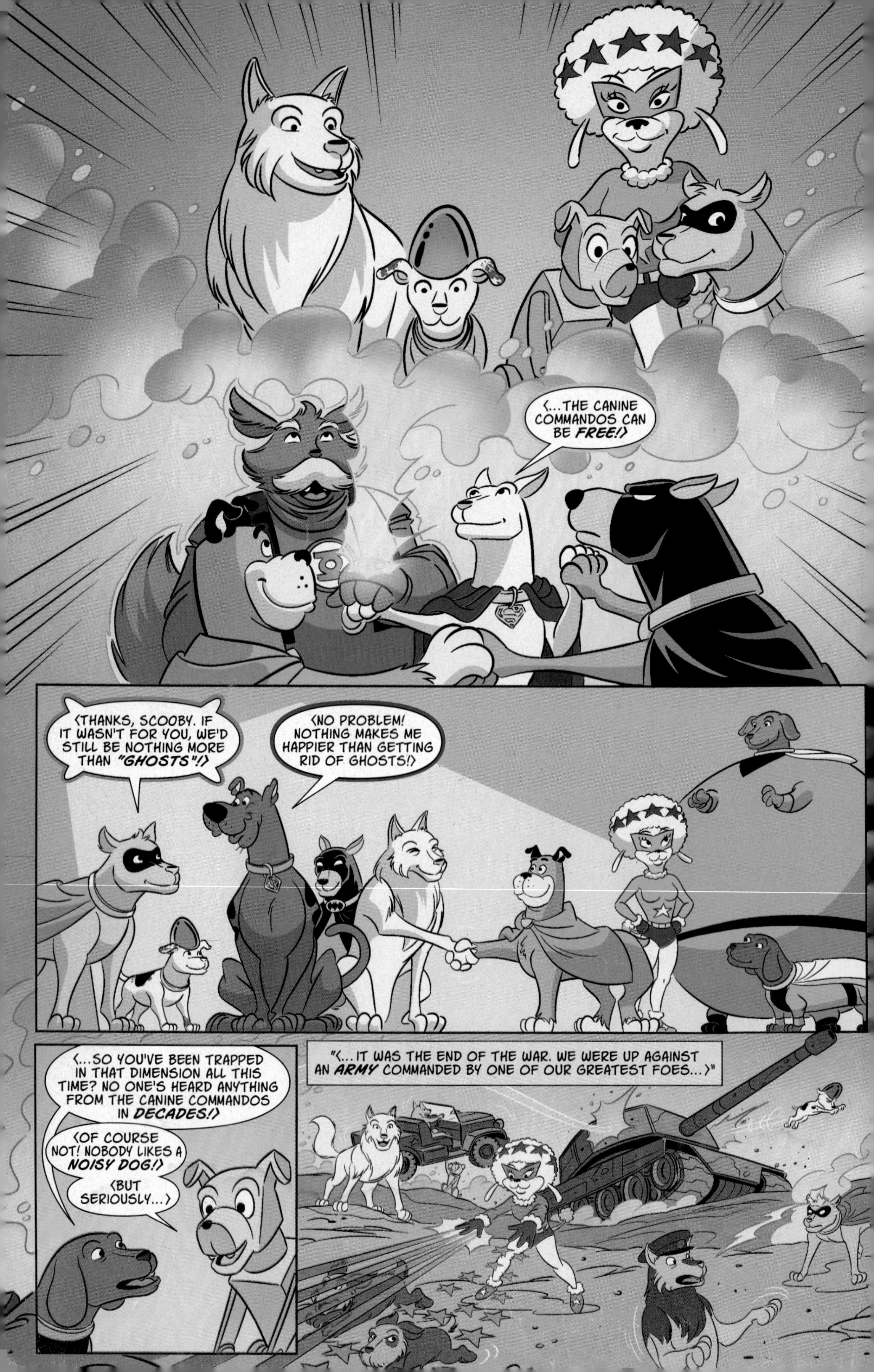
⟨...THE CANINE COMMANDOS CAN BE FREE!⟩
⟨THANKS, SCOOBY. IF IT WASN'T FOR YOU, WE'D STILL BE NOTHING MORE THAN "GHOSTS"!⟩
⟨NO PROBLEM! NOTHING MAKES ME HAPPIER THAN GETTING RID OF GHOSTS!⟩
⟨...SO YOU'VE BEEN TRAPPED IN THAT DIMENSION ALL THIS TIME? NO ONE'S HEARD ANYTHING FROM THE CANINE COMMANDOS IN DECADES!⟩
⟨OF COURSE NOT! NOBODY LIKES A NOISY DOG!⟩
⟨BUT SERIOUSLY...⟩
"⟨...IT WAS THE END OF THE WAR. WE WERE UP AGAINST AN ARMY COMMANDED BY ONE OF OUR GREATEST FOES...⟩"

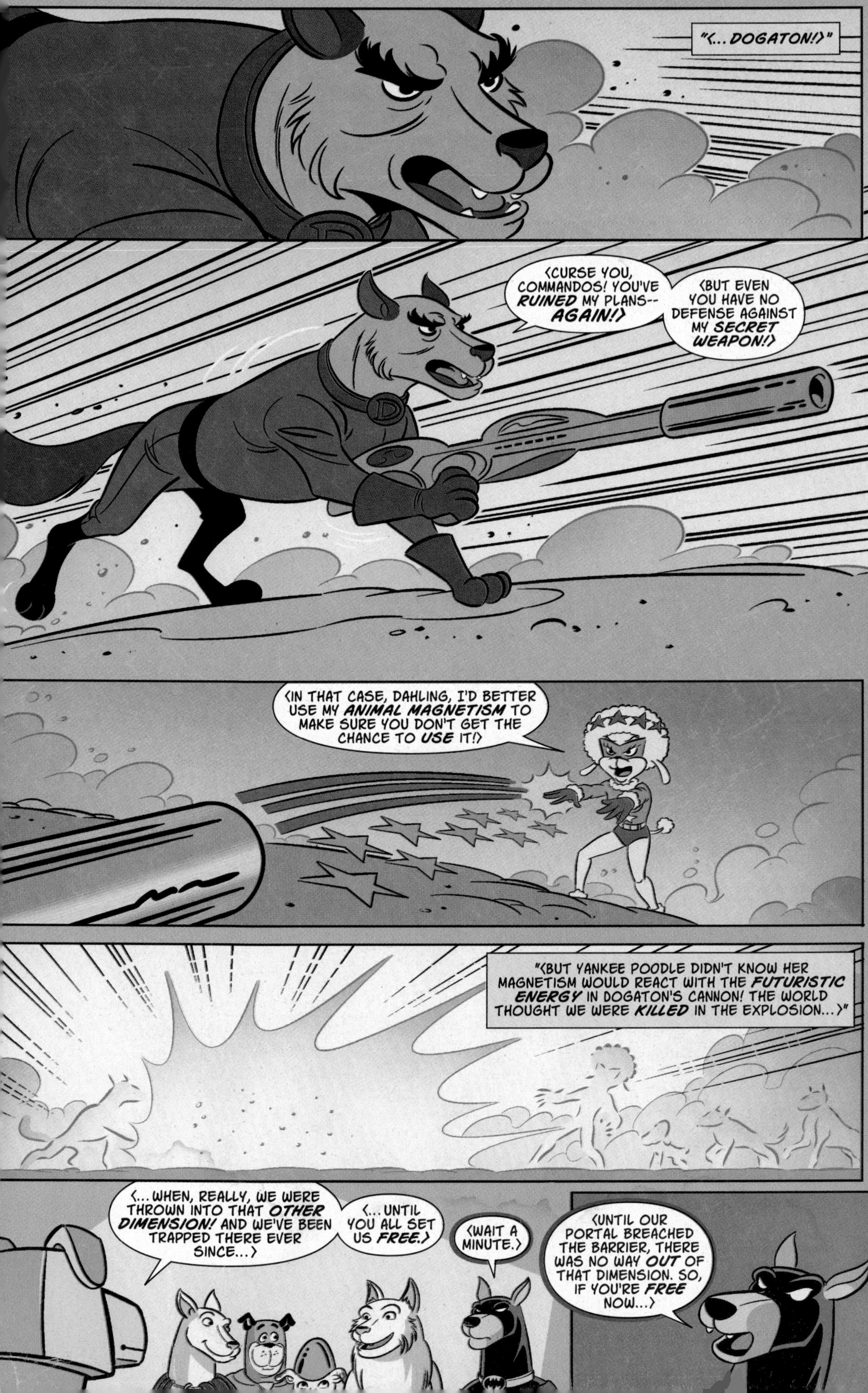
"‹...DOGATON!›"
‹CURSE YOU, COMMANDOS! YOU'VE RUINED MY PLANS-- AGAIN!›
‹BUT EVEN YOU HAVE NO DEFENSE AGAINST MY SECRET WEAPON!›
‹IN THAT CASE, DAHLING, I'D BETTER USE MY ANIMAL MAGNETISM TO MAKE SURE YOU DON'T GET THE CHANCE TO USE IT!›
"‹BUT YANKEE POODLE DIDN'T KNOW HER MAGNETISM WOULD REACT WITH THE FUTURISTIC ENERGY IN DOGATON'S CANNON! THE WORLD THOUGHT WE WERE KILLED IN THE EXPLOSION...›"
‹...WHEN, REALLY, WE WERE THROWN INTO THAT OTHER DIMENSION! AND WE'VE BEEN TRAPPED THERE EVER SINCE...›
‹...UNTIL YOU ALL SET US FREE.›
‹WAIT A MINUTE.›
‹UNTIL OUR PORTAL BREACHED THE BARRIER, THERE WAS NO WAY OUT OF THAT DIMENSION. SO, IF YOU'RE FREE NOW...›

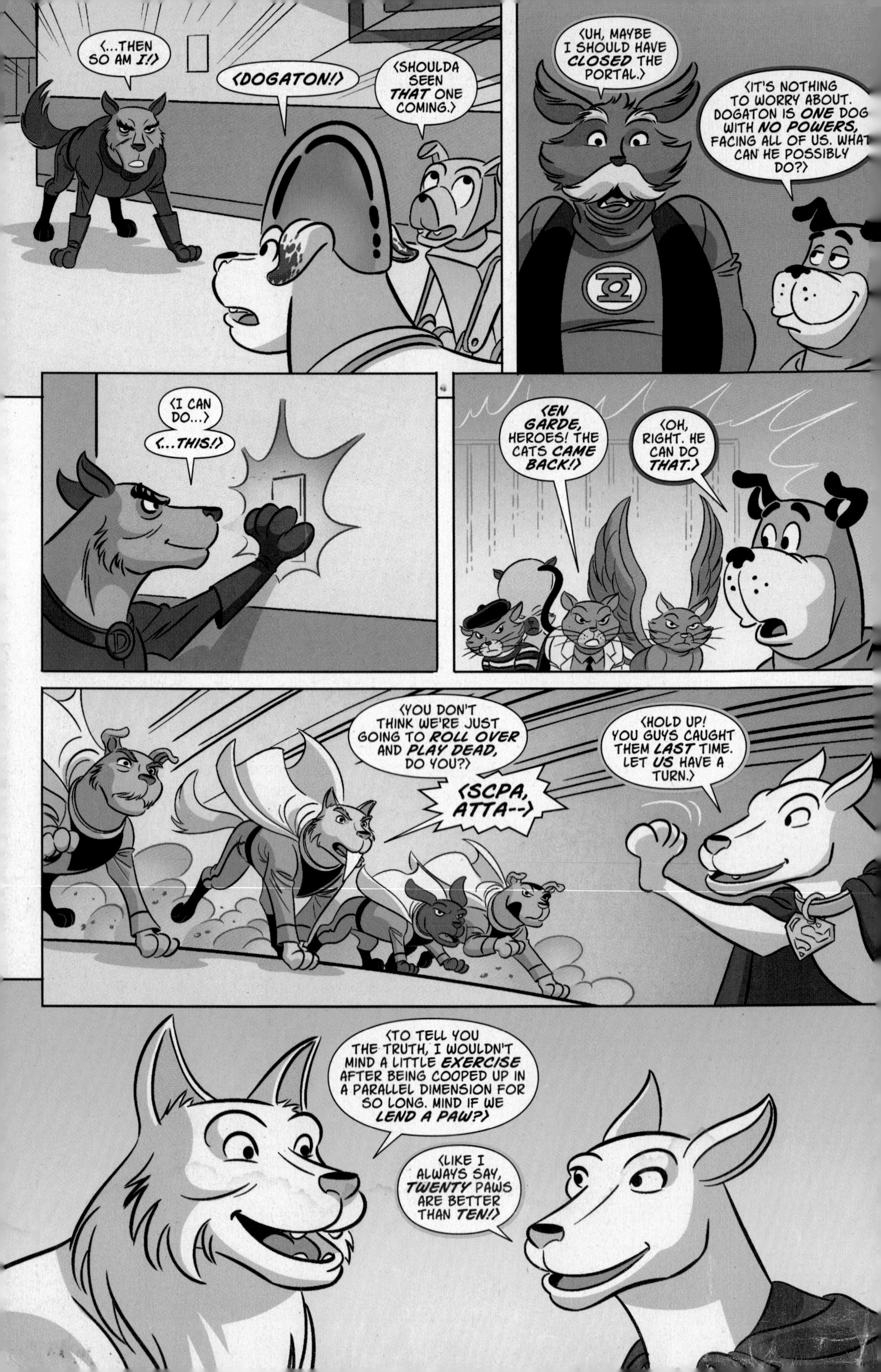

‹...THEN SO AM I!›
‹DOGATON!›
‹SHOULDA SEEN THAT ONE COMING.›
‹UH, MAYBE I SHOULD HAVE CLOSED THE PORTAL.›
‹IT'S NOTHING TO WORRY ABOUT. DOGATON IS ONE DOG WITH NO POWERS, FACING ALL OF US. WHAT CAN HE POSSIBLY DO?›
‹I CAN DO...›
‹...THIS!›
‹EN GARDE, HEROES! THE CATS CAME BACK!›
‹OH, RIGHT. HE CAN DO THAT.›
‹YOU DON'T THINK WE'RE JUST GOING TO ROLL OVER AND PLAY DEAD, DO YOU?›
‹SCPA, ATTA--›
‹HOLD UP! YOU GUYS CAUGHT THEM LAST TIME. LET US HAVE A TURN.›
‹TO TELL YOU THE TRUTH, I WOULDN'T MIND A LITTLE EXERCISE AFTER BEING COOPED UP IN A PARALLEL DIMENSION FOR SO LONG. MIND IF WE LEND A PAW?›
‹LIKE I ALWAYS SAY, TWENTY PAWS ARE BETTER THAN TEN!›

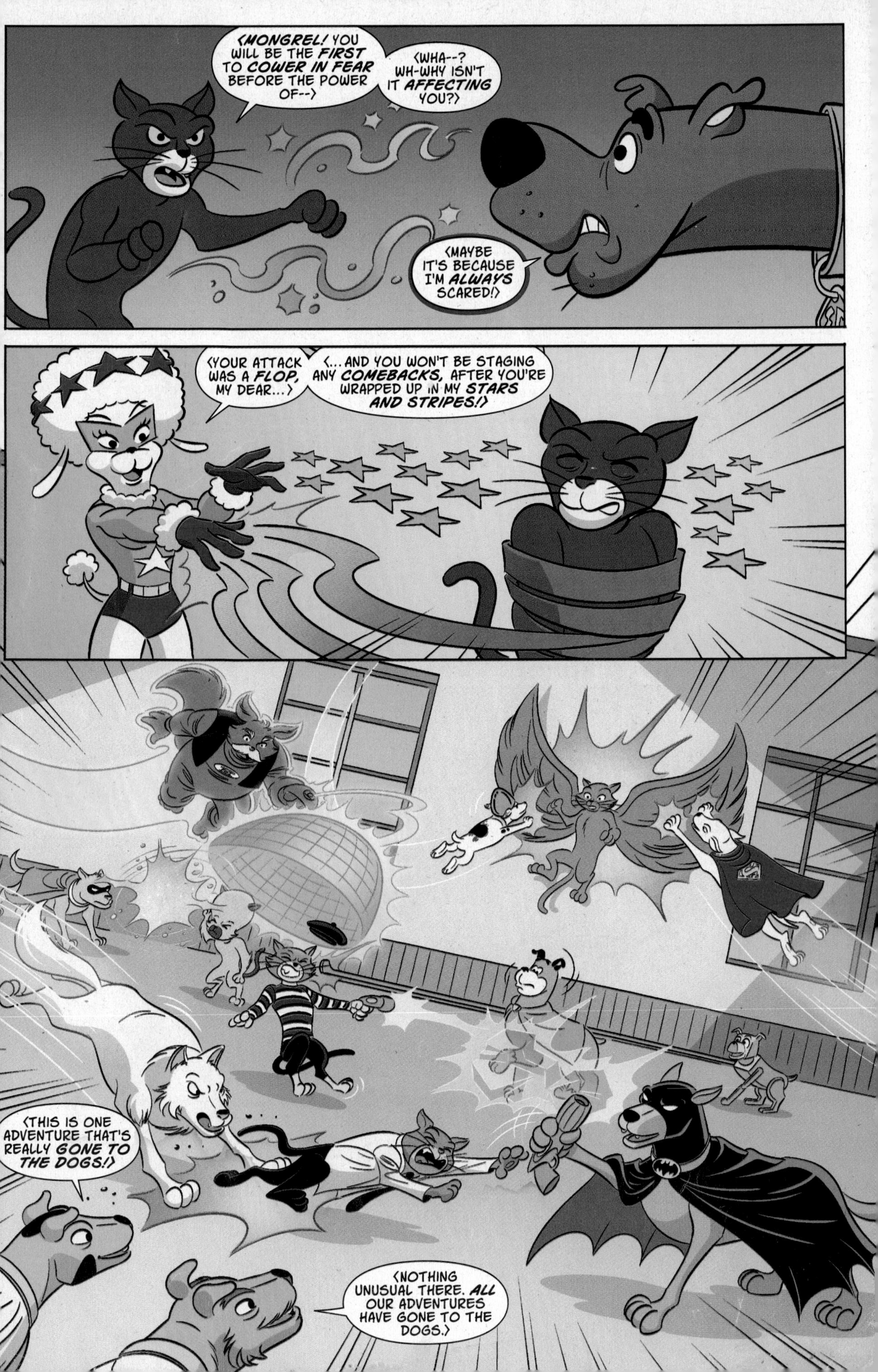
<MONGREL! YOU WILL BE THE FIRST TO COWER IN FEAR BEFORE THE POWER OF-->
<WHA--? WH-WHY ISN'T IT AFFECTING YOU?>
<MAYBE IT'S BECAUSE I'M ALWAYS SCARED!>
<YOUR ATTACK WAS A FLOP, MY DEAR...>
<...AND YOU WON'T BE STAGING ANY COMEBACKS, AFTER YOU'RE WRAPPED UP IN MY STARS AND STRIPES!>
<THIS IS ONE ADVENTURE THAT'S REALLY GONE TO THE DOGS!>
<NOTHING UNUSUAL THERE. ALL OUR ADVENTURES HAVE GONE TO THE DOGS.>

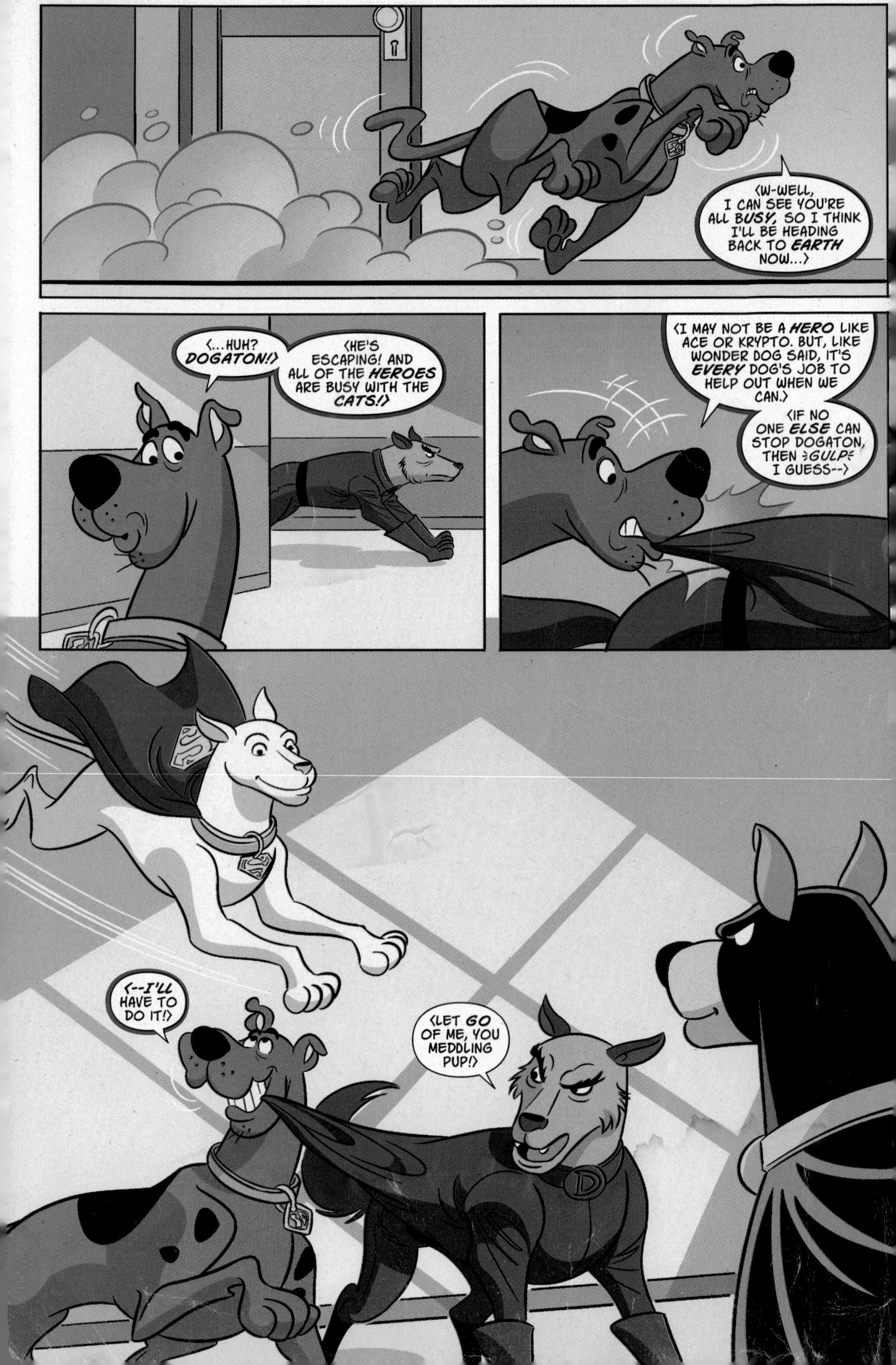
⟨W-WELL, I CAN SEE YOU'RE ALL BUSY, SO I THINK I'LL BE HEADING BACK TO EARTH NOW...⟩
⟨...HUH? DOGATON!⟩
⟨HE'S ESCAPING! AND ALL OF THE HEROES ARE BUSY WITH THE CATS!⟩
⟨I MAY NOT BE A HERO LIKE ACE OR KRYPTO. BUT, LIKE WONDER DOG SAID, IT'S EVERY DOG'S JOB TO HELP OUT WHEN WE CAN.⟩
⟨IF NO ONE ELSE CAN STOP DOGATON, THEN ≡GULP≡ I GUESS--⟩
⟨--I'LL HAVE TO DO IT!⟩
⟨LET GO OF ME, YOU MEDDLING PUP!⟩

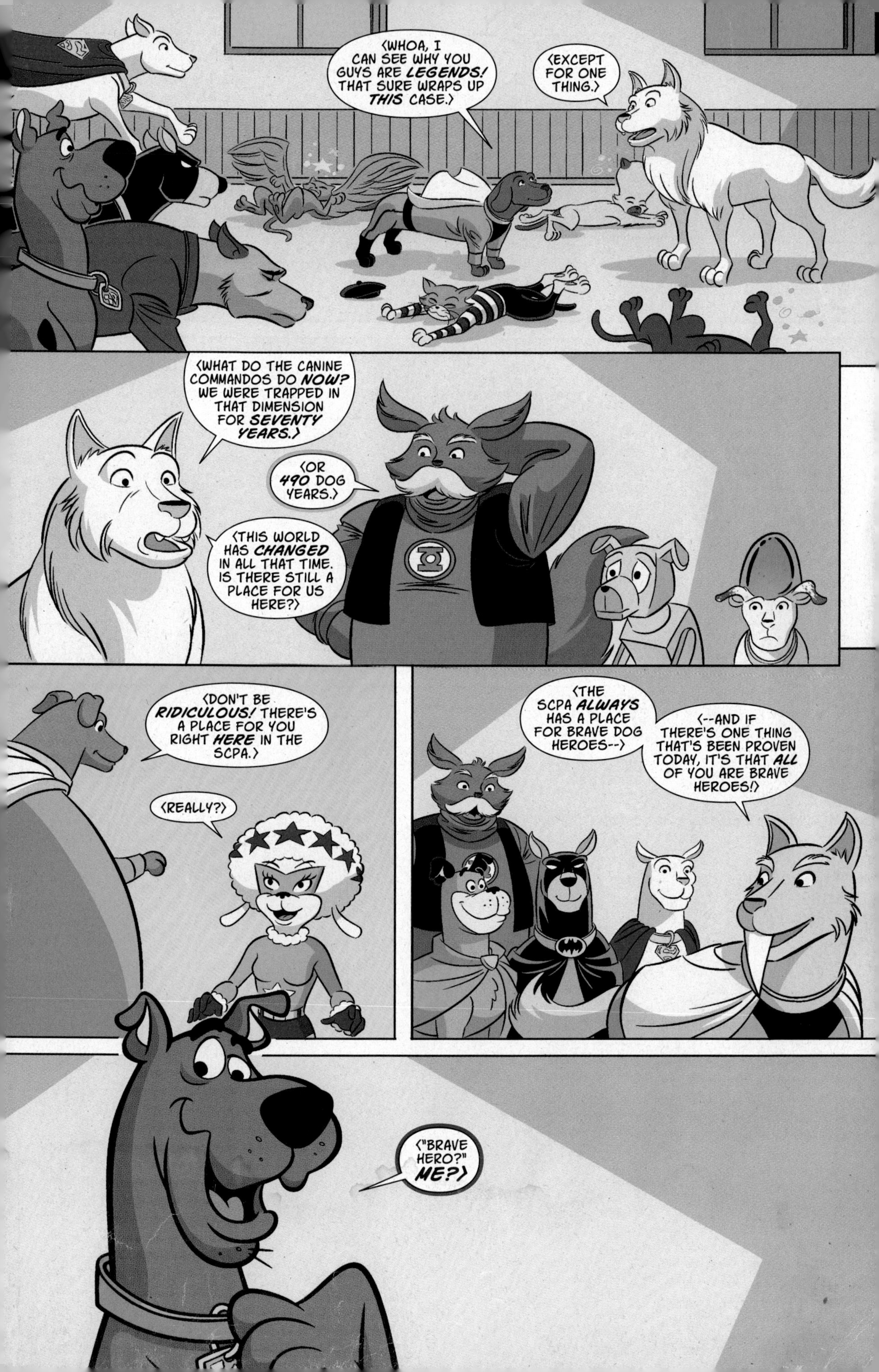

‹WHOA, I CAN SEE WHY YOU GUYS ARE LEGENDS! THAT SURE WRAPS UP THIS CASE.›
‹EXCEPT FOR ONE THING.›
‹WHAT DO THE CANINE COMMANDOS DO NOW? WE WERE TRAPPED IN THAT DIMENSION FOR SEVENTY YEARS.›
‹OR 490 DOG YEARS.›
‹THIS WORLD HAS CHANGED IN ALL THAT TIME. IS THERE STILL A PLACE FOR US HERE?›
‹DON'T BE RIDICULOUS! THERE'S A PLACE FOR YOU RIGHT HERE IN THE SCPA.›
‹REALLY?›
‹THE SCPA ALWAYS HAS A PLACE FOR BRAVE DOG HEROES--›
‹--AND IF THERE'S ONE THING THAT'S BEEN PROVEN TODAY, IT'S THAT ALL OF YOU ARE BRAVE HEROES!›
‹"BRAVE HERO?" ME?›

...AND SO, BY CONSIDERING *DNA* EVIDENCE, THE CURRENT PHASE OF THE MOON...

...AND RECENT TRENDS IN THE WHOLESALE PRICE OF *TAPIOCA* PUDDING...

...IT'S OBVIOUS THAT THE *FREAKY PHANTOM OF FINSTER FALLS* MUST REALLY BE--

LIKE, *LOOK OUT!* HERE COMES THE *FREAKY PHANTOM* AGAIN!

THAT'S NOT THE FREAKY PHANTOM! IT'S *SCOOBY!*

HEY! AREN'T YOU GOING TO TELL US *WHO* WAS PRETENDING TO BE THE FREAKY PHANTOM?

IN A MINUTE. FIRST, WE HAVE TO SAY HELLO TO OUR *DOG.*

I HOPE YOUR TRIP WAS A *SUCCESS.*

SURE WAS! WE DEFEATED A GANG OF *DESPERATE SUPER-VILLAINS,* FREED A TEAM OF HEROES WHO'D BEEN TRAPPED FOR *SEVENTY YEARS* AND PROBABLY SAVED AN ENTIRE *SOLAR SYSTEM!*

NOT BAD. DID YOU PULL OFF ANYONE'S *MASK?*

WELL, IT SOUNDS LIKE YOU WERE ALL *GOOD DOGS*--AND THAT YOU EARNED YOURSELVES SOME *SCOOBY SNACKS!* WHO WANTS...

...HUH?

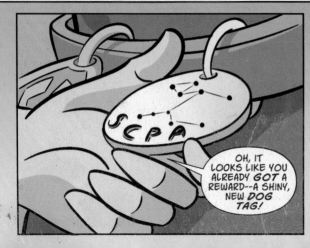

OH, IT LOOKS LIKE YOU ALREADY *GOT A REWARD*--A SHINY, NEW *DOG TAG!*

SCPA

BUT WHAT'S THE *SCPA?*

THE END